Dark Justice

A Novel

By

Mary Jane Wijtyk

Dark Justice

Cover design by Zenon Wijtyk

Published in the United States of America by Alpha Publications

Fiction/Crime/Detective

10.20.18

Dedication

It is so very wonderful to have a partner in life that encourages me to be the very best that I can be. My husband believes in me, even when I do not. I cannot ask anymore than that.

I also am very blessed to have a friend that pushes, shoves, and pulls me to be where I should be to accomplish my goals. Though writing is a passion, the day-to-day minutia can hold you like quicksand. Thank you SrS for keeping me going!!

I also want thank my sister Ruth, for all of the valuable information and statistics on family abuses. As an RN, she has encountered many such tragedies and she has seen the horrible effects that this has on so very many people.

Warning

What is your opinion on premeditated murder? When you read a newspaper clipping or hear a story on the television regarding this heinous crime, do you cheer for the murderer or do you sympathize with the victim and his or her family? This story may take you into that gray area we hate to enter, and it might cause you to question your own values.

It never occurred to Jadyn Martyn that she would enter so very many gray areas in her lifetime. Although she came from a dysfunctional family, she had excelled in school, work, and life. It never dawned on her that she would become someone who was capable of murder. Things of that nature never crossed her mind. Jadyn must face dark days, with twists and turns she cannot anticipate.

The only pleasant part to the horror she must face is the time she crosses the path of Detective James Carter. A very conscientious young man with very firm opinions on the subject of murder, he is the only one who seems to genuinely care about what has happened and what can be done about it. But beware the determined man, Jadyn. He does not give up, he does not lose sight of his goal, and he knows how to catch—a murderer.

Twenty - Twenty

The innocence of youth,
The passage of time.
Leads to a sad wisdom,
Developed from behind.

Regret can follow reckoning,
Of decisions made today.
Tears dropping by the wayside,
As you follow your chosen pathway.

Chapter I

"Mother, where's my new sweater?" Rachael yelled down the stairs to her mother, who was in the kitchen making supper. "I know I had it a couple of days ago, but now it is gone."

"Look in your bottom drawer, honey. I put it back for you yesterday." After a brief pause her mother yelled up the steps, "Did you find it?"

"Yep—I did, thanks Mother."

Mrs. Dickerson went back to the kitchen to finish making the meatloaf they were going to have for supper. A well-rounded meal with vegetables, meat and salad was required by her husband every night. "And so he should—he works hard every day to provide for his family," Mrs. Dickerson was so often heard saying. They seldom went out to dinner, mainly because Mr. Dickerson said that his wife's cooking was too good and he was spoiled by the taste. Although Mrs. Dickerson was an excellent cook, that was not the reason that Mr. Dickerson did not want to go out to eat; he found it hard to spend money on something he considered a duplicate. Why pay a restaurant to cook for him, when his wife could do so and more cheaply?

To describe Rachael in one sentence: she was a knock-out. She did not look like her parents; she was tall and lithe, having long blond hair and beautiful blue eyes; she was always in demand. She was very seldom was without a date for all the various particular functions she attended. But tonight was different. She continued to lay out the clothing she was going to wear to the dance. She was actually excited as she had never been on a blind date. All that she knew was that the guy was good looking and came from an excellent family from Connecticut. Gloria, Rachael's best friend said that he and Fred, her boyfriend, attended the same Ivy League school, which was hosting the dance that they were to attend shortly. Rachael knew the dance was starting at 7:30 pm, giving her about two hours before Fred and Gloria would pick her up. There was no hurry to get ready.

"Will you have time for something to eat, before you go dear?" her mother had asked.

"No, I'm not hungry. They will have stuff at the dance. Afterward, we will go get something to eat,"

"Well, I know you are nineteen, but I still worry about you. Especially since you will be going with a total stranger," her mother said—half out loud and half to herself. Mrs. Dickerson worried about everyone. She could not get used to the idea of her daughter being old enough to make her own decisions; whether right or wrong.

This was not the first time Rachael had had this conversation, nor would it be her last. Her mother was kind and loving, but she did not trust boys. Rachael had dated some very nice boys in high school. Her mother was not too worried because they came to ask permission to take Rachael to this or that event. However, college boys were a different type. Self-assured, smart, wealthy—or at least some of them. Rachael had dated very regularly since she started her schooling two years prior. Mrs. Dickerson was not so sure about these young men and was not afraid to mention this to Rachael.

Rachael's father was usually at the store during the day. He owned Dickerson's Hardware in town and ran it with two employees. This kept them very busy most of the time as the store was the only one of its kind in town. Their town was not large enough to attract a megastore like Walmart or Home Depot, so, Dickerson's was convenient for the locals and Mr. Dickerson was looked upon as a friend by most in the community. As far as children, he left most of the parenting to his wife; he had all he could do to rear a store.

About an hour later, the house phone rang and Rachael ran to pick it up, "Hello?"

"Hey Rachael, are you ready?" her friend's voice climbed out of the receiver as if to visually ensure that Rachael was taking this date seriously.

"Of course," Rachael replied, "I know what I am wearing and have my hair done and nails polished."

"Oh, that sounds very efficient," Gloria Swanson answered. "By the way, we are going to pick you up a little earlier than we planned. Charles wants to be picked up at seven o'clock. He really wants to meet you."

"Okay. What time will you be here?"

"We will pick you up at 6:30 pm and then drive over to pick up Charles. He lives on the other side of the county," Gloria explained.

"Well, you better let me go if you want me to be ready on time," Rachael stated.

"Oh, okay. See you in half an hour!"

Gloria seems more excited than I am, Rachael mused. I hope he is really neat, because she sure has played this up. Rachael finished dressing and brushing her teeth. Makeup on and hair fixed, she was ready to turn the heads of all she met. She felt very confident and self-assured about her looks and her mind and she was thankful for both. Gloria was one of her few friends that was not intimidated by Rachael's looks and brains. It was good to have a friend like her.

Time moves quickly and it was not long after she had finished prepping that a horn blew out front of the house. Rachael descended the stairs quickly, sweater on her arm.

Her mother met her at the bottom. "Be sure to eat something for supper, dear. You know how you get if you don't eat." She did not wait for a reply before saying, "And be careful of strangers, honey. Not everyone is as nice as your father."

"I love you, Mother," Rachael said as she leaned over and kissed her mother on the cheek. Then she quickly went out the door before her mother could think of any more warnings to place on her shoulders.

Gloria and Fred were in the front seat of Fred's Ford Taurus, talking very earnestly. Rachael opened the back door and climbed into the black sedan. "Hey you two, why so serious? This night should be fun!" Rachael interrupted their talk with some light-hearted cheer.

"You betcha!" Fred offered up. "Sorry about the time change, but Charles seems to have his own time frames."

"No problem, I was almost ready anyway." Rachael knew Fred felt bad about it.

Soon the car was moving out of the town and toward the country. All three sat in silence for a few minutes, obviously in their own thoughts. Then Rachael and Gloria started to say something at the same time. Both stopped and laughed.

"Maybe I am a little on the nervous side after all," Rachael offered.

"Well, you don't have to be nervous about this date, Rachael. Charles will definitely show you a good time. He knows how to have fun and spend the money!" Fred was trying a little too hard for Rachael's benefit and it sounded like it.

"Oh, I am not worried about that. With the dance and all, we should have fun," Rachael answered, "I just don't want him to be disappointed with his date."

"Disappointed!" Gloria turned in her front seat to face Rachael, "He is going to love you from the very first moment."

"Well, time will tell." Rachael settled back into the seat and started to look at the scenery that was streaking by the window. "It is really lovely out here."

"Yes, this side of the county is very picturesque," Fred returned the observation. It was not very long until Fred slowed the car, and started looking at the addresses on the mailboxes at the bottom of the driveways. "I know it is along here somewhere."

"Is there a mailbox or sign or something to mark the house?" Gloria wanted to know.

"Yes, there is a large, ornamental gate near the end of the drive with two large eagles on the posts."

Just then, Gloria pointed and said, "There it is!"

Fred swung the long car into the driveway entrance and stopped at the gate. There was a small box mounted on a three-foot post, sitting on the side of the drive. It had a large round button sticking out of the middle of the front with the word "push" written underneath. So Fred pushed the button.

"Yes, may I help you?" a voice with a rather thick accent came cautiously out of the box.

"Yes, we are here to pick up Charles," Fred replied to the query.

"I will open the gate. Mr. Charles is will meet you out front."

The gate slid back upon itself allowing the car to proceed on its way. "What a long drive!" Gloria felt a little out of place.

"Yea, I would not want to shovel this!" Fred joked to relax the girls. He had been here once before, so it was not as intimidating to him.

After driving up the wooded drive, they came to a clearing. It was like driving up to a football field. Wide open grass ways, with shrubs and ornamental trees scattered about in what seemed to be random patterns. The large house seemed to look small when they had first spotted it—such was the distance of the driveway. As they continued driving, it grew very quickly and Rachael felt her chest tighten up. Driving around the circle that was laid out carefully in the front of the magnificent mansion, Fred pulled to a stop, but before he even needed to blow the horn, the dark double doors on the front of the house opened and Charles Martyn came strolling down the steps. He was dressed in a very rich looking sports jacket with tan slacks and dress shoes. A tie was knotted around his throat and he looked every bit a young lawyer to be. Rachael was very impressed.

Noting on which side of the car Rachael was sitting, Charles strolled around the back of the car and climbed into the back with her and exchanged words with Fred and Gloria.

With a little hand flourish, Fred introduced him to Rachael, "Charles Martyn, meet your date for the evening, Rachael Dickerson." Then looking at Rachael, Fred continued, "Rachael, may I present Charles Martyn the Third, your date."

Rachael offered her hand expecting it to be shaken politely, but was surprised when it was swept up to Charles's mouth and was kissed ever so formerly.

"Good evening Rachael. So very nice to make your acquaintance." Though Charles's mouth spoke few words, his eyes were speaking volumes. There was no mistaking that look.

Rachael had seen it before, although with much less intensity… I will have you.

"It is very nice to finally meet you." Rachael felt a little self-conscious at this point. He was so handsome and acted so formal. Why would anyone like this need a blind date?

"You must be wondering why I felt it necessary to go out on a blind date." Rachael wondered if he could read minds. Charles continued, "The answer is very simple. I was not really interested in anyone at my school, as they all know my name and background. I wanted to meet someone who did not have any predetermined ideas about me. So I asked my buddy Fred to find me the most ravishing woman on his date's campus." After a slight pause he added, "He seems to have succeeded."

Rachael blushed at the obvious ploy to disarm her. Well, nuts, it worked. She was baffled by how she felt about this. Her emotions had started to take over all thought, and the most she could hope for was to not stutter an incoherent reply. Gone was the self-assurance. Gone was the confidence. Rachael hoped she would not feel this confused the entire night, or this would turn out to be agony.

"Okay everyone; let's get going to the dance!" Fred announced as he set the transmission lever from park to drive. The car slowly completed the circle and proceeded back down the long drive. Charles did not take his eyes off Rachael the entire length of the driveway, which unsettled Rachael all the more. Usually she liked the attention of men, but somehow this particular man set her nerves on edge. He was entirely too intense and powerful. Oh, not physically, although he did look great, but mentally. Yes, that was it, she concluded. He was intense mentally.

The drive to the dance took almost three-quarters of an hour. Fred and Charles's college had a beautiful campus, and both Gloria and Rachael were quick to mention this when they stopped in the large parking lot that Charles had directed Fred to park in for the dance.

"Yes, the school is very old, but the buildings have been modernized to the requirements of any university," Charles offered. He got out of the car quickly and went to the opposite side of the car to open Rachael's door.

"Thank you kind sir," Rachael said as she slid out of the seat with very graceful movements.

Charles offered his arm and they walked up to where Gloria and Fred were standing. Together, all four headed toward the large greenish-colored stone building that had open doors and many other young people strolling into the structure. Music could be heard as they approached and Rachael relaxed a little bit. Maybe this would not be as nerve-wracking as she expected. After all, who could be so very intense while jumping around at a dance?

As they entered the auditorium that was to be the dance floor, Charles escorted Rachael over to some tables that were sitting along the side of the room. Several of the tables had sweaters, purses, scarves, and other miscellaneous materials on them to reserve the seating. Charles guided her to a table in the far back corner of the room. Rachael was amazed that it was not already reserved as it was fairly private and the lighting was a little darker than elsewhere. When they got to the table, Rachael noticed there was a sign on it – Hold for the Mister. This was puzzling to Rachel, but she assumed that Fred or Gloria would ask Charles what that referred to, so she decided to wait. She turned to see which chair Gloria wanted to take and found she was alone with Charles. "Where did Fred and Gloria disappear to?"

"Here, put your things down on here. They will be perfectly safe," Charles directed without answering the question.

Rachael did as she was instructed, placing her purse and sweater on the table. Charles removed his jacket and then taking Rachael's elbow gently, escorted her back out to the floor. The band was quite good and it was not long until Rachael made another discovery—Charles was a very polished dancer. She was able to keep up with him, but just barely. She occasionally saw Gloria and Fred dancing in amongst the crowd, but she did not get a chance to speak to them for several dances, as Charles was determined to keep her moving.

After half an hour, the band announced they planned a small break and that records would be played in-between. Charles asked Rachael if she would like something cold to drink, and she gladly headed with him to the refreshment table. Fred was there ahead of the pack, getting something for Gloria, who was standing along the side of lines. As Charles joined the queue to acquire their drinks, Rachael joined Gloria on the side.

"Well, what do you think of him?" Gloria was awash with curiosity.

"I am not sure what to think. He is wonderful and scary at the same time."

"Scary?" Gloria was worried, "Has he said something to scare you?"

"No, it is, well…" Rachael trailed off. "He is very intense and perfect."

"Oh, is that all. Yes, he is rather marvelous, isn't he?" Gloria agreed, "But he seems to be the perfect gentleman."

"Oh, to that there is no argument. He is by far the most gallant of dates I have ever had. I am enjoying myself very much. Thank you and Fred for setting this up."

"Oh, don't be silly. We could think of no one that was more suited than you two."

At that point, Fred, who was far ahead of Charles in the line, returned with drinks and a plate of nibbles for Gloria and himself. "Great dance, isn't it, Rachael?" then without waiting for an answer, he continued, "Charles is a marvelous dancer, isn't he?"

"Wonderful, Fred. I can scarcely catch my breath in-between dances."

"I told you that he would show you a good time. You certainly won't be bored," Fred stated with a little knowing look on his face.

"No, I don't think that would ever be an issue with Mr. Charles. But hey, why did you not sit with us—not that we have sat very much—but our table is in a great location," Rachael wanted this answered before Charles came on the scene.

"Charles told us he wanted you all to himself." Gloria stated a little flatly.

Just then, Charles joined them with some snacks and drinks. He had chosen wisely, although he had not asked her what she liked. She took the proffered napkins and plates and headed to the table, while Charles followed carrying the drinks. They wove their way around the other tables to the back of the room and setting down the items, Charles held her chair out for her.

"This looks very tempting, Charles. Thank you," Rachael said.

"Well, it is not the Ritz, but we will survive until we can go to dinner."

Rachael took a small bite of the cracker laden with a cheese spread. She wanted to have conversation with him, but decided to let him open the conversation. She did not have long to wait.

"Rachael, I did not mention this in the car, but you look very lovely tonight."

"Thank you, Charles. You look very dashing." Rachael felt dumb. For some reason, she felt the conversation was very tilted. She was becoming out-of-sorts again while sitting next to the very intense, dark-eyed young man. She looked around the room at people sitting at the other tables and noticed that many were watching them and speaking to each other as if she was the main topic.

"Don't let that bother you," Charles offered.

Rachael was amazed that he could tell what she was feeling and thinking. No one had ever been able to read her face this quickly. Rachael decided to play ignorant to what he was referring, "What do you mean, Charles?" She enjoyed saying his name… even that sounded formal.

"People here know me and are naturally curious about the people I am with."

This caused Rachael to be even more curious, but she did not want to ask direct questions, so she began with a general request, "Charles, tell me something about yourself. I don't know very much about you or your family."

"Well, there is not very much to tell. I was born to Irish parents, who are both from the medical field. My father is a cardiologist with his own practice and my mother used to be a nurse at the

General Hospital here in town. My father did his internship there and they met and fell in love. Father is not home very much during the day as he has a very large practice, but my mother retired from nursing when I was born, and has elected not to return. She did not need to as Father does very well."

Charles paused to gather his thoughts and to take a swallow from his soda. He then continued, "Mother is a very precise and organized woman. She keeps us all on an even keel and runs the house for my father. Although I love my father, I did not feel quite the same about the medical field, so I elected to be a lawyer." He paused and took another swallow.

This gave Rachael an opening to formulate a specific question, "Charles that does not really explain why everyone is looking at us. They act as if you are a celebrity. What you have told me does not really explain that."

Charles looked at Rachael for about twenty-seconds before answering, which made her extremely uncomfortable. She was sorry she became so bold as to ask that type of a question, but it was too late now. Charles seemed to be deciding something as he took a couple of chips and popped them into his mouth.

Before Charles could finish chewing, another student came over to the table and asked Rachael, "May I have the next dance?"

"No, you may not, Clive. She is spoken for tonight!" Charles answered for Rachael before she could even consider a reply.

The young man retreated quickly and soon Charles and Rachael were looking at each other in silence. Rachael could not fathom what being spoken for meant when you were on a blind date for the first time. She thought that Charles's decisive answer was very possessive. She felt flattered that someone so obviously refined would care about whom she would dance with or what she did. After all, he did not really know her and yet he wanted to warn off any other competitors.

"I am sorry about that, but I do not want to lose even a moment of your time." He then took her hand and they went back to the floor to dance to a very rhythmic song from South America.

It was slow and very intense, and before it was over Rachael was afraid. Afraid that she was going to fall in love with this young man, before she even had a chance to get to know him. But I don't care. Although this is just one night, and I probably won't hear from him again after this. Hmm, I never did get an answer to my question. She continued to dwell on these thoughts, while moving to the music and gazing into his intensely dark blue eyes.

However, Rachael did hear from Charles again. The next day, he called Rachael's home and requested that she accompany him to a polo match, later that day. He apologized that it was such short notice, but that he did not think of it the evening before.

Rachael accepted and it was not long before he picked her up and they drove over to the polo club to which he and his parents belonged. The day was warm and breezy and they both seemed to be having a pleasant time. Charles looked like he was born to ride and seemed to be able to control the field while he was playing. In-between matches, he was very attentive and Rachael was more relaxed than she had been the night before at the dance. Toward the end of the afternoon, as Rachael watched Charles in his final match of the day, a young man about the same age as Charles, strode over to her table.

"Excuse me, but is this seat taken?" he asked.

"Well, it is and it isn't," Rachael replied, "its owner is playing in the match over there." Rachael pointed to the galloping group that seemed to ebb and flow back and forth over the field not unlike the tide.

"Well, Charles won't mind, I am sure." He sat down with his drink in his hand. "Oh, by the way, my name is Alfred, but you can call me Al," he informed Rachael.

"Rachael," was all she offered back as he had not offered his last name. He seemed to know Charles, or so he inferred.

"How do you like watching the ponies fly around the course?" He started his conversation very generally.

"It is very interesting. There does not seem to be as many rules and regulations as there are in football or soccer. Do you play?"

"No, I am an observer only. It requires skill and manual dexterity—both of which I sorely lack." He stretched his arms over his head and then signaled the server to bring him another iced tea. "Can I get you anything?" he asked politely.

"Oh, I am fine for now." Rachael was not sure why this Alfred person had sat down with her. There were plenty of seats and tables around the open field, but maybe he did not like to sit alone —or so she speculated.

Soon the match was over and the horses were given over to the grooms to manage. Charles headed directly to the outside stand to retrieve something to drink and then walked over to the table where Alfred and Rachael were sitting. His face looked very different and Rachael could not tell if he was pleased that they had won, mad because someone was sitting in his seat, or just plain tired because of the exertion that had just taken place. His face was masked, which was a little unnerving.

"Well, Al, I see you have found my Rachael."

Rachael was flattered that he referred to her as his, although a little taken aback. Ownership usually was a mutually agreed upon event. They had had only two dates. Taking a sip of her tea, Rachael began to wonder what to say to this.

"Yes, I did and she is lovely. Where on earth did you find such a beautiful creature?" Al answered with total calm. He rose and looking down at Rachael he added to Charles, "Keep your eye on her, old man, or someone will sweep her away from you."

Rachael was amazed that they were talking about her as if she was not there. It must be a man thing. She had always been taught that it was rude to do such a thing.

Charles took the seat vacated by Al and proceeded to take a long drink from his glass, not looking at Rachael, but looking out over the empty field.

Rachael felt a little silly just sitting there waiting for Charles to speak, so she started off the conversation, "Your friend seemed very pleasant."

"My friend? Oh, did he? Yes, he can be very charming." Charles put down his glass and turned toward her with those intense blue eyes. His whole being had changed. Before he went into the match, he was gracious, attentive, and full of smiles. Now he exhibited a completely different demeanor and Rachael was worried that she had done something terribly wrong to make him feel so defensive, or hurt, or whatever this was.

"Are you upset, Charles? I did not mean anything by it. He came over and asked if he could sit at the table during the match."

"And of course you did not mind having a handsome man invite himself over to your table, did you?" Charles's voice held a sharp, sarcastic edge to it.

"I did not have much choice. He more or less invited himself and said you would not mind." After a moment she added, "He called you by name, so I thought he was a friend." Rachael looked down at her hands and felt very awkward and totally at a loss. She did not want to offend Charles, but he was acting terribly possessive for only two dates. She looked down and stared at her hands, motionless in her lap. She was not sure what to say and she definitely was out of her element as far as being treated this way. She was not used to being anything but confident and straight forward. Now, she felt as if she was on the verge of failing at something that she did not understand. She knew she was losing control of her feelings. He held them in his control and she was on the defensive for the first time in a dating relationship.

"Well, it is time to go," Charles announced abruptly. He stood up, coolly held her chair so she could get her pocketbook from under the tablecloth, and then escorted her from the area. When Charles dropped her off, he escorted her to her door and then said, "I hope this day has been educational for you." He then turned before she could answer and descended down the small flight of stairs off her front porch. He did not look back at her as he left, just climbed into his car and pulled rapidly away from the curb.

Rachael was dumbstruck. She had never seen anyone act this way before. It was flattering that such a man would want her in the first place. He was handsome, rich, educated, from a good family, and most of all, seemed totally enamored with her. But now, he seemed cold and yes, even angry at her. She had no

14

control over what Alfred did–whoever he was. She was just sitting and watching the match.

She did not know that Charles was smiling as he drove away from her neighborhood. She did not know that he felt very confident and full of himself. She thought she had hurt him deeply in some way. It must be her fault. She was too naive about such things, and she felt that she had learned a very hard lesson, and had lost someone she was falling in love with all too quickly. Well, perhaps it is for the best, she mused. However, she did not really feel that way. She felt very dejected. Slowly she ascended the stairs to her room to be alone with her thoughts.

Too Late

A tiger is not bound,
By bars of black and tan.
His confidence exudes,
His eyes see across the land.

He crouches low, blending in the grass,
His eyes fixed on his prize.
You don't even know that he is there,
Until you look deep into his eyes.

Chapter II

"How was your date, honey? It did not last very long. I thought he was taking you to dinner," her mother had a way of asking things and stating things all at one time.

"I did too, mother," Rachael answered softly. She hung up her dress, sat down on her bed and said, "Mother, may I ask you a question?"

"Of course dear, anything you would like." Mrs. Dickerson came and sat next to her daughter on the side of her bed.

"Charles has been wonderful. He is smart, funny, polite, and so much better than most of the dates I have gone out with, thus far."

"Yes, so what is your question?" Her mother did not see a problem as of yet.

"Well, today he changed," Rachael began. "He was great until his last match. He rode beautifully and the match went well. But when he came back to the table, he was sullen and quiet." Rachael left out the part about the other gent who had seated himself in Charles's chair at the table. "He would not look at me and then abruptly, he said we had to leave. He was very cold when he dropped me off. I really don't know what this means. I don't know if I will ever hear from him again." Rachael realized that she was very close to tears, but did not know why.

"Well, sometimes I can't figure out your father, when he gets in a mood, but he usually comes out of it and so I just ignore it. I will go bake him something he likes or fix a special meal for him and he comes right out of it." Mrs. Dickerson thought for a moment and then continued, "I think perhaps Charles was tired from his match. Maybe he did not feel good or something happened out on the field you could not see or hear. It might be it had nothing to do with you at all." Mrs. Dickerson patted her daughter's hand and said, "I bet you hear from him tomorrow. Come on downstairs. I have some cookies that are just the right temperature for nibbling."

She stood up from the bed and led the way to the door. Rachael had no choice but to follow.

****

The next day was Sunday and Rachael decided to take her bicycle out for a leisurely ride on a trail that wandered along the river, as a designated hiking and biking trail—no cars allowed. She loved to go there when she wanted to lose herself in nature. Although she could not think of anything that she had done to hurt Charles, she knew that she had done something. She thought perhaps she could figure it out if she were not distracted by household things.

She dressed quietly and left her room. It was seven-thirty in the morning and she did not want to wake her parents, especially her father, since this was his only day off. Now that she thought about it, when did her mother get a day off? Well, she did not really have a job, so I guess that is okay. Or so her father felt. "If you don't have to be somewhere all the time, then you live in the lap of luxury," he would repeat whenever her mother mentioned how tired she was. Father always had an answer to the problem—but Rachael did not think that it helped very much.

She went downstairs and grabbed a glass of milk. A little chocolate and it was the perfect breakfast to Rachael. She left the glass in the sink, took some paper towels from the counter, folded them into her pocket and went out the door to get her bike. It did not take her more than fifteen minutes to get from their home to the trail that she loved. She did not get a chance to come here very often, with college, dating, and friends; she felt she was fortunate that she did not have to work to pay for school. Thank you Dad, she silently mouthed as she peddled down the trail.

Now to review what had happened at the polo match. I got up and had breakfast. Then he called me. I wore what I hoped he would find acceptable for going to a polo club. She had never known anyone who had attended these things, so she had no one to ask as to what was appropriate. He seemed fine when he picked me up. Smiling and joking. His usual self. He must have thought the dress was okay, so that was not it.   Hmmm… then what happened? Oh yes, we stopped to get gas in his car, because the club was two towns over and we had a fairly long drive.   No, everything was fine then.

Rachael went over everything in her mind twice and by the time she returned home, she had come to the conclusion that he was a little insecure and that he must have felt threatened when she spoke to another man. This made him seem vulnerable and sweet in her mind. He must really like me, she thought. However, no matter what, she was determined not to call him. Let him call me if he really wants to see me again.

Two days later, Rachael now doubted her resolve. After all, it was her fault.   If she had said no to that guy, she and Charles would be together right now… or so her thinking had now progressed. She was going to wait until supper, and if he had not called her, she would give him a casual call pretending nothing was wrong, and she was just checking to see how he felt after such a vigorous polo match.

That afternoon after her classes, she drove home and fixed a snack. While she was eating some cookies, the familiar ring of the phone caused Rachael to jump up and run to the hallway where the phone was stationed.   "Hello?" she said trying to sound casual. Inside her hopes were anything but casual.

"Hello, Rachael?" the familiar male voice came across the line.

Relief swept over Rachael. She swore in her mind, that if he had called her, she would never do anything to make him mad or hurt again. "Hi Charles," she replied, hoping to sound calm and rational.

"Rachael, I must see you. Can I come over? I want to talk with you."

"Oh, I guess that would be okay. My mother is not here right now, but we can sit on the porch until she gets back."

"I will be there in twenty minutes. Please don't leave," Charles pleaded, "I know the other day was terrible and I want to talk about it."

They hung up and Rachael immediately went about fixing her makeup and hair. She was thrilled to have a chance to recover their relationship and she really was not worried about anything else. She could fix this and make him happy again. She just knew it.

Charles drove up shortly thereafter and they settled themselves out on the swinging glider located on the side of the front porch. Her parents used this most summer nights, when they wanted to cool off from the heat that dominated the house. Both just looked at each other for a moment and then Charles scooped up Rachael's hands in his. "Rachael, I am so sorry."

Rachael was now confused. She thought she would be the one apologizing. Why would he apologize? After all, it was her fault. "Charles, don't apologize. It was my fault. I certainly never meant to hurt you."

"No, no—it was me. You see," Charles seem to hesitate before he continued, "you are so special to me. I don't want anyone to come in-between us."

Rachael started feeling more confident. He really does like me. She felt so relieved that she smiled and said, "Charles, that won't happen, unless you want it to happen." She never really gave what she said, any thought. Young love is very trusting and vulnerable.

They both sat and smiled at each other. The world was right and all that was going on outside their little sphere was of no consequence. They made small talk for a few more minutes and then Charles asked her if she would like to come to his graduation the following month. To Rachael, that seemed to indicate I plan to be with you for longer than a few dates, and it pleased her. "Yes, that would be great."

The ordeal was over and quickly forgotten as the young couple talked and laughed and planned. The planning encompassed the entire summer and Rachael now understood that Charles planned to see her most of the time. Wow! This really sounds like he is serious.   She was to accompany him to all of his family social functions, and oh, she must meet his mother and father. When her

20

school let out for the summer, they could go up to the lake for a day on the water with his boat, etc., etc.

Rachael loved the idea that she would be busy with him, but wondered what she would wear to fit into this sphere of the social world. What was she getting into? Rachael worried about all the wrong things, and soon was not worried at all. She was in love and knew it. Two dates and that was all it took. He was really special, wasn't he?

By three in the afternoon, her mother drove up out front. Rachael went down to lend a hand carrying the groceries up the steps. Charles trailed after her and so Rachael decided this was as good a time as any to introduce him to her mother. She wanted to sound a little more formal, but it was hard to do so when her mother beat her to the punch line.

"Oh, and this must be Charles, the one I have heard so much about."

"How do you do, Mrs. Dickerson?" Charles took Mrs. Dickerson's proffered hand and gave it a small shake.

"Well, you are really correct about this one, my dear, he certainly is handsome."

Turning a slight shade of pink, Rachael felt embarrassed that her mother was so quick to reveal that she had been discussing Charles with her; however, that was the least of things that her mother could have said, so she remained quiet.

"Do come in and have some lemonade, Charles. I would like to get to know this mysterious young man that so engages my daughter's thoughts." She turned, picked a few packages out of the car and went up the front steps and into the house.

Rachael did not look at Charles for fear that her red face would show more than it already did. She grabbed up a bag and a carrier of soda and trailed behind her mother. Charles secured the remainder of the packages, and closing the car door, trailed after the two ladies.

Charles was very satisfied. This day was one of his best. After all, he wanted Rachael for his own and one of the best ways to do that was to be perceived as helpful. She had come around to his way of thinking and seemed to be ready to become involved. He knew now that he could influence and control her thoughts. She was the kind of a girl that would do as told because it would please him. He found that she had reacted just the way he had wanted her to. Yes, all was right in the universe.

****

By the end of summer, Charles and Rachael were an accepted item in the society pages. Charles's mother seemed to accept Rachael as her son's girlfriend, but Rachael could not tell if she would accept anything else. Charles's father was very busy and she seldom saw him. When she met him, he was very cordial and seemed genuinely interested in their relationship. However, being a cardiologist, he was away to conferences or was operating or was doing any number of other things that occupied his time. Although she thought he was very nice, it did appear that Mrs. Martyn ruled the roost as the expression went.

One night, about two months later, as they were walking hand in hand along the beach, Charles popped the question. Rachael was convinced that he was the right man for her. She could overlook his moods and tempers. Her mother taught her that these did not matter; only his love mattered. Rachael accepted and could not wait to tell her friend Gloria, that the events she and Fred put into motion had turned into a major event. Her friends would be thrilled.

Although Rachael was going to college for teaching, she could do so married, couldn't she? She did not have to give up her career, just because they were going to set up house together. Charles still had three more years of schooling to do, so they would both be studying at night together. How romantic, she thought.

Rachael's parents were not happy about the marriage taking place so early in their daughter's life. She was only nineteen and only halfway through school. What if she dropped out? What would happen if her husband needed her to move to another state for his work? Would she ever finish her degree? Her father said, "All that money. You took this schooling with the understanding that you would finish before you married."

"We will pay you back, Dad, all of it," Rachael comforted, "but I want to marry Charles as soon as we can arrange it. He is so wonderful and I don't want to wait until I graduate. Besides, his parents will help us out. They don't mind at all and are happy to help." Rachael stretched the truth on this one. She was in hopes this was the way they felt, but Charles had not elaborated on this subject—he merely said that they were going to help them.

However, Charles had spoken with his parents the night before he proposed and merely informed them of his decision to marry Rachael. He listed several reasons, but ultimately it was because she was exactly what he wanted in a wife. Charles's father was very pleased as he truly liked Rachael and enjoyed her company. He asked a few questions and then turned the floor over to his wife. All that Charles's mother had said was a slightly reserved question, "Are you sure you know what you are doing, Charles? After all, marriage is forever." But Charles weathered the questions and gave nice, concise answers. In the end, all three decided that they had discussed it enough and retired to their respective bedrooms. Although not expressed in front of her son, Mrs. Martyn did have a very pronounced opinion that she railed upon her husband as she sat down at her dressing table, "What on Earth is that boy thinking? No, that is just it. He isn't thinking." Turning around suddenly to face her husband, who was in the process of pouring himself a nightcap from the bedroom bar, she accused, "This is your fault! You were not firm enough with him. You are never around, and so he has had to learn to fend for himself! He made a very poor choice in that girl. No money. Low family. My word, you might have thought he did this deliberately to make me crazy." She stood up and started to pace slowly around the room.

"Calm down and have a drink, darling. I am sure that Charles knows what he is doing. He always has and the older he gets, the more I see your, ah …determination in him. He will do what he wants and get what he wants," he swallowed a big gulp of liquor and finished, "so don't worry about him." This was more direction than he had given her in a long time.

Rachael was correct to assume that Mrs. Martyn ruled the household. She more or less bent, folded and manipulated (as the expressions go) her husband, if he dared question any of her decisions. So he avoided these kinds of talks by being absent. Then his wife could run things the way she wanted and no one argued with her. It was much easier to listen to her inform him of this or that instead of having to actually voice an opinion, which most certainly would be wrong.

On October 14, 1974, Rachael Dickerson became Mrs. Charles Martyn. He was so handsome in his tuxedos and satin waistcoat and so pleased with the way the wedding had gone. He must have liked the arrangements that her mother and she had planned. They had not had long to prepare, but everything was done very tastefully. Capon under glass, champagne fountain, and a band that seemed to be dressed to go to an orchestral event, were all in place.

Charles seemed to catch his breath when Rachael walked down the aisle. Her dress flowed beautifully with seed pearls all over the gown reflecting tiny lights from the church's chandeliers. She was certainly one of the most beautiful women he had ever known and now she would be his and his alone. He smiled at that thought; he had won the prize.

The honeymoon was spectacular, as Charles's father spared no expense enabling them to start their wedded bliss correctly with ten days in the Bahamas, touring from island to island. Charles had made arrangements with his class schedule to make up the work that would be missed, and Rachael notified her counselor, but waited until they returned to see what was going on in her classes. Her father's worst fear was coming true; she was not as focused on school as she had been. Charles was now the center of her universe and so everything else took second position. Her college professors were very understanding and offered to help her with a tutor if she needed. However, Rachael was a very smart girl and she quickly fell back into step with her classes.

Life at home was wonderful. Charles's father and mother had rented an apartment near Charles's school for them to use. They claimed it was cheaper than paying his board at college, although Rachael thought that they were being extra nice. Charles's mother had not said much when he had announced his engagement to Rachael as she was afraid that if she protested too much, that he would elope or do something rather stupid.

After all, the girl was pleasant enough, even if she was not from the right crowd. It would not affect Charles's plans for college and career. At least not up front. But she had warned Charles not to get Rachael in the family way until he was out of school and had joined the right law firm. "It will add too much pressure to your lives," was all that she offered.

But as these things go, the best-laid plans never work. Rachael became pregnant in January in her junior year of college. Charles was attending to his full-time program and very, very busy. The pressures to keep up his studies and take care of an often sick wife were starting to affect their relationship.

"Charles, I am so sorry I can't go tonight. I just don't trust myself. What if we arrived and I became nauseated again? It would not look good for you and that is the last thing I would want." Rachael was three months pregnant and feeling very poorly. She was still going to school, but often had to leave her classes in the middle of a lecture or not show up at all.

Charles was so busy that he hardly had time to eat, let alone clean the apartment, cook, or shop. "Look Rachael, as happy as I am to be having a family with you, I don't see how I can keep all this up. You are going to have to pick up the slack. I know you feel awful, but think of me. I have two more years of law schooling and then I must take the bar. I barely have the time I need to accomplish all that I have to do; I can't keep doing all of your work for you. You will have to find a way to manage it all."

Rachael did just that. She decided to leave school for a few years, at least until Charles had completed his studies and their children were out of diapers. She could then pick up where she left off in her junior year, without too much course alteration—or so she hoped. Her parents were very disappointed that she had chosen to stop her schooling, but were ecstatic about the prospect of grandchildren, so they did not protest too much.

Charles thought it a most sensible solution. He was far too busy to do anything but his own schooling and career. He socialized with the students that came from the best of families as it could not hurt to know someone who might be able to recommend him to a father or friend in a top-notched law firm. So cultivating these acquaintances was necessary. When Rachael did not feel up to these social excursions, he was more than happy to leave her behind, although he was very careful to not let her know. She was, after all, a very beautiful, if not very pregnant woman. She drew everyone's eye, even though she was draped in maternity clothing.

Charles's parents invited them over to the family home often for formal dinners with all the right people. They were very interested in Charles's career and schooling. Charles's father seemed disappointed that Rachael had stopped her schooling, but Charles's mother only smiled and kept her own counsel. Although she had never warmed up to Rachael, at least she was not intrusive— merely tolerant of her son's choices. However, she let her husband know exactly what she thought about all of Charles's decisions and she fully expected Mr. Martyn senior to take the responsibility. She did not care that Charles was an adult. If he did something foolish, it had to be her husband's fault. After all, they were both male.

July 6 was a particularly hot and muggy evening. When Charles and Rachael had finished supper, Charles said he had some studying to do and would be in his office. Rachael finished the dishes and went into his office to ask him if he would like to go out and get an ice cream cone at the local farmer's mart. "No, I cannot go now. Do you not see I am very, very busy?" he had replied in exasperated terms.

"But you study all the time and when you don't, you are away at some boring function. I never really see you anymore. I thought you would have summers off like normal students."

"You don't really understand anything do you? I am under tremendous pressure to complete this schooling with the absolute highest honors. I can't take off any time my wife thinks she needs something sweet." He paused his little berating session and then added, "Have you looked at yourself? You don't need anything to add to what is already becoming a giant balloon." He gave her a disgusting look and then went back to his books.

Rachael felt terrible. She felt guilty for hoping he would like to go for a ride and get a sweet treat. Sure, she was craving it, but why on Earth would she think he would be interested. He was so busy and had to study so hard. His parents were being so nice to provide them with the apartment. She really should stop thinking of herself and make amends. "I am sorry, Charles. I was not thinking. I will leave you in peace to study." She turned and went out of the office and back to the kitchen.

Rachael decided to call Gloria on the kitchen phone, so as not to disturb her husband's studying. It only had to ring twice and Gloria's friendly voice came over the receiver, "Hello?" Rachael was so relieved that Gloria was home. "Hi Gloria, how are you doing?"

"Rachael, is that you? My word, I have not heard from you in such a long time! How are you doing? How do you feel? How is married life treating you? When can we get together and catch up? I feel like we have lost touch." Gloria had been saving up her questions and they all came out at once.

"Well, I am not doing anything now. Are you free? I feel like some ice cream."

"Oh so do I, Rachael. I will pick you up in about twenty minutes, if that is o.k. It is so hot that going for something cold sounds great."

"Okay. See you then." Rachael hung up the phone and went upstairs to freshen up and comb her hair.

"Who was that you were talking to?" Charles appeared at the bedroom door.

"Oh, I am sorry. I did not want to disturb you. I called Gloria to catch up with her. She wants to see me and she thought that getting some ice cream on such a hot night was a valid idea. So we are going. I hope you don't mind, but we have lots to talk about. I have not seen her for several months," Rachael added this last part to help her husband understand that they had a great deal to discuss.

"I thought I made it clear that you were to forget the ice cream idea. You seem to want to get me upset!"

"No!" Rachael protested, "It just sounded like something to do. Charles, I am stuck in this apartment all day; we only have the one car and justifiably you need it for school. But I do get a little bored. I just wanted to see a familiar face and have an hour or two of girl talk."

"So, you are bored. You weren't bored when we first moved into here. You did not protest when my parents gave us the furnishings to this place. You seemed happy to be here and now all of a sudden you are bored with me and my need to finish my degree." Charles seemed to be building into something illogical.

Rachael could only stare at him in silence. Once again, he had confused her with illogical conclusions. His jealousy was understandable when it came to men, but Gloria was her best friend. How could he object to her seeing Gloria? But as always, Rachael capitulated, "I am so sorry, Charles. I will call Gloria and cancel. You know what's best for me and I am appreciative."

Rachael went back to the kitchen and dialed Gloria's phone again. Although it rang and rang, Gloria did not pick up. Now Rachael was worried. She did not want Gloria to make the trip over for nothing, but on the other hand, she did not want her husband to become any more upset than he already was—over what? Something. She did not know what, but just wanted to keep the peace.

It was not very long before Gloria was knocking on the door. Answering it, Rachael said, "Let's go for a walk. I can't go for ice cream tonight, but we can still talk."

They stepped outside the apartment and went down the flight of stairs that lead to the main lobby. Gloria did not say anything until they were away from the front door, but then asked, "Why can't we go get some ice cream? And why are we going for a walk in this heat?"

"I don't want to disturb my husband's studying. He is under so much pressure."

"That may well be, but why can't you go anywhere?" Gloria was a good friend and could see Rachael was upset.

"Charles is such a good provider. I need to think of him. He needs me to be home right now.   Besides, I am pregnant and should not eat so many calories."

"Rachael, are you okay?   Is everything with Mr. Wonderful okay?"

"Yes!" Rachael agreed a little too quickly, "Everything is fine." She walked a little ways forward and Gloria followed.   Rachael changed the subject, "How is Fred? Has he found a great job yet?"

Gloria sighing, gave up and answered, "No, but he did get a job with Moyer's car rental agency. It will be good training for him, but he hopes to get into a different kind of business. However, you never know, he might learn to love car rentals!" Gloria kidded back to make Rachael relax.

They walked and talked for half an hour only as the heat was too oppressive; then turning back, they headed to the apartment. "Gloria, how about I give you a call sometime next week, during the day. Or you could call me, anytime before 2:30 pm and we can talk or go out, say for ice cream."

Gloria looked into Rachael's eyes to see if she could read anything into what was being told to her. But alas, Rachael had masked her thoughts and feelings. The only thing that Gloria could tell was that Rachael needed to see her when Charles was not present. She wondered why. They all used to be such good friends and it did not seem that that much time had passed by. But then, how much time is needed for friendships to change?

They parted in the lobby with a quick hug and a promise of a phone call. Rachael headed up the stairs and Gloria went back into the heat to find her car and sped away to get the ice cream she had been denied with Rachael.

Rachael went into the apartment and closed the door as quietly as possible. She did not want two things: to disturb her husband's studies and to disturb her husband. He had been acting a little peculiar lately and she did not think that today was one of his better days. Even if she had floated in on a breath of air and he would have heard her. As soon as she entered, he stormed up to her sticking his face about four inches from her face and accused, "You just felt the need to ignore what we talked about and went with Gloria to get goodies anyway."

"No, we just went for a little walk around the block. I tried to call her, but she had already left. I could not reach her. So we just went for a walk." Rachael thought that the truth was innocent enough to appease him.

Smack! It happened so fast that she did not even have time to turn to deflect the blow. Although Rachael felt the palm of Charles's hand hit her face, she could not believe it had happened. She reached up instinctively, her eyes round and fearful. Charles's eyes were now a dark pit of anger. He turned from her and as he strode away he said, "You should not push me when I am under so much pressure! You should not act like everything is about you!" Then lowering his voice he turned toward her and added, "I bet you both had a good laugh at my expense."

Tears streaming down her cheeks, Rachael fled from the room and into the bedroom. She hurled herself onto the bed and started to cry in earnest. About five minutes later, she heard the door to the apartment slam and she knew she was alone. Once again, alone, but for once she was glad. She had to think. She had to figure out what she had done to make him so mad. She knew he was under pressure, but to have struck her… well something was going on and she needed to find out what it was and soon.

However, no matter what Rachael considered, she could not understand why Charles had struck her, although it had not been too hard. Nor could she find an answer as to why he did not want her to see Gloria.

Rachael's mother was always very philosophical about such things and so Rachael decided not to be too concerned by this incident. She figured that she had pushed him too far by exerting her will. She would apologize when he came back, if he did not look too angry to talk.

Rachael would have a long night waiting, as Charles did not reappear until the next afternoon after his classes had concluded. He came home about an hour later than usual and as soon as he had come into the apartment, he went directly to the kitchen to find Rachael. He took her into his arms and said nothing for a moment. Rachael was so glad that he had come to his senses. Whatever it was that set him off was obviously over and she was his love once again.

"Darling," he began, "I can't tell you how sorry I am. I should never strike you, no matter how angry you make me. For that, I am truly sorry." Then reaching into his pocket, he took out a small jeweler's box. Rachael was surprised. Where did this come from and why? "I feel so bad that I lost my temper like that, so I bought you a little something." He handed her the box and she could not wait to see what was in it. She was not disappointed. Inside was a beautiful pearl ring. The pearl was almost the size of a pea and it glowed with the soft opalescence that true pearls seem to exude. Warm colors skidded over the surface as she turned it around in the light.

"Darling, I don't know what to say…" she stated in truthfulness.

"Well, just say you are sorry, that you like it, and we will not speak of this incident again. I forgive you and love you," he stated with the final instructions.

"Oh I do love it—how could I not? And I am so very sorry. I would not ever deliberately upset you.   Please forgive me?" Rachael wanted to make sure that he was back to normal.

"I said I forgave you. Now let's not speak of it again." He turned from her and peered into the pots that were on the stove, "What is the delicious smell that is wafting around here?"

Rachael was thrilled with the ring and wore it every time they went out. It was not long until the incident was just a memory. From that time on, Rachael made sure that she did all of her personal socializing during the day and devoted all her energies to pleasing and helping her husband, when he was home with her. She was feeling better; the morning sickness seemed to have passed and she was now able to attend most of the functions that he attended. Although she felt self-conscious looking like what she knew he thought she looked like, she managed to hide her feelings. It would not be forever and she would be able to return to her normal size.

It was true, she was very large; Rachael did not know it yet, she was carrying twins. Nothing like a true surprise to shake things up. It is amazing that she could function at all. But she was determined to not disappoint her husband. Not ever again. And so the days passed in relative peace.

However the day of delivery was anything but peaceful. Rachael's water broke about four in the morning, waking both her and Charles. "Great, nothing like an early morning wake up call," Charles chided as he put on his pants and shoes.

"Well, I did not do it on purpose. I was asleep."

"I'll call the doctor and let him know we are on the way to the hospital." Charles was efficient if not sleepy.

"I don't have any pains yet. Just a little backache. Don't you think it is too early?" Rachael really did not want to wait in the hospital for hours and hours.

"I can't wait – I have an exam to get ready for and you need to be at the hospital in case something happens." Charles made it clear that there was to be no discussion.

"Okay, I will get ready." Rachael did as she was told and dressed as best she could. Although she had a sore back and a huge belly, she was ready by the time Charles came back into the room to get her overnight case. "I am just about ready. All I need to do is find my slippers," Rachael mumbled quietly as she looked from the closet to the end of the bed.

"You just had them last night. They could not have gone anywhere. Think!" Charles obviously was not in a very good mood this early in the morning. Rachael remembered that he had not had much sleep—he did not come to bed until almost 2 am. It was such a shame that he had to get up so early to take her. "Charles, do you want me to call my mother. She can take me to the hospital and you can come over later, after your exam." She thought about it for a moment, then continued, "As a matter of fact, she really seemed like she wanted to be there when I had the baby. Why don't you go back to bed and I will go out on the sofa. I promise I will be quiet. I probably will sleep a little myself."

Rachael thought this was a good plan and apparently so did Charles. "Are you sure you don't feel any contractions? It will take your mother over an hour to get here," he stated with a frown on his face, "and you don't want any surprises in the car."

"No, I will be fine. The first child usually takes the longest to come, so I am not worried."

"Who says?" he retorted. He was relieved that he could go back to sleep. The exam was being given at 10 am and he could really use the rest. However, he felt a little guilty at the thought of not being at the hospital with his wife. Oh well, may as well make the best of it. "Never mind. I am going back to bed. Call if you need anything," he turned back to undress and climb into the bed.

Rachael had not found her slippers in the bedroom, so she paddled barefoot out to the sofa in the living room. Settling herself into as comfortable position as she could, she turned on the light next to her and picked up a magazine. She was not sleepy at the moment; she was very nervous. This was a scary time. She did not know what to expect and her mother had given her scarce information. She had said, "The pain is bad, but just when you think you cannot handle it anymore, you'll deliver." Thanks, Mom. No, sleep would not come to her easily. So she read and worried.

The alarm clock sounded in the bedroom, waking both Charles and Rachael. Now she had a neck ache and a backache. She must have dozed off reading, because she still had the magazine in her lap and the light was still on, although the sun was now streaming into the room. She heard Charles get in the shower and so she decided to get up and make him some coffee. As she stood up (a chore in and of itself), the first contraction hit with a vengeance. Rachael doubled up and sat down on the couch much more quickly than she had stood. It did not last too long, but she knew she had to make a phone call to her mother. Nuts, she thought, I am going to have to stand up again. But when she did, nothing happened and she relaxed a little and waddled out to the kitchen.

Dialing, she contemplated how she would start the conversation. The answering, voice of her mother sounded wide awake. "Hello?"

"Good morning, Mother. Are you up for a little trip?"

Her mother was quiet for a few seconds and then asked, "Is it time?"

"Yes, I think so. How soon can you come over? I have only had one contraction, but it was a whopper."

"I will leave in a few minutes. Let me get your father's lunch packed and I will be out the door."

Rachael sighed and agreed that would be fine. "Don't drive too fast, Mother. I need you here in one piece."

They hung up and Charles came into the kitchen to see who it was that she was talking to so early in the morning. "Who was that?"

"I called Mother. I had a contraction about five minutes ago, but not since, so I don't know if it was the beginning or just a warning."

"Well, you had better find your slippers. You're going to need them," he added, his eyes searching the floor. "You had to have left them somewhere your feet could reach." Turning, he headed back to the bedroom to finish dressing. Concern for Rachael was not first and foremost on his mind. Rachael would have noticed if she had not become accustomed to his ways.

34

Charles left with coffee in hand, to head to the school library. He had one more thing he wanted to look up prior to the exam. Rachael sat down to wait for her mother. It had been about twenty minutes and she was beginning to wonder if she was going to have any other contractions. She did not have long to wait after that for the second one to hit. She really wished someone was there with her, when this happened. It was amazing that her body could hurt this much. As she sat there waiting, she wondered why they had not planned this out better. Charles usually has everything planned down to the millisecond. But this had more or less been her responsibility. So here she sat, by herself. Once the baby comes, I am going to have to get more organized.

And as time progressed and her contractions started to come closer and closer, her mother arrived. Although she felt nervous, her mother seemed very calm. Soon they were off to the hospital, with the pains coming every five minutes. Arriving in time was definitely a relief for Rachael. The doctor arrived as Rachael was being wheeled into the delivery room. "Hello, Rachael. How are we doing today? How often do you feel the contractions?" he was asking her and holding her hand to comfort her at the same time, "Where is Charles? Is he coming?"

"Hello doctor. Charles will be here after his exam. We were not sure when the baby was coming, so he went to take his exam. My water broke…." She stopped talking abruptly to face another onslaught of pain. Grimacing and holding her breath, she started to push from within.

"Don't push yet, Rachael. I know it feels like you want to, but we have to check a few things first." The doctor started to put on his gown and mask while the nurses prepped Rachael. "Don't worry Rachael; everything is going to be fine. Just relax in-between pains. You will need all your strength for what is to come."

The first baby came twenty minutes later. The doctor said it was a healthy baby girl weighing six pounds four ounces. Rachael smiled and as they started to clean the baby up, Rachael said,

"Doctor, I'm getting another contraction." She clenched her teeth and pushed again.

"Rachael, surprise! You are having twins!" the doctor stated with obvious pleasure. He loved surprises.

Rachael continued for another ten minutes and soon a second little girl was born. She was very similar in appearance, but not identical. The doctor handed the baby to the nurses and continued to help Rachael. She was obviously exhausted and in need of fluids. He ordered a slow drip to help her stabilize and become more comfortable. Then Rachael, twins, and drip were wheeled into a private room for nursing mothers.

Rachael's mother came into the room beaming from ear to ear, "Darling, look at what you did! Twins! Oh, honey, we are going to have such fun with these babies. I will come over every day and help. Twins! Wait till I tell your father. He is going to be very happy with this news."

Rachael smiled. She felt much relieved that the ordeal was over, but she still was tired and sleepy. "Thank you Mother, for bringing me and being here with me. I love you. Give Dad my love too." Then after a brief pause, she said, "If I doze off, please forgive me. It was an early day and rather tiring." Rachael was telling the truth as she was very tired. But what she did not tell her mother was that she was worried about how her husband was going to react to having fathered twins. He was not really prepared to deal with one baby, let alone two crying babies.

"Don't you worry about a thing, dear. I will talk to the doctor and get your instructions. And I will keep an eye on the babies to make sure they are fine. When you wake up, you can feed them. They are as tired as you are right now." She walked over to the two separate, small bassinets that had been wheeled into the room. Both girls were sleeping happily. By the time she had checked on the babies and walked back to her daughter's side, Rachael had fallen asleep. "Your husband should have been here with you, you poor lamb. He sure is a strange one," Mrs. Dickerson murmured quietly to herself. She felt so sorry for her daughter. But now, with the children would come company and Rachael would not be lonely anymore. She hoped that Charles would be as happy about the children as she was—but her motherly intuition that Charles would not be happy, was nagging at her when she pulled up a chair and settled down to wait.

She was all too right. Charles, the great chameleon, never issued a word of negativity when he arrived. He came into the room while Rachael was feeding the firstborn of the twins. He smiled and leaned over to kiss her on the forehead. "Darling, you look marvelous." He acknowledged his mother-in-law sitting in the chair and then noticed the two little beds. "Why are there two beds?" he asked with a wrinkle on his brow.

"Charles, maybe you had better sit down—there has been a development." Mrs. Dickerson stood up to offer the chair.

"No, that's all right." Then turning back to Rachael he asked, "What development?"

"Well, nothing bad darling," she began, "it's just that we have had twin girls!" She smiled her brightest smile and hoped that it would be infectious. It was not.

"Twins? How did that happen?" he turned to Mrs. Dickerson and asked, "Do you have twins in your family?" He looked more surprised than concerned. But pleased would not be an expression that Mrs. Dickerson would use to describe his reaction when she told her husband later. "Well, yes. But they were a few generations back. We never expected our children to have any, however," she swallowed as she met his accusing look head-on, "it seems that you have them now."

Charles realized that Mrs. Dickerson was looking at him oddly, so he changed his look and his words for her benefit, "Well this is such a nice surprise. I thought Rachael was really large to be carrying a baby, but I just thought it was one big baby." He turned to Rachael, "Well no wonder you had such a hard time getting around-there were three of you."

He went over and took her hand in an apparently loving manner. Mrs. Dickerson stood up and stretched her arms, "Well, I must be getting home for now. I have your father's dinner to get on the table. I will be back tomorrow morning to see how you are doing."

She leaned over her daughter and gave her a kiss on the cheek. "You did marvelously dear. Do get some rest if you can."

Just then, as if on cue, the second baby started to make little noises. She was not sure how to cry, so she attempted to do so in a squeaky sort of a way. Rachael handed her mother the first baby and asked her to hand her the second baby. The first was still hungry, but Rachael would not have enough milk to fill both babies for a couple of days.

A nurse came in and said she would get some formula to give the babies to supplement Rachael's milk. When she left to get the bottles, Mrs. Dickerson said, "Well, I'm off. You two will have to come up with names pretty soon. I always found that the hardest part." Smiling, she turned and went out the door.

That left Charles and Rachael alone. Charles looked at Rachael and his smiling loving face morphed into something quite different. "You never mentioned that twins were a possibility." He was obviously upset.

To change the subject, Rachael inquired, "How did your exam go?"

He did not fall for the change, "Now what are we to do? Two babies at the same time! How on earth am I supposed to get my work done?"

"Charles, my mother has told me that she will come over every day and help out. You don't have to do anything. Just study and keep up your grades." She smiled, happy that she had an answer to his obvious worry.

"You think this is funny?" he accused.

"No, quite the contrary, I think this is serious. But I can't get all flustered over it. It is too late anyway. They are here." She sat up in her bed and looked down at the little girl, who was now fast asleep in her arms. "She is so beautiful. They both are. Oh, one good thing," she added as an afterthought. "They are not identical twins."

"You wanted kids right away, didn't you? You wanted to be a mother. Well, you got your wish." He turned and stormed out of the hospital room, almost running into the nurse, who was returning with the additional formula for the babies. After the nurse had left, Rachael was alone with her thoughts. She now knew that Charles held her responsible for all the added stress that two babies would bring. I wonder what his parents are going to think? She will probably think I had a litter. But he will be happy. Mr. Martyn always seemed please to see her. Maybe he would come to see her, before she was discharged to go home. Hmm…. home. They would need a lot more stuff, now that there were two babies. An extra bassinet, more blankets, clothes. Well, her mother and father would help, she was sure.

But she was not sure about Charles. She felt very bad at the moment. Guilty that she had had twins. Why had she not told him that there were twins in the family? He is really upset, but he will just have to get over it, she mused. After all, what is done is done. He is just going to have to learn to deal with it. My, I must be feeling terribly brave. She turned on her side so she could face the two little beds, thinking of names for each one; she soon fell into a troubled sleep.

Acquiescence

My life is not my own,
It passes by at its own speed.
I try to control it,
But it still controls me.

I guess I can't change the past,
Lord knows I would if I could.
But love controlled my destiny,
I must accept as I should.

Chapter III

"They play so well together." Mrs. Makim commented as she watched the twin girls playing in the sand-box designated for small children in the Long Island Park.

"Yes, I think so too," Mrs. Downy agreed as she peered at the girls through her thick-rimmed glasses. Her friend, Mrs. Makim sat beside her on a park bench about ten feet from where the girls were playing with their dolls.

"I am amazed as to how close they seem. I know they are twins, but they have the same mannerisms, the same likes. It is like looking at a mirror and watching one child instead of looking at two, except they are not identical," Mrs. Makim continued.

The day was very sunny; although a chilly breeze was coming across the park from the direction of the Long Island Sound. Large billowing white clouds obscured the sun, occasionally causing a strobe light effect on the ground. Though winter was a promised event, November had its cold moments. The children were bundled up in matching warm coats, hats, and mittens and seemed oblivious to the cool breeze.

"When will Mrs. Martyn be out of the hospital?" Mrs. Downy asked in a very tentative tone.

"Soon," Mrs. Makim paused to think how to begin, "Mr. Martyn said she would not be in the hospital for more than a few days. It was such a terrible fall," Mrs. Makim paused with a tentative look on her face, "I really don't see how she could have done it the way he described it, although it must have been that way, don't you think?"

"Well, it is hard to tell nowadays, just what to believe." She straightened her scarf with a firm tug and continued, "Respect is not always the same for everyone." Mrs. Downy added with a knowing look, "I just hope that this is the last fall that Mrs. Martyn encounters."

"Me too!" Mrs. Makim agreed with an emphatic nod of her silver pate. She wore a plain black woolen cap that suggested a

French tam.   Her long coat covered her slacks down to her knees, keeping her warm while she watched her young charges.

"Well, it is a little too cool for me. I think I am going home to get a nice cup of tea. Would you like to come with the girls and have tea? I have some hot chocolate that they will love and a fresh angel food cake," Mrs. Downy rose while speaking.

"That sounds grand!" She answered her friend, and then turning, she said to the girls, "O.K. children, Mrs. Downy has asked us to tea. Gather up your dollies and things and let's put them in your dolly coaches." Mrs. Makim helped the girls collect all the little clothes, bottles, brushes and other assortments that were strewn across the blanket upon which they sat. Then all four turned and headed out of the park and toward Mrs. Downy's home.

When they had settled down on the sofas and chairs with their tea, hot chocolate and cake, the girls seemed very quiet. To make them feel at home, Mrs. Downy asked, "So what did you two do yesterday?"

"We were playing," Margot answered flatly with her eyes never leaving her plate of cake. She continued to munch rhythmically.

"I know that you played, honey, but I mean what did you do when you first got up? Did you color or watch some cartoons?" Mrs. Downy persisted, partially out of curiosity and partially out of concern. She turned to Jadyn and asked the same question, "What did you do yesterday when you got up?"

Jadyn stopped chewing and stared at Mrs. Downy. She seemed to be analyzing how to answer the question. Finally she answered, "We watched Bugs Bunny." Although her mouth stated this item rather nonchalantly, her eyes remained direct and forbidding.

"Well, that sounds like fun." Mrs. Downy decided to change the subject. "Who wants some more hot chocolate?"

And so the little tea party continued for another forty minutes. Mrs. Makim knew the children were getting a little tired of listening to the grownup talk, so she stood up and said, "Well girls, I guess we had better get back to the house."

Exchanging glances with one another, the girls stood and held their plates out to Mrs. Downy. "Thank you for the cake," Jadyn said quietly.

"You are more than welcome. Please come and visit with me again and maybe we can play a game," Mrs. Downy encouraged.

As the three of them exited the comfortable little home, Mrs. Downy touched Mrs. Makin's arm lightly and said, "Be careful my old friend. The waters seem to be getting a bit choppy."

Mrs. Makim nodded toward the girls and said, "Yes, I will. I fear it is going to get worse." She turned to escort her two young charges back to the empty house from whence they came. It had been such a relaxing afternoon. She hoped it had relieved some of the tension that the children had exhibited when she came to work that morning.

There were just some days that you could not tell what was in store. When she had arrived that morning, at her usual time, to the large decorative brownstone, Mr. Martyn had met her at the door to explain that his wife was in the Long Island General Hospital and explained why she would not be released for a few days. He looked a bit under the weather as would be expected if a beloved spouse had suffered a horrible accident during the evening.

Later, as she prepared breakfast for the girls, she noticed odd, solemn behavior in both. Normally, they were expressive, happy children. But the absence of their mother had seemed to affect their behavior more than it should have, under the circumstances.

Also, there seemed to be a complete lack of curiosity about their mother's condition. It was as if they had been told the answer to every child-like question that they could possibly conceive. It was if asking questions would open a door the children did not want to look through in waking hours or sleep.

Mrs. Makim had finished up the household chores and quickly dressed the children for a day out in the sun, hoping to lift their little spirits; she could not think of anything else to do. Mr. Martyn said he would not be home until 8:00 pm due to a late meeting in the city. Mrs. Makim was used to long days with the Martyn family, but since Mrs. Martyn was in the hospital, Mrs. Makim was surprised he was not going to visit her first, before coming home. However, this was not the first time he had late meetings. Some went well into the night. He had very rich and powerful business associates that always seemed to keep unusual hours.

And so the week progressed. The mood of the two girls did not seem to lighten up until Thursday, the promised day of Mrs. Martyn's return. Mr. Martyn said he would be working for part of the day and then would pick her up from the hospital on his way home. He seemed genuinely pleased that she was returning, which lessened Mrs. Makim's anxiety slightly. She planned a wonderful meal for the family and started dinner at around 3 o'clock. By five, Mrs. Martyn arrived by taxi.

"Where is Mr. Martyn?" Mrs. Makim was surprised that he had not brought her home since he had seemed so concerned.

Rachael Martyn, whose back was to Mrs. Makim as she took off her hat and coat, seemed deep in thought. As she removed her scarf, she looked up into the mirror that was hanging in the hall. A very bruised, drawn and sorrowful face stared back at her. She wondered if that could really be her own face. She hoped there would be no scaring, although she thought that most of it would fade…in due time.

When she looked up into the mirror, Mrs. Makim drew in a sharp breath and then covered, "Oh, you poor dear. That must have been a dreadful fall!"

Rachael did not reply. She slowly folded the scarf and laid it on the small table that stood under the mirror. Suddenly, from upstairs, two excited little girls pounded down the steps. They did not appear as shocked at their mother's appearance as Mrs. Makim was, but then again, they had seen her right after her fall.

"Mommy, we missed you so much!" Jadyn was the most vocal and was not to be contained as she wrapped her arms around her mother's legs.

"Yes, Mommy, you were gone so long," Margot added with authority, "and we could not come to see you."

Rachael seemed to snap out of her reverie as soon as she saw the two girls. "Oh, yes my darlings! Mommy was gone too long from

44

her darlings!" She stooped down and hugged them both and then each in turn as she gazed into their little, expectant faces.

Mrs. Makim remained silent as she witnessed the happy reunion. She did not want to pry…. well, actually she did, but did not dare at the moment. She decided to talk about something else. "I have made a nice roasted chicken with stuffing and small onions, mashed potatoes, and cornbread." She stated this knowing that Mrs. Martyn loved cornbread and she wanted to see her reaction. She was disappointed.

"That sounds lovely Mrs. Makim, but I don't have much of an appetite at the moment."

They all walked into the family area and Rachael sat slowly down on her favorite rocking chair. The girls sat on the floor near a central coffee table and continued on with dolly dress-up, chattering away in small, clear voices. You would never know that anything was amiss. But Mrs. Makim knew, after seeing Rachael Martyn's face, that this family was headed for disaster. She felt so helpless. She loved this little family as if it were her own, even though she was more or less a governess for the girls. At least until they became of school age, then Mrs. Martyn thought she would be able to handle them and her busy schedule.

"Mommy is really tired today, girls, so I think I am going to go upstairs and lie down for a little while," Rachael stated flatly to the twins, although they were not particularly paying attention.

Mrs. Makim was not going to let this go completely. "Will Mr. Martyn be home at his usual time tonight or shall I feed the children first and get them into bed?" She could not fathom that he had not picked up his wife from the hospital. She had to take a cab!

"Yes, Charles will be home by 6:30 pm. He is just so busy, that I did not want to interrupt his day by forcing him to take care of an invalid." Rachael seemed to be taking on the blame for what had happened.

Mrs. Makim was not buying it for a moment. "Very well, why don't I bring you a nice cup of tea after you have settled in upstairs? Meanwhile, I will feed the children and get them ready for their bath. They will need it after all the playing outside we did today."

Rachael looked up at Mrs. Makim, seeming to realize for the first time that she had been absent for a few days from the home. "I am so sorry, Mrs. Makim. I guess you were stuck for everything. I will see to it that you get an extra bonus for this."

Mrs. Makim had heard this before but knew that it did not matter what Mrs. Martyn promised, Mr. Martyn never followed through. She had a suspicion that he did not allow Mrs. Martyn to make very many decisions. "Don't worry about that my dear; just get yourself well and I will be a happy camper." Mrs. Makim always said something like this when the promises were made as she did not want Mrs. Martyn to feel bad when it never happened. She really did care for them and really did worry.

It did not take long for Mrs. Makim to fix a plate of supper for each of the girls, and brew a nice cup of tea. She knew that Mrs. Martyn liked a specific English afternoon tea, so she prepared it with great care and carried it up the stairs.

"Just set it on the dresser over there," was all that Rachael Martyn said when she had knocked on the door and entered. "I will drink it in a bit." She was sitting in front of a mirror at her vanity, calmly brushing her hair with a dazed or distracted look on her face.

"Mrs. Martyn, I don't want to pry, but I am so worried about you and the girls. Is everything here okay?"

Mrs. Martyn stopped brushing her hair and continued to stare at her own reflection. "Of course, Mrs. Makim, everything is just fine. I had a little fall, but now everything is fine. I will be fine. The girls will be fine. My husband adores the children. They will be just fine… don't you worry."

Mrs. Makim gave up. She could not continue to probe her employer when she was in this frame of mind. Perhaps tomorrow would be a better day. She turned slowly from the room and retraced her steps to the hallway. She felt sick inside and did not know what she could do. Maybe he would feel guilty and not repeat whatever it was that he did. Perhaps he would recant his behavior and change. Perhaps, she thought. She left the room, closing the door behind her.

Downstairs, the girls were finishing up supper and arguing over what color their new bikes should be. "Are you getting new bicycles, girls?" Mrs. Makim asked a bit surprised.

"Yes, Father promised us new bikes," Jadyn answered.

"When did he tell you that, Jadyn?"

Jadyn looked up at Mrs. Makim as if to decide what day to answer. "Monday, before he went to work."

Mrs. Makim had a funny feeling this was bribery, but she smiled and said, "Oh, how wonderful! But how will I ever be able to keep up with you if you are riding a bike?"

"We will ride very slowly for you," piped in Margot.

Just then, a familiar sound came from the hallway. Charles Martyn entered the hallway with a newspaper under his arm and a briefcase in his hand. He put down both on the hallway table, and noticing his wife's folded scarf, turned toward Mrs. Makim, who had entered from the other end of the hall. "Is she upstairs?" was the only thing he asked.

"Yes, she is resting." Mrs. Makim turned and started to walk back into the family room, as Mr. Martyn walked slowly and deliberately up the stairs. Nothing he did was ever quick or sudden, at least as far as Mrs. Makim had ever seen. Although, she was never around for the exciting segments of their lives.

Mrs. Makim, turned her head as she was walking down the hallway and stated, "I have your supper in the oven, whenever you are ready for it."

There was no reply. Mr. Martyn was too occupied with his thoughts to even think about his supper. As he ascended the stairs, he prepared what he was going to say when he went into the bedroom. He was sorry that he hit her as hard as he did. He had no way of predicting that she would fall against the counter like that.

He opened the door to the bedroom and looked around for Rachael, before entering. The room was darkened and so it took a minute for his eyes to adjust to the lighting. "There you are," he said as he spotted her on the bed.   Walking into the room, he quietly closed the door behind himself and then went over to the bedside.

Rachael was lying on her side, staring out toward the windows. She did not look up at Charles as he approached. Nor did she even seem to blink, or at least as far as he could tell.

"Darling," he said taking her hand, "I was so worried about you. I am so sorry that I struck you so hard. I did not mean to." He paused, waiting for her eyes to move or blink or something. But his comments elicited no response, so he continued, "I really did not mean it, but you made me so angry. You keep asking for more money. I am not a well of funding, you know. I am a junior member of the firm, not a partner." Ah, there it was—she blinked. He knew how to draw the attention of a jury, and once he did so, he usually won.

"You just pushed me too far on a day that was very taxing on me, to begin with. My boss is not happy about how my current case is proceeding and he did not hold back his thoughts when he verbalized it to me."   Charles now stood up and proceeded to pace the room as he continued to talk.

Rachael was now listening with all her attention. Poor Charles, no wonder he was in such a bad mood. And to top it off, I did needle him about money. But he always seems to have money. His parents are quite generous with him. Maybe he has told them he does not want their help. Maybe he is being independent of them. I wonder. Rachael was now fully attentive and ready to back him up.   He was very good at persuasion; he was, after all, a lawyer.

"He said I was incompetent and naïve to think that what I was doing was going to free my client." Charles was now in a full lie. His boss had spoken to him, briefly, but only to tell him that his approach to this case was very unusual and he was looking forward to seeing the outcome. But a lie or two in life was not going to bother Charles.

"Rachael, I don't know what is going to happen. I am worried about my position and supporting you and the children."   He

48

stopped and looked at her with his most earnest look. It worked. Tears welled up in Rachael's eyes and she had stopped looking like a zombie. Remorse was written all over her face. He had won this trial and he knew it.

"Charles, I am so sorry. I definitely would not have pressed you about anything had I known about your day." She sat up and drying her eyes, she took a very deep breath. She had to tell him. She knew he had a right to know but was now the right time… she had no way of knowing. But perhaps he would be feeling bad enough to take it a little better. "Charles, I have something to tell you."

Charles walked over to her and sat down on the bed. Taking her hand he said in a smooth, caressing voice, "You can tell me anything. Anything, but don't leave me. I love you and the girls. I need you."

"Oh, no, it is nothing like that," she stated with alarm, noticing that she was causing him discomfort, "I am pregnant." She stopped to witness his reaction, as best she could in the lower light.

But there was no facial reaction. His face had gone from reconciliatory to blank. He put down her hand and looking into her face he asked, "How did you find out?" Then, before she had a chance to answer he added, "What did you tell them in the hospital? How long have you known this?" His manner was now demanding and defensive.

"I found out while I was at the hospital. Whenever there is an accident of any magnitude, they said they always check. They are afraid that a young mother might not know that she is pregnant and complications can erupt without warning." She stopped and looked back into his eyes to show him she was telling the truth.

"Why did this happen? I thought you were on the pill!" He stood back up and started pacing again.

"I may have missed a few last month," she offered. Now she was the one on trial again. "I needed more pills, but the girls also needed shoes. I had heard that you won't get pregnant for up to a month after you are off the pill, so I thought I could skip it for a week or so until you got paid." The reasoning had sounded so good in her own mind when she had first thought it up. But now it sounded lame and in hindsight, a poor choice.

Charles just looked at her with a disgusting look. He loathed her at that moment. Stupid woman. Why on earth would she think that she would not get pregnant? Well, one thing was for sure. He would make sure that she did not get pregnant a third time. After this, he would see to it that she had a surgical procedure performed. With these happy thoughts, he turned silently from the room and walked out into the hallway. Yes, we will never have any more children.

****

Rachael had a large, strapping boy by the name of Thomas John Martyn in July 1980.   The four-year-old twins were enraptured with the new baby brother. They wanted to take care of him and to play with him constantly. Rachael had to remind them almost daily that they were not to look upon him as a doll or a toy. He was a living being with feelings and needs just like the girls. But the girls loved him anyway and as he grew, it made the job of watching him easier for Rachael. The girls were glad to supervise his whereabouts and his doings. They entertained and taught him constantly.

But no one was more attentive to him than Charles. He loved having a male child in the family; someone he could lavish his attention on and someone to whom he could make and pass on a legacy. His son. His seed. Yes, Charles was a happy man. He even became a little more attentive to Rachael but in the wrong way.

"Rachael, why did you put a night light in his room? It will make him a weakling. He needs to learn the dark won't hurt him." Charles knew what was best for his son. "Rachael, don't feed him that way. It makes him expect entertainment when he eats. He needs to learn to eat because it is time to eat."

And so the time passed. The girls, reaching school age, needed new clothes and shoes to attend school. "Charles, could I have a little extra money to take the girls shopping for school supplies and clothes?" Rachael did not know how much her husband made at the prestigious law firm that had snatched him up after he had passed the Bar, but she knew that it had been enough to maintain the brownstone that they were living in and to acquire a new car for his impossible commute to the office in New York City. So she hoped that there was enough left over for the girls.

"Rachael, all you do is spend, spend, spend. Don't I give you enough money to take care of the children? I have to work so very hard to accomplish this and yet you want more, more, more. You don't work. You get to stay home and laze around all day and play with my son."

"Charles!" She turned to face him directly after this accusation, "You did not give me enough to keep Mrs. Makim, so I do everything around here. I cook, I clean, I do the laundry, and I take care of the children and take care of you. How can you say such things?" Her feelings were hurt and she felt as if he underestimated her efforts.

"Rachael, where is the pressure in that? If you don't clean the steps or the hallway, who is going to fire you? Or bring you up before the board and embarrass you?" Charles very patiently explained. He never realized that she could not possibly feel spoiled and taken care of in the marriage.

"You are the pressure!" Rachael was now frustrated and confused. Somehow the subject had turned from the need for more funds to get clothing to her inefficiencies. How did he do that? She wondered. Noticing the look of anger on his face from her remark, Rachael conceded, "Never mind. I will make do with what I have." She gave up the quest and walked out of the room. Rachael was a very good steward of the funds that Charles allotted her each month, but he did not give her nearly as much as she truly needed. She was expected to run the house, give dinner parties, maintain her wardrobe and the children's all on almost half of what she should have used.

Their home was beautiful. An old brownstone, it sat majestically back off the street. Although it was an old home, the interior had been meticulously refurbished with hardwood floors, inlaid banister and stairs, high ceilings and large open rooms. It was perfect for entertaining, which is why Charles had chosen it. Plus it had ample room for his ever-expanding family.

Charles always had a reason for not wanting to give in to her, but seldom expressed it. He always seemed able to work his way out of the conversation and to make her feel guilty in the process. Rachael had considered getting a job to bring in the extra funding, but she had not completed college, so the money she could earn presently would not cover the daycare (as if Charles would allow Thomas to be in daycare), and a car and gas and, well everything that she imagined that goes along with working. So she gave that idea up.

Then she thought about running a daycare in the house or taking in one or two children at least. But here again, she would have had to purchase insurance, purchase more educational toys, and turn one of their already occupied rooms into a playroom. Charles would not appreciate that. Rachael continued to rack her brain for some way to acquire more funds. Then she had an idea! She would throw a special Going to School party for the girls. She would invite both sets of parents and have refreshments and cakes. It would accomplish two things. It would make the girls feel special and grown up plus the in-laws would definitely contribute some gift money—of this she was certain. It was brilliant. And Charles should be happy to see his parents. He might even enjoy seeing her parents.

Her parents…. She could not remember the last time she had seen her mother. It seemed every time she tried to set up a get-together, Charles could not make it. She knew Charles liked her parents—hadn't he told her so over and over? Well, anyway, she would use the party as an excuse to see them.

Charles had left to go to the office so she would have to tell him about the party (but not the motives) tonight when he came home. Yes, maybe after supper. He usually was in his office looking over books and making notes. Oh, this was her best idea ever; she just knew it would work out wonderfully. It also would turn a little

52

attention from Thomas to the girls. It seemed that Charles only saw Thomas when he was home. He always said hello to the girls, but did not try to play with them or kid with them or do the things that Rachael thought he should do with all the children equally, not just Thomas.

Rachael prepared some oatmeal for the children and herself. She always wanted the children to have a nice hot breakfast. While they were happily chattering away at the table, Rachael grabbed a pad of paper from her miscellaneous drawer and began to write down things she must do to prep for the party.

"Whatcha doing, Mommy?" Jadyn noticed that they were not the center of their mother's attention.

Rachael looked up and realized she had not thought about whether she should tell the girls about this or not. If she told them, they would be very excited and enjoy the anticipation for the week that she would need to prepare. However, a surprise party is always fun too. The look on the children's faces when they realize something happened without them being aware. Decisions, decisions. Well, she knew one thing for sure. She had better get permission from Charles to do this. He might have something going on, the day that she was planning to have it. Or he might need to do something with clients or entertain someone. But most importantly, he was very funny about her inviting his parents over for frivolous causes. They were far too busy to attend nonsense functions, according to Charles.

Her own revere was broken when Jadyn asked again, "Mommy, what is that?" she indicated her subject with a pointed finger.

"Oh, sorry Jadyn," she glanced up to her oldest twin, "I am making up a shopping list. I don't want to forget anything." Then she came back to reality and said, "Jadyn, don't say 'whatcha doing'. Your father wants you to always speak like a lady. It should be what you are doing." Rachael corrected Jadyn constantly. Jadyn, for some reason, deliberately like to go against the wishes of her father. She was extremely bright, as were all the Martyn children, but she was the one with the iron will.

"Yes, Mother. I will remember," Jadyn acknowledged quietly.

Rachael put the little tablet in her apron pocket to prevent the children from seeing its content. Although the girls had not entered school as of yet, they were able to read, print the alphabet, and count up to fifty. She was so proud of them. She knew that they would excel at everything they did. She just hoped that Thomas was as bright. However, he was a boy and his development might be different. She was not sure.

Rachael knew time would tell. She collected the dirty clothes from around the different bedrooms and started a wash. Then while this was going on, she washed the dishes and planned the evening's meal. Once done, fill the dryer and mop the kitchen floor. She had not done that for a few days. Lunchtime for the children, baking dessert, more clothes in the washer and dryer, folding and putting clothes away, pick up toys around the house, start supper, read to the children, and to top it all off-set the table before her husband arrived home. He was very punctual and expected her to be so also.

Tonight, she wanted everything to be perfect. If she did not fail him today, (although most days she failed in one aspect or another) perhaps he would let her give the party. She was starting to worry. Although her reasoning could find no flaw in the theory, she knew he was very unpredictable. He also was very good at sniffing out a motive. But then, he would have to be wouldn't he?

By 6:30 pm, the table was ready; the children were fed, washed and ready for bed. She had prepared a wonderful meal—his favorite. Looking around, there was nothing she could think of that would displease him. Good. I have done the best I can. That is all I can do, she reasoned. She heard the key in the lock and the front door open. Charles entered, took off his hat and coat, which he hung in the hall closet, and entered the sitting room, paper in hand.

"Good evening, darling. How was your day?" Rachael started off the evening's conversation in the usual way.

"Oh, I guess it was a typical day. Very busy and very productive." Charles turned toward the kitchen with his nose slightly up in the air, "Is that Beef Wellington that I smell?"

"Yes, I thought that you have been working so hard, that I would give you a very nice treat."

Charles put down his paper on the coffee table and walked into the dining room. He noticed the beautifully laid table and asked, "Are we having company or are you buttering me up again?"

"No, darling, I just wanted it to be a very nice setting for your favorite meal."

"I thought you did not have money for such meals, or so I was led to believe."

"Well," Rachael began, "I had bought most of the ingredients and the meat when you asked me to have the Michaels over a week ago. But they postponed, so I thought it would be nice for you and me to have a quiet dinner." She looked him directly in the eyes to avoid being suspected of ulterior motives.

"Rachael, you should have saved the meal. The Michaels will be coming to dinner soon enough and we will have to buy more meat," he chastised.

Rachael knew that this was boo boo number one. She hoped the grand flavor of the meal would get her out of the situation she had entered. Just then, three children in their pajamas came bounding into the room to see their father. Thank heavens! Rachael thought. It sidetracked her husband's interrogation and gave her time to flee to the kitchen on a pretense of checking on the meal. She hoped that serving the meal would soothe his mood.

After Charles acknowledged all three children, the girls left the room. There was no use hanging around after the initial acknowledgments as they knew that all of his attention would be focused on Thomas. Fortunately for Thomas, the girls loved him. Jealousy can make life unbearable for young children when it dominates their behavior toward one another. But Rachael had been very good at convincing the girls that their father loved them very much, but did not know how to play with little girls. He was afraid he would hurt them. Father was not afraid of hurting Thomas because he was a tough old boy. The girls accepted this, mostly. Their love for their little, sweet-tempered baby brother did the rest.

Charles played with Thomas for a few minutes and then his hunger got the best of him. Looking up from his son, he raised his voice allowing Rachael to hear, "When will you be serving?"

Rachael knew this to be her queue, "Almost at once, darling. But let me stick the children in bed. Why don't you get comfortable too? You have time." Rachael knew he did not like to eat later than seven, so she shooed the children up the stairs and into bed. She did not hear her husband come up the stairs and did not know he was watching her every move from a distance.

Finishing with the children, she returned downstairs to find her husband in the living room. He looked at her accusingly and asked, "How often do I have to remind you that Thomas needs to learn to brush his teeth for two minutes, also. Just as we make the girls."

Rachael froze in her tracks. Nuts, she thought, strike two. I hope these boo-boos don't continue. Recovering, she said, "I am so sorry darling, but I wanted to get downstairs to serve supper and forgot." She thought for a moment and then added, "He does brush longer most nights. Tonight I made a mistake."

Charles glared at her and said, "His teeth are just as important as the girls' teeth, and don't you forget it." He turned and headed for the dining room. There was no love in his voice, no thought about all she had done. She would receive only his constant reminder of her short-comings. He sat down at the head of the table and sampled the wine in his glass. "It is a bit warm. You know I like it chilled."

Rachael felt totally deflated. Her chances for getting the party seemed to be floating away on the back of her insipid stupidity. She turned back to the kitchen to retrieve the salads. Once served, she sat down and they both ate in silence. Then Charles decided to fill up the conversational void, "Look Rachael, you know I love you. I am just trying to make you a better mother. You know I have your best interests at heart." This was more of a statement than a question.

Rachael looked up and acknowledged that she knew this. But she did not really say anything. She was too despondent. After the salad dishes were cleared away and she had served the beautiful meal, Charles seemed in better spirits. He even told her that the meat was just the way he liked it and that she had done a good job on the meal. She was elated. She waited for an opening to bring up the subject that had weighed on her mind all day.

The moment came just before she served dessert. Charles, still seated at the table, was looking over something in the newspaper while Rachael was clearing the dishes and leftover vegetables. He noticed an article in the society section. The Blakely family was moving from Boston to Long Island. They would be hosting a party to get to know some of the families in the area: the best families that is—and the paper said it would be held the following month. Charles looked up at Rachael and said, "We have not given a party for a long time. Maybe it is time we gave one also."

Rachael could not believe her good fortune. She knew this was not what he meant, but the subject was broached, so she plunged ahead, "Now that you mention it, I have an idea for something that would be fun to do, party-wise." She waited until he looked up from his paper again and then continued, "I would like to throw a party for the girls. A Going-to-School Party. It would make them feel more grown-up or special." She had said it. Now to wait. She did not have long to wait.

Charles stared at her for about two minutes. He did not say anything. He did not even blink. He just stared at her. Her mouth became dry and her hands started to sweat under that gaze. Why was he just staring at her? She could not hold his gaze. She looked down at the cake that she had served for dessert and pretended to be eating it.

Finally, after what seemed forever to Rachael, Charles spoke in a very quiet and controlled voice, "You have been thinking about this for a long time. All day I bet. As a matter of fact, you think you have come up with a way to undermine my authority around here, haven't you?" He did not move, although Rachael was glad to see him blink once he had said this. "You want my parents to give you money for the girls, don't you?"

Rachael's worse fears had been realized and so she wanted to pick her defense words carefully, "Charles, I wanted to make the children feel special. I also know that you work very hard, and it is not right that I should constantly nag you about money. I just thought this would be a great way to accomplish both." She waited for a response that did not come. She then made the mistake of thinking he was actually thinking over what she had said. She continued, "What would be so wrong in giving a little party for the girls?"

Charles rose from his seat, his water glass in his hand. He went closer to his wife and thru the water directly in her face. This caught Rachael off guard and it took all of her wit to get her eyes closed before the water hit. She jumped up so suddenly that she knocked over her chair. The loud crash made Charles even angrier. To make matters worse, Rachael could hear Thomas start to cry. He did not handle it well when he was woken from a sound sleep.

Charles drew back his hand and slapped Rachael across the face —not so hard as to knock her over (he had learned his lesson regarding that), but hard enough to hurt her. Rachael reached up to the reddened cheek and stood frozen, with her eyes closed, waiting for the next blow to hit. She did not dare run or he might get extremely violent. Oh, why had she tried to be so sneaky? Why was she so stupid? She could not think fast enough to make this better. All she could do was to take whatever punishment he felt she deserved.

But when she opened her eyes, Charles was done. He did not want his wife to be marked up in any way. She was beautiful and she adorned his little family tree quite nicely. But she had to be taught a lesson. She had to learn to obey him without question. Charles stared at her and then said, "We will discuss this later. I have work to do and you have your kitchen to clean up." He turned from her and walked into his study and closed the door.

Rachael just stood where she had risen as if rooted. She was afraid to believe her good fortune. After being so stupid, well, she felt lucky. She deserved much worse but had gotten only a light slap. Charles is right. I did try to undermine his authority. He

58

works so hard trying to take care of us and I was devious and sneaky…. The thought process continued as she slowly cleared the table and went into the kitchen to put away the leftovers and to wash the dishes. She railed against herself for over half an hour until she was thoroughly exhausted.

When she had finished, she went up to the bedroom and prepared to take a shower. Bed sounded so good right now, but she was not sure that she could sleep. She was still afraid as to when they would discuss this event again, as he had promised. She hoped it would not be for a few days. However, she knew her husband all too well. It would not be long now.

But Charles loved to be unpredictable. The next morning, Rachael woke to an empty bed. Charles had not slept with her during the night. She got up and after putting on her dressing gown, she went downstairs to start the coffee. No Charles. He apparently had left for the office before she had even woken up. Sloth, she thought. You might know I would oversleep. She made coffee and noticed the time—it was only six in the morning. She was not late at all. Charles must have gone in very early, she reasoned. She did not dare call him at work. He was angry enough at her. She did not need to add fuel to the flames.

She decided to continue with her day. There was nothing she could do and the children would be up soon, hungry as all growing children are. She would wait for the evening and see what happened then. Charles would come home and they would talk this out. She would apologize and make this right. She was determined to smooth this over. She went about her usual chores with extra determination. Make the place shine. That's the ticket!

But the evening proved to be a disappointment to her. Charles did not come home at his usual time. Now she was alarmed. Had something happened to him? A car accident perhaps? A client meeting? Had he gone to his parent's home? Did he want a divorce? Did he hate her? Her mind was building up question after question without answers. What was she to do? She finished cleaning up the floor in the girls' bedroom as she was thinking all these lovely thoughts. She had not noticed that Jadyn had entered the room. "Mother, why did Father hit you last night?"

Rachael was stunned. She did not know how Jadyn knew about this, but she did not want her children to be influenced by this event. "No, honey, he did not hit me—you are mistaken. What made you think he did?"

"We saw him hit you. You told us it is not nice to lie." Jadyn looked accusingly at her mother and continued, "We heard you talking and then we heard a loud noise. We were watching you. We saw." She finished with a definite close and Rachael knew her best excuses were of no avail to this very precocious child.

"How did you see us? You were in your room?"

"It is easy. We watch you through the grate." Jadyn pointed to the large, square, grated hole in the floor. The home was very old and was built to have central heat down on the first floor. To help heat the bedrooms, large grated openings were placed between floors. The grate they were looking at was the opening to Jadyn's and Margot's bedroom and it looked directly into the dining room.

Rachael was not sure what she was going to say at this point. She did not know where Charles was for sure and she did not want to make the girls or Thomas afraid of him. She started with a thought, "Did you ever see the cartoon characters that are on Saturday mornings? Remember how they hit each other over and over, but never get hurt?"

Jadyn nodded but did not take her eyes off of her mother. Her face did not give away her thoughts and her eyes penetrated Rachael's heart.

"Well, it was like that. I said something that made your father angry and he just tapped me. It was not a hard hit, just a tap…. To remind me of something." Pausing to see what effect her words were having on her daughter, she then continued, "I did something very wrong and he was upset. You and your sister and brother never have to worry about your father doing that to you. He loves you very much and would never hurt you."

"Doesn't he love you, Mommy?" Jadyn was far too smart to not draw the logical conclusion—if he loves us and won't hurt us—he must not love Mommy because he hurts her.

"Oh, yes darling, he does love me. But grown-ups handle their love differently. He is teaching me to be a better wife and mother. But, sometimes I do things so wrong that he gets upset." Rachael could see by her daughter's eyes that this ruse was not working. Actually, she did not know why Charles got so angry all the time. Sometimes she wondered if he needed more sleep. "Well, when you get older you will understand," she ended with the old standby of an answer. She finished straightening up their room and left to tidy up Thomas's room.

Margot and Thomas were playing blocks on the middle of his floor when she entered the room. Looking up, Margot asked, "Mommy, can we have a swimming pool someday?"

Rachael did not take this too seriously and answered casually, "Well, we will have to see about that. They are very expensive." She stopped working about the room and looking directly at Margot asked, "Honey, what made you ask that question?"

"Well, Susie Thompson is getting one. I just thought we could get one, too."

"Let's just wait and see, honey." She continued to work around the children until she heard a noise downstairs. Charles was home. She had heard the lock in the front door and knew only too well the sound of the door opening. She was not sure how to act. She was defensive and relieved at the same time. She was happy that Charles was okay, but now she had to think up her apologies. She quickly told the two children to go down and say hello to their father.

Then she went into the girl's room and looked for Jadyn. She was sitting quietly on her bed, staring at her hands. "Jadyn, why don't you go down and see your father before you have to go to bed?"

"I don't want to go down. I don't feel like it." Jadyn was acting differently than she had half an hour earlier.

"Don't be silly, honey. You love your father. You can't be mad at him."

"I am not going down tonight. I will go brush my teeth and go to bed."

"Very well, you can skip it tonight. I will tell your father that you don't feel well." Having said this, Rachael decided to go down and see if her husband hated her or forgave her. It could go either way.

As she descended the hall stairs, she heard giggling and nonsense coming from the living room. She walked into the room and was delighted to see Charles wrestling with Thomas. "I am happy to see you two enjoying yourselves," she offered. Looking over at Margot, she noticed that she was seated on the chair watching with very intent eyes. She seemed to be thinking very deeply.

Charles and Thomas continued the roughhousing for another couple of minutes and then Charles told the two children it was time for bed. Margot took Thomas's hand and they both ascended the stairs. Charles took his jacket from the back of the couch, along with his tie, and laid it over the banister of the stairs. Returning, he looked briefly at his wife as if deciding something. Rachael waited for him to speak first so she could gage her apology according to his mood.

"Well, what do you have to say for yourself?" Charles asked rather pointedly.

"I am so sorry, darling. Really I am. I had no intention of undermining your authority. I was just trying to help."

"Well, I have decided to leave it be for now. You can have your party, but you may not ask my parents or yours. If you want to give a party for the girls, I will allow it. But it is to be just us four. No one else—after all you don't have much extra money for such nonsense, do you?" he asked in a cutting tone.

"As you say, Charles," was all that Rachael offered back. Tomorrow, she would have to get her sewing machine out and try to fix up some of the dresses and pants for the girls for school. School shoes, well that was something else again.

"I will give you money for the children to get new clothes, but only one hundred dollars. That is the limit."

Rachael was deliriously happy with this. She could do a lot with one hundred dollars. Shoes too. This was marvelous. Maybe getting a slap in the face was worth it if she was able to get the money she needed. Maybe. But the money was not in her hand and she knew Charles could change his mind on a whim. Or if she messed up again. She was not going to mess up.

"Thank you, Charles," she started, "that is very generous of you. I will take the children out on Saturday and start getting the things they need."

"Well, I don't know about generous," his face changing from a matter of fact look to a malicious smile. "I do have some other requirements."

Rachael tried to keep her smile on her face but did not succeed. Charles noticed it and was very pleased. He would make her pay with her own pound of flesh. "You see my darling Rachael, I want Thomas to have new shoes and new clothes too. His are much too shabby."

"But Charles, he has not outgrown his play clothes or shoes. We just bought him several outfits three weeks ago. The only thing he will need this fall is a new jacket for winter." Rachael stopped, ready to kick herself. Why had she not kept her big mouth shut?

"You know what," Charles said, elated that Rachael had mentioned the jacket, "I am so glad you mentioned that. He does need a new jacket. Good idea. Let's put it on the list."

Rachael was deciding how to answer this when Thomas called down the stairs, "Mommy, Jadyn won't kiss me good night. She's being mean."

Rachael rushed toward the stairs and answered her son as she was going up the steps, "Don't worry about it Thomas, she doesn't feel well and does not want you to get sick too. Let's go brush teeth and wash faces and all that fun stuff," Rachael tried to brighten up her own mood as well as that of her petulant son.

Charles went into the kitchen to see what Rachael had fed the children for supper. He knew that she would have a plate made up for him in anticipation of his coming home, but he had met with his father for a wonderful dinner of lobster and steak before he had come home. It was very good to get away from the children and wife and have just man talk. After satisfying his curiosity, he went into the living room to read his paper. He would look into the children's rooms later. No use running up and down the stairs right now.

Rachael came down about half an hour later, looking very pensive. "Jadyn is not quite herself tonight."

"Is she sick?" Charles asked, not bothering to put down the paper.

Rachael sat quietly. She knew the children could not see them through the vent when they were in the living room, but she was not sure if they could hear.   She decided to lower her voice, "Charles, she is upset over our fight the other day."

Charles's eyes looked as if they would bore right through her. "What did you tell them?" he hissed through his teeth.

"Nothing, absolutely nothing!" Rachael defended. Looking over into the dining room she pointed and said, "They can hear us and see us when we are at the dining room table. The grate in the ceiling opens into the girls' bedroom."

Charles looked amazed for a moment and then decided that he would have to fix this issue immediately. Standing up, he went into the dining room and looked up at the grate. Next, he went into the kitchen and taking a measuring tape out of the catch-all drawer, proceeded to measure the opening. Writing everything down, he put the information into his briefcase. He would get the necessary materials on his way home tomorrow to block up the grated vantage point that the children had so cleverly discovered. They had no need for the heat as the house had a baseboard heating system.

Rachael sat quietly on the sofa and did not offer any comments. She knew she was on thin ice and did not want him to have any excuses to keep the money or add more demands. She knew that Thomas did not need a new jacket right away. It was still summer-like outside. Later, much later, he would need one. If they bought one now, he would probably outgrow it before he actually was able to wear it. No, she must think of something else to buy Thomas to placate her husband. And she had better think of it quickly!

Pete and Repeat

The Merry-go-round spins,
On the path to which it was designed.
It has no preconceived notions,
Of taking a different course through time.

Is not everything as it should be?
Your circle is complete.
If you feel you are spinning out of control,
Remember it is your chosen fate that you must meet.

Chapter IV

Jim Thorpe region is a typical town in Pennsylvania coal country. The mining in the area had sustained the local economy for many years.   But the mining industry was dwindling.   Only certain mines still were producing and many of the miners had moved on to other areas or found other opportunities.

The Blodger family was one such family that still depended on the mines for their livelihood. Today, they were having a typical breakfast. Well, typical of them.   "Why do I always have to eat this slop, Kate?" Harold Blodger asked in a not so pleasant tone.

"It is not slop, Harry. I made oatmeal today for breakfast because I need to get more eggs at the store. We ran out and I wanted you to have something hot before you went to work. I couldn't think of anything else," Kathleen Blodger defended. She was used to Harold's complaints and was not able to do much about it today. She would just have to make up for the disappointing breakfast at supper time.

"I work hard, Kate. Is it too much to ask if I want a little meat for breakfast? You know I hate this," he continued. Harry looked around the room to see if there might be some biscuits left from the day before. Not seeing any, he picked up his dish and walking over to the counter, tossed it none too gently upside down into the sink. The oatmeal went everywhere, splattering in the sink while coating part of the counter. Harry did not even look at the mess he made. He turned back to the table where his wife and three of their five children sat eating their breakfast.

"Don't think this will work, Kate. You can't expect me to labor all day on an empty stomach." He picked up his lunch pail and headed out the door. Everyone sat in silence waiting to hear the car start and their father drive away.

"It's okay kids," Kathleen began. "He has time to go over to the diner and get some eggs before he goes to work."   Everyone continued to eat their breakfast in relative silence. Each had their own feelings when these things happened, especially Kathleen.

Her two oldest children, Theodore and Jim, were away today and did not witness her shame. It was my fault, after all. I should have had more eggs. I knew I was getting low—why was I so lazy? It wasn't too late yesterday to go out and get eggs and sausage. Walmart is open all night. I could have gone. She rose from the table and removed all the plates and bowls. The children scattered from the room to retrieve their coats and books for school. Within fifteen minutes, Kathleen was alone with her thoughts.

Harold went off to the diner and was soon eating a super hardy breakfast with some of the other workers from the mine. He enjoyed their company and was glad for any chance to socialize with them. His wife was a good cook, but he found that it paid to get mad at her over a meal. The subsequent meals became feasts to make up for her assumed shortcomings.

Harold enjoyed his work. He went to work for the United Mining Company after he quit high school. He was sick of the principal always calling him into the office for such stupid little details. He knew that the school had it out for him. When he would skip a class to go outside to smoke, he knew he could make up the work. Why did they not leave him alone? His friends were his own business. He knew who he was comfortable hanging around with, so they should keep their opinions to themselves.

He quit school in the eleventh grade and went to work at the age of seventeen. He lied to the company and told them he was eighteen and they believed it. He did look older than he was because he refused to shave the stubble that grew on his face. That, combined with an aggressive attitude got him a job loading carts with coal and dirt. He loved getting paid to work and soon became one of the management's favorites. He loved the camaraderie that was shared between the miners and felt much more at home with them than his own parents and family.

Then he saw Kathleen. She was working after school at the Delvine General Emporium and Drug Store. Harry was walking around the town one Friday after work. He was supposed to meet a few of the guys from work at the local pool hall, but when he looked into the drugstore window, there was the prettiest girl he had seen in a long time. He could tell she was young though. Well, that was okay because he was not so old either.

He went into the drug store and decided to buy some aspirin. One could always use aspirin and so he loitered about the store randomly looking at this and that while stealing glances at Kathleen. When he went up to the counter, he looked at her with his most mature look. Or so he thought. Kathleen rang up the item on the old register and handing him the bag with his purchase said, "Thank you for shopping at Delvine's." She did not even seem to notice him. She definitely had something on her mind.

Harold was fascinated by her. Most girls loved to see him. He was tall, with dark black hair and cool green eyes. Very macho looking with a slight swagger when he walked. But this girl was merely polite and did not look him up and down like most of the girls he knew. Well, he was going to have her and that was that.

He left the drugstore and met with his friends. He asked them if they knew who the new girl was in the drug store. "Nope, haven't a clue," was the only response he received from his friends.

"Well, I plan to find out and I will let you know," he announced. And so his campaign to meet her started. He would buy things at the drugstore, meet her accidentally on the street, bump into her in the grocery store, or farmers market. Pretty soon, she felt like she knew him. When the town held its local festival with a dance, he felt confident enough in his conversations with her to ask her if she would like to go.

She said she would and this became their first date. By now, Harold was really infatuated with Kathleen. She was pretty and smart, but very shy. She did not seem to have any interest in hanging out with girls her age, giggling or chasing boys. She seemed more mature. He knew she was only sixteen, but he did not care. She was the one he wanted. And he always got what he wanted. It was not too long and not too many dates later, he was able to get her into the back seat of his car. By now, the naive Kathleen really loved him and would do anything for this young man who seemed to really love her. Although he had never said so, he certainly gave her all of his attention.

He took her as if he owned her, in the back seat of the car. Halfway through, Kathleen became frightened and wanted to stop, but Harold was not going to have any of that and he slapped her lightly on the face. She was stunned. Even her father had never hit her. She did not understand it and did not know how to react to it. This gave Harold time to finish what he was doing and then figure out how to make her understand. He told her that he loved her so much that he could not help himself. He needed her and wanted her.

Kathleen relaxed a little bit after he told her he loved her. After all, that is what most girls want—someone to love them. He continued to caress her and told her of all his plans. She thought that they included her, so she listened and wondered if he would want to marry her before she got out of school or wait until she finished. As he talked, he noticed that she was listening to his every word. He felt such power at that moment and he was addicted to the power. The power also made him feel a need again, so he started to kiss her and caress her all over. This time she did not fight it. She knew he wanted to spend the rest of his life with her…. She just knew it.

Two months later, Kathleen started to worry. She was late with her period and Harold had not called her for almost a week. He was thrilled to see her when they went out; didn't he tell her so? But now she was worried. He can get so mad and if I am in a bad way, well, he might drop me. What will my family say? What will Mother say? They do not like Harold. But they do not know him. If they took the time to get to know him, they would feel the same as I do. He is so wonderful. Hard working, handsome, and comfortable in his own skin. Her musings went round and round.

Kathleen prepared for school with these happy thoughts bouncing around in her head. Her friends teased her about going out with an older man, but she did not care. What did they know? They were just jealous. Besides, she knew he would call her soon. But how should she tell him? She would have to make him understand. She decided to go see Harold's company doctor.

She would not tell her mother or father. The company doctor did not know her, and she could pretend she was the daughter of one of the miners. She could say she thought she was pregnant and did not want her parents to know, yet. The doctor would have to be discrete, especially if he did not know who she was. She also would not tell him who the father was until she was sure that Harold would take the responsibility for the child.

After school, she rode her bike over to the company doctor's office. The nurse looked familiar, but she did not think she had ever met her. Maybe she was a customer that came into the drug store. She told the nurse she wanted to be tested and an hour later, she rode home to await the phone call. It came two days later confirming that she was indeed pregnant. She hung up the receiver and went into her room to think.

Friday evening, Harold called asking her to go to the drive-in movie with him. She agreed and spent the next hour making herself look as pretty as she could. It must have paid off because Harry's eyes popped when he saw her come to the door. "Wow, you look spectacular!" was all that he managed. "You know we are only going to the drive-in movies? Why so dolled up?"

"I just felt like it," she lied and went out the front door and down the driveway to the car. Although she was very nervous, she had to find out one way or another. Harold followed and they were soon on their way to the movie.

"You're kind of quiet tonight, Kate. Are you feeling okay? You look great, but you are not acting like yourself." Harold thought that Kathleen was angry because he had not called her that week. Good, I don't want her to be too comfortable.

"No, I am not sick or anything." Kathleen hesitated and then launched into her rehearsed speech, "I am with child, Harry. Your child."

Harold did not look at her but kept driving down the road. At first, he thought she must be kidding, but when she did not laugh, he became nervous… then mad. How could she be pregnant? We have not been together that much. Geez, now what am I supposed to do? I bet this dumb girl thinks I am going to marry her and settle down with her. Oh Geez! But he said nothing and his face did not give his thoughts away.

"Did you hear me, Harry?" Kathleen was not sure what else to say. She had not intended to tell him until after they had seen the movie and gone out to park. She wanted to help him satisfy his needs before she broke this over his head, but it just came out. So there it was and he was just sitting there—driving.

"I heard you. I just can't believe it. How could you do this to me?" He answered with an edge to his voice beginning to creep into his usually relaxed speech.

"I did not do this to you, Harry. If anything, you did this to me."

At that moment, Harold brought his right hand off the steering wheel and backhanded Kathleen directly on the nose. She screamed and grabbed her face, ducking down and away from the offending hand. Harold, startled by her scream, swerved the car and lost control, hitting the nearest telephone pole. They came to such an abrupt halt, that both were thrown forward into the windshield. Unconscious, both flopped back into the seat, leaning at odd angles.

The noise of the collision brought a farmer and his wife out of their house to see what had happened. He directed his wife to call an ambulance and he went out with some towels to see if he could help until the medical team arrived. The ambulance arrived quickly as the drive-in movie was on the outskirts of town and they were close.

Kathleen's parents were relieved when the doctor told them that she was not hurt too badly. They were not as pleased when he added that the baby was also going to live. This news came before Kathleen woke in her hospital room. Her parents went out into the waiting room to have a rather terse conversation. Later that night, their daughter woke up and her parents behaved as normal parents do when they are relieved to see their child awake and starting to recover, although it pained them to see Kathleen's face all bandaged on one side like a mummy's. The doctor told them that the scar would be permanent unless there was extensive plastic surgery.

"How is Harry?" Was the first thing that Kathleen asked.

"He seems to be fine, although we are not his parents, so the doctor has told us very little. Just that he will be fine," her father answered.

Leaning back against her pillows Kathleen stated, "Good, I am glad. I don't want him to be afraid for me or anything." She did not remember much about the crash or what had precipitated it. She only remembered that she was carrying his child and that she loved him. Her parents decided that now was not the time to broach the subject of her pregnancy. They would wait and continue with small talk.

Two days later, Kathleen's mother picked her up when she was released from the hospital. She had been nominated to ask questions to find out about the pregnancy and what Kathleen and Harry had planned to do about it. The conversation was stiff and unhelpful to both. Kathleen had not seen Harold since he had picked her up for the movie. She was not even sure he had heard her informative statement about her pregnancy. She wanted to see him desperately, but was not allowed to call him; her father planned to handle this.

The next night, Harold knocked on the front door. Upon entrance, he came directly to the living room sofa and took Kathleen's hand. "Kathleen, will you marry me?"

Kathleen was too aghast from this query to answer. No hello, no how are you, no I love you. Nothing, but the one sentence. She also saw her father standing at the front door, looking quite grimly in her direction. She was not sure what was going on, but she did not want Harry to lose any momentum in his proposal. "Yes, I will marry you," she answered as directly as the question.

Harold looked at her with rather intense eyes and then stood up and turned to her father, "Sir, I wish to marry your daughter. Will this be acceptable to you?"

"Well, under the circumstances, I guess it is the only thing to be done."

Harold turned back to Kathleen and added in short, choppy sentences, "Kate, I will get you a ring. I was not prepared for all this. I hope you are feeling better. I will come back tomorrow to see you." He left the house almost as abruptly as he had entered.

Kathleen's mouth was still open when her mother came out of the kitchen and asked, "Who was at the door?"

Kathleen's father answered rather flatly, "Oh that was Harold. He just proposed to our daughter." He then turned slowly away from the two ladies and went up the stairs to the bedroom. Both Kathleen and her mother heard the bedroom door close.

Kathleen's mother came into the room wiping her hands on a towel. "Honey, I know this is hard right now, but it will be fine later on once the events all fall into place."

Kathleen closed her mouth and looked down at her bruised hands. She was not so sure about everything being fine later. She had a feeling the hard times were just about to begin.

Kathleen and Harold's marriage consisted of a small, quiet ceremony at a beautiful park with a lake that was located not too far from the town. Kathleen was all smiles and very happy that she was not showing her condition very much; she was able to hide it with the dress she had chosen. Harold was very handsome in his rented tucks although, when she commented to him about how he looked, he just grunted and said it was all part of the package. He was not in a bad mood, just a sober one. He knew his life was about to change forever and he was not sure how he felt about all the changes. He really liked Kathleen, but he had never thought about a forever relationship. Forever. Well, nowadays that might have a different meaning. He would see. It might be fun to have someone to do the housework and cook. Like having a maid, but with some perks.

These lovely thoughts were going through his mind right up to the moment he said, "I do." He was not worried too much about money at this point. He had a place for them to live and it was large enough for a kid. Kate could work until she was too big to fit in the counter area, so they would actually have a little extra money. The company benefits would include her, so the baby birthing expenses were of no consequences. No, Harry was not too worried. Just sober. However, his friends would see to it that his

74

sober thoughts would be remedied at the reception following the wedding ceremony.

Harold and Kathleen went on a short honeymoon to Niagara Falls that was provided by Kathleen's father and mother. When they returned, they settled into a comfortable routine that revolved around Harold's work at the mine. Getting up at a set time, with Kathleen cooking him breakfast and packing his lunch. After he left for work, Kathleen would eat and get ready for her work at the store. She had asked and received a small raise in pay as she now worked every day at the drug store. The Delvines, the owners of the drug store, loved Kathleen and wished they could do more for her. But the best they could do was to adjust her hours to fit in with her husband's needs and give her a small raise. It was a shame she had dropped out of school, but under the circumstances, they understood.

Kathleen loved married life and adored Harold. He worked hard and seemed to genuinely care for her. Although he did not dote on her every word, he did answer questions when she asked him and seemed to listen to her—at least most of the time. So she felt fortunate. She was confident that they could make a good life together if only Harry would stop drinking with his buddies. She worried that he would get hurt or drunk.

But Harold was merely following his old life. It was nice to come home after working in the mine all day, shower and be fed a nice dinner. However, he would be very bored if he had to stay home afterward. So he did what he used to do before they were married; he went with his single buddies to the pool hall and drank beer and shot pool. It was the perfect win-win situation for Harry. He did not even mind that his wife was now showing her condition.

After several months of this routine, Kathleen started to become unsure of her situation. She knew Harold loved her and would not leave her—at least she hoped that he would not. She decided to have a talk with him as she was lonely at night and starting to wonder if he would ever settle down. She decided that she would try to fix the situation. That night she would fix him a special dinner and dessert, hopefully putting him in a good mood. Then she was hoped she would be able to have a talk with him about the weeknights.

Harold came home and was thrilled that she had made such a splendid meal. He showered and ate with many compliments to the feast. Kathleen thought that now would be as good a time as any to broach the subject.

"Harry, could you stay home tonight? I made a special dessert to go with this meal and I was hoping we could have it with coffee on the back porch." She waited for him to stop chewing and reply. When none came, she continued, "I really need to talk to you."

"Well, what are we doing now? We are talking, aren't we?" Harold was not sure where this was going, but he did not want to be caged into anything that might change his routine. He stopped eating and stared at her, which made her feel especially uncomfortable. Noticing her discomfort, he decided to glare at her and see what effect it would have on her. Marvelous, she is really nervous now. Good. I don't want her to ask me to stay home tonight. Harry continued to glare at Kathleen, without saying anything.

Kathleen decided that she had angered him enough for one night and dropped the subject. She would have to talk to him about this a little later in the week. Besides, when she had the baby, she was sure he would be happy to stay home with them and to play with the child and perhaps notice her again. So she rose from the table and proceeded to clean up the main course and make room for dessert.

However, they did not have the conversation again. Kathleen went into the hospital a month and a half later and delivered a large, baby boy. They decided to name him Theodore, after Kathleen's grandfather. The healthy baby grew quickly and was a joy to both his parents. Typically, Kathleen had gained weight when she carried Theodore and was now having a hard time getting rid of it.

Harold loved to make fun of her and decided it was very effective to make her feel less than attractive. He still kept going

76

out most nights and was amazed that Kathleen seemed to be hurt by this. After all, he had been doing this for their entire married lives together—why change now?

Predictable in life, nothing stays the same and after two years, Harold's company was not as busy as it was when he first joined it. Because it was slowing down, he was not getting as much overtime and that meant not as much money. This meant more time around Kathleen and their son Theo. Harold loved Theo, but he felt that he could not play with him as he was too small to really do anything with, so Harold merely talked to him and then went to eat dinner. Harry's disposition had become unbearable until he had eaten something. The lack of extra money did not stop him from buying his beer and cigarettes, which made it harder and harder for Kathleen to get extra food money for the necessary little things such as diapers, baby products. As Theo grew, he had a ravenous appetite, and it was not long until he was eating solid food, drinking from a juice cup, and demanding attention from his mother on a constant basis.

Kathleen wanted to go to work, but a babysitter would cost almost as much as she would make, so it was impractical. Although she had lots to do at the house, she wished she had more children. She decided that she would ask her husband about that after supper that night. After all, he had told her he wanted a large family when they had first started dating.

Harold came home in an exceptionally foul mood. He had had an argument with his boss at work, which left him feeling that he might be on the next layoff listing. Plus, he was down to his last five dollar bill until payday, which was two days away. Gas or beer? Some choice. So he would have to stay home tonight with Kathleen, something he did not really enjoy.

Kathleen was not aware of these circumstances, so she was humming in the kitchen and talking to little Theo, who was playing in his highchair. She had given him some little Cheerios on his tray to play with calling them peep-peeps. He was delighted to finger, stack, and eat the little round items. But as with all little ones, he was soon throwing some on the floor and swirling them around. Isn't that what peep-peeps are for? Kathleen mused. They occupied Theo while she was preparing dinner, so they had done their duty.

Harold came into the house and went directly into the bedroom to shower. Kathleen was surprised he did not say hello first but thought he might be exceptionally dirty. Working in a coal mine did not lend itself to clean clothing. So she continued humming and waiting for Harold to appear. When he did not come out and the dinner was ready, she went into the bedroom to find out what was keeping him.

The blinds were down and the curtains pulled tight, darkening the room and making it hard for Kathleen to see where Harold was sitting. He had flopped down in the bedroom chair, not showering or changing or doing much of anything. He was obviously sick or upset, but Kathleen could not tell which. She went over to him but did not want to upset him by touching him until he was ready to talk. "Harry, is everything okay? Are you sick? What's wrong?"

Harold looked up at Kathleen and for the first time, she thought he looked like he wanted to spit at her. "Harry, don't look at me that way," she managed to say. "I am not trying to upset you, but dinner is ready and I can't leave Theo in the chair by himself long. I just want to know how to help."

"If I wanted you or your help, I would have come out to see you," Harry said in a very quiet and menacing voice.   "I don't want to talk to you now. My life was great until you got knocked up, and now look at it!"

Kathleen was not sure what he was talking about as she thought he seemed content with his life, as long as he was free to go out at night and do what he was used to doing. But something in his look told Kathleen to not ask any more questions. He almost looked dangerous. Would he hurt her? No, she decided. He would not.

"All I want to know is if I should set the table. I can't leave Theo. Do you want food or not?"

Harold was feeling sorry for himself and had shifted his circumstances and problems to Kathleen. All he wanted to do now was to lash out and make her leave him alone. "Get out!" he yelled, "I don't want to look at you right now."

Kathleen turned abruptly and headed back to the kitchen. She was angry and afraid at the same time. Harold had a bad temper, but he never looked like he wanted to beat her until today. This was a new side to him and she did not like it. She thought that he must have had a bad day so she would leave him stew in his own juices as her mother used to say. There is no talking to someone who is feeling like this.

By the time she reached the kitchen, Theo was crying. He did not like being alone in the chair with no one to dote on him. Kathleen cleaned up the mess on the floor with a broom and decided to eat in the kitchen. She was very upset, but the meat would get too well done if she did not take it out of the oven.

When Harold did not appear for dinner, she fixed him a plate and cleaned up the remainder. After washing up the dishes, she decided to take Theo for a stroll. Harold was obviously feeling too poorly to be civil, so she put a sweater on Theo and out the door they went.

Hearing the front door close, Harold realized he was alone in the house. Furious at the world and still feeling sorry for himself, he took off his dirty clothing and dropped it unceremoniously on the floor in various little piles, instead of putting it in the wash basket as he usually did. Punishment. That was much more to his liking. When he thought about it, he decided that making as much work for Kathleen as he could, would be fitting for his current state of mind.

After his shower, he dressed and went into the kitchen. Kathleen and Theo had not returned, so he thought he would look to see what was for dinner. He found his plate in the oven, warm and fragrant and he devoured its contents quickly, wiping it clean with the soft biscuits she had baked that day. He left the plate on the table and went into the living room, now ready to entertain himself, at Kathleen's expense. But she was not there, which made him angry again.

He switched on the television and sat on the sofa, not really watching the program, but planning his next move when Kate came home. Shortly thereafter, Kathleen opened the front door holding Theo and trying to balance her purse, the child, and his toys that strolled with them.

Harold decided to ignore her and not speak to her—after all, it was all her fault. She was the burden he had to carry and if she was not here, he would have more money to play with and less nagging to listen to; or so he determined in his mind. If he did not speak to her, she would get upset. Harold liked that idea, and if she was unhappy, he would have exacted a little punishment. He remained glued to the ever-changing screen on the television.

Kathleen came into the room and asked, "Do you want to hold Theo for a while? He misses you." Kathleen leaned over to hand Theo down to Harold but stopped when she saw his face. No, obviously he did not want to hold Theo, who was reaching out to go into his daddy's arms. Theo started to cry when Kathleen straightened up, keeping him in her arms.

"Shut that kid up or take him somewhere else," Harold snapped.

Kathleen took Theo into his bedroom and sat down on the rug with him. Loose, Theo forgot all about the slight from his father and went after the first object he saw—a large teddy bear leaning up against his toy chest. Soon he was happily talking in the unknown language that babies speak in, to the teddy bear. Kathleen smiled and hoped that Theo would not become as moody and cross as his father had become. She had no idea how much Harold's behavior would impact Theo and what it would form him into as he grew. If only she knew….

Just then, Harold called her in a tone that made her jump from her happy reverie. She stood up and went into the living room, closing the baby gate on Theo's room, which she had baby-proofed. Theo would be fine playing with Teddy.

"What Harry," Kathleen said when she entered the living room.

"Don't you take that tone with me," Harold admonished, "I work hard all day to keep you living in comfort." He glared at her and decided that this felt good so he would step it up a notch. "All you have to do all day is play with the kid and watch TV. If I was not working and killing myself all day, you would be stuck in that drug store, trying to support yourself."

Kathleen was starting to get upset as Harold was obviously in the mood to orally attack her. She put her hands on her hips and retorted, "Look Harry, I don't want to fight, but you are acting very weird tonight. What exactly is your problem?"

Harry stood up abruptly and turned the TV off.   He turned to Kathleen and said, "You fat cow, how dare you talk to me that way! I own you! You owe me everything!" He started toward Kathleen, who was still annoyed with him, but starting to become a little frightened also. She stepped back to keep a distance between them and said, "Harry, I don't know what your problem is, but don't call me that!"

Harold was on a roll. He was enjoying this too much and knew how he wanted it to go. "You stupid pig," he stated while stepping even closer. "Don't for one moment think that this is my fault. You do nothing but sit and eat, eat, eat.   If you had any self-control, you would not look like you do."

"My looks are not the subject here, Harry, you are. You come in and act like a hermit and then turn into some mean spirited person. You are not acting right and I think you are sick." She knew something must be wrong with him because this was just plain irrational.   She was half afraid and half disgusted with his behavior.   His insults were not new, but the aggression and language were.

Harold crossed the room and grabbed Kathleen by the arms and shook her so hard that she bit her tongue.   Crying out in pain, she tried to break free of his hold. Her cry was loud enough to startle Theo, who had crawled over to the gate looking for attention. He did not know what was happening, but even he could feel the tension in the air.

Harold let go of Kathleen at the same time she gave a heave backward to get free. She fell over and ended up on the floor next to the sofa. She just sat there and stared at Harold as if he had two heads.

Harold, annoyed that this seemed finished, turned and stormed out of the house.   Actually, he had enjoyed himself and was disappointed that it was over.   It sure beats television.   Plus, his anger was abated.   He felt much more in control of his life.   At least at this moment.   He started down the street on foot, not really going in any one particular direction… at least not one he was conscious of at the moment.   However, it did not take long for him to realize that he was headed toward his favorite bar.   Ah, well, this would work out after all.

Kathleen sat on the floor until Harold was completely down the steps of the front porch and headed down the sidewalk.   She was absolutely shocked at his behavior.   He had never grabbed her or treated her this way before.   She absolutely did not like this new Harold, but what was she to do?   She could not leave him as she had nowhere to go.   Her parents had made it very clear that her life was her own doing and she would have to deal with all the consequences of her wrong choices.   At least her father had indicated that he was no longer responsible for her.   Her mother just sat quietly and said nothing one way or another.

No, she could not leave him.   Besides, she was not really hurt.   Just a little bruised.   She got up and went into Theo's little bedroom to pick him up.   At least she had Theo.   She hugged him, deciding to bring him out into the living room for some playtime until he got sleepy.   It was almost eight o'clock at night and soon Theo would be asleep in his little bed.   She wished she could say the same for herself.

****

Years later and several children later, things had not really changed.   Harold would goad Kathleen into an argument and then he had an excuse to hit her or push her or whatever he felt he could get away with at the time.   The children often witnessed these altercations but kept the incidences to themselves.   Harold informed his children that they should be quiet about it because the fights were their mother's fault.   She always said or did something to make him mad and if they told someone, the police would take their mother away.

As youngsters, they believed that his threats were true. Later, the girls sided with their mother, while the boys sat on the fence. Theo was very interested in what his father did at all times. He thought his father was wonderful and could do no wrong. His mother should learn to keep her mouth shut when Dad became ticked-off.

But Kathleen was a fighter and was not going to let Harold push her around without an argument. Knowing this, Harold would set her up for a fight and then use it against her later, proving it was her fault. Kathleen knew she was being manipulated but did not know how to avoid the fights. Harold said such dreadful things to her and made her feel like she was low and useless. The comments he made were getting worse and worse. Kathleen was afraid she was going to have to leave Harold someday, but not right now as the children needed their father. She would have to stick it out until the children were out of school. For now, she would have to endure his scathing remarks and physical abuse. For the sake of the children.

Drowning Fates

Can you outrun the encroaching tide,
As it makes its way on shore?
Can you see it steadily rising,
As it comes ever closer to your door?

Run if you can, no time to waste,
Don't make the effort to look back.
For the tide is advancing rapidly,
Intent on catching you in its lethal trap.

Chapter V

As with all families, both functional and dysfunctional, the raising of children and living of life disguises the passing of time. Charles, now a full partner in one of the best legal firms in New York City, was often away at night. He maintained an apartment in the city to allow him to get into court early in the morning without missing too much sleep. His schedule was such that it allowed him to get home on Thursday night, late, and remain home until Monday morning.

The twin girls had grown into lovely young women. Fulfilling her propensity toward the sciences, Jadyn entered Berkley for a degree program in Biology, while Margot felt that she would enjoy nursing and went into a nursing program at a specialty school located near home in Long Island.

It did not take long for the professors to realize that Jadyn was gifted in many areas. She excelled in her science work but also did exceptionally well in Math and English. Soon, she was able to take extra classes, doubling up her workload. She seemed driven to anyone who was watching; and there were plenty of people watching, for this beautiful woman drew attention whenever she entered a room.

But Jadyn hated her looks. She felt that beauty was a handicap for someone with any brains. No matter how hard she tried to discuss this point or that point with another student, if he were male, he would invariably ask her out. This was very annoying to Jadyn. She liked the young men at school for friends; however, she had no interest in getting to know them socially. She graduated early from her classes and entered a graduate program in the field that was slowly catching her interest: nano-technology.

Jadyn was interested in the medical implications of this new process and decided early on to acquire a degree in it. Very few schools in 1996 had the degree programs specializing in this area, so she knew she had to be the best at everything to be admitted. Fortunately, Berkley did have the program she wanted and her professors encouraged her to pursue her goals. She would never allow herself to perform less than one hundred and forty percent—and it paid off.

Thomas was four years younger than his two sisters. Although Charles tried over and over to get him enthused about the legal fields, Thomas leaned toward the arts. He loved music and played both piano and horn. When he graduated from high school, he and his father had a large argument as to his field of choice for a career. Thomas decided to go into the social sciences and later received a BA degree in Social Services. This would allow him to help people in a different way than what his father thought he should do.

Nicknamed T. J. by his peers, the good looking young man was very popular with both male and female friends. He took his studies seriously, but always had time to socialize and relax. His philosophy was that you only pass this way once, so look around and enjoy the view. He loved his older sisters but found he had more in common with Margot than Jadyn. Margot liked helping people and so did he. Jadyn, on the other hand, wanted to take everything and everyone apart and see what made them tick. She was brilliant, so they allowed this to be her eccentricity. As long as she did not expect them to behave as she did, they all got along very well.

Thomas had decided to go to school while living at home to save on expenses, whereas Margot had decided that it was easier to stay under Charles's rule than to try to argue with him about rooming at a college dorm. However, there was no stopping Jadyn – she had picked a school as far from home as she could get. Berkley was a bit far from Long Island to commute. Her acceptance had stunned and irritated Charles, but he let her go in the end. She was very hard for him to control. He never seemed to be able to intimidate her as he could her mother or her sister. Nor could he manipulate her into believing his lies as he thought he could with Thomas. She seemed to be able to see right through him.

Rachael was still a very attractive woman, but starting to show her age. The stress of family life with Charles had prematurely grayed her hair, but she had kept this a well-covered secret, never allowing her roots to show her true hair color. She had wept very hard when her mother and shortly after, her father passed away; she felt great guilt because she had not seen them very much after she had married, had children, and had family responsibilities. Now that the two girls were of adult age, she felt even more alone.

Charles was gone during the week and this made it easier for Rachael—less nerve-wracking. When he came home, instead of trying to engage Thomas in activities (he had wearied of this when he found that Thomas had an empathic personality), he seemed content to go with the local influential men to clubs and polo matches.

Rachael went with him if he requested it but usually stayed at home to work on this or that project. She was always doing something with her hands and found she had an artistic gift. Her husband merely grunted at her work as if it was a hobby that did not warrant even a comment.

She was not too worried about whether Charles liked her art or not. She was tired of being a stay at home housewife. She was bored and needed something to help fill the time when she was alone. She took art lessons and soon was adventuring out into art galleries and art shows.   She loved the art world more than she liked her own life. She could see beauty in the art world; she only experienced loneliness and ridicule in her own.

Charles had grown tired of his wife. She seemed to have aged right in front of his eyes. To top it off, she had ruined his son. Look at him. He does not think of his own future or the power he could have. All he does is date, help people and make friends. If that kid applied half his efforts toward his studies, he could have made a very persuasive lawyer.   Charles fumed about this constantly, until finally one day he gave up the notion of having Thomas in his law firm. His eyes were on a different prize, and she was a knock-out in the courtroom. Charles started to extend his time in the city and extend his attention from one woman and then to another.

As Charles became more unfaithful, Rachael's life became easier. She was crushed at first when she realized he was not coming home to see her, but at the same time-relieved. It never dawned on her that he was being unfaithful. He would not do that to them. Didn't he tell her that she was his forever and did that not imply the reciprocation? His attention to everything she did seemed to tell her that he loved her. However, now that he was not there very often, she started to make friends and socialize with people her own age. When Charles took the apartment in the city, she had to have a car. She was also given a small gasoline allowance, of which she made the most of over the course of the month.

She finally realized that Charles was unfaithful one weekend when she called him at the apartment and she heard a female voice in the background. Stunned, she asked Charles who was the person with him in the apartment? Ever the lawyer, he asked her how she could possibly ask him that? How dare she imply he was cheating on her and that they would discuss this when he returned home next Thursday. She knew what that meant. He would discuss and she would cower.

Thank heavens she had been able to keep most of their difficulties from the children. Charles seldom yelled. Mostly he hissed through clenched jaws and tightened teeth. Plus, he always waited until the children were out of the room…but the children knew. Children always know. Now that the children were growing up, Rachael was determined to make sure that they did not know of her husband's philandering. She would never want them to know about his indiscretions, whatever they may be.

****

"Jadyn, you have just got to meet the guy I met last week. He is very cute and really funny," Margot stated as the twins strolled around the block on the street where they had lived for the last eight years.

"Well, I guess I have time to do so as this is the winter break from school and I have an official vacation from work."

"He was born in Jim Thorpe, but attended school at Penn State."

"How did you meet someone from Penn State?" Jadyn asked amazed at the number of people her sister had time to see and to date while going to school.

"He was walking around the Museum of Art the other day and we sort of bumped into each other at the gift shop. Well, not sort of, actually, I almost fell over him. He bent over just as I was walking up to the counter with a book I was going to buy for Mother. It was on the masters and how to copy them. I thought Mother would love to imitate some of the old-time masters, just to see if she could," Margot explained.

"I am not interested in the book, Margot, just the details of your mishap with this guy."

"His name is Theodore. He had bent down to tie his shoelace and so I did not see him." Margot looked dreamy in the eyes for a moment and then went on with her story, "Anyway, he apologized and offered to buy me a coffee at the little restaurant across the street. He seemed very nice, so we finished up and walked over."

"So what makes him so wonderful compared to your other boyfriends?" Jadyn was already bored with the conversation, but this guy seemed to have reached her sister on a whole new level. She really did want to know the details.

"Well, he is very charming and seems to be interested in the same things I like. Did I mention that he is good looking?" Margot asked, but did not wait for an answer, "He asked me out to go see a movie at the old State Theater. He said they were running something old and funny. Who could resist?"

It was obvious to Jadyn that Margot could not resist. "So if you just met this guy, how do you know he is so wonderful?"

"Well, we have seen each other most nights ever since."

"Is he working? What does he do besides trip people?" Jadyn was warming up to a quiz.

"Well, after he graduated with a degree in business, he moved into this area and started working in a store. His father is a coal miner and has to work really hard. Theo does not want to have to stay in that area or do that kind of work. Besides, he says there is very little work up in that area. He likes this area and plans to stay here." Margot had that dazed, unfocused look again and Jadyn was getting a little annoyed.

"Well, if he comes around within the next few days, I should still be here. I don't head back to California until mid-January. Then, if I haven't met him by then, I will know he was just a passing fancy for you."

"You'll meet him tomorrow night—he is coming to dinner. I asked Mother if he could," Margot announced.

"What? You are actually going to invite this guy to meet our-ah-unique family?" Jadyn put on a hesitant face to show that this could be a disaster.

"Ha ha, very funny. We are normal. Well, as normal as most. I have seen worse at the clinic." Margot insisted.

"Be that as it may, you are committing a first intro to our parents. They might get some sort of odd idea," Jadyn warned.

Margot changed her expression from silly to serious. "Jadyn, I really like this guy. I don't know what is in store for us, but I am about to find out." She looked down at the sidewalk as they strolled further along the street. She did not say anything for a few moments as she seemed lost in thought. Although Jadyn did not interrupt her reverie, it was not long before Margot continued, "Jadyn, you have a wonderful life ahead of you. You have your new sciences and wonders and you probably will end up in some exotic field that no one has heard of, doing incredible things. I am so excited for you. But for me, I don't even have the nerve to move out of the house. I watch Father bully and intimidate Mother, whenever he decides to grace the house with his presence, and I can't even leave or stand up for her."

Margot looked so lost at that moment and Jadyn wondered what had caused this sudden truthful discussion. She hesitated to interrupt Margot, as it seemed as though she needed to talk. Margot continued, "Jadyn, promise me that you will always do as your heart dictates. Promise me! Don't let Father or a guy or anyone tell you what to do or who to do it with."

This brought a smile to Jadyn's face, "No problem Sis, I am the born rebel, remember?"

They continued to walk for another twenty minutes or so before they realized they were at the small ice cream parlor that their mother had spoken about. Even though it was cold outside, they could not resist going inside for coffee and a sundae to round out the day. It was so wonderful to be able to spend such an intimate time together. It also would be the last time that Jadyn would be alone with her sister in this way. Life has a way of using up our precious moments.

When they got back to the house, their mother was nowhere to be found. T. J. was sitting on the sofa scrolling through the TV channels with a worried look upon his face. The girls came in and sat with him on the sofa, one on either side. "Why so gloomy, Gus?" Margot asked. "And where is Mother?"

T. J. answered without turning his head to look at the speaker, "Mom is upstairs, sleeping."

"Sleeping?" Jadyn queried.

"Yes. She and Father had one of their little instructive talks again. Or should I say he talked and she was instructed." There seemed to be no love lost between T. J. and his father. T. J. did not like the way his father treated his mother but was at a loss as to what to do about it.

"I am going to go check on her. Sometimes his little sessions leave marks." Jadyn headed up the steps with a certain amount of urgency.

"Margot, whatever you do, don't ever marry anyone like Dad," Thomas admonished his sister. "Promise me!"

"I promise." Then after a moment, she asked, "Why did you not tell the same thing to Jadyn?"

"Because I know Jadyn. She would have someone's head on a platter if they tried any of that crap with her."

"Your lack of faith in me is touching, brother dear."

T. J. stopped working the remote and turned toward his older sister. Although he was the youngest of the family, he was under no illusions about some of the things in life that happen when you least expect it. "Look, you and I, well, we are alike. We don't like to rock the boat or start confrontations. We are more susceptible to being duped into a lie." He had such a serious look on his face that Margot started to smile. Thomas, seeing her look, added, "Look, this is not funny. I don't want you hurt. I would not be able to live with it."

"Don't worry silly."

Just then Jadyn came back into the room. "Well, she really is asleep. I did not see anything wrong, but I don't like that she went to bed so early. I think she may be depressed."

"Aren't we all?" T. J. asked with a bit of a smile on his face.

"Where is Father?" Jadyn asked in a none-too-friendly tone.

"Sorry old thing, but you missed your chance with him," Thomas said with a pretend British accent. "He feigned anger, which gave him the excuse to packed his overnight bag and trot off to his little get-a-way in the city."

"More than likely, he headed off to a mistress somewhere," Margot stated in an uncommonly trite tone.

"Shhh," Jadyn admonished. Although they all knew about their father's little trysts, they wanted to pretend that they did not have a clue for their mother's sake. She had worked so hard to prevent them from knowing anything; which is why they knew almost everything.

"Well, wherever he went, he did not say much when he left. He was picking on Mother about something, but I could not quite hear it. He is so good at being just out of ear-shot. I could tell from his tone, he was trying to get her upset." T. J. turned off the television and turned toward Margot, "Did you ever notice Father's pattern?"

"Pattern?" Margot asked, one brow rising slightly in the query.

"Yes, he has an attack pattern."

"Like what?" This came from Jadyn, who had resettled on the other side of Thomas on the sofa.

Thomas stood up from the large leather sofa and stretched. Then he walked around the dark mahogany coffee table and sat in the chair that was positioned across from the sofa, for conversational convenience.

"I have noticed that he pretty much behaves the same on the days he wants to escape from the family. He gets up at his usual time, showers, comes down and fixes himself a cup of coffee."

"He does that everyday Thomas," Margot added.

"Yes, true, but then he comes into the dining room, where Mother has laid out a beautiful breakfast and complains. The subject of his gripping varies; today it was the coffee. He thought it was bitter."

"His complaining is not unusual, T. J." Jadyn offered to the conversation.

"Yes, right again, but let me continue. He sits down with a disgusted look on his face and eats without any conversation. Then he gets up, leaves his dishes for her to clean up and stalks about the room, pacing. You can tell he is building up to something." Thomas stopped talking for a minute to gather his thoughts. He then continued, "He finally looks at Mother and says there is something that he wants to discuss with her, out in the kitchen."

"Yes, well that part we have all seen, so what do you mean by a pattern?" Jadyn was really interested to learn. She had great respect for T.J.'s ability to observe.

"Well, I have noticed that when he is about to attack Mother with something particularly nasty or painful, he takes her out of our hearing range."

Margot and Jadyn both sat still waiting for Thomas to finish. They knew he was on to something, but were not sure just what he was thinking.

"They go somewhere to talk privately. He is the one who talks the most. If Mother answers him back, then he gets madder. He always tells her that she does not know what she is talking about and that he does so much for her and for us, and she has to start to act appreciative for everything he does. By now, he is talking louder and hissing a lot. Then he waits for her to answer him back and then he storms out—justified in his anger toward her."

Both the girls sat in silence thinking about all the times their father and mother had had one of these little private sessions. Although Jadyn was not around as much now that she was attending school on the West coast and working full time at a Research and Development Lab, she did remember some of what her father had done before she left.

To Margot and Jadyn, this all made sense. Their father would belittle their mother on general items with them present, but when he wanted to escape to his other world, he would take their mother aside to have a special little discussion. It was his way of being particularly nasty to upset her and then he could pretend to be the wronged party if she defended herself, and storm off—justified and in control of the entire affair. In more than one of these sessions, his wife would end up with a bruise or a mark in a very inconspicuous place. Never on the face, anymore. He had learned his lesson on that score.

Jadyn broke everyone's silent thoughts. "Well, I sure hope that this all works out for you, Margot. The new friend and everything. Life can be so unpredictable."

"Margot has a new friend?" T. J. piped up.

"Yes, I do, T. J. as a matter of fact, he will be coming to dinner tomorrow night. Hopefully, Father will be here," Margot stated without much conviction. "I would like him to meet everyone."

"Well, if you tell Mother, she will call him and let him know. I have a feeling he will come back very quickly if he thinks you are getting serious about someone," Thomas added.

"I am not sure I am serious about Theo, but I do want to see how it all goes. He is very wonderful."

Changing the subject, T. J. looked at Jadyn and asked, "So Jadyn how goes the world of R&D? Have you made any breakthroughs yet? I still can't get over my big sis being a scientist." It was obvious to all of them that Jadyn was the brainiac of the group, and Thomas was so proud; he loved to talk about it to his friends. He

94

was never sure about what she was working on—it was usually a subject too technical and secretive to be discussed.

"I am pursuing some interesting things." Jadyn looked at her little brother, who was not so little anymore and said in a quiet, confidential tone, "You know things are going to change in the world of medicine for everyone. Miniaturization is going to make it possible for a surgeon to correct major health issues with tiny robots that will do the work for them. The surgeons will be more like programmers than cutters."

Margot was looking from Jadyn to T. J. and then back to Jadyn again. She was in the medical field right now and doctors were constantly talking about the latest and greatest thing coming up, but this was not sounding familiar to her. "Jadyn, what makes you think people will want little tiny robots wandering around in their bodies? How on earth could you control it or stop it if it did not do as you want?"

"Well, it is not a robot as you have seen on TV. It won't wander around. It will be programmed like our computers, to perform a task. Simple tasks at first. Then, later, perhaps a series of tasks." She stopped briefly to collect her thoughts to make a very complicated idea simple. "Suppose you have a cancerous tumor in the liver. Now as you know, cancer cells in the early stages, come from the same cells they originate with—so they would look like normal liver cells. They really are liver cells that go berserk. Well, we will be able to code the little robots to cut out cells that have certain traits. We might be able to biopsy the tumor, feed the information into the little robots, and tell them to go kill that cellular material."

"That sounds a little like a science fiction book, Jadyn. What is to stop them after they have eviscerated the bad cells?" T. J. was now looking a little concerned about the subject. He could see the little robots getting carried away and people's figures or toes falling off.

"Well, this is all speculative, but we could give them a life expectancy."

"Jadyn, you are talking like this is now happening. Is this what you are working on?" Margot was fully aware that Jadyn was far ahead of the pack when it came to the newest technology.

Jadyn smiled and said, "Well, I did propose it to the team. Keep this confidential as I don't want anyone to start on something I thought up.   I will let you know if anyone takes me seriously." Then changing the subject, she cleared her throat and asked Thomas, "So what are you working on as of this moment?   Has Father started to speak to you civilly yet?"

"Well, as you know, I intern for the local welfare department. I actually counsel people to help them obtain more education and jobs. I am trying to put myself out of business, but unfortunately, I know I have job security.   There are many people that have it rough. It is amazing how many want a better life but have no way to obtain it—at least not without help.   It makes me feel much needed when I am at work; it is like I might make a change somehow. Even if I help only one person, that is one person who will be better off having met me.   I think it is called having purpose. I enjoy my work, but it does not have a lot of growth potential.   I want to do more, but I am just biding my time and gaining experience."

"How about you, Margot? How is your job going?" Jadyn had not really had a chance to ask Margot about this as Margot was too focused on the discussion about Theo.

"Oh, I love my work," she answered. "It is a little hectic going to school and working at the clinic because they cannot afford more nurses and technicians. But we get everyone taken care of before we go home. Sometimes we have to send the people next-door to the hospital, but most of the time, we can take care of the issue."

"How many doctors do you have on staff?" T. J. asked.

"We have two that are there most of the time and one that comes in when he is not scheduled at the hospital. We have long hours, but we all feel it is a very much needed facility in the community." Margot paused and then added, "I see a lot of abuse within the less fortunate groups of people.   You would think that for us, our

96

family's stature and peer group, and the education factor would stem this. But it hasn't." Margot seemed looking for an answer that was eluding them all. Why did their father abuse their mother?

"I see it too often at my location too," added T. J. "It seems to go hand-in-hand with other factors, though," T.J.'s brow wrinkled together as he mentally ticked off a list, "like drinking or job loss or drugs. But I work within a world that is barely wringing out a living from hard rock. I don't understand Father any more than you do."

Changing the subject, Jadyn got up and said, "Why don't we make dinner tonight for Mother. We all know how to make something special." Turning to T. J. she said, "You make a great Chili—why don't we have that and a nacho salad and bread."

They all agreed and within a few hours, had supper ready and had happier thoughts. When Margot went upstairs to wake their mother for dinner, she found her dressed and ready to come down.

"I smelled something wonderful coming up the stairs and decided to come down to investigate." She finished straightening out her hair and continued, "I must really have needed a nap. I fell asleep very quickly and did not stir for over a couple of hours."

"That is good, Mother. You needed some sleep and had the sense to get it," Margot stated. She did not want to let her mother know that she thought she was clinically depressed, and with good reason.

Supper was a much livelier affair than it would have been if Charles had been present. Everyone seemed happy he had elected to vacate the premises. Rachael loved having her children (now all young adults) together at one time. T. J. and Margot were still living at home, but Jadyn had started a new life so far away. Rachael missed her more than she could express. Jadyn was the personality that Rachael wished she could be: strong of character, determined, unafraid of anything. Rachael hoped that Jadyn would stay that way and never change.

Margot was a different subject. Rachael loved her as much as she did her other children, but worried more about her. She seemed to have inherited her own naive outlook on life. She found the best in everyone and did not look for the dark, repressed feelings that could be under the surface. Rachael hoped that Margot would be a better judge of character when it came to finding a mate. But only time would tell in that area. Tomorrow night, she would meet the young man that had so captured Margot's feelings. Perhaps he would be as wonderful as Margot thought he was…. perhaps.

"Mother, what do you think we should serve for dinner tomorrow night?" Margot inquired, while they were cleaning up the table and kitchen after their feast.

"Well, what does he like?"

"No clue. I have only seen what he orders out. Maybe that will help." Margot offered and then with a face that expressed deep thought she stated, "Well, he has taken me to a couple of Italian restaurants. Perhaps that would be a good place to start."

"Excellent, we can have my famous three meat three cheese lasagna," Rachael said with a mock look of pride.

"Did I hear we are having lasagna?" Thomas walked back into the room and did not want to miss out on one of their favorite meals.

"Yes, we have decided to have that tomorrow night when Margot's friend comes to dinner," Rachael offered.

"Great! Once he has had the family's secret weapon, we can grill him for dessert!" The mischievous look on T.J.'s face was definitely a giveaway if anyone was looking; however, Margot was able to hear, but not see, as she was taking a large tray of dishes into the kitchen.

"T. J. you brat, you will not play inquisitor with my friend, do you hear?" Margot came back into the dining room trying to look stern, but unable to hold the pose for any length of time.

"Don't worry, Margot. I am sure your brother will be the ultimate host and gentleman, won't you T. J." Mother looked at Thomas with a firm but loving expression.

"Well, I for one am dying to meet this marvelous guy," Jadyn commented while picking up loose linens and glasses left on the table.

And so the night progressed with light banter and conversations. Whenever the three siblings got together, there was always the reminiscing of past events that took place with much laughter. Rachael loved these times and almost seemed to come out of her depression. Almost. But down below the immediate surface, the stress continued. What would Charles do? Would he come home for the dinner, beg off, or not even acknowledge that he had received the message regarding the meal? She almost hoped he would not come home for the official meeting. After all, this new boyfriend might not last. So many had not.

The phone rang and Thomas answered it in the living room. When he returned to the kitchen where the ladies were finishing up, he stated with a very neutral face, "Father will be home tomorrow night for supper."

"Okay. That is wonderful," Rachael offered back without much enthusiasm. She knew deep down inside that Charles would not let this opportunity pass. When it came to the family, he had to control everything. Poor Margot, Rachael thought.

Rationalization

I have climbed the mountain,
I have swum the sea.
I have created all the choices,
That I happily set before me.

I know not what will come,
I only know what is now.
My heart rules my head,
My life must follow it somehow.

Chapter VI

As the time approached for Charles to come home and retake possession of the household mood, everyone began to tense up, each for a different reason: Margot, because she wanted her father to like her new friend. Thomas, because he did not like scenes and confrontation; he also empathized with his mother and her thoughts and feelings—he knew she was nervous. Jadyn, because she was having a very hard time not telling her father exactly what she thought of him. And lastly, Rachael, who knew tonight could go very nicely, but probably would not. She too was unsure as to how to handle the situation. She not only wanted Margot to have a nice time but also hoped they would not scare off her new friend with their sometimes unusual behavior.

At two o'clock, the door opened and Charles came back into the house. After taking off his outer coat and gloves, he walked directly up the stairs and went to the master bedroom to change. He was not about to talk to his wife or family yet. He wanted to keep them in suspense as to his mood or thoughts. When he had left, he had pretended to be angry with Rachael, but he did not know for sure if anyone else knew of the situation. He doubted that Rachael confided in them, as she usually tried to keep them in the dark, so he decided to play it cool and not let on to his latest issue with his wife.

Issue. That was slightly amusing. He created these issues to escape into his current lover's arms. But more importantly, he liked the ability to upset his wife. Controlling someone else's emotions was very pleasant, making him feel strong and domineering. After all, wasn't she his wife? Wasn't she there to serve and please?

Charles decided to dress a little more formally for this so-called meeting with a special friend. He wanted to control the night just as his mother seemed to be able to control the dinners and parties at her own home. Charles smiled. His mother was the dominant one, but you would never know it at the parties—his father seemed to be head of his own castle. But Charles knew who controlled that head of state. His father seemed to hate confrontation. Maybe that is where the weak lineage came from and why Thomas never seemed inclined to fight back. He was a weak link too.

Once Charles had dressed and ensured his hair was in perfect place, he went down the stairs and into the dining room. The table had been set formally: Wine glasses, water glasses, and all their best china and silverware. Hmm… this guy must be someone special that Margot wants to impress. She is old enough to be thinking of someone but too weak to choose any one of a decent background. We will see about this.

Walking into the kitchen, he caused everyone to stop what they were doing and look at him as he made his entrance. Each was curious and worried in his or her own way. They wanted this night to be special for Margot. She asked so little of life and each wanted her to have this as an exceptional evening. Charles sensed all this the moment he walked through the door. A slow smile played around his lips as if it was testing the waters to see if they were dangerous. His smile looked dangerous; it was so seldom displayed coupled with that look in his eyes.

Margot's heart started to beat harder in her chest. What was he up to? What would he do to them? He had a way of doing nothing special and ruining the evening by innuendo alone. Please don't let this be one of those nights.

Thomas knew from the look in his father's eyes that he was not going to let this be a quiet and enjoyable evening. No, he won't let Margot or Mother have any peace this evening.

Jadyn spoke first, "Good evening Father. How was your trip back from the city?" Although she was not afraid of him, she was worried that he could ruin the night for Margot.

Charles stared at his wife with that look that said she owed him. "Fine. It was fine." He then looked at the one who had asked the question and said, "This seems to be a fancy affair. Is our guest someone of importance? All the best of everything."

"Father, Theodore is a very special person to me," Margot interjected. "I would like him to get to know us because I am hoping to see him often."

Charles gave Margot a glancing blow with his eyes, then turned and went to the living room. He had not finished the paper this morning and thought he would let them all wonder about what would take place. Actually, he was not sure what he planned for the evening. On the one hand, it would be nice to get one more girl out of the house. If she married, someone else could take care of her for a change. Save him some money and time. However, he was not sure he was ready to give up ownership of one of his children. Thoughts about this cruised through his mind as he sat in his favorite chair, staring at the front page of the New York Times.

Rachael came in from the kitchen and sat across from him on the sofa. She was determined to defuse any potential situation that was to come, although she knew she would pay for the attempt later in the day. "Charles, I am sorry that I caused you any unhappiness yesterday. It was not my intent. Can you forgive me for being so stupid?" She knew no other way to start the conversation other than to take the blame for something she knew to be nonsense. Rachael was starting to catch onto Charles's methods, but for Margot's sake, she thought she would placate him enough to make the evening a little better.

"Don't worry my dear," Charles said in a nonchalant tone as he turned the unread page and went back to glancing at headlines. "I have forgiven you of that. However, I was a little annoyed that you planned this little soiree with so little notice to my calendar. I have a very large trial coming up and need to prepare my case. You should have asked me first what day and time would be convenient."

"Margot set this up, not me." Rachael did not want to be wrong on this point. He would not get as put-out with Margot as he did with her. He did not expect as much from his children as he did his wife.

After a small pause, Charles stated, "I will speak to her about this." He behaved as if that was not going to happen within the immediate future, so Rachael noticeably relaxed.   Mistake. Charles had excellent peripheral vision and was not going to have that. "Please send Margot to me at once," he requested in a very small tone.

Rachael just looked at him. She was debating with herself as to whether she should say something or just do as she was instructed. Finally, discretion won the toss and she rose quietly and headed into the kitchen. With all that she was trying to prepare and plan, she did not have it in her to argue with Charles before the meal.

A few minutes later, Margot opened the swinging door from the kitchen, walked through the dining room, and came quietly into the living room. "You wanted to see me, Father?"

Charles laid the paper in his lap and looked at her with curious eyes as if seeing her for the first time. He more or less studied her or appeared to do so. Then he said, "Margot, you seem older. It seems that only a week ago, I was holding you in my lap. How odd the way time goes by." He shifted his position in his seat as if he was truly interested in the conversation. "Margot, tell me about this young man that has interrupted my week so suddenly."

Margot knew to pick her words carefully. Her enthusiasm for Theo should not be as apparent as she had made it to her mother. "Well, I met him at the art museum a little while ago and we seem to have a lot in common. We get along well and I am hoping to make a good impression on him."

"Simply put, Margot. Very simply put. Tell me, what are his intentions? Besides a free meal, I mean."

"Father, this is just a social get together. Not an engagement party or anything so dramatic. I like him a lot, but that is it for now. Please, don't misconstrue anything. He is very pleasant to talk to and I enjoy his company. Period. Nothing else for now."

"So you called me in off an important case for a little social get-together?"

Margot sat quietly trying to think of what to say. However, it did not matter for Charles reopened his paper and began reading again. Margot was not required to answer. She knew he was annoyed with the dinner and surmised he would mess up the
104

evening with attitude, much to her dismay. Oh well, Theo may as well know all about her family. If they were to have a relationship, it must come out sooner than later. She rose and went back to help in the kitchen.

All eyes turned toward her as she walked through the door. "Well?" they all seemed to ask in unison.

"I don't know, but I think he is ticked off about having to come home for the dinner," she said very quietly. No need making him any angrier by talking about him while he could hear. "He acted weird," she whispered to them.

"He always acts weird," Thomas whispered flatly.

"Quiet – the both of you!" Rachael admonished, "You don't want this to get any worse for the slippage of the tongue."

So for the next fifteen minutes or so, they all worked on some part of the preparation in silence and in their own thoughts. Rachael hated them to feel this way when their visits together were so few and far between. After all, it would not be long and they would be married and with their own families raising their own children. She did not want them to have the life she had, and she certainly did not want them to not enjoy this vacation together.

A few minutes later, the doorbell chimed the standard Big Ben impersonation that people seemed to love. Margot dashed out of the kitchen but slowed when she approached the living room that housed Charles and his newspaper.   No use ticking him off any more than she already had by acting as if she was more excited to see this new gent than she was her own father. She checked her hair and makeup quickly in the hallway mirror and then opened the front door.

There he was, smiling and radiating that wonderful charm she had come to love. "Good afternoon, Margot," he said simply.

"Good afternoon to you kind sir," she returned. "Won't you come in and warm yourself?"

He crossed the threshold and walked down the hallway a few feet, looking around at the beautiful old, wooden accents on the ceiling and on the large staircase leading up to the second floor.

"This is a lovely old home. You can see the craftsmanship displayed here in the entranceway."

"Yes, it is. It has large rooms and plenty of them," Margot added, only slightly conscious of anything around her, other than his presence. She felt foolish, but when he was present, she was not really aware, nor did she care about her own surroundings. "May I take your coat and gloves?"

Handing her the gloves and smoothly removing his coat, he noticed that she brushed it off with her hand absent-mindedly and hung it on a large coat hanger in the hall closet. She then smiled up at him and said, "This way into the parlor. Everyone is looking forward to meeting you." She said this with a very happy look on her face, but in her head, she was saying well, maybe not everyone……

As they entered the living room, Charles stood up to make sure the young man was aware of his physical presence in the room. A presence that always set the tone to any conversation. Charles had height and stature, with a little touch of gray at the temples, which made him look distinguished and sophisticated. "Well, this must be the young man who has made such an impact to everyone's schedule." Holding out his hand he continued, "I am Charles Martyn, head of this little band."

Taking Charles's hand, Theodore decided to allow this gentleman to have the upper hand for the moment. He relaxed his grip to a medium level, "Good afternoon sir. Theodore Blodger."

Margot never had a chance to introduce Theo or her father. She just stood to the side nervously biting her lip. She had no idea what would come of this meeting and was not going to interject anything until the positioning of the two men had been established. It seemed to her that Theo was allowing her father to set the tone. That was unlike him. Whenever they had gone out, he set the tone and made sure everyone followed it. She wondered if he was intimidated by her father. Well, why not? After all, aren't young men supposed to be nervous around their date's father?

"Come in and have a seat," Charles indicated the sofa to the side.

Theo looked over at Margot, to see if she was going to join him. When he caught her eye, she suddenly stood up straighter and announced, "I think I will let you two get to know each other a little, while I go into the kitchen and see about supper." Turning, she more or less fled from the room.

Theo noticed her apparent nervousness and smiled. It looked as though his thoughts about her were correct—she was used to being ruled by men. She did not try to interject herself in matters that were to be between men. She knew her place. Good. Turning and sitting down he said, "You have a lovely daughter. I truly enjoy her company."

Charles sat and stared at Theo for about thirty seconds, to see if it made this man nervous. He was surprised when Theo returned his appraisal without any qualms. "You know she goes to school for nursing," Charles began.

"Yes, I think that is excellent."

"She seems to like helping people. What is your line of work?"

"I am currently selling shoes in a store downtown. I like it, although I think the owner is running it into the ground." Theodore waited until Charles commented. He was not going to run a one-sided dialog.

"What makes you think that the owner is doing such a poor job?" Charles asked, thinking this was a rather bold statement for someone who did not have any investment in the store.

"Well, I realize that I am not the owner, but I do have a degree in business from Penn State. Trends in business are changing constantly and the owner of the store is an older gentleman who does not like current ideas." Theo looked down in order to think of the correct phraseology needed to get his point across. "You see, most businesses have moved to malls or strip malls. The common shopper likes to park once and shop in a variety of stores. And, if he does not offer online shopping, he is no longer competitive." Theo looked up again into Charles' dark eyes. He was not sure if he had made a good impression or not. Oh well, time would tell.

But Charles was merely studying the young man. Although he looked exceptionally fit, with broad shoulders and obvious strength, he also seemed relatively intelligent. Maybe a little too confident, but that might be a front. I wonder what he is like when no one is around and it is just he and Margot.

The kitchen door opened and Margot came into the dining room with a handful of linen napkins and extra ladles. "How are you two doing?" She asked rather tentatively.

"How do you think we would be doing after only just meeting, Margot?" Charles asked with a slightly annoyed tone.

Margot looked at the table and decided to skip asking polite questions. Her father obviously was not in the best of spirits.

"Do you need any help?" Theodore asked her, to smooth over the feathers that seemed to be ruffled.

"There is an army in the kitchen, Theodore. They don't really need anything." Charles answered for Margot, who promptly turned on her heels and reentered the kitchen.

Theodore looked back at Charles with only a hint of a smile on his face. He knew this man was similar to his father in some ways, which was good. But he was not sure exactly how he was going to react to his marrying Margot. "Margot has told me that you work in the city. I appreciate you taking the time to come down to meet me." Theo thought that this would be received with a certain amount of politeness.

This time it was Charles's turn to smile. He knew that Theodore did not know very much about their family or interrelationships. "Yes, well, it was difficult to get away right now, but I try to make it home whenever I can during the week."

Theodore knew this was a lie. Charles was a good looking, aggressive, successful lawyer with a true dominance over his family. The odds were that he had a mistress. Theo would if he had to work away from home all the time. It really is nice to have power and a commanding way. His father demanded a lot from his mother but did not have power. True power that is. Theo suspected that Charles did and perhaps would pass to him some of those qualities. "How long is the drive when you go into the city?" It was now time for some small talk and a little less posturing.

The conversation that followed allowed the tension between these two males to abate. Charles did not want to like this man but had to admit that he seemed to reflect some of the values and thoughts that he had at that age. "Where are you from, Theodore?"

"Oh, please call me Theo. Theodore is too formal," Theo warmed up to the next topic, "I come from the Jim Thorpe area originally, although I have now made my home in Long Island," he answered simply. "I think there are a lot of possibilities for business in this area and very few in the Jim Thorpe area. It is too remote to ship product economically and too low in population to make a killing in sales." Theo felt on firm footing with this conversation, since he was from that region.

"Well, I am not sure about that, but I will defer to your expertise." He looked slightly taken aback, and Theo wondered what he said that was wrong. Actually, Charles was doing what he loved to do best. Control the mood of the conversation. If he could make this confident man feel off balance, he would be content for the moment.

Rachael came into the dining room with two plates full of steaming vegetables, followed closely by Thomas with two casseroles filled with lasagna. Margot followed with two baskets of freshly baked rolls and Jadyn came in with chilled wine and cold water, to fill the glasses.

"The feast is ready," Thomas announced with a broad grin as he anticipated eating his mother's marvelous lasagna. He could even endure his father if his mouth was filled with something that good.

Charles stood, cocked his head toward Theo and said, "Shall we?" He then strode to the head seat at the table. Margot leaned over to Thomas and requested, "Can you sit at the other head of the table?"

Thomas knew why this was being requested. If he or Jadyn sat across from their father, he was more likely not to target his wife. "Sure."

As everyone found a seat, Rachael started the passing of the food in Theo's direction. She wanted everyone to be chewing and not asking questions. Once they mellowed out with the happy carbohydrates, she hoped that it would be a smooth night.

But the best-laid schemes of mice and men, as Robert Burns volunteered, never seem to work out. As soon as Charles had filled his plate, he leaned back in his chair, staring at his wine glass with a look of distaste. "Who chose the wine tonight?"

Without missing a beat, Jadyn claimed the title. "I happen to like this particular type of wine. And it is red," she added as if to justify her choice.

Obviously, it would not have been Charles's choice, but he just stared at his glass as if it would change into something else through his sheer concentration.

"We really could use two bottles of wine, dear. Would you like me to get you something else?" Rachael added hurriedly, just to keep peace.

"Yes," Charles added rather flatly. "Get the bottle that I put on the sideboard the other day." Charles knew that either wine was acceptable, but he wanted to show he was the true master of the house. His every wish did not even need to be verbalized and his wife would jump to please him.

"I'll get it, Mother. You worked very hard on the meal, and I know where you put it." Margot wanted to show that she liked to please also.

Jadyn sat looking down at her food. She did not dare look up at Charles, knowing that everything she thought would race across her face like a teletype. She was furious that Charles would deliberately make a big deal out of this. He was trying to show his superiority and to needle her mother at the same time. How she hated his ways. If he wanted something else, he should not have acted as if he had been served poison. Why could he not let one meal go by without criticism?

Margot returned with a clean glass filled with the alternative wine, and the bottle. She set the glass down in front of her father and removed his poison glass. Sitting down next to Theodore, she started a conversation. "I hope you like lasagna, Theo. It is one of Mother's famous recipes."

110

"I love it," Theo punctuated the sentiment and took another large mouthful to prove the point.

"Once you start eating it you can't get enough of it," T. J. affirmed and chewed contentedly.

"If you continue to love it as you do, you will be the size of a barrel, Thomas." Charles was in a mood to annoy anyone and everyone.

But T. J. was not to be drawn into an argument at that moment. Between the wine and the carbohydrates, he did not really care what his father said. However, Rachael did. She wanted this evening to be special for Margot and she was hoping the usual sniping by her husband would end. And so the evening passed with tension and hope at every turn. The food was wonderful—so much so that Charles could hardly complain.

After dessert, Charles excused himself and went upstairs to make a phone call. When he returned, he announced that he had to leave and go back into the city. He then looked at Theodore and said, "My daughter is mine. I expect you to respect that."

Theodore knew what that meant and nodded affirmation. Charles owned Margot, at least for the moment. Theodore was determined that the ownership would pass into his hands soon. However, he had no illusions that he would ever be close to Margot's father. He and Charles were too much alike. Too many character traits were vying for dominance and he was going to win, ultimately. They shook hands and Charles, without saying anything else to his family, put on his coat, picked up his briefcase, and strode out the door into the cold, winter night.

Theodore noticed that the minute the door closed, calmness fell over the room. Rachael started to clean up the table, with Jadyn and Thomas working with her. Margot was left alone to entertain her guest. "I am sorry that Father left so abruptly," she offered in hopes that Theodore would not think it was something he had done.

"No problem, my love. I am used to fathers that act oddly. How about we go for a little ride?" Theo wanted her alone so he could expand on their relationship. Her father may own her now, but he was going to start the process of taking her away from her father.

"That sounds wonderful. After that big meal, the cold air might wake me up. I will get my things." She went into the kitchen to let her mother know she was going for a ride, and then returned to retrieve Theo's coat and gloves as well as her hat, gloves, and coat. Together, they left the house and headed for Theo's two-year-old Altima. Theo held the door for Margot and then entered the driver's side. Once he warmed the engine slightly, he pulled away from the curb and headed down the street. The sidewalk lights formed a soft glow against the black and white setting of darkened buildings and freshly fallen snow.

Margot leaned back against the cold leather seat and wondered what Theo thought of her family. Would he still want to see her after tonight? "Theo, about my father," she started.

"Margot, I like your father. Don't think anything about it. He is only being protective of what he … loves." He definitely did not want to use the ownership word. "I am very much like your father. I know what I want and I would protect those I love with all my being."

Margot loved hearing this. Well, the protecting part. The fact that he thought he was similar to her father in any way was ludicrous—wasn't it? She did not have any fear of Theodore. He seemed kind, thoughtful and attentive. How could he think he was like her father?

Theo drove on in silence, not wishing to expose any of his thoughts to her at that moment. He drove over to the little park that they had enjoyed during these cold, winter days. As he drove into the park, Margot realized where she was and stopped thinking of anything in particular. The park was well lit and beautiful in the snow.

Theo parked the car along the street situated next to a small pond, a favorite haunting place for many swans and geese. Theo turned off the car and swiveled in his seat toward Margot. He had decided he wanted to take this young woman away from Charles, sooner than later. It would be his pleasure to deprive Charles of

112

this particular chattel. "Margot, I totally understand how your father feels. You see, I love you too. I don't plan to mince words or beat around the bush as the expressions go. I want to marry you. I want you with me for the rest of our lives." After all, this came out, he took her gloved hands in his and asked, "Margot, will you marry me?"

Margot was totally shocked. She knew she really cared for this man, but she had not thought about the long term. She had had many boyfriends and dates. Because she was beautiful, outgoing and fun, many had tried to become more serious with her than she had wanted. But it was easy to push them away. She had not really felt drawn to them. But this man was so different. Magnetic would be a good word. She was really hoping to be with him for a long time, but marriage… She was totally caught off guard. It was just the way Theo wanted her. "I don't know what to say Theo; this is really out of the blue. We don't really know each other. Once you know me, you might regret this impetuous offer."

"No, I won't. I already know you. You are Margot Lynn, a beautiful, witty, thoughtful, smart, kind, appreciative," he paused to place emphasis on the last word. "lady." .

"Please, don't continue. I am sloppy, confused, and easily distracted. Don't paint me out differently. I have negatives too, like everyone else."

"I am in love with the negatives and the positives. I know them all and I want them to be with me. Can't you understand how I feel?" Theo knew she was wavering.

"I don't know Theo, let me think about it."

"Fine, you think and I will drive. But I am not going to leave until you agree that you love me and that marriage would be appropriate for two people who love each other. N'est-ce pas?" Theo looked directly into her eyes when he spoke to her, although the lighting was a bit dim for the effect he was hoping to exude; however, you can't have everything… or could he? He turned the car on and guided the car back onto the streets. Because of the time, there were not very many cars on the street and he did not have to worry about her having any distractions. She could sit and think.

Silence was hanging on the air. Theo turned on the heater since neither of them had noticed that the car had become very cold. He glanced at her and said, "We don't have to get married tomorrow you know. We could wait until summer or fall if you like. I just know that I want to marry you."

"Theo, I do love you. But have you dated many women? You haven't even gotten to know me." Margot mumbled for a second time.

"We have covered that before. I know what I want and don't have any doubts that we could have a most glorious time together." Theo thought he could hear her heart beating, rhythmically and rather quickly. He smiled. He had won and he knew it.

And so they continued on, with only their thoughts crashing in on the silence that surrounded them. Margot noticed that he had turned toward the country and they seemed to be driving in a random pattern. I guess he really is waiting for me to make up my mind right now. She was not sure how she felt about having this kind of pressure. It was very flattering that he wanted her for a wife. Long term commitments were not for everyone and she was not even sure it was for her, as her father had truly messed up her perspective as far as happily ever after. But, Theo is kind and attentive. He is not like Father at all.   No, he is not and I am sure of that.

"Theo, I have made up my mind. I would love to marry you. But let's not rush into this.   How about we plan a summer wedding? But if you, for any reason, want to call it off, I will not be the least bit angry." What Margot did not say was that she was giving herself some time, in case she changed her mind.

"That sounds sensible. I won't change my mind. However, if you do change your mind, let me know. I will not be the least bit angry either. I want only your happiness."

Smiling, they both settled into a comfortable silence. Margot did not know what would happen next. She fully meant it when she said she would be happy to marry him, but she did not really

114

know how she was going to break it to her family. Her father may not take it very well. Everyone else would be happy for her—or so she thought. Maybe she would not have to tell anyone just yet. After all, she did not want a big wedding. Therefore the arrangements could be done quietly, over the next few months without her father knowing. Maybe.

Interrupting her reverie, Theo announced, "I will speak to your father next week after his big case is over."

Margot's eyes widened into fear as she tried to mouth her objections, "Theo, please wait for a while, before you discuss this with Father. I want to gentle him into the idea." She paused, looking for the right words, "After all, to him, we have just met. He will expect us to court for a while longer."

Theo sat quietly, letting the fear in Margot's heart dissipate slowly. No need to tell her my plans anyway. "Don't worry my lovely; I will wait for just the right moment."

Now Margot's mind was racing into imagined dangers. Her father could be very vindictive. Her life could turn into a living hell if he decided it should be one. Oh, why did she start dating this man? Why didn't she just let him go like all the others? If she had, she would not have to face this upcoming potential nightmare. She looked at the man next to her, wondering if she could call it off now before he decided to talk to her father. No, he is just too wonderful to give up because of the cowardice of my imagination. I will just have to bear up under the brunt of the storm. I've seen Mother do it, so I can do it too. Ugh! Why does life have to be so complicated?

Margot noticed that they had made a circle around the town and that they were headed back into her neighborhood. She did not say anything but wondered if he thought she was afraid of her parents. She had no need to worry on that account, as Theo knew she was intimidated by her father and was counting on that very fact.

"Margot, I am going to take you back now. I have had a wonderful night and I am very pleased you will be my wife. Don't worry about anything. I will take care of it in a way that your father will be pleased that you and I are to marry."

Margot could not imagine what that would be but said she would not worry. Fat chance of that. Oh well, I may as well go in the house and see if there is any more dessert available. Margot suddenly had a huge craving for chocolate.

Theodore, always a gentleman, walked Margot up the stairs of her porch and opened the door for her. In the hallway, he kissed her lightly on the forehead and said, "Don't worry. You look like you are about to have an apoplexy attack. I will not tell your father until you are ready, okay?" His voice dripped with assurance.

"Okay," Margot managed to whisper.

"Tell her father what?" Came a voice from up at the top of the stairs. Charles started walking down the stairs slowly, not taking his eyes off of the two young lovers.

Silence. Theo was debating how to approach the truth of it without making Margot faint. He had no intention of being intimidated by this man. "Well, Sir, we feel a great deal for each other and have decided to take our relationship to the next level."

Charles took his eyes off of Theo and shifted them over to Margot as he approached. His dark eyes bore down on her while she started doing the best imitation of a shrinking violet he had ever seen. Her behavior was kind of funny, but Charles certainly did not want to laugh. "What does this mean, Margot?"

Margot did not look up; head down and her mind racing. What should she say? Where could she go?

"We are going to become engaged." Theo decided to end the nonsense. This was to be his wife. He would control her emotions from now on.

"If I wanted to hear from you, I would have addressed you." Charles averted his stare long enough to make sure Theo was paying attention. Then he looked back at Margot and said, "What on earth could you possibly be thinking? Do you have no appreciation for what I have done for you? Why would you do this? Sneaking around and keeping secrets?" Charles was truly enjoying her discomfort.

Margot knew that her life was not going to be worth much now. She had no answer to these questions and she thought she was

116

becoming dizzy from the look her father was giving her. "Father, we were not sneaking around. We have been dating for several months now."

Just then, Rachael came into the hallway. She had heard voices and knew from the strain in her daughter's voice that trouble was about to break out. "Well, Charles, I did not know you had returned," she stated rather flatly.

Charles turned around to face Rachael. His complexion was now reddish and his face was very grim. "Did you know about this?" He pointed to Margot and Theo and back to Margot again.

"Know what Charles? What is there to know?" Rachael was feeling confused and defensive at the same time. No new feelings for her when it came to Charles.

"Tell your mother!" Charles demanded, turning back to Margot.

Margot found telling something to her mother much easier. She looked up, straightened her shoulders and seeing her mother's puzzled face started her tale. "Although Theodore and I have only been dating for a few months, we feel that we belong with one another. Tonight, Theo asked me to marry him." She stopped and looked earnestly in her mother's eyes. How could she make them understand how right this was?

Rachael saw the pleading look in Margot's eyes and capitulated, "Margot this is so wonderful!" Then turning to Theo she said, "Congratulations and welcome to the family!"

Charles by this time had lost a certain amount of momentum and interest. If he could not scare Theodore, and Margot was now avoiding his look, he may as well continue with his packing upstairs. He shook his head at Margot one last time, as if he was thoroughly disgusted with her, then turned and went back up the stairs.

"Don't mind him, Theo," Rachael mouthed silently. At this point, Rachael had not really had time to absorb the information. Her little girl was going to get married. Boy, I hope her marriage is kinder to her than mine was to me, she thought. However, this was not the time to worry. Not yet. "Margot, this is so wonderful. I hope both of you will really try to make it all work."

"Make what work?" came a different voice from the dining room.

"Great news Jadyn, Theodore has asked me to marry him." Margot was now warming up to the announcement.

"You're kidding, right?" Jadyn's serious response felt like a slap in the face to Margot.

"What's wrong with that?" Margot was now getting a little upset with people expecting her to do things because they said so. It was her decision and she had chosen Theo because he was perfect for her. She had already forgotten that Theo had done the choosing out of the blue.

Jadyn just looked from Margot's face to Theodore's face and back. Theo smiled and returned her look with a look on his face that seemed very self-satisfied. He knew it was going to happen and he was content. Now this beautiful creature, which he had been seeing for the last four months, was to be his.

Thomas felt lonely in the kitchen and entered into this oddly staring group. "What gives everyone?"

Rachael answered her son instead of Margot, "Theo and Margot are getting married."

"When?" T.J.'s response came from happy lips. Then everyone looked at Margot.

Margot realized all eyes were on her and she turned slowly toward Theodore and while looking at him, she answered their question, "We have not really gotten that far. We will let everyone know as soon as we do."

"Yes, and we may have a little hiccup in all of this as your father does not seem thrilled by the announcement," Theo added in a fairly quiet voice.

"I am not surprised," was all Jadyn added.

"Well, I am sure it will all work out." Rachael said and then asked, "Does anyone feel like coffee, tea or maybe something a little stronger?"

"I do," added T. J. and all walked back toward the dining room, which contained the server and the only liquor in the home.

As they all were standing around the table asking questions and sipping brandy, they heard the front door slam and knew Charles had exited the premises once again. I wonder why he came back? Rachael thought while she was still calming down from her nervous encounter and intercession between Margot and her father. It would take more than one drink to calm her jitters. I certainly would not want to be his latest girlfriend tonight! With that ugly thought, she smiled and went back into the conversation.

Quicksand

I saw you smiling as you walked,
You looked so very calm today.
As if your stroll through life,
Could not ever be made to go astray.

But dangerous, hidden shoals abound,
Unseen by the predictive eye.
Don't ignore the subtle warnings,
You see, no one will hear your fatal cries.

Chapter VII

After the holidays, Jadyn had returned to Berkley and to her work in San Rafael, while T. J. continued his work in social services at their community center. Rachael's world seemed to have settled down to painting and taking care of the home during the day and to planning the wedding with Margot during the evenings. She was so happy for Margot. She seemed a completely different girl now. Serious, happy and full of hope. Rachael remembered how she felt when she was planning her own wedding. But that was a different time. Rachael knew how certain she felt that Charles was the only one for her. Goes to show how misguided you can be in life if you are not careful.

The date for the wedding was set for June and Rachael knew that Charles was just going to have to accept it. Because Margot had graduated with honors, receiving a BS in Nursing, she had been recruited from the clinic and now had a wonderful position in the new hospital being built outside of Smithtown. Margot was so happy that she did not notice that her father seldom was home and when he was, he seemed extremely quiet, even for him.

Two weeks before the wedding, Jadyn came home for a vacation from all her activities. She had finished up her schooling, which would be a continual thing, and wanted to kick back and relax. She was happy for Margot, but a bit worried that she made such a major decision in such a short period of time. However, Margot was grown up like she was—so it was not her business.

One evening shortly after returning home, Jadyn walked down to the ice cream parlor that they all loved. When she went into the little store, she saw several friends and neighbors had decided to do the same thing. It was very nice to sit with them and reminisce. Then above the casual conversations that she was having at her table with the group of friends she had joined, she heard someone arguing somewhere behind her. She did not pay much attention until it became clear that the two were Margot and Theo. Jadyn did not even know that they were in the crowded parlor, as they were sequestered into the very back corner.

As Jadyn turned, it was very apparent that Theodore was doing most of the talking and Margot was doing most of the listening. Where had she seen that before? Three easy guesses. Suddenly, Theo got up and walked out of the parlor, without looking back. Jadyn peeked up over the heads of the people to see if Margot was alright, but she was not in the booth where she had seen her.

She must have gone into the ladies room. I had better not let her know I saw the argument. Jadyn excused herself from her friends and went to the counter to pay for her ice cream. While she waited, she noticed Margot coming down the aisle toward the counter where Jadyn was standing. Margot was so distracted that she never even noticed that her sister was standing in front of her.

"Margot, it is too funny," Jadyn started the conversation.

Margot looked up and seemed to finally focus on her surroundings. Seeing Jadyn standing there, she tried to smile and asked, "Oh, hi. What's too funny?"

"You and I getting hungry for ice cream at the same time. It must be a twin thing."

"Yeah, I guess so." Margot was still not sure what to say. She did not know if Jadyn had seen her and Theo fighting. She did not want Jadyn to see any chink in his armor. She loved Theo, but sometimes he could be so stubborn. He would not even let her explain her side of it. What was with that? Oh well, probably premarital jitters. "Yes, tonight seemed the perfect moment for something cool," she began again.

"Yepper. How are the wedding plans coming? You should be about done now since it is in two weeks."

Margot paid for her sundae and headed out the door with Jadyn. They walked for a little while before Margot answered. "Yes, the plans are all made, but Theo wants to honeymoon in the Bahamas and I want to go to Canada."

"Well, that is quite a difference. So will you guys come up with a compromise?"

"Oh, I suppose I don't really care. He can pick it since he has to pay for it." She seemed to hesitate and then added, "He was here with me until we got ready to leave. We were arguing over it and he got up and left." She looked down at the sidewalk as they continued.

"Hum. Well, men seem to have very distinctive ideas about honeymoons. They usually are tropical if they can afford it. I think they like the idea of seeing their new wives in a bikini," Jadyn added with a large smile.

Margot looked at Jadyn and seemed to feel relieved. She took her sister by the arm and smiled. "I love you, sis."

They continued for the remainder of the walk, each in their own thoughts. Jadyn was worried. The way that Theodore was addressing Margot reminded her of her own father and his way with Rachael, although not quite so extreme. Boy, I hope this is not another big mistake. But she kept her peace.

****

The wedding day was spectacular. Margot looked so beautiful that even Charles made a pleasant comment. But if he was not in control, he was not really interested.

Rachael was so proud of her grown daughters and very happy for Margot in particular. Rachael, even though she was not in a happily married situation herself, still believed in the sanctity of marriage. Each marriage was special and deserved to succeed, even though over fifty percent did not.

Jadyn was the maid of honor and Theo had asked Thomas if he would be the best man. Keep it all in the family was his motto. Jadyn and Thomas were enjoying the festivities, but holding their breath until Charles gave away the bride—if he would. They were almost surprised that he condescended to attend the wedding; however, Margot was persistent if not convincing. She truly wanted a traditional wedding.

When Charles and Rachael invited the soon to be in-laws for cocktails and a small get together the day before the wedding,

Charles was the ultimate host and it relieved Margot that she did not have to run interference. Rachael looked very pleased with her husband at that moment. He could do no wrong, in her eyes, if he made her children happy.

So the day progressed. The Blodger family members were definitely impressed by the wedding and the surroundings since it was being held at Charles's parent's family mansion. His mother insisted on it. Once she became involved, the catering, tables, decorations all came under her purview. That was fine with Rachael and Margot. They had all they could deal with in the other details. Theo's brothers and sisters thought the home must be owned by some sort of a tycoon.

As for Theodore, he was dazzled by the beauty of his lovely bride, the thoroughly planned ceremonies, and the prospects of his marriage to someone who would do anything for him. This was just what he knew he should have to be happy—at least for a while. He could not wait for the honeymoon!

Once the couple had escaped catching their flight to the Bahamas, Rachael decided to stop trying to be the mistress of ceremonies and socialize a bit. She did not have much time during the earlier part of the day to greet and speak with many of their guests, of which there were many. Charles had done all the hosting and she dealt with photographers, caterers, and directing traffic in general.

Suddenly, Charles was by her side. He tapped her on the shoulder and once she had turned to look at him, he whispered, "Very nicely done, my dear. I suppose we will have to ransom the house to pay for it."

"It is not as bad as you might think, Charles. Your parents were very gracious to allow us to use their home and grounds. And everything your mother ordered, she paid for so we would not have to do so. It was very nice of her to do that! Margot seemed so very happy. How beautifully it all has gone." Rachael's eyes turned from Charles's eyes and surveyed the dwindling crowds.

"Well, while you tend to the dismantlement of all this, I must leave."

124

"Charles, it is your parent's home," Rachael started. "Surely you are not going to leave all this to me?"

"Well, absolutely. After all, I paid for a lot of this, too. What did you pay for with the money you earned?"

Although this was to be a slap in the face, Rachael had a comeback. "I bought her wedding gown."

Charles stopped turning to go and looked at her. "Where did you get that kind of money?"

"My paintings have started to sell, Charles," was her simple reply.

"That nonsense?" he slurred. "Someone actually likes it?"

"Oddly enough, yes. At least enough for a wedding dress." Rachael did not want him to know that many people liked her work and she was now able to support some luxuries that she could not have before. Better cuts of meat, dining out with the kids once in a while, going to a play or show once in a while with her friends. Life was much better than it was, but she did not want Charles to know this. He would find a way to kill her small gains.

"I want to see how much you have sold, my dear," he said simply. Turning, he walked up the paved walkways that lead to the patio. Once there, he went into the house and disappeared from sight.

Rachael did not dare show the alarm she felt, in case Charles was watching from the window. She had been very careful to keep records of all sales. This year had been an exceptionally good year so far, and she did not want him to know just how well she had done. She would have to get creative. It was hard to hide money from Charles. For tax purposes, she had kept him in the dark. After he had submitted his tax information to his accountant, Greg, she would call him and add her figures. Greg would add them in and complete the documents for filing. Charles never looked at the supporting documents. He only looked at the bottom line.

The event was over for everyone and a slightly anticlimactic feeling entered for the family. The wedding had taken up so much of their spare time; they felt a little bit lost. Or perhaps bored. Jadyn flew back to the West Coast to her research. T. J. started to put out feelers for new employment that might not require night work and would have more opportunities for him. He wanted to stay in social services but at a larger facility. Once he did, he could move out and get his own pad. He hated to leave his mother all alone, as he knew that it would not be long until Margot and Theo got a place of their own. Theo had a new and promising job that would certainly allow him to work his way up the ladder. He was that kind.

Though Rachael would be alone, as Charles stayed in the city more and more, she was content to be so. She enjoyed her paintings and art friends. She socialized often and seemed to always have something to do. When Charles had social functions in the City, she would drive in with him to attend. Thomas wondered what their conversations were like in the car. Poor Mom.

It took about two more months of searching for the right place to live. Margot was working now full time at the new hospital. Theo continued with his work and also found a great starter apartment located between the two work situations. Margot was delighted and they moved in as quickly as they could. She worried about her mother but was happy that T. J. was still at home. At least he would be the last one to leave the nest and not her.

Charles did look over the records that Rachael presented to him. The funds contained just enough to buy a wedding dress, but not enough to make him want to cut the household allowance. She kept two sets of books and certainly hoped he never found out the truth. If he did, she would definitely rue the day. However, Charles was not home during the week, and his law practice kept him close to clients and the courts in the City. It also afforded him pleasurable company when he felt like it. He was a contented man and did not suspect the ruse.

A few months after Margot and Theo had moved into their new apartment, Theo seemed to change. He did not ask Margot for her opinion on decisions as he had before—not that he always took her opinion seriously. Margot noticed that he seemed a little edgier. He did not seem as happy as he did when they first got married.

126

"Theo, are you okay?" Margot asked him one night when they were eating supper.

Theodore finished his mouthful and replied, "Sure. Why wouldn't I be okay?"

"Well, I've noticed you don't seem as thrilled to be here as you were. Or maybe your work is becoming a little tougher than it was."

"Margot, just because I don't dote on you every minute of the day, doesn't mean that I am not happy." Why do women always have to verbalize everything, anyway?

"I don't mean you don't pay attention to me. I just mean that you seem a little preoccupied. You do not seem as enthusiastic for new things and our new life. That's all I mean."

"I am fine, Margot. I am just tired." He shifted in his chair and looked at her for a minute without saying anything. Then he asked her a question, "How is your work going? You really have not said much about the people you work with—just about patients and their symptoms."

"Oh, well, I work on one floor of the hospital. I do more paperwork than anything else, or so it seems. I make up the medications, visit patients, and do paperwork. There is a team on my floor—two additional nurses, two LPNs, and a medical coder. The doctors come and go, but no one particular one is on our floor."

"Good," was the only comment that Theodore made before he resumed his meal.

Margot thought that this was an odd comment, but she did not know if he meant good regarding her job or good that there were no doctors around. She did not want to push it anymore and so she let it drop. She knew Theo was not himself. After supper, she cleared the dishes and loaded the dishwasher. Theo was in the living room watching his favorite news channel. It would be a quiet evening.

The next morning, when Margot was getting ready to go to work, Theo acted like he was bugged by something. As Margot held him close in her arms, she looked at him and said, "Darling, I love you."

"Do you? I hope so. Life would be just too hard without you." Theo kissed her and then turned to finish dressing for his work.

Margot went out to her car and started the engine. She did not drive right away, but sat and wondered, What was all that about? Pulling away she decided to do something especially nice for her husband that night. Maybe an extra spicy, romantic night would help him get out of this new mood. She would think up some extra fun for the bedroom. With that happy thought, she went to work.

Theo also was pleased. He would start to have a little fun like his father seemed to, now that they were settled into a routine. He would say things off and on just to evoke a reaction from Margot. She had a very creative imagination and would definitely come up with something to make him happy.

It worked better than he had hoped; when he arrived home, Margot met him at the door in a very revealing outfit. As he ate the fabulous meal she had made, he could hardly concentrate on the taste, as she was much too exciting dressed as she was. When they had finished and went into the living room to relax, that was the last thing Theo could accomplish. "Margot, you are making it hard for me to watch the news."

Margot was pleased that he seemed to enjoy her new outfit. "Oh?" She said, "Well, this is only the tip of the iceberg, my love. Wait until we retire for the night!"

Day vs Night

It is said that no matter how much life changes,
It always remains the same.
We chase our dreams all during the night,
Not really knowing from whence they came.

But when we wake, and daylight calls us,
To the harsh reality of life.
We long for the time of peace and rest,
That comforts us during the night.

<h1 style="text-align:center">Chapter VIII</h1>

Jadyn's work seemed to be in the most amazing field she could have chosen. She loved her work and excelled at it, combining cutting edge nanotechnology and microbiology. Once her boss, Dr. Farnot, realized her gift for developing products in this new field, he left her on her own. She was part of a team which developed viruses to carry and deliver medicines within the human body, but Jadyn wanted to use non-biological materials to do the same thing. She wanted to develop a non-viral delivery system for cancer treatments.

Her immediate superior, Dr. Farnot, was considered brilliant in his specialty. Being middle-aged did not seem to slow down his abilities to impress his superiors. And if it meant cheating, he was not averse to seeing what others had done, to borrowing the work, and to take it to the next step. Because he had a reputation for doing this, Jadyn did not share all her information. She kept it in a private file on her home laptop that was not accessible by others— she did not want someone to take credit for her ideas.

As time continued on, she started to have some successes with her delivery viruses. But her non-biological delivery systems were much more complex and difficult to engineer. She wanted to develop a system of miniature robots that could carry a chemical to a specific target location-based on a grid. Program it to travel to the x,y,z coordinates and deliver it. Part of her issue was being able to see the object she was developing.

Jadyn needed to develop the item on a larger scale and then downsize it to enter into the human system quickly, in order to avoid triggering an immunological response. At least until it had finished the delivery… but then what did she want it to do? Hmmm.

It took her almost a year of puttering around with this until she got the idea of constructing the item partly out of the medication that she wanted to dispense. IF she could encapsulation the material within a part of the robot, she could then have the item explode in the target area. The medication would be released and what was left of the little robot would flush out of the system through the regular channels, depending on the location of the tumor.

She found this much more feasible, although the programming would be a little trickier. She was way ahead of her time and she knew that if she could get this to work, she would be able to get whatever research grant monies that she would need to finish up the project. But it still had a long way to go. Plus, she had to be able to deliver the little robots into the system, which was another issue: inhalation, ingestion, or inoculation—too many choices. Swallowing it was the least effective way unless the target organ was the stomach or small intestine.

But one thing at a time, as she must first construct the bot (as she called it), which will require designing with engineering specs. Jadyn would have to make a feasible bot design and then use her nanotech background to downsize it. Jaden worked on this little mechanical item at home on paper and computer. She did not want anyone to get an idea of her goals at this point; not until she could present it to many people at once, not just her boss.

Jadyn was surprised that the delivery bot idea was easier to develop than she expected. Because the bot would contain the medication in part of its construction, only the explosive device was needed in the programming. Then it dawned on her to make the outer shell of the area that contained the medication water soluble. Thick enough to be a timed release, but thin enough to dissolve before being flushed. Yes, that would work.

She next decided she would need multiple delivery systems: Inhalation for the cancers within the lungs and pulmonary system, injection directly into the correct arteries to reach the approximate area; the little bot would then transport itself to the cancer site, and ingestion if the cancer was within the digestive tract.

The little bot was more of a challenge than she knew because she did not have the specialty electron microscope at home to do trials. To use the one at work, she was required to register the work for which it was used. That would have to come later in her development.

It took Jadyn about another six months to complete her initial designs and be fairly sure that she had covered all her bases. She packaged up her presentation and set up a meeting with her boss, several colleagues, and two other department heads (as she would need their aid in the final development).

Her boss, Dr. Farnot, was very irritated with her for not giving him a presentation first. "Jadyn, what is the meaning of this? You are not high enough in the pecking order around here young lady, to call a meeting of this scale! Who do you think you are acting as if you are some sort of departmental head?"

"Dr. Farnot, I certainly did not wish to step on your toes, but my idea will require the input from others in order to evaluate its merit. Engineering is one of them. I have been working on this for over six months on my own time and hoped it would be an answer to the research we have been working on since the beginning of the year."

"You had better hope your idea has merit, or you probably will not be doing your research here. I am to be your extra set of eyes! Not everyone else!" Dr. Farnot snarled to add emphasis and a touch of threat.

"Yes, sir, I will remember that for next time," Jadyn answered quietly. She turned around and headed out the door before he could muster another volley of words. Jadyn was pleased, as she knew he wanted to control or get credit for her work. She did not care if he threatened her or not; she was going to control at least this presentation.

Two days later, she was placing documentation around the table in the conference room, when Dr. Farnot entered very quietly. "Jadyn, don't bother to set this up. I have canceled the meeting."

Jadyn was too stunned to know what to say at first. Dr. Farnot was going to control her one way or another and she knew he would attempt to steal her project. She slowly started to gather up the materials she had so carefully laid on the large conference table.

"I'll take one of those since you need to get me up to speed on this immediately!"

Jadyn could not think of a way to circumvent her situation at that moment. He was her superior and if he was not so sneaky, she would not have minded showing him the research first. But now she felt very much like she used to feel as a child at home.... outmaneuvered and no options. She handed a packet to Dr. Farnot and continued to retrieve the other packets.

"Jadyn let's go over this once I have had a chance to peruse it. Come to my office at eleven and we will discuss your next move—if any." He was watching her face as he spoke to see if she looked effectively cowed. He could see she was thinking of what she could do to prevent this. "Oh, and you are not to give this to anyone else until I tell you. You work for me and I own everything you do until you are head of your own department! Do you understand, Jadyn?" His small, piercing dark eyes stared at her and spoke the silent words or else.

"I understand only too well. It is a shame you feel you have to bully everyone into compliance." Her little attitude started to work on the defense/offense.

"Women!" He snorted, "You always have to have the last word." He turned and started toward the door. Just before he passed through, he turned his head and said, "You have been warned!" Passing through the door, he left Jadyn so furious that she could not think of what she would do next. Her humiliation and frustration had reached new levels, but she had no other alternative...for now. She would have to wait and see how this played out before she could decide what to do next.

Dr. Farnot was not used to being circumvented by subordinates. He knew Jadyn would not give up and he had to find out what the value of her project would be and how to spin the work to look like his initiation. Walking hurriedly into the outer office, he gave instructions to Sally, his secretary, to hold his calls.

Sally watched him stride quickly into his office and close the door. Hmm, I wonder what he is up to now. Sally had been his secretary for four and one-half years, so she knew when he was doing something she would not like. However, she did like her job, so she tried not to get involved in the politics of the research departments. I wonder what that binder was that he was carrying. Nothing I put together for him, that's for sure.

Sally went back to typing up the memo Dr. Farnot had dictated to her earlier, stating that all employees in his department were required to get his expressed permission prior to scheduling any departmental or intradepartmental meetings. Sally knew that was about Jadyn's meeting; she had received a memo and had scheduled it on Dr. Farnot's calendar, as she did with all his meetings. After he had seen it, exploded orally at her for putting it there, he had left the office. Sally knew Jadyn was in for it that day. Poor girl, she should have known better. Sally went back to her typing and did not give it much more thought. She too had seen these things play out and wanted no parts of it.

****

Jadyn walked slowly back to her office area… deep in thought. He had outflanked her, but she would never give up. Fortunately for Jadyn, she had withheld most of the engineering portions of the project—they were set up to be displayed on a PowerPoint presentation. She knew that it would be unwise to put the information on her work laptop, so she had completed everything at home and kept it on a small drive, which was happily sitting in the bottom of her lab coat pocket.

As she neared her office door, she realized that he would notice most of the most critical information was not in the packet that he had forced her to give to him. He would ask her for the rest of it and take her laptop and office paperwork if he felt it was there. He would not stop until he had acquired all the information. She needed to get the jump drive out of the building and somewhere safe. But where and for how long? For all she knew, when he asks for the remainder of the information, and she does not give it to him, she might be terminated.

134

It was a very unfortunate situation. She did not mind if the company obtained the rights to her bots, but she wanted to get the credit. It could lead to much wider possibilities in her future endeavors, with other labs and corporations. It was going to make headlines and she wanted to be included in the scheme of things. If Dr. Farnot got a hold of it, he would make sure that he was on the cover of News Week with a big, self-important grin on his face (and a big fat check in his pocket). She would probably not even get a mention if he followed the pattern that he usually used with other junior lab personnel.

Jadyn went into her office, removed the drive from the lab coat and put it in her pant's pocket. She reached into her desk and retrieved a copy of her presentation, which she folded and put in the top of her pants in the back. Then she pulled out her pocketbook, walked across the room, picked up her briefcase, which contained her laptop, and turned off the lights. She knew she had only a few minutes before he would come looking for her. As she walked passed the young receptionist that was stationed in the hallway, she said, "Grace, I am not feeling well. I think I will go home and lie down for a while."

Grace was amazed at this announcement because Jadyn never took any time off during the usual business hours, except for her vacations. She looked at Jadyn more closely and asked, "Are you well enough to drive yourself or should I take you home?"

"Oh, I will be fine. I just have a bad headache that I don't seem to be able to shake."   Jadyn turned from the desk that Grace occupied and headed down the hallway, toward the escalator that would take her down into the lobby and ultimately out the front doors. She knew that she had to act normally, but she suspected that she could be stopped by security at any time if Dr. Farnot called them.

As she rode down the escalator, she saw the security man on the phone watching her. By the time she reached the bottom, he had left his desk and walked over toward her. "Ms. Martyn, a word please."

Jadyn knew this was going to be a shakedown ordered by Dr. Farnot, so she smiled happily and said, "Of course."

"Dr. Farnot said he thinks you have some papers that you might have inadvertently picked up off his desk. I need to check your briefcase and laptop?"

"I thought you were looking for papers?"

"Yes, well I thought you might have put them into your briefcase, so I need to check that. And your purse. I will need to check that too," he was curious and determined that she had something belonging to Dr. Farnot. He opened the briefcase, looked under the laptop. No papers. Then he turned to her purse.

"Well, I don't have any papers in my pocketbook, but you are welcome to look."

The guard took her purse and rummaged through it thoroughly. Finally satisfied that she did not have any papers, he said, "I guess Dr. Farnot has misplaced them somewhere else. Sorry for the delay, Miss."

"No problem. I have a headache, I won't be returning today."

"Sorry to hear that Miss," the guard added looking at her like he wanted to search her, but not necessarily for anything belonging to Dr. Farnot.

Jadyn exited the magnificent, glass-fronted building and descended down the cement stairs just outside the doors. When she reached the bottom, she turned and looked back inside the building through one of the huge glass windows. The guard was back on the phone and did not appear to be very happy about the conversation. Jadyn turned and half walked, half sprinted out into the parking lot and across to her car. Once she was inside the car, she took the jump drive of her pant pocket and slide it into her pocketbook. No use sitting on all the research. She was not sure where she should go or to whom she should confide; however, sitting in the parking lot was not her first choice.

She started her Toyota Camry and pulled quickly off the company property. She felt a little better about the situation, but she knew that the project that she had worked so very diligently on could be taken from her anytime. She needed advice as to what to do but was not sure who to trust. While she drove through the main sections of San Rafael toward the highway, she made a decision; she would go see her old professor/mentor at Berkley. He would have a better idea as to how to handle the legal quagmire that she was now embroiled in with the company. He also might have enough connections to steer her toward someone to help her with the final engineering portions of her designs.

Jadyn was now convinced that her boss was going to try to steal her project or he would not have been notifying the guard in the lobby to keep an eye out for her. Her apartment had her personal laptop and more of her research, so she headed to San Pablo, to retrieve it before she received any unwanted visitors. After a thirty minute ride, she parked out in front of her building. Fortunately, she did not need very long to pick up all of her necessary materials and pack a small overnight bag—just in case.

Twenty minutes later, she climbed back into the car and headed down the street and away from the area. It would take her about another twenty-five to thirty minutes to get to her campus. She hoped the professor would be in his office, although it was approaching lunchtime and she knew he loved to sit under the trees on campus, to eat his sandwiches. After parking in her usual parking lot, she took her briefcase, which contained her laptop and the conference notes and headed across campus to the large shaded tree area just behind the science center. It was very beautiful this time of the year, as the rains had freshened the grass and flowers were out in full force.

She did not have to look very long before she saw a familiar gray pate and hunched shoulders that were so distinctively Professor Bate's. As she approached, he looked up from his peaceful repose and smiled, "Jadyn, you are a sight for sore eyes! When did you get back on campus?"

"Well, I am not really back for academics, sir. I need some serious advice and am not sure who I can ask." She took a seat next to him on the large bench and waited for him to start speaking.

"I don't know if I will be able to help, but I will certainly try. What is going on?" He asked while chewing his sandwich.

Jadyn looked around to ensure no one was within ear-shot, and then started her story, "About eight months ago, I started working on a little project at home, off-site from the company. It was more or less a science experiment when I first started, but I soon realized that if I could get the engineering part solved, I had a real live amazing project to give to my company."

"Well, I am with you so far. You did some experimenting at home and developed something that the company might like to look at." He paused and then added, "Am I correct so far?"

"Yes, but the only problem was how to present the project to the company without my boss taking the credit for it. He is very good at feathering his nest and I knew he would take all the credit for what I had done, even though he had not a single bit of input into the entire proposal."

"Are we talking about that jackass, Farnot? Is he still there?" When Jadyn nodded her head, he continued, "I would have thought the company would have dumped him years ago."

"Well, unfortunately for me, he is still parading around like he is King Tut. To be truthful, I don't really think he knows as much as he pretends to know."

"He was not much of a student when it came to the sciences, but his ability to make friends and influence people high in the pecking order of the school was amazing. They gave him such glowing recommendations that he acquired his position with the company as soon as he graduated."

"Well, he is my problem right now. I am not even sure if I still have a position with the firm, as I left very abruptly and under a cloud I am sure." Jadyn proceeded to give the highlights of her project to the Professor, who only interrupted to ask questions on various points.

Professor Bates, having finished his lunch, sat quietly thinking. After about three minutes, he sat up very straight and said, "Wait here. I am going back to my office to make a phone call. I will be back out shortly."

Jadyn knew that he was very clever and so she decided to sit and try to relax for the duration of her wait. However, after about thirty minutes, she started to get a little concerned—she trusted Professor Bates entirely, but was worried that he might have called the company to make some inquiries and inadvertently tipped them off as to her location. Just when she was planning to bolt to her car, she saw him exit the science building from the rear door. "Whew," she said when he got within earshot. "I almost gave you up for lost."

"Oh, no need to worry on that account. I could find my way around this building with a blindfold on; I have been here too long. He paused to get his breath due to the extended walk he had just performed. "I know what you must do."

Jadyn was amazed at this revelation—not so much because it was the professor, but because he was so very absolute in his statement. "I will do what you suggest as I am at a loss as to how to proceed."

Looking Jadyn directly in the eyes, the professor said, "Go back to your job."

"What?" Jadyn thought she did not hear him correctly.

"Yes, go back to work as if nothing has happened. You will be called into the CEO's office toward the end of the day...he is a little busy before that time. Your boss, Farnot, will think you are going to be called on the carpet, but instead, you are to take your entire presentation with you and present it to the CEO privately."

Jadyn sat very still in her seat waiting for some sort of bad side to this announcement. When none was offered, she decided to play devil's advocate with his suggestion. "Yes, but won't the security guard nab me when I go back into the building?"

"No, that has all been taken care of—you will not be accosted in any way. Even your boss will leave you alone. He thinks he has made his point to the CEO and you will be dealt with according to his wishes." The Professor sat back into his bench seat and smiled, "The idiot is so puffed up in his own mind that he cannot conceive that anyone could get the better of him. I will enjoy this," he said with a grin. Then as an afterthought, he said, "Give me a call tonight. I want all the juicy details!" His eyes twinkled while he enjoyed his little private joke.

"Professor, I am scared, but I will do as you say." Jadyn rose to go, gathering up her briefcase and fishing in her pocket for her keys.

"Relax Jadyn; I think you will be amazed before the end of today." There was that twinkle and smile again.

Jadyn thanked her old friend and walked quickly to her car. When she had deposited her briefcase in the backseat, she got into her car and started the engine. She only sat debating for an extra minute and then reversing out of her space, she accelerated out of the lot. It did take her a little extra time getting back, as traffic was increasing. When she finally pulled into the company parking lot, even though she had rationalized it all in her mind, she felt the butterflies in her stomach come rushing back. Oh well, no turning back now, she mused.

As she entered the building, she noticed that a different guard was at the receiving station. He looked up with a smile and said, "Welcome back Miss Martyn. I have a message for you before you go up to your office." He handed her an envelope and then gave her a clipboard on which there was a form requiring her signature verifying that she received her message and the time at which she did.

After signing, she opened the sealed envelope and stood with her mouth open, almost gasping. She was extremely upset, which became apparent to the guard. "Is everything all right, Miss?" The guard noticed that she had turned a very pale shade of white.

Jadyn looked at him with vacant eyes and said, "Yes, everything is fine." She turned and walked over to the escalator not really looking where she was going. When she got off at the next level, Jadyn walked past Grace's desk with only a brief nod of her head, entered her office and closed the door. Jadyn was heart-broken. She felt betrayed and lost. She opened the letter again and reread it.

By now, Jadyn felt sick to her stomach. She put the letter down on top of her desk and looked around for something that she could put her personal items into as she knew she would be escorted off the property at the end of the day.

At three o'clock, there was a soft knock on her door. "Come in."

"I did not want to bother you. I thought you still had your headache or something, but I have a message for you that needs attention." Grace handed her the yellow message that was torn from the message pad that she kept next to her phone.

Jadyn saw the inevitable words: Come to Dr. Jeffries office at three-fifteen today. By now Jadyn was passed shock. She nodded quietly to Grace and said, "I will go over in a few minutes."

Grace looked at what Jadyn had been apparently doing-gathering her personal pictures and items and shoving them loosely in a box."What's going on Jadyn? Why are you cleaning house?"

"Please, not now Grace. I will tell you more if I can, after my meeting with Dr. Jeffries."

After Grace left, closing the door behind her again, Jadyn looked around the room for her presentations. She had left them in a pile on the top of the credenza. Not there. Surprise, surprise. Humph, well, I have one in my briefcase and I don't even know if I will be allowed to speak as it stands now. Jadyn picked up her briefcase and after walking past Grace as if going to the firing line, Jadyn detoured to the ladies room.

She washed her face and combed her hair. May as well look my best. They are not going to get the better of me! Determination was starting to kick in and she decided that she would set the atmosphere with this meeting—not Drs. Farnot and Jeffries. If she was to present her work to Dr. Jeffries, she wanted to look like a professional. But if they were going to fire her, she would not allow them to try to intimidate her, too.

As she walked down the hall, towards the elevators that went to the upper levels, she looked far different from when she went into the ladies room. There was strength in her stride and a serious, almost angry look on her face. She reached the outer door to the CEO's office, opened it and walked in.

Dr. Jeffries's secretary looked up from her computer and smiling broadly said, "Good afternoon Dr. Martyn. Good to see you. Dr. Jeffries is waiting for you."

Jadyn was confused slightly by the smile and warm greeting. You would think that if someone was being fired, the secretary would know it. Jadyn smiled back and opened the inner office door. Dr. Jeffries was sitting at his desk, with the phone to his ear. He was not speaking, more or less just listening. He signaled Jadyn to have a seat in the large office armchair on the other side of his desk. Mouthing silently, in an exaggerated way, he indicated he would be with her shortly.

After about five minutes of intense listening, he stressed, "As I said at the beginning of our conversation, I will let you know my decision after I speak to her. And no, you may not come up and interview her. This is my show now. You should have all you can do to be looking for a replacement" Hanging up, he looked at a slightly perplexed, slightly angry Jadyn. Smiling a very warm greeting he said, "I hope I have not interfered with your day by calling you in for this meeting."

"Meeting?" Jadyn was just warming up to her mentally rehearsed speech. "I have never heard of being called on the carpet referred to as a meeting."

Her scowl and tone told Dr. Jeffries everything. "What makes you think that you are being terminated?"

Too angry to answer, Jadyn pulled her briefcase up on her lap, opened it slightly, and pulled out the letter from Dr. Farnot. Handing it over to Dr. Jeffries, she said, "This certainly does indicate that termination was your intention."

Dr. Jeffries scanned the letter briefly and said, "I don't see my name on it."

"So you are not going to fire me?" Jadyn was now passed confused.

"Not today, my dear. That was Dr. Farnot's letter. But fortunately for many in this firm, I get to over-ride his decisions." Clearing his throat he continued, "Now that we have that out of the way, why don't you show me the presentation that has caused Dr. Farnot to get so very worked up."

Jadyn's face began to show signs of hope. She opened her briefcase lid and handed Dr. Jeffries the only presentation folder that she had left.

"I have already seen this, Jadyn. Dr. Farnot presented it to me after lunch."

Jadyn did not know how to interpret his facial expressions. It was too matter-of-fact for her to even guess what Dr. Farnot had said when he gave it to Dr. Jeffries. "Well, what I did not include in this very generalized proposal, were the exact details. I have been working on this at home for over eight months, and I am certain of what I know and what I don't know."

"Continue, and feel free to express yourself regarding Dr. Farnot, the lab, the company, and staff."

"I have no complaints regarding anyone but Dr. Farnot. I believe he wished to take credit for the project."

"So he did not write up this proposal? His name is on it."

"What!" Jadyn was now furious again. How dare that little creep put his name on her hard work!

"Calm down Jadyn. I don't for a minute believe this belongs to him…the ink is too fresh on the page, so to speak."

Jadyn had to take a minute to do as he had requested but then managed to start her true proposal. "I have a PowerPoint show on my jump drive. May I show it to you?"

"Yes, let's use my computer." He moved his chair off to the right of the center of the desk, and pointing to another wheeled chair, he said, "Have a seat."

Jadyn pulled the drive out of her briefcase, went around the desk and pulling the chair in behind her, sat down and inserted it into the USB port. She booted up the informational PowerPoint presentation and started to explain, in detail, what she had been working on for such a long time.

After about half an hour, drawing it to a conclusion, she finished with, "As you can see, when the engineering portion of this project is perfected, the company stands to make a huge amount of money and millions of people will reap the medical benefits of this type of pharmaceutical actives delivery system."

Dr. Jeffries leaned back into his chair with a look of intense thought. He did not say anything directly to Jadyn at first. He seemed to be chewing on the ideas she had presented. Finally, he said, "Professor Bates, my friend, was not incorrect in his assessment of you or your project." Then smiling he added, "And he was not incorrect in his lavishing of colorful metaphors that he offered about Dr. Farnot."

Jadyn could not say anything at the time, so Dr. Jeffries decided to fill in the quiet moment. He lifted the receiver and asked his secretary to bring into some tea. Then turning back to Jadyn he offered, "I have a proposal of my own if you would be interested in hearing it."

"Sir?" she asked quietly.

"How would you like to be in charge of the project? In your own lab. On the East coast?"

Jadyn still had not found her voice, but her eyes were starting to indicate that the information was getting through. "Sir?" was all she managed.

A knock on the door and Dr. Jeffries's secretary came in with a tray of tea, cups, and all the fixings. After she sat it down on the

144

side of his desk, she turned to leave. "Thank you, Joyce. I have been looking forward to this all afternoon," Dr. Jeffries informed her. Turning to Jadyn, "How do you take your tea?"

"Just a little honey," Jadyn managed to answer without sounding too dazed.

Pouring a cup and handing it to Jadyn, Dr. Jeffries started up again with his proposal. "Our company has a sister company that is doing some amazing research for the military. The labs are extensive and very, very well funded. I think your work would fit in perfectly with what they are trying to accomplish. It would be a two-fold win—you would help the medical community immensely with your findings and the military might be able to use it also." He stopped for a moment when he saw her brows drawing together. Then starting up again, "I know that you probably don't want the military to use this, but they might be able to carry some of these little bots in the field to help stem blood loss or help with some of the other issues that they face." He did not elaborate on what some of the other issues might be.

He took a drink of his tea, which reminded Jadyn that she had a cup also. She picked up a spoon and added a little of the honey, stirring absentmindedly as she thought about what he was saying. Military too. Well, they do have the bucks. My own lab. And near home and Mother. That would be nice.

"Sir, if it does not seem too bold, it sounds as if you had this all prepared."

"The tea?" he asked. "Joyce always has it ready for me in the afternoon."

"No, the promotion. The lab, the offer, and well, everything. But this just happened this afternoon."

"Yes and no. We have a large facility just south of Boston. We are always looking for great ideas and top-notched staff to place there. Today, when Farnot gave me your proposal, I knew he had hit on one that would mesh very well with my East Coast Projects." He leaned back again, grinning and said, "Besides, I love to goad him. He has wanted to go over to that facility for nearly ten years. Often he has said that he had a new idea; he is desperately hoping to be relocated, prestige and all that, and although he does have an original idea once in a while, I can tell the ones he has liberated from a junior staff member."

"So when you called me into your office, it was to offer the position? But you had not heard my proposal, or at least not any details."

"You underestimate the influence of Professor Bates. He heard most of your proposal and relayed it to me.   He knew the implications of such a project and the ramifications if we let this opportunity go by the wayside." He leaned forward toward Jadyn and continued, "Are you interested in doing this?"

"Absolutely!" She had found her voice and her convictions.

"Good. How long will you need to pack? We will find you a suitable apartment by the time you arrive and arrange for someone to move your furniture and pack your belongings." He seemed to be in a hurry.

"Well, fortunately for me, I rented a fully furnished apartment. I merely have personal items, pictures, odds and ends, plus my personal lab equipment. I am very particular about them; I will pack them."   She thought for a moment and then asked, "What time frame did you have in mind?"

"Next week, if possible." He smiled again at her surprised look. "We don't want anyone else to try to snatch you up!"

Jadyn stood up and asked, "Am I allowed to tell anyone or is this a secret?"

"Let's keep this on the Q.T. for now. I don't want Dr. Farnot to have any idea that you are receiving his dream job. He might try to muddy the waters for you. Just tell people, like Grace or your other team members that you are leaving for medical reasons. That should be sufficient as I am going to have you escorted out. The guards can help you carry your stuff to your car and it will make Farnot think you were canned." He seemed to inwardly smile and then added, "Won't he be surprised."

Jadyn could not believe how her afternoon had finished. She walked back to the elevators and went down to her own office on the second floor. Grace was still waiting at her desk, hoping to see Jadyn before she left for the day. "Grace, why are you still here?"

"I wanted to make sure you were okay. There have been some terrible rumors going around and I did not want you to come back to your office alone."

"Grace, that is very kind of you, but I am fine. I am leaving here of my own free will and I will miss you terribly… you and the rest of my team. But I have some medical issues to attend to and have decided to take care of them now." Jadyn hated to lie to Grace but was not sure if anyone else was within earshot.

"I will miss you too," Grace said, tears welling up in her eyes.

At that moment, two guards approached. They looked politely at Jadyn and the oldest one asked, "Are you ready to go?"

"Yes, in a moment. If you would help carry my little boxes, I will follow with my briefcase."

"Leave your computer and drives!" a sharp voice jumped through the door from just outside the office. Dr. Farnot was standing there with his hands on his hips, expecting an argument.

"No problem," Jadyn answered. She had transferred the data on the jump drive to Dr. Jeffries's computer and then left her personal drive with him. He had promised to send it back to her after he reviewed it with his colleagues at the new facility. She had a copy of all the material on her computer at home, so she was not worried about it. Jadyn picked up her briefcase and took her laptop out, laying it on the desk.

"And the drive!"

"Dr. Jeffries took that. I do not have that anymore."

Dr. Farnot looked slightly concerned but was not about to give up his preconceived advantage. "You got what you deserved and I hope you are satisfied!"

Jadyn did not look at him but stole a glance at Grace, who was appalled at his behavior. "Grace, I will call you in a week or two and let you know how I am doing."

"Thank you, I would really like that."

Jadyn walked around her desk behind the second guard, who turned and preceded her out of the office, more or less forcing Dr.

Farnot to get out of the way. Jadyn walked deliberately close on his heels, not giving Farnot a chance to engage her in any kind of debate. She had had enough of him to last a lifetime.

Once inside her car, the guard placed her box of personal belongings in the back seat. "Good-luck Miss. We know you will be brilliant," the older of the two stated.

Jadyn was amazed. They must have known what was going on and were there to keep her from being hassled by Farnot. Thank heavens for Dr. Jeffries! She hoped she would not let him down. But only time would tell.

Tread Lightly My Dear

I have my life and I have yours,
To control both will require thought.
Learning to predict—setting the tone,
Making you believe and never getting caught.

I dance a fine line as I walk this narrow ledge,
I cannot let you know my history or my past.
I must keep you in the dark, I won't let you go,
Believe all is well and your life might truly last.

Chapter IX

Theo was very ambitious when it came to his position with the new department store. He introduced some new marketing strategies to the managers that were very successful—so much so, that they promoted him to a buyer. It gave him an opportunity to expand their lines to compete with some of the very large department stores, many of which he visited for ideas, trends, and price comparisons.

As time went on, Theo also discovered new ways to unnerve Margot, without being too obvious. A distrustful look here, a little innuendo there, and most of all, the lack of conversation. Margot was beside herself; she just knew it was her fault. Theo was the most respectful, loving husband... he would not do anything to hurt her. It must be that she was doing something.

Theo was increasing his game. When he was on the road traveling, he would call Margot at least three times during the day, just to check in with her to see what she was doing. At first, Margot was delighted, even though it interrupted her work and through her off schedule. Later, Margot started to wonder if he was checking up on her instead of checking in. Did he not trust her?

One afternoon around 2:00 pm, Theo just showed up on Margot's floor to see her. She excused herself with the head nurse and went into the cafeteria to have a coffee with him. After they had sat down, she asked, "Theo, this is really nice but unexpected. Is anything wrong?"

Theo answered, "No, I just wanted to see you. I have to leave this afternoon for a conference that my boss signed me up for and I wanted to see you first before I left." Then he started to look around the room and spotted a young man dressed in greens, sitting at a table about midway from the back of the room. He did not seem to be paying any attention to them as far as Margot could tell, but Theo started to glare at him, then turning to her asked, "Do you know that one?"

"Yes, that is Dr. Tippen. He performs gastric surgery here and in Boston. He is very busy, considering his age."

Now Theo had some ammunition, "How do you know so much about him? I am sure that he does not tell everyone that. Did he hit on you?   Or did you make discreet inquiries because you thought you could hit on him?"

Margot put down her cup of coffee and tried to concentrate on what Theo had just said. It did not make any sense to her, so she asked, "What are you talking about, Theo? I don't understand the question."

"It is a simple question Margot, do you have interest in him?"

Now Margot was becoming alarmed. What on earth would make Theo think she was interested in anyone other than himself? "Theo, why would you even think those things? I never even look at other people except to talk to them regarding work. It is way too busy around here for anyone to worry about such things." Although Margot meant this as proof, it was the wrong thing to say.

"So, where is it that it is not too busy?"

"Nowhere…Theo, that's enough. I love you. I have no interest in anyone else."

Changing tact, Theo looked straight in her eyes and said, "You better make sure you stay that way too!" He finished what little was left in his cup, got up and walked out of the cafeteria, leaving Margot to dispense with the cups and napkins. Finished, she looked up, but he was nowhere to be seen. Dejected, she headed back to her workstation to check on her patients. She could not figure him out and was a little tired of trying. He came here for some reason, but I never did get to find out why.

When she got back to her floor, Bonnie Culpepper, a young nurse about her own age, looked up as she passed her station. "That was quick. You guys must have inhaled your coffees." Margot looked as if she could not understand what Bonnie was saying, so Bonnie started again, "Margot is everything all right? You look, ah, confused, to say the least."

"I don't understand men sometimes, Bonnie. I think they are a little on the nutty side."

"Well, you'll get no argument from me, Margot. It is a given to the species."

Margot stopped and smiled at her friend. She had known Bonnie for over three years. Although she never had socialized with her outside of work or school, they had studied for tests, cringed over finals, and had some wonderful conversations over lunch. The cute, petite little nurse always had a way of making Margot feel as if she was worrying over nothing.

"Bonnie, I don't want to take up any time right now, but after work, would you be interested in going over to Charlie's for a drink?" Charlie's was a wonderfully warm and friendly restaurant and bar on the outskirts of town. Although Margot had only been there once, she noticed that many of the hospital staff frequented the location.

"You're on. How about I meet you down in the front lobby around 4:00 pm. You'll know me because I am the pixie midget with the silly smile on my face."

"Great, I'll see you then!" Margot turned and walked down the hallway toward her area of work feeling much, much better. Bonnie was always a great sounding board, even though she was not the least bit interested in marriage. She said she was going to be a free spirit until the right spirit whisperer came along.

By four fifteen, they both jumped into Margot's car and headed off to Charlie's. Upon arriving, they entered and walked to a booth on the far side of the room. It did not take long until a waitress came over with menus and water. "Take your time, I will come back to take your orders unless you know what you want already?"

"I know I will need some time," Margot said.

"Yes, me too—I'm starved!" Bonnie added. The waitress left and Bonnie took a minute to peruse the menu and then, looked up at Margot and asked, "How is it that we have not gotten together before this? It has been ages since we got together to kibitz."

"Well, it was hard for me to get away since my marriage. Theo likes to have supper with me at the end of his day. However,

152

tonight he is on the road. I think that is why he came by to see me, although he ended our get together rather abruptly."

Just then, the waitress reappeared and Margot stopped long enough for them to order. Bonnie took advantage of the interruption to ask a question after the waitress left, "Why did he leave so fast? You came back from your lunch break fifteen minutes later!"

"I don't really know. We picked up our coffee, sat down and he started playing quiz about one of the doctors that was sitting on the other side."

"Which one?"

"Dr. Tippen."

"Well, he is very nice looking. Perhaps Theo was just upset he could not be with you tonight. Or do you think he is jealous because you work around a lot of men? You are gorgeous you know."

"Bonnie, I am not gorgeous. I'm a married woman and not interested in other men." Margot looked down at her water glass and did not say much more for a minute. Then she looked up and said, "Bonnie, it almost seems like he wanted to have an argument with me…like he was looking for an excuse."

"Why on earth would anyone want to have a fight? That is irrational. Besides, you are so good-natured that I don't see why he would want that to change."

"I can't figure it out either. This is not the first time he seemed to pick a fight. He has done it on many occasions since we moved into the apartment. I try so hard to make it right, and although he seems better the next day or two and then wham… it starts up again."

"I love Theo and I don't understand his behavior. His health is good and the only quirk he seems to have is his nasal spray. He always feels that his nose is dry and he is afraid that it will not protect him from germs I might bring home if he does not moisten it on a regular basis. He has a favorite brand of spray that he keeps in his cabinet at home and in the car.   Heaven help me if I don't keep it in supply for him!"

Bonnie and Margot stopped talking when the waitress brought over their salads and breadsticks. Everything looked too good to talk through, so they decided to eat first and enjoy the meal, then talk seriously over coffee. It was a good plan, and Margot was so very happy to be there with Bonnie. She almost never was on her own and did not realize that she was a little smothered in the marriage. Maybe he feels the same way too… maybe we just need to see friends outside of our usual social activities.

"Bonnie, do you think he just needs some space? Maybe he misses some of his friends, too."

"That is a good guess. Have you ever suggested that he meet up with some of his friends or does he hear from his friends from school or work?"

"No, as a matter of fact, he always says—when he is talking to me—that he only wants to spend his spare time with me."

"Well, when he gets home, you could suggest it to him. Tell him I want to have you go shopping with me this Saturday. And oh, by the way, that would be true. I need to find a really nice dress for my friend's wedding in two weeks, and I can never figure out what I look good in, or better yet, what makes me look taller."

"Bonnie, you're not that short."

"Margot, I am only four foot eleven. Compared to most of my friends, I am on the short side. Look at you! A giant—comparatively speaking."

They both laughed and decided it was getting late. Margot said she would call Bonnie and let her know what time she would be over to go shopping on Saturday. She was determined that she would join Bonnie; it was time she had a little freedom in this marriage. After all, she did not want to live like her mother did her entire marriage.

They paid the check and departed in high spirits. Margot forgot all the fuss in her head about Theo. She knew it would pass over and she could make it better between her and Theo, once he came home from his trip. Special treatment, special meals. That would cheer him up and make him feel like he was special to her. No more of this jealous bit. That was just silly. She would never give

154

him cause to doubt her. She jumped into her car and headed to the apartment, about twenty minutes away from the restaurant. When she pulled into her assigned parking space (the complex allowed two spaces per apartment) Theo's car was not in its spot. She knew he was on his trip, so that made sense to her.

She took her keys out of her handbag and walked up the stairs to their second-floor apartment. When she opened the door, she noticed that the apartment was totally dark. That was odd because she usually left the curtains open and the parking lot lights offered enough lighting to see to get across the room to the floor lamps. She closed the door and turned on the hall light, hung up her coat in the small closet in the entranceway, and walked carefully into the living room area.

Suddenly, the table lamp turned on and a voice said, "Where on earth have you been?"

Margot jumped, let out a startled cry, then realizing who was speaking—gasped, "Theo! You scared me to death! What are you doing here? You said you were going on a trip."

"You could not wait for me to leave, you rotten whore!" Theo stood up and approached her slowly with dark, menacing eyes and a look of pure hate written across his face.

"Theo!" Margot had never been spoken to like this before and was totally shocked.

"You knew I would not be home and you took advantage of me."

"Theo!" Margot could not manage to say anything else. He was scaring her and she could not really think of what to say, right at that moment. Finally, when he was about two feet from her she said, "Theo, I just went out to dinner with Bonnie from work. I don't know what you are thinking, but it is wrong."

Theo raised his hand and brought it down across her face so hard that it knocked her backward. She fell to the floor with nothing to help break the fall except her hand. When she hit the hard wooden floor, her wrist snapped and she let out a yell of pain. She was terrified of Theo. What was wrong with him? What on earth could possibly make him act this way? Was he on drugs? Was he bipolar and did not tell her? She was totally afraid, confused and hurt. Her hand and wrist were killing her and she knew her face must be bleeding too. Such a hard hit would leave a very bad bruise at the very least.

Theo had not intended to hit her so hard, but it did make him feel powerful. However, he did not want to lose her and more importantly, he did not want to go to jail. Knowing what to do, he crumpled to the floor next to Margot and looking at her with a look of true regret, he drew her into his arms and cradling her, rocked back and forth stating, "I am so sorry, so sorry, so sorry. But you make me so crazy. I love you so much and I don't want you to leave me for someone else. I know how beautiful you are and how men look at you. I love you and need you."

Margot was afraid to say anything and her arm hurt so badly that the rocking just seemed to make the pain worse—but she did not want him to stop. She was so happy he was repentant that she would endure almost anything at this point. Maybe he was just having a hard time with his job and did not like traveling away from her. Or maybe he felt she was too remote when she was home with him. Who knew…she was just happy he still loved her. Did he not just show her just how much he did love her.

Margot moaned when Theo moved his position next to her and he realized there was something else wrong with her. "Honey, your arm is hurt. Let me look at it."

Margot did not want to have him look at it but allowed him to see it while she held it with her other hand. "I think it might be broken. I hit the floor pretty hard." Margot looked up at him very intensely and added quietly, "I thought you were going to kill me"

"Darling, how could you even think such things? I adore you. I will never hit you or try to scare you again. I am so sorry. Here, let me help you up." Theo got up and held out his hand for Margot's good arm. Slowly, she got to her feet grimacing as she rose. When she was standing, Theo said, "We will have to get that looked at—but not around here." When Margot looked at him quizzically, he added, "If anyone finds out I was involved, even if

156

it were not my fault, I would be thrown in jail." Theo decided to test the waters as far as what Margot would say.

Margot was in a lot of pain and right at that moment, all she wanted to do was get her arm strapped up and take some ibuprofen. "All right Theo, but I have to get this x-rayed and quickly."

"I'll go get the car and we can go into the emergency room over in Huntsville."

"Theo, that is almost an hour away. Can't we go somewhere a little closer—it really hurts."

"Do you want me arrested? We have to go somewhere that neither of us is known." Theo turned and went to the hall closet to get her jacket. He put it over her shoulders and then, putting on his own coat, he held the door for her and closed and locked the apartment up.

Without conversation, they proceeded down the steps and out into the cold night air. Margot's arm was starting to throb and all she wanted to do was to stop the jostling that came with walking and to get into the car. Once inside, she tried to settle into a semi-comfortable position and wait. Theo started Margot's car and pulled out of the parking lot. He headed out of town and toward the hospital that he had mentioned and did not speak for about fifteen minutes. The silence was actually comforting to Margot. She could not really concentrate on anything, but the pain.

"Darling, what are you going to offer as a cause to the hospital personnel when you go in for the x-ray?"

Margot then realized that he was testing her. Would she tell the truth? Or would she lie and make something up. If she told the truth, he could go to jail. It could end their marriage, as he would probably not forgive her. IF she said something else, like she had fallen on some icy steps at her apartment building, they would never know the difference. It was too far for the local police to check and they would not know her stairs were on the inside of the building. Yes, that would work. As long as it did not repeat itself.

Margot answered, "I will tell them I fell on icy steps at the apartment complex."

Theo exhaled an obvious sigh of relief and said, "Darling, you know I will never do anything like this again. You won't make me do this again, will you?"

Margot had no idea how she had caused this, but at this point, it did not matter. The pain was just as sharp as it was ten minutes before and she did not really care to reason out who was at fault. Somehow she doubted it was her fault, but she kept her opinions to herself. "No, let's not do this again," she answered him.

Unexpected Winds

See the sails folding and billowing,
As they seize the wayward wind.
They have not a care or sorrow,
Their purpose fulfilled as soon as they begin.

Beware the pleasant feel of the breeze,
As it gently caresses your face.
For suddenly it may turn against you,
Never to leave a single trace.

Chapter X

After Thomas Martyn had graduated from college, he started working at a local social services center dealing with the homeless and abused. His heart went out to people who had so little control over their lives. Many of the homeless women and children came from broken homes and they did not have the wherewithal to get back on their feet. Instead, they would be out on the street and in a shelter at night.

Thomas loved helping these people and found many of them were willing to do almost anything to stand on their own two feet. After a year, Thomas acquired a position with the state of New York. He was able to start a retraining program for people who were interested in learning new, practical trades. Often the people needed to learn to improve or their ability to read or do simple math. It was a wonderful program and it soon was filled to capacity. This brought attention to the program at the state capital level, and Thomas was asked by several state senators to implement similar programs within their districts.

Thomas was not only thrilled to do so but found it amusing that he was rubbing elbows with the cream of political society when his father thought that only being a lawyer would bring him any notoriety. Thomas did not really care for the lime light unless it brought in more money for his programs. He could not wish for anything more than to make this a statewide program throughout New York.

Although he was extremely busy, he always found time to call Margot and Jadyn once a month. To keep everyone in touch, he made a conference call so all three of them could talk and catch up. It worked out great, and if one could not make the call at that time, they would reschedule it to a convenient time.

But this month's call took on a totally different tone. The girls had so much going on, that Thomas was only able to listen with amazement. Jadyn was moving to the Boston area to work in a top-secret lab and Theo had gotten a better position in a large retail chain, still located on Long Island. They had moved from their apartment and now lived close to where Theo was working. It was wonderful. Now all of them would be on the same coast and not so very far away.

It was a shame that Margot had to leave her hospital; she loved it and had friends there. She was very sad about that but happy that Theo was finally being recognized for his talents as a buyer. But now he would be traveling more, so he did not want her to have to work. He wanted her to relax at home and have children.

Jadyn thought that this was a shame—Margot went to school and had a wonderful career ahead of her, no matter what state she was in… so why did she have to stay home? She decided to get settled into her new apartment first, and then have a serious conversation with Margot concerning this. "It may not be my business, but something does not sound right," she confided in Thomas later in the week.

"Well, it is up to her and Theo. It is their marriage and life."

"Yes, but did you notice the way she phrased everything when she was telling us about it? It was Theo this and Theo that. Not what she wanted, just what he wanted. Sounded a little too much like speaking to Mother."

"True, but I think we are a little overly sensitive about that kind of thing because of Mother's relationship with Father. They had or I should say have such a sad life that we may be projecting it onto Margot."

"Well, Thomas, you may be right…but I still plan to play quiz with her later. Right now, I have my own problems… keeping my head above water at this new facility. I am mixing with the best in all fields. To be honest, I am a bit overwhelmed that Dr. Jeffries felt I belonged here. Truthfully, I am a little scared."

"Will you be working on your little home project, now that it is out in the open?"

"Well, Thomas, one thing has changed. I cannot talk about anything I work on from now on. It is all top secret."

"No fun, I used to love to hear about what you were doing. But I guess you had to give up some things to get to the East Coast.

I'm thrilled you are here. It will be great for Mother, too. Hey, let's run down to see her the first weekend you're available. All three of us."

"That sounds perfect. I can go this weekend. I live alone and don't have any kind of a schedule that I have to meet, as long as I am back to work on Monday on time."

"Great! I'll call Margot and see if she can come. Maybe you two could ride down together and you could play quiz with her then."

"Thomas, that's a great idea! Call her and see if she can come on such short notice. She is not as free as we are."

The next morning, Thomas called Margot on his way to work. "Hey Margot, I had an epiphany yesterday."

"Oh, what might that be little brother?"

"Well, since we are all on the same side of the world now, how about the three of us going home to see Mother and Father- if he is there."

"That sounds marvelous! Can Jadyn come? She has just moved in and is really busy."

"Yes, she said she would not miss it."

"Oh, I can't wait Thomas! This will be such a nice surprise for Mother. It is a surprise, isn't it?"

"Yes, we are definitely keeping it quiet. She won't be expecting it at all. Also, Jadyn said she would pick you up and you two could drive down together if you would like."

Margot did not answer right away, but when she did it was in a different tone of voice, "No, I think it best if I drive myself. I don't know if I can stay the entire weekend."

"All right. I will let Jadyn know. We are going over Friday after work and meeting at the ice-cream shop first. Then all three of us can drive over as a group. It will be so much fun. I did call Mother the other day and she did not have any specific plans, so I think we are good to go. Meet you at the ice-cream shop around six-thirty pm or so, okay?"

"I will be there with a yellow ribbon in my hair!"

It sounded like the old Margot and Thomas was really pleased with himself, to have come up with the idea.

Friday at six, Jadyn pulled up to the ice-cream shop, parked, and went inside. It was fairly busy as they also served hamburgers, cheesesteaks, and french fries. It was a local hang out for working folks from the area. Jadyn spotted Thomas sitting in a back booth, waving happily at her.

"Hey Thomas!" Jadyn exclaimed as she ran over to hug him.

Thomas jumped up out of the booth and embraced his sister tightly. "No sign of Margot yet, but it is early. She probably has to get some things ready for Theo for meals, etc. She will be along soon."

They both ordered some coffee as they knew it would be a long, talkie night. Jadyn wanted to know how Thomas was doing with his new position as head of the state's Unemployed Rebranding Department. "The work is so wonderful and I get so many letters from the people we have been able to help. I feel like I am truly making a difference!"

"I am so proud of you, Thomas. When I left, you were a very popular free bird on campus, and I was not sure what you would become…in the long run."

"What, no T. J. ?" Thomas was amazed that his nick-name was dropped.

"No, it does not fit the distinguished man you have become."

"Thanks Sis, but I had to work really hard to come even close to what you are accomplishing… even though I have no idea what it is," he stated with a sly look on his face.

"Well, I have not accomplished much yet. Everything I am doing is in its baby-stages. But I have high hopes."

As time went on, Thomas started looking at his watch wondering why Margot had not shown up. At seven o'clock, it was becoming clear something had impeded her trip in to see them. Thomas said, "Let me give her a call and see if she is stuck in traffic somewhere." He left the booth and went outside to hear more clearly. His cell phone reception was dodgy at best, but outside it would be better. New technology always started out with problems, but later would be indispensable. When he returned to the table, his crestfallen face said it all.

"She's not coming, is she?" Jadyn remarked.

"Well, yes and no. She said she was sorry, but she can't drive down tonight. She said she will be here tomorrow by lunchtime, for sure."

"What was her reason?"

"She said she had too much unpacking to do, and Theo thought it best she stay home this one extra night."

"Humph, I'll bet he did," Jadyn snorted out.

"Now, now, Jadyn, we can't judge what is going on unless she tells us. Suspicions don't count."

"Well, let's get going. The least she could have done was call and let us know."

Thomas agreed, "Yes, true, but maybe it was a last minute decision."

The two of them got into their cars and drove the few blocks to their childhood home. They could see the lights on in the front room but did not hear any television. The two of them ran up the front steps and raced to be the first to ring the doorbell.

"This place brings out the child in us both!" Thomas declared with a big grin.

"It sure does. So many nights we sat on this porch playing games and telling stories."

Just then, the front door opened and Rachael Martyn peered out to see who was there. When she saw the kids, she cried a joyful welcome and told them to come in the house. She was so happy to see the kids. Well, not kids, but her kids nonetheless. "Oh, Jadyn, it has been so long! You look marvelous, dear. And Thomas, handsome as ever."

She took their coats as if they were guests, and then directed them into the kitchen. "Have you had supper yet?"

"No, Mother, we were planning to take you out to a late supper, if you don't mind." Thomas filled in the information.

"Oh, well I look a fright. I have been painting all day."

164

"No worries. The Dracock Hotel serves a wonderful meal and is open until ten."

"Okay, but you two have a seat in the living room while I change into something a little less scary."

Jadyn and Thomas waited happily in the living room and fifteen minutes later, a more presentable Rachael announced she was ready. All three piled into Jadyn's new car and they were whisked away in the smooth machine. "Jadyn, this is a lovely car. Did you just lease it or buy it?" Rachael was awash with curiosity.

"No, Mother. It is a company car."

"Yeah, Jadyn is an important lady now, Mother. She works on secret stuff and cannot tell anyone what it is about."

"That really bothers you, doesn't it little brother?" Jadyn asked teasingly.

"No, well, maybe a bit," he cleared his throat and added, "but only a bit."

"You two should have let me know you were coming and I would have made some lasagna for you."

"You will have your chance as we are here until Sunday night. Then it is back to the old grind." Thomas was so happy that they were with their mother, but secretly he felt guilty that Margot was not there. "Let's head out to that nice restaurant in the hotel."

After they had ordered their meals, Rachael started her quiz, "Jadyn, I knew you were back on this coast, but I did not expect to see you so soon. Tell me about how you got your transfer here and all that is going on with you."

Jadyn filled in her mother and Thomas on the shady dealings with her old boss and how Dr. Jeffries and Professor Bates had worked to fix her problem. She said she was so very grateful as she really did want the company to get the research as long as she got credit for the development. She loved her new facility and whatever equipment she needed, they supplied it happily. "You have got to love working as a subcontractor to the military."

"You work for the military?" Jadyn's mother was intrigued.

"Well, not directly. I work in a lab that they fund, but I work on projects that they may or may not need for military use.

Remember, I am a medical biologist. I want to help people in Margot's field, more than the military. But right now, they are a necessary evil."

Turning her gaze over to her son she asked, "Thomas how is your latest promotion? Tell me how all your plans are being implemented on the state level." Rachael wanted both of her children to have equal time, much to their amusement.

After about two hours, they decided to go back to the house and check in with Margot… just to ensure that she was coming in on Saturday. When she did not answer, they assumed that she had gone to bed early, probably exhausted from unpacking. They all said good night and Jadyn and Thomas went into the two guest bedrooms, which were once their bedrooms as children. It was nice to be home in these surroundings. It was also very nice that their father had elected to stay in the city for the weekend. Oh well, too bad.

The next morning after breakfast, Thomas gave Margot a call. She answered after several rings, sounding remote or tired or something… Thomas could not tell. "Hello, Thomas. How is your visit with Mother?"

"It was very nice, Margot, but would have been much better if you had been there."

"I know, but it is a very hard time to get away right now. Theo wants to do a lot around here before Monday when he goes into work again."

"You are still coming down today, aren't you?" Thomas knew the answer before he had it confirmed.

"I don't think so. Not this weekend. Maybe next time, when I am not so busy." Margot then hung up before Thomas could even ask her any questions.

He went back into the living room where Jadyn and her mother were happily looking at some pictures and talking about Margot's wedding. "She looks so happy. I hope she can come in this weekend," Rachael continued.

"She's not coming," was all that Thomas said when two faces cast inquiring looks in his direction.

166

Jadyn's face, clouded in a mask, said it all. She was not allowed to come. Jadyn knew it. Thomas knew it. Only Rachael seemed oblivious to the problem, "Well, they have only been in their new home for a month or so. She must be very busy putting up shelves, sorting out furniture and sprucing the place up for company. I hear Theodore is very important in his new position."

The weekend passed by very quickly. Jadyn and Thomas were amazed at how well their mother's paintings had been selling. They knew she was talented, but this went way beyond good. Galleries were inviting her to do shows on a regular basis, but she seldom took the opportunity. "If your father knew how much I had sold over the years, he would not feel as obligated to support me," she admitted by Sunday morning. "I would have no way of going to the showings in New York City. I would be too afraid that I might be seen by him, or worse, he might come in with one of his latest friends and embarrass the heck out of me."

Her honesty about the situation was refreshing. Both Thomas and Jadyn thanked her and informed her that they had known about the problems that their parents had had over the years. "We know you are no stranger to pain and suffering. But hey, I have a great idea!" Thomas was at it again, "Why not have a showing near me in White Plains or near Jadyn in Boston? You could say you were going for a visit if he bothers to ask, and he would be none the wiser."

"Not a bad idea, Thomas. I will give that some thought. I would love to come for a visit, even if I am not having a show. I am getting a little housebound as the expression goes."

They hated that time seemed to have no problem swimming by and soon they made their way back to their homes. Thomas said he wanted to continue the conference calls with the two girls and promised to call his mother in a week or so. Rachael was sad to see them go but very happy to know that she would see the girls more often. She already saw Thomas at least once a month, which she thought was really good, since he was a man. Her impression was that sons don't usually visit as often as daughters. She was just lucky with Thomas.

****

Margot was very unhappy that she had to miss the get-together at her mother's, but the fight that ensued when she informed Theo that she was going for a visit was just one of many new battles. Theo said they were too busy to socialize at that very moment. He felt she should concentrate on fixing up the house for company and plan a party for his fellow workers. Margot did not mind helping Theo further his position in the company, but she did want to see her family, especially since her twin sister was back on the East Coast.

This made Margot even more determined to go back to work. She decided to bring it up one night, at the dinner table during dessert. She thought she would plant a few seeds and give Theo a chance to get used to the idea. But it would not have mattered when she told Theo that she wanted to go back to work, he would not hear of it. They discussed it at length, well, Theo talked and she sat and looked at him with a blank face. She did not dare let him know that she thought he was acting very selfishly. She did not want another blow to her head. She had had enough brain rattlers for one lifetime.

When they went to bed that night, Theo started to tell Margot about this wonderful sailboat that his company owned. "They let management take it out for short runs and weeklong sails, during the summer. I have signed us up for the third week in August. We can have it for the entire week. In a month or so, we will take it out for a spin, just to get a feel for it."

"Theo, what do we know about sailing?"

"They show you what you need to know and they ask that you keep the shoreline insight if you are not used to sailing."

"What kind of a sailboat is it? What size?"

"I don't know. All I know is that we can handle it and it has a cabin that sleeps six."

"Theo, what brought this on? What made you want to do this?"

168

"Margot, we must start thinking of the future… not living in the past. You have to remember that I am getting to be very important in the company and I want to look and act the part."

Margot was getting sleepy and decided that it would be a few months before she had to worry about this. "Good night Theo, I am too tired to absorb all that you are saying."

"I'm not tired Margot and do you know what I feel like?" He extended his hand over to her side of the bed to make sure she understood his meaning.

"Theo, I am really tired. I have been unpacking and rearranging furniture all day."

"A man has needs and a beautiful wife should be happy to take care of them, whenever and wherever. Maybe we will even do it on the boat—what a kick that would be."

Margot groaned inwardly and turned to do as Theo wished. It was so much easier and less painful if she just did as she was told.

****

A few weeks later, Margot was tired of Theo's excuses for not allowing her to go see her sister, who lived so very close (or at least close compared to California).   So, when she got up and fixed breakfast for Theo before he headed off to work, she decided that today would be the day. "Theo," she began. "I am going to go see Jadyn today. We are meeting for lunch in Providence. Is there anything you want me to pass on to her while I am there?"

Stony silence was Margot's answer. Theo could not think of a good excuse to keep Margot home and away from her sister. He just looked down at his breakfast while he thought about what he could say. Finally, he came up with an angle, "Did you plan to take the ferry across? That is a big expense."

"Well, not as much as driving all the way around through New York City. Besides, Jadyn said she would pay for my tickets. All I have to do is pick them up at the office."

"All right Margot, you go and have a nice time while I am working to support us. But I expect supper at the usual time, and I expect to be treated to something special!" The implication was there and Margot did not miss the hint.

"Don't worry; I will have a very special dinner ready for you when you get home." She did not mention anything else.

When Theo left for work, he slid out the door while Margot was in the kitchen cleaning up the dishes. No goodbyes. No kiss. No nothing. She knew she was in the doghouse for whatever reason he had conjured up; however, at this point, she did not care. She was getting out of the house!! She called Jadyn's number and after a few rings, she heard Jadyn's voice, "Hello."

"Hey sis, what are you up to today?"

"Working as usual. Why?"

"Well, I am out and about and thought we could have lunch together," Margot's voice sounded very upbeat and excited.

"Great! I have a better idea—I will meet you at eleven-thirty and I will take the remainder of the day off. Where do you want to meet?"

"Well, I kind of lied to Theo and told him I was taking the ferry and we were meeting in Providence. I told him you were paying for my trip, but you don't have to worry about that; I have some money squirreled away for a fun day."

"That sounds great, Margot. We can go over to the mall and have lunch and then just buzz around." Jadyn was amazed at the sudden visit and hoped that Margot's plan would work.

"Super!" Margot responded, "Where shall we meet?"

"How about at the Oh-Kay Coral? It will take me a little time to get there, but I came into work early. I can take off at ten just to make sure I am on time."

"Great! See you soon." Margot hung up her phone and decided to take a shower and get ready. Although she had time, she should catch the earliest ferry that she could. Once ready, she grabbed her handbag and keys, locked the front door, and went down to the curb where her car was sitting. Something did not look quite right with the car, but she was not sure what—at least not right away. Walking around it, she saw what was making the car look a little off; her tire was flat on the driver's side.   Now how did that happen? It was fine yesterday.

She went back into the house and called the local garage. Twenty minutes later, the man from the garage came to pick up her tire and take it back to repair it. He said that it would take several hours as they were extremely busy. Margot called Jadyn to tell her that she might be a tad later than planned and she would keep her posted. Thirty-five minutes later, the man from the garage called her and said, "I have bad news, Mrs. Blodger. The tire is ruined."

"What! How?"

"I tried to repair it, but it looks like you ran over something large and sharp. Either that or someone took a knife to it. It has a very large gash in it."

"Well, just hold on to it until my husband comes down or calls. I will tell him about it when he gets home. Thank you and we will call you in the morning."

Margot was not about to give up on her lunch with Jadyn, so she called for a rental car to be dropped off and headed to the ferry. By the time she crossed the Sound in the ferry, she actually arrived only about ten minutes late; Jadyn already had a table and ice tea ordered. They hugged and sat and grinned at each other with true pleasure.

Jadyn was the first to speak, "I am so glad you got your tire fixed. If not, I was going to come over and pick you up."

"Truthfully, the tire is ruined. We will have to replace it; I will have to tell Theo about it and he can get a new one put on. He is going to kill me for ruining the tire, but I have no idea what I could have run over.   I don't really go anywhere but around town.   I rented a car and took the ferry to New London," Margot added when she saw Jadyn's brow wrinkle.

"Well, I am paying for the car rental. I make plenty of money and I don't really go anywhere nor do anything so I can take care of your car's cost. That is no problem."

Margot was very thankful but embarrassed that she needed help. She knew that Theo made enough money for her to rent a car, but he would not like that she did it without asking. However, Margot was full of questions and decided to skip over her issues with Theo for now. "So, tell me about your new job. How do you like it on the East Coast? What kind of projects do you work on?" They had not seen each other since Christmas and time was short.

"Margot, I am so happy to be back on this side of the country. Less pollution, more variety of scenery. I also like four seasons; I really missed that. As for my position with the company, I love that too. I have my own lab, two assistants, and several colleagues. I can't tell you about my work as it is top secret, but I can tell you that it is going very well and I will be doing some beta trials very soon!"

"Jadyn, that is wonderful! Your own lab and everything! I am so proud of you." Margot's face went from joyful to sober very quickly. "I wish I was still working. I miss the excitement of the hospital arena. Always something new to deal with."

"Margot, why don't you go back to work? You must be done unpacking now."

"Oh, heavens yes!" Margot's face went blank while she finished her thoughts, "But Theo thinks that his wife should stay home."

"Don't you have any say about that? Doesn't he know you want to go back to work?"

Margot rapidly changed the subject, "What made them transfer you here? Is this facility more along the lines of what you work on?"

Jadyn knew Margot did not want to talk about her situation, so she told Margot about her new place and how she was enjoying the area. She also told her about what had precipitated her transfer—Dr. Farnot's duplicity and Dr. Jeffries and Professor Bate's role on her behalf. Margot became very incensed when she thought about what Dr. Farnot had tried to pull.

"I don't believe that Farnot guy! I wonder what he is thinking now…"

"He does not know I am over here. He thinks I was fired. We have decided to keep my transfer and promotion a secret, for the time being. He could cause me trouble over here if he wanted to—

and he would if he knew. He has wanted to come to this facility for several years and they keep rejecting his requests.”

They kept talking as they walked the mall, looking at this and that while they strolled. It was such a pleasant afternoon, that Margot hated to end the time. “Jadyn, I have to get back home. Theo was not too happy with me this morning and when he finds I have ruined the tire, well, I just want to get home to fry up some chicken and smash some spuds. Then he will be a happier camper, I hope.”

“Margot, how is it going with you two?” Jadyn did not know how to phrase it delicately, so she just blurted out what she was really thinking. “Is he as nice to you as you are to him?”

Margot did not answer right away. She knew if she lied, Jadyn would know it. Yet she did not want people to feel sorry for her. “Well, his new job and promotion have made him a little tenser,” she started out with that excuse. “He seems to be able to focus on his issues and problems just fine, but he is not really interested in anything else.”

Jadyn did not say anything, just nodded and said, “Oh.”

“I don’t want you to get the wrong impression; I am sure he loves me and wants me to be happy. But I don’t always know what to say or how to act.” Margot made a face indicating she was truly in a quandary, “He always makes me feel like second best.”

Jadyn was sure Margot did not want to hear what she really thought, so she just let Margot unburden herself. “He gets mad real easy, so I try not to bring up anything that might set him off.”

“Has he hit you, Margot?”

No answer. The look on her face told Jadyn everything. “Margot, that is unacceptable and you know it. When we used to see what Father did to Mother, we all swore we would never let that happen to us. Now you have fallen into the same trap that Mother was in—only she has it a little better now that he is not home much.”

“Jadyn, you don’t understand. He does not mean it—he is just tired and overworked.”

“Margot, you know it will only get worse if you let it.”

"No, the last time he struck me, he promised he would never do it again, and I believe him."

"The last time? How many times are we talking about?"

"Jadyn, I don't want to talk about it, okay? I have to go and get supper started. Please, don't tell Thomas. He can be a pest about such things. Please?"

"No promises. For now, maybe, but you have to come and see me more often so I can make sure you are okay."

They walked in silence for a few minutes, and then Margot added, "I wonder what happened to my tire? It does not make any sense. I would have known if I ran over anything large yesterday. Maybe someone slashed my tire for kicks—some kid or something like that."

"I wouldn't know. Do you have much of the tire slashing going on in your neighborhood?"

"No, not usually, but there is always a first." Silence fell again and Margot felt the strain of not telling her sister all that had happened to her over the last few months. She was even starting to wonder if Theo had maybe slashed the tire. No, that would be stupid. Why would he do something like that?

Jadyn must have read her thoughts, because she added, "Maybe the slasher is a little closer to home." She did not add anymore and they walked the parking lot to Margot's rental car. "Sis, you be careful, okay? I don't want you to get hurt."

"I love you, Jadyn!" Margot said with a little tear starting to form in her eye. She knew that her sister meant only the best for her.

They parted, each thinking their own thoughts and worrying about the other. Being a twin could make life wonderful or it could make the pain more real. Margot did not want Thomas to get involved as he might report Theo to the authorities. Jadyn did not want her sister to continue being a victim. She knew it would not get better if they did not seek counseling. Jadyn had no idea the fate that awaited or she would never have let her sister out of her sight.

174

Jadyn was truly worried about Margot. She knew that if she admitted to being hit more than once, that she probably had been injured more often. But how to find out? She knew that Margot did not want Thomas involved, but she wanted Thomas to do some research on it. It was time to drive down to see her brother. Jadyn did not turn to go home but headed out toward White Plains to see Thomas. Hope he does not have plans for tonight.

****

Margot set about making a fabulous supper for Theo. She did not want him to be mad at her for the tire as well as going out while he was working. She rationalized that he would not be too upset after seeing all the time and preparation she spent on the evening meal. Maybe he would not ever know how long she had been home. As the evening approached, she finished all the preparations and started to fry the chicken. All the side dishes were complete and she knew he would be delighted with the meal.

But when six o'clock came, no Theo. Margot wondered if he was delayed in traffic or at work. She set the table and then went upstairs to fix her hair and make herself look presentable. By seven, she was now starting to be concerned about what was delaying him. Although she had the meal in the oven, keeping it warm, if he did not come soon, it would be too dry. She decided to call his office to see if he had left.

"Hello Mrs. Blodger," came the silky voice of Theo's young secretary. "How can I help you?"

"I was just wondering what time my husband left the office—I am trying to time a special dinner for him."

Silence hung in the air for at least twenty seconds. It sounded like Vanessa had covered the mouth-piece and had a small conversation before she answered. "He left a couple of hours ago, Mrs. Blodger. He should be home soon."

Margot did not know how to react to this disconcerting conversation, so she merely said, "Oh, okay Vanessa. I guess he is picking up something at the mall."

"Is there anything else you need, Mrs. Blodger?"

"No. Thank you."

Both parties hung up, but Margot was not feeling nearly as satisfied with the conversation as Theo was, "Great job, Vanessa. As usual." He leaned over the side of her desk to kiss her squarely on the mouth.

She tilted her head back to receive the expected kiss and then said, "Won't she be worried or suspicious?"

"Worried yes, suspicious, no. That is the beauty of all this. She always thinks things are her fault. She will fret for hours. Then when I go home, she will be ready to apologize in so many ways. I know what I am doing."

"You are such a bad boy, Theo," Vanessa said with a smirk on her face. She really enjoyed Theo's company when they went out for their little trysts, but she was amazed to find that she enjoyed his treatment of his wife even more so. It was a type of vicarious voyeurism, she guessed. No matter, she still relished the pleasure it gave her when he shared the details.

"Bad boy?" Theo asked as he bent over her again. "You have no idea how bad I can be."

They continued their passion for another thirty minutes and then Theo realized he was hungry. "I guess I had better get home to put her out of her misery. I don't want her too upset, as we have our sailing adventure coming up. I have special plans for that."

"Okay, go home to your wifee poo. I will see you tomorrow morning."

Theo kissed her beckoning lips one more time and then headed out the door to go home. It was now about seven forty-five and he had truly worked up an appetite. It would take at least half an hour to get home, but that would give him enough time to plan his evening's entertainment.

As he pulled his new sports car up into the driveway, he noticed that Margot's car only had three tires on it. One tire was missing and it rested on a no-move jack. She must have called the garage after I left, he mused. Pity, she missed her luncheon. He hit the garage door opener and drove into the space reserved for his new sports baby.

Margot, hearing the garage door opening, breathed a sigh of relief and headed to the kitchen side door, which led to the garage. She did not get the door open before Theo slammed through it and said, "What is wrong with your car?"

"Theo, I was so worried about you. Why are you so late?"

"I had to work." He answered tersely and then added, "Don't sidestep the question. What happened to your car?"

Margot did not want to tell Theo that she had called the office, so she just answered his question, "I had a flat tire this morning. I had the garage pick it up to repair it."

"So why is it not on the car? Does it take all day to repair a tire?"

"I did not want to upset you before you had a chance to eat, but the garage said the tire is no good. Too large a cut in it. I think we have been vandalized."

"That is an unlikely event, Margot. This area does not have vandals. More than likely, you ran over something because you were not paying attention."

Margot knew there was no way to prove her innocence one way or the other, so she decided to change the subject, "Why don't you get comfortable and I will fix your plate. I made your favorite meal and it should still be warm."

Theo shook his head in disgust and went to change out of his suit. Margot again breathed a sigh of relief and hurried to the kitchen to make up Theo's dinner. By the time he sat down at the table, she had everything he could possibly want for that meal. He did not say anything, just grunted and started to eat. Margot put a second plate down on the table and started to eat silently, waiting in anticipation of the inquisition that would begin; she did not have to wait long.

"So, was Jadyn upset that you missed your little luncheon?"

"No, it was okay. I rented a car and was able to meet her." Margot saw Theo's eyes and hastily added, "Jadyn paid for the rental."

"You mean to tell me that you ruined a car tire, spent money on a rental, and then spent money on lunch?" He plopped down his napkin next to his plate for effect. "What do you think I have to do to make that money? I work!"

"Well, now that you have brought that up, Theo, I wanted to let you know I am ready to help out with the money."

"What do you mean?"

"I can go back to work at a hospital and make enough to take some of the pressure off you." Margot thought that sounded slightly noble, but was under no illusions—Theo would be resistant.

"Margot, we have had that conversation before. You are not going back to work. I know you would like to see some of those doctors that you worked with before, but no way José…. You are not getting your way!"

Margot knew that it was going to be a long, tense night and she was determined it was not going to ruin the day she had spent seeing Jadyn. She would bear up under the innuendos and accusations, once again. Maybe if she just thought of something else while he was ranting, it would not be so bad. Yes, that is it. Distance myself from the may-lay. Margot would have had to take a trip across the state to avoid the tirade that Theo unleashed on her, but in the end, she won; he had not struck her nor had he shoved her around. What a victory, she thought.

****

"Hurry up Margot; we don't want to miss the tide!" Theo was already dressed in his shorts, sweatshirt, deck sneakers, and hat. He had all the trappings he needed to go sailing.

"I want to take some sun tanning lotion and I can't find it."

Theo rolled his eyes and said, "Margot, you have on long sleeves and a hat. You don't have anything exposed to get burnt."

"Well, I am dressed in layers, in case it is warm on the water. I thought there was a storm off the coast somewhere…are you sure today is a good day to take the boat out?"

178

"Yes, yes, fine. Besides, we are scheduled for today. I have been practicing for a week in the off hours and I am ready to go." Theo stated with finality. He did not mention that he had been taking lessons for a month and was a naturally proficient sailor.

"Okay, I will be ready in five minutes." Margot was not looking forward to the sailing adventure. She knew Theo had some grandiose ideas and felt he could impress the bosses at his work if he sailed the big boat. He had been acting so unusual these last few days that she thought he might have given up on the idea of sailing. No such luck. He could be aloof and distant from her one moment and demanding and scrutinizing the next. She thought she would love another afternoon with Jadyn—just to even out her life's pressures. Jadyn always had a way of putting things in perspective. Besides, she always made her laugh.

Margot locked the front door and stepped down to the curb, where Theo had pulled the car. He sat looking annoyed at her tardiness but said nothing and Margot did not volunteer anything either. They pulled away and it only took about thirty minutes before Theo turned the car into the yachting club. Margot had to admit she was a little more excited than she thought she would be. She had packed a nice picnic luncheon and a very nice bottle of wine to accompany it.

Theo drove over to the general parking lot of the wharf, where the boat was docked. A security guard came toward them, watching to see who was getting out of the car. As soon as he saw Theo, he broke into a smile and said, "Welcome Mr. Blodger. The Princess Lea is all ready for you."

"Thank you, Teddy. We are looking forward to a nice sail."

"Oh, I see you have different company today. I trust she has her sea legs?" Teddy's eyes danced with a conspiratorial wink.

Theo did not want this conversation to go further, so he said, "Yes Teddy, and they are all mine." Turning away from the nosey guard, he popped open the hatch on his sports car and picked out the basket. Margot grabbed her bag and the drinks cooler and followed Theo silently toward the wharf.

"What was he talking about, Theo? He had a weird look on his face. I don't think I like him."

"Well, the good thing about that is that you are not required to like him. He secures the boats and preps them for outings, like the one we are having today." Theo ignored the first part of Margot's question.

Margot fell silent and let Theo lead them to the side of a large sailing vessel. "The Princess Lea is a beautiful, sleek racer-cruiser, about thirty-four feet long and can get up to about thirteen knots if the wind is right and the sea cooperates." It was obvious that Theo enjoyed his newest hobby. Margot was worried he would start wanting one of these babies for himself. Margot had no idea what a knot translated into, but she put on the appropriately impressed facial expression and handed up the cooler and her bag to Theo after he jumped up on board.

"Can one person sail this? It is much larger than I thought it would be."

"One can sail it, but it would really take two to race it," Theo stated.

"Race it?" Margot was perplexed, "I thought this was a sailboat."

Theo once again rolled his eyes and indicated with an abrupt thumb gesture that she should head to the cabin section of the boat. "Take the food and drinks down into the galley. It has a portable refrigerator that will keep everything cool enough." Theo then started to go over the checklist that the guard had left on the deck chair. He made sure he had enough gas in the tank in case the wind quit, checked the rigging and then untied the mooring lines and pushed the nose of the boat away from the dock. He then proceeded to the back of the boat to start the motor.

Margot came up on deck and walked over to the side of the cabin that looked the safest to sit upon. "Theo, it has an engine?"

"Yes, you can't sail it in and out of dock. Too unstable for control. So you run it out to get into open water, and then drop your sails."

This unusual and patient explanation was amazing to Margot, so she sat nodding a general understanding. She could see that Theo was truly enjoying his mastery of this type of craft and was in a very good mood. She started to relax. The day was beautiful and the seas were calm… or at least as far as she could see from the inlet in which the pier was located. She walked to the second attached deck seat that was located near where Theo sat guiding the large vessel out to sea. This may be the perfect day to discuss things with Theo. Maybe his mood will afford me time to make my case.

"What did you pack for lunch?" Theo's mind was on every detail of the trip.

"Hard-boiled eggs, cheese, fried chicken, cucumber salad, and some of the apple pie I made the other day."

"That sounds fine. I hope you remembered the salt."

Margot was proud of her luncheon and nodded affirmation to the query. She knew he loved chicken and so she made a point of bringing it. She really wanted him in a good mood.

It did not take long to reach the entrance to the Great South Bay and sail into open water. Obeying the speed restriction and rules he had learned, Theo guided the vessel through the floating markers indicating the deepest waters in the channel. He had no desire to do anything that would tarnish his standing with the company, which included failing his use of the company boat. After passing under the bridge, Theo cranked up the throttle and guided the boat out of the bay and into the open water.

The water started to rock the boat slightly as the wave action gently lifted the nose up and down. Margot had expected this, so was not alarmed. Theo started to smile very slightly and Margot took this as a very good sign   He must be pleased with himself. She watched him as he stopped the engine and then went forward to unroll the large sail. There was one big mast in the middle of the boat and a smaller one in front of that one which was fastened to the front of the boat. This made a large triangle with a peak in the middle of the deck. Very pretty, Margot thought.

"You're going to have to help me with some of the sailing, Margot." Theo was used to having Vanessa as company. At least she knew what to do. Theo enjoyed telling the women in his life, what he wanted them to do. But today would have the added bonus of Margot being afraid of what was happening during the sail. She had never been on a sailing vessel when it tipped sideways and looked like it was going to sink. She will be frightened out of her mind. This thought made Theo smile, although he did not say anything.

As they went further out, away from the shore, Margot noticed that the wind seemed to change. Theo did not appear to be worried, so she tried to relax as the big sail grabbed hungrily at the proffered breeze. It was quite beautiful in its design; she just hoped it would not be too much to handle. "What can I do to help?" Margot offered, hoping that there was nothing to start with until she got her sea legs.

"Nothing right now, but if the wind gets too strong, we will have to trim the sails as well as steer. I will do that and you can hold the wheel for me."

Margot relaxed as that did not sound too bad. How hard can that be? Margot looked toward shore and noticed it was fading from view. "Theo, are we supposed to go this far from shore?"

"Don't fret your little self, Margot. We are not that far out. It just looks that way. I want to get away from the land breeze and take advantage of a good sea breeze."

Margot was not sure why one breeze was different from another but decided to change the subject. "Theo, I would like to speak to you regarding some things. I thought we could do that over lunch if you don't have to steer this boat all the time."

Theo did not answer but nodded his head acknowledging that he heard what she said. As he guided the boat across the gentle waves, he glanced at Margot to see if she appreciated how efficiently he was able to handle the boat. Margot was looking out over the waters toward the shoreline, or at least where she assumed it was located. Theo was still headed out further from the shore and enjoyed the fact that she was getting uncomfortable with the distance.

After another half an hour, Theo swung the boat to the right and changed direction, keeping an eye on his compass. He was now headed northeast, about six miles out from the coast. The water was getting choppy, which added a thrill to the sailing experience. "How about we eat some lunch?"

Margot looked around the deck but could not see a table. The sunken floor, where they were standing and sitting only had room for the two deck seats on the side, the steering wheel and some of the instrumentation. "Do you want to eat below or up here? Can you park this while we eat?"

"Park it? Really Margot, do you see any parking places?"

"Well, no, but it will be hard for you to eat and steer at the same time."

Theo looked at her and then said, "I will lower the sails and let her drift. We can eat below. Come here and take the wheel and I will go do the sails."

Margot stood up from her seat and walked slowly and carefully over to the wheel.

"Now keep the wheel in the position it is in right now. Don't let it turn on you. Once I get the sails down, it will not give you a hard time."

Margot nodded and grasped the wheel with two hands, determined to make Theo proud of her. Theo turned and walked gingerly along the side of the cabin to the mainsail, past it, and forward to the smaller sail. Theo lowered it and wrapped it around the guide wire that kept it in place. Once secured, he went to the mainsail and lowered it. Margot noticed the wheel was much more easily handled when the mainsail was lowered. She relaxed and waited for Theo to come to the back of the boat.

"Okay, you can let go of the wheel now. The boat will drift some, but will not go too far from where we are now." He then headed down into the cabin to the galley fully expecting Margot to follow. When she did not, he stuck his head back out through the opening and said, "Well, are you coming?"

Margot walked around the wheel and over to the cabin entrance. As she climbed down the stairs to the deck below, she thought that the galley and eating area reminded her of a large camping RV she had seen at a dealership they had visited, when Theo thought he wanted to be a camping guru. Thank heavens that phase passed before it took charge or they would have had a huge RV parked out front of their house.

"Get out the food and I will open the wine." Theo was in charge of this also.

Margot moved to the refrigerator, handed one of the wine bottles to Theo, and then took out the containers that housed all the goodies for lunch. She heard the cork pop quietly and the gurgling sound it made when he poured it in the glasses. She was surprised how quiet it was below the deck. Outside, it was very noisy, with seagulls flying about and the sound of the wind and waves slapping the side of the boat.

Margot fixed two plates of food and placed them on the table where Theo sat comfortably drinking his wine. She sat down and they began to eat their meal with silent relish. Sea air seemed to make them both very hungry. After the first ten minutes of eating, they started to talk about the trip: How did Margot like her first voyage thus far? Was she finding her sea legs? Did she want to do this again? He hoped so, as they were scheduled to take it for a week later in the month. Theo seemed interested in her opinions on the subject, so she answered as best she could, in-between bites of chicken and salad.

The conversation soon shifted to revolve around Theo's work, taking the boat out from work, and Theo succeeding in learning all about it. Theo wanted to impress his superiors—showing he was an equal. He did not leave Margot any openings that might allow her to ask about her going back to work. No money was brought up... Margot thought she would take a different tack, "Theo, do you think you would like to get a boat of your own? How much do they cost? Would you need one this large?"

Theo took the bait, "Yes! I would love to have one. No, not as large, as this one sleeps six. We could do with one that sleeps three

184

or four. Also, it would cost less to tie up at a smaller pier." Theo was obviously excited about sailing, for whatever reason, and from his speech, he already must have been thinking about it. She knew that Theo would do whatever it would take to get a boat.

Margot smiled and began, "Well, that may be not as expensive, but I don't know if we could do it on your salary alone." She appeared to be thinking as she continued, "However, if I started working again…"

Margot never got a chance to finish. Theo realized her ruse and slammed his fist down on the table. "I told you NO!"

Margot got up from the table and cleared the paper plates, knives and forks and miscellaneous materials, placing them back into their bag. She did not look at Theo, who by now was so furious at himself for allowing her to ensnare him, that he stormed out of the cabin and back up on deck. Margot soon heard the sails flapping in the breeze and felt the boat begin to move through the water. However, Margot was not done with this topic yet, as her day with Jadyn had given her new courage; plus she had drunk enough wine to be certain she was going to tell Theo how she felt. She was determined that she was going back to work.

The boat was rocking back and forth as if on a large swing. The waves had increased tremendously as they cast back and forth in the wind. Theo would not look at Margot when she climbed back up to the deck, pretending to be interested in the compass and the heading, although he knew where they were.   Theo was now angry at Margot for multiple reasons: she had tricked him, she had baited him, she had disrespected him…the list continued to grow as he stewed. By the time she had come up on the deck, he had decided he was going to make her regret her little games. She was going to pay for ruining the day. Vanessa never made him so angry —why did his wife have to do so?

Margot took one look at Theo's face and knew he was building up to something painful. She decided not to allow him to scare her away from having a discussion. She may not get what she wanted, but at least she should have the right to discuss it. "Theo, we were not done talking about this. Just because you don't feel I have a right to a life outside of our house, I do!"

Margot never saw it coming. Theo tacked the boat to one side, which caused the sail boon to swing very fast in Margot's direction. It hit her squarely in the head and she was propelled over the side of the boat, into the water. Theo smiled, thinking that her surprised face and fear looked funny, like a cartoon. Then, he realized that he would have to answer for this as she would definitely tell her mother and father, if not the police. No, he could tell her that it was an accident, as he always had before. As for the police or her parents, if it came to that, he could claim that a rogue wave hit the side of the boat and made the sail fly that way when he tried to compensate. He was new at this sailing thing; he did not know it would do that. Yes, he had run this scenario in his head, just for mental amusement. Now that he had actually followed through with his imaginary plans, he decided to follow it through.

He wondered where Margot had gone, as he did not see her floating anywhere. The sea was rough enough to make hunting for her difficult and the sky was darkening in the distance. A storm would be moving in soon. Theo was concerned about how losing his wife overboard would look to his superiors at work. Would they be sympathetic or annoyed? In-between these lovely thoughts, he would re-visualize her flying overboard with that panicked look on her face and would grin to himself. It was comical looking and he may as well admit it to himself. He might even admit it to Vanessa when it was over.

He secured the wheel, took down the sails, and went down into the cabin to call the coast guard. After ten minutes of hunting around on the dials for the frequency, he made the call and was received. The coast guard told him to drop a marker as the seas would be getting very rough. A storm was brewing further out to sea and although it was not going to come on shore, it was definitely going to affect the waves.

Theo went below to find what they had described as a marker. He did not find it in any of the cabin's closets or drawers, so he

186

decided to look on the deck in the storage locker toward the back of the boat. When he lifted the large cover, he saw a pack of markers on the side of the unit. Snatching up two, he unrolled them, dropping the weighted tag and line into the water, followed by the barbell-shaped marker. They floated beautifully and started flashing.

There, that should show my good intentions, Theo mused. The boat was drifting along with the waves and soon the markers, which remained in place, were out of sight. Theo heard the large coastguard cutter approaching and he knew they would do all that they could to find his wife. He donned his frightened and panic look, much the same way he would put on a hat, and prepared to face the oncoming barrage of questions as best he thought he should. No use alarming them or making them suspicious.

The coast guard looked most of the night and then a replacement crew joined them in the morning and continued to look. Theo, who was now aboard the second cutter, sat on the deck with a blanket around his shoulders, looking depressed. After several days, the coast guard declared that they felt she was gone and stated they would keep an eye open for any persons who might wash up down the coast. However, Theo was not to get his hopes up.

Theo had called Margot's mother and explained all that had happened. Margot's mother, Rachael, said nothing at first. She was so shocked that she could think of nothing to say except, "I will notify her father. He will know what to do and who to call for more help with this."

Hanging up, Theo thought that this would work out even better than if he had planned it. Her father would get her declared dead and Theo would get the insurance policy. She wondered where the money would come from for me to get a sailing boat, well, guess what Margot—you have provided. Theo went back to work a solemn and contrite man. Everyone was sympathetic and comforting, especially Vanessa. Theo and she decided that they should not see each other as they had been, at least for a while. Discretion was now called for in light of the accident.

Theo was a little nervous inside, but after all, it was an accident. Even if they found the body, the marks on it would show she was hit by the sail boom. They had found blood on the sail boom. It is not like he could have picked that huge thing up and knocked her in the head with it. Well, not with normal methods. No, Theo was only a little nervous. He had no idea how long it would be until she was declared dead. So he would have to keep up the depressed appearance and not let on that he was now a free, single, good-looking man, moving up in the world, and soon to have enough money to be considered desirable by the right kind of women. Theo smiled to himself. Yes, he owed Margot a debt of gratitude. It was she who was helping him meet all of his goals.

Guiding Veracity

Truth lies somewhere in the perception,
It changes throughout the light of day.
We see it from our own perspective,
Guiding others to see it our own way.

Beware the serpent who tells his truth,
He controls his words as he glides through.
And when he has finished what he has to say,
You think you have heard what is really true.

Chapter XI

Jadyn was making excellent progress with her goals on her little bots, as she called them. The design was simple in appearance—something like a paramecium with a hundred little legs to propel it. The engineers that she worked with on the design, loved the way that this was coming together. The body of the little cell, although curved, was a dissolvable circuit board with coding to proceed along a certain path until it reached its target. It would penetrate the target and then dissolve, freeing all the active ingredients that it carried inside of itself.

It looked like a hairy little football, except you could not see it unless you looked under a very special microscope. Jadyn had mastered the biocircuit board at home partially, and then at her new lab; however, she needed help with the little moveable legs. She programmed the board to move the little legs along a certain path, and it worked very well in the test solutions. Although it did not carry much because of its size, it would be very effective when there was three or four million of them.

Jadyn wanted to create little bots that could do seek and destroy, also. That way, if someone had cancer, but they did not know where it was, the little bots could go find it and destroy it. Jadyn knew it would not be long before she could program the board to do more complicated tasks than just move the little legs on a programmed path. She put long, tiring hours into the project because she knew she was very close to being able to tell the bot to go and deliver medication. But she had already started to work on the project that would enable the bots to seek and destroy—similar to our own white blood cells, but more effectively. She knew she would have to tell them what kind of cell to look for, which would depend on the type of cancer. More complications.

The best part was that when the little bots did what they should, they would then dissolve and be flushed out of the body without affecting other organs. That made them much safer than most of the chemo drugs currently on the market. Of course, the military had other plans for her little soldiers, but that was inevitable. After all, they were funding all this expensive research.

The military overseers were ecstatic with her progress and could not throw money at the project fast enough. The only thing they were annoying her about was security. She loved to work at home at night, but they would not allow any information to go out of the building or on any private computers as they would be too easy to hack. So, for now, her work had to be done at the lab; she was not home very often. Time flew by and although the project was encompassing most of Jadyn's time, she still worried about Margot.

She had gone to see Thomas and he had promised to look into the records to see if he could find out if Theo had ever put Margot in the hospital. Jadyn had not heard from him for several weeks, so she decided to call him when she got home that night. If he had any information, she was not sure what she was going to do with it; however, she needed to know desperately. She was having a hard time sleeping because she felt that something was wrong; twin sensitivity?

After she ate a light supper that night, she reached out to Thomas. "Hey brother of mine, I have not heard from you for a while. Did you find anything out about Theo and Margot?"

Thomas was quiet for a moment as if he was organizing what he was going to say. "It is as you expected. Margot has been in two different hospitals, both of which are not located anywhere near where she lives. I could not get many details, but she paints it out as if she is clumsy and falls down steps or runs into doors. She was hurt pretty badly the weekend we got together at Mother's house. That is probably why she did not show up. Too bruised. Jadyn, what do you want me to do? Report it or put them on my watchlist; I set up one up to cover all around the state for abuse cases. What?"

"No, not yet. She did not want me to tell you for that very reason, so just keep an eye on the reports. We will have to keep a closer eye on her too. Maybe we can plan another get together soon. Maybe at the beginning of next month. We can tell her that it is because she missed the last one. What do you think?"

"I think we have a problem and she has a problem. It is not going to go away unless he gets therapy or is thrown in jail. Sometimes that wakes them up to the consequence of their actions. But if she does not press charges, he thinks he can just keep on with it.   Our hands are tied for the moment unless we move forward with the reports." Thomas sounded very frustrated.

"Well, I will call her this weekend and see what weekend would be good for them to come over to Mother's. Thanks, Thomas. I don't feel better, but at least we have the start of a plan. Good night for now."

"Night Jadyn. I will let you know if she shows up on the reports again."

Now Jadyn was sure that her twin sensitivity was spot on and that Margot was in danger. But unless the victims of the abuse admit that there is a problem and take steps to get it changed, there was not much that anyone could do. At least for now. Jadyn settled into bed in preparation for another restless night.

****

Two weeks later, the phone call came in around two-thirty in the morning waking Jadyn from a fitful sleep. "Hello?"

"Jadyn, its Thomas. Sorry about the time of night, but I just received a call from Mother. Margot is dead."

Jadyn was not sure that she was awake. Could she have heard this correctly? Thomas? Oh no. Thomas! "What do you mean, she is dead? When? How?"

It was obvious that Thomas was having a difficult time speaking, "All I know is what Mother told me. She and Theo were out on a sailboat on the Atlantic Side of the bay.   Somehow Margot went overboard and they can't find her. The coast guard said they thought she was dead and have stopped looking for her. They told Theo there was little hope as of this date, because of the water temperatures."

Jadyn was sitting up in bed, trying to absorb the information and wake up at the same time. "Thomas, when did all this happen? I just spoke to her the other day. She mentioned that Theo had a sailing trip planned. I did not know it was this soon. Is that how it happened?"

"I don't know anymore. Mother and Father are going over to see Theo this morning, sometime. Dad will advise Theo as to what to do for a death declaration."

"He would…. Geez! What if she is not dead, just recovering somewhere and does not remember who she is or something like that?"

"Mother will call me tomorrow after they see Theo, so let's not try to figure this out. Let's wait."

"Well, how about we wait together. I have to go into work for an hour or so to set up our next trials, but then I will come to your place if you are going to be home."

"Yes, I will be home. I want to speak with the Coast Guard in the morning and the police. I just don't have enough information, and I don't expect Theo will be as forthcoming as he could…just because he may not know or …."

"Or what, Thomas?" Jadyn was fully aware of what Thomas was thinking, but she wanted it to be out in the open, as she had had the same suspicions about Theo for a long time.

"Well, I guess there is no use speculating until I make some calls. We are already suspicious enough, without fanning that fire. I am sorry I woke you, but Mother wanted me to call you because she was going to call Father again. He is on his way home, but she will try his cell phone. I think she was a little afraid to call you as you are a twin and might not react the way that you are, calmly and rationally."

"Humph, Mother ever the coward."

Thomas changed the subject, "What time do you think you'll be here?"

"Around eleven at the latest. You might have some news by then; I won't believe that she is dead until there is a body! Good night Thomas." Jadyn may have sounded relatively calm, but that was far from the truth.   At that very moment, she had at least five very strong emotions gripping her: fear, anger, guilt, regret, and sorrow.   Why didn't we take a more active role to protect her? Why did we assume that Theo would protect Margot on a boat? Why did we not follow our instincts?   No, Jadyn was far from calm and rational.   She was just getting started.

Jadyn was up before the sun, showered and dressed for work. She drove to the lab without really thinking about where she was going; she had driven this way so many times that it did not require thought.   It gave her a chance to concentrate on the problems at hand: Would they find Margot's body, what would the coroner report, when did she really die, and how exactly was her death going to impact Theo's life?

As she approached the parking lot, she reprimanded herself for thinking negatively.   After all, we don't really know if she is dead. I must keep good thoughts.   She might turn up and surprise us all. Jadyn went into the lab to find all eyes following her.   "We don't know anything and I am hoping she is fine and resting somewhere. We are staying positive about this."

The lab personnel, all of whom worked directly under Jadyn, had heard bits and pieces of the incident on the local news channel; they converged on her in unison expressing their heartfelt thoughts and wishes.   Jadyn appreciated all their efforts in the lab, but right now she needed to concentrate on what she was going to set up prior to leaving for Thomas's place.   Jadyn ran the gauntlet of well-wishers and headed directly toward the door.   It became very quiet in the lab as she prepared to exit; she turned and said, "Oh, I will be setting up the next set of trials that we need to perform to keep on schedule.   After that, I will be leaving to join my brother to await any new information.   You will be able to reach me on my cell phone."   Smiling, she turned and went into her office and closed the door.

She phoned her immediate superior and after listening to more sympathetic overtures, told him that she would be leaving shortly, but would have all the projects scheduled and hopefully, she would be back in the office in the morning unless they discovered

194

something regarding her sister. She would let him know if that happened. He told her to take as much time as she needed—the trials would be ready for her when she came back.

Jadyn sat quietly in her chair for several minutes thinking about her sister's last conversation with her. How stupid could I be? Then, realizing that this kind of thinking was not going to speed her on her way, she booted up her laptop and went to work. It took over three hours setting up the protocols, procedures, and schedules. She sent a copy to her boss and then sent copies to the various lab personnel that would be directly involved with the projects. Closing her laptop, she grabbed her briefcase and headed out of the office.

She was halfway to Thomas's house before she realized that she had not heard from anyone—not her mother or father or Thomas. Surely they must have heard something by now. When she pulled up in front of Thomas's stylish Cape Cod home, he came out onto the front porch to meet her. His face did not look encouraging.

"Hey Sis, how was the drive?"

"Quiet. Have you found anything out?" His face looked strained and she could see he had some news to tell her.

"Let's go inside and sit down." They went in the house in silence. She turned to the left and headed into the living room. Sitting down on the sofa, she looked up expectantly at Thomas for information.

"I called the Coast Guard this morning to go over what they had found. They did not recover a body, but they said it could be several days before it would wash ashore IF she were not alive. The prevailing currents would take her much further down the coast before bringing her into the shoals, so we must wait."

"Have you spoken to Mother? Have they gone over to see Theo? Did you speak to the police?" The news was not coming fast enough to suit Jadyn.

"I did hear briefly from Mother. They are still over there now and I could tell she did not want to talk in front of everyone there. We will have to wait until she is alone to get her to take on this."

"What did the police say?"

"Well, they said that there is nothing they can do until a body is found. Nobody, no crimes as it were."

"I hate this not knowing." Jadyn turned and stared at the phone as if willing it to ring. It did not work.

"Well, let's have something to eat while we wait." Thomas stood up and headed to the kitchen. Jadyn remained posted near the phone awaiting news. Fifteen minutes later, Thomas came back in with sandwiches and coffee. "No news yet?"

"Thomas, what if they never find her? What if he did something to her body? Cut it up or buried it somewhere pretending he lost her at sea?"

"I don't have any answers, Jadyn. But time will tell one way or another. I am sure of that."

****

The coastguard stopped looking. The police stopped looking. Charles went back to the city to be consoled for his loss by his current mistress. Rachael, Jadyn, and Thomas got together on the weekends to give each other comfort and company. The loss was too great to bear alone. After two weeks, they had almost given up hope of ever having any kind of closure. However, a knock on the door one Saturday afternoon changed everything. By this time, Rachael answered it with no anticipations. "Mrs. Martyn, I am James Carter. Do you remember me?"

"Yes, of course I do, detective. Please come in."

His voice was deep and very quiet. He entered into the hallway and looking directly into Rachael's questioning face as he said, "Mrs. Martyn, we think we have found your daughter. We have notified her husband, but I thought it best if I came to see you myself." The young detective, James Carter worked for the Long Island Police Department. Rachael had met him when they were speaking to the police regarding Margot's disappearance. He seemed to be the only officer who truly cared about her missing daughter.

"Is she okay? Where did you find her?"

196

"Let's sit down." He took her elbow and escorted her into the living room. Thomas came into the dining room from the kitchen and crossed over to the living room.

Detective Carter seemed reluctant at first to answer any questions. Looking at Rachael, he started slowly, "Have you heard from Theo lately?"

"No, we have heard from no one!" Thomas answered abruptly, even though the question was addressed to his mother.

"Well, a body has washed ashore near Smith Point Park. The reeds and vegetation had concealed the remains, but some kids went clamming nearby and discovered the body." He stopped to give her time to absorb the information.

In a very weak voice Thomas asked, "How do you know it is her?" He sat down as he asked, not quite able to stand to hear the answer.

"She was wearing the jewelry that her husband had described. The hair color and general features match the picture we have."

Just then, Jadyn came down the stairs and entered the room from the hallway. James Carter sat bolt upright when he saw her. They had never met, but he felt that he knew her from her mother's descriptions… of Margot and the picture he had been given. He did not realize that there were twins involved.

Rachael, through tears, saw the detective's disconcertion and managed to say, "Detective, this is my other daughter, Jadyn Martyn." Then adding sadly, "They were twins."

James Carter hesitated only a minute before he stood up and shook Jadyn's hand. "I am sorry for staring, but you surprised me. I thought I was looking at your sister."

Jadyn shook his hand but was looking at her mother's face. "Mother, what's going on?"

Rachael could not utter the words. She threw her face into her hands and started to weep. It was Thomas who was the first to speak, "Jadyn, they think they have found Margot's body." Then turning to the detective he asked, "When can I see the body?"

"I would be glad to take you over anytime you wish. It would be helpful to have collaborating identifications."

"Mother, we can go if you don't feel up to it right now. Then Jadyn and I will make the arrangements, but only if you wish it." Thomas was taking the lead at this point and Jadyn and Rachael were glad to let him do so.

"No, I don't want to go right now. I will call your father and wait for him to come back." She sat up, drying her eyes and nose, and then added, "We will make the arrangements for her." Looking up at the detective and she asked, "When can she be removed?"

"Well, the coroner is going to perform an autopsy first. Although the death looks accidental, we want to make sure."

Thomas and Jadyn both looked at him sternly through tear stained eyes. Jadyn spoke first, "Is there any doubt to that statement?"

"No, not as of yet, but we have just recovered the remains…. I mean your sister." He was obviously having difficulty looking at Jadyn without staring.

"Let's go now. I want to see my sister!" Jadyn was excruciatingly sad and angry simultaneously, both of which almost hurt.

Detective Carter nodded and then turned to Rachael, who was staring off toward the fireplace. "Mrs. Martyn, I will let you know what we find."

The three of them went out the door to the detective's large sedan. After he sequestered Thomas and Jadyn in the back seat, he pulled smoothly away and headed towards The Coroner's Office and Morgue.

Three-quarters of an hour later, they arrived at the office. Detective Carter led the way to the back of the offices. "Wait here, please. I want to make sure all is in order before we go in. Coroners do not like being interrupted."

Thomas and Jadyn waited a short time in the hallway, which smelled mildly of alcohol and bleach. The detective stuck his head out the door and said, "Come in. He has finished what he was working on." The coroner was in the far corner of the room, putting recently sterilized instruments away in a drawer of a roll-away cabinet. He looked up as they came in and regarded them with serious, but sad eyes. He kept looking at Jadyn very closely. Detective Carter started the introductions, "Dr. Corson, this is Thomas and Jadyn Martyn, the decedent's brother and sister. Jadyn is the decedent's twin sister."

Dr. Corson nodded his head and said, "It is nice to meet you, but not under these circumstances. I am sorry for your loss. Forgive my staring, but you two look so very much alike." Neither Jadyn or Thomas said anything, but they each took turns shaking Dr. Corson's outstretched hand. Clearing his throat and looking slightly abashed, he continued, "Your sister is over here." Turning, he led them to the large, solid wall containing stainless steel drawers. He went over to one of the ones in the middle and checking on the label in the front, he pulled the weighted drawer open, exposing a sheet-covered figure. He carefully turned down the sheet, revealing Margot's swollen, bruised, and partially eaten features.

Thomas said nothing while looking on her face, but Jadyn, inhaled abruptly when she first saw it, then turned to the coroner and asked, "Have you completed the autopsy as of yet?"

"Yes, it is complete. The results are that she appears to have been struck on the head with a large, wooden object, which is consistent with the statement made by her husband that the boom of the sailboat swung around and struck her on the head. We can find no other marks on her. The cause of death was drowning."

"So she was alive when she went overboard." Jadyn made more of a statement than a query.

"Yes," was the short answer from Dr. Corson.

"Thank you, Dr. Corson," Thomas said. "I think we have seen enough."

"I take it that you agree that this is your sister?" Detective Carter was looking for more confirmation.

Both Thomas and Jadyn nodded in unison and turned to walk out into the hallway. Once outside the doors, Jadyn asked, "Detective, I don't know much about sailing, but could the boom be made to swing from one side to another, intentionally, by changing the direction of the boat or heading into the wind or something like that?"

The detective was slow to answer. He did not want to open that can of worms without some sort of evidence that contradicted the existing theory. "Yes, I suppose it could, but it would be nigh on to impossible to prove, unless her husband left a recording or noted it somewhere, which is unlikely."

Jadyn and Thomas looked at each other and then Thomas said, "What if Theo had been abusing her? What if it had happened more than once or twice? Would that make you look a little closer?"

"Do you know that he was abusing her?"

"Yes, I have data that shows the number of times he put her in the hospital or sent her to the Outpatient Care Centers. I work for the Social Service System of New York. We started to become suspicious over three months ago, but unfortunately, we did not do anything—she did not want us to even know about it." Thomas's face looked both guilty and sorrowful.

"How did you find this out? When Mr. Blodger first reported her missing, I checked all the local hospitals for current or past visits. Nothing was reported back to me." The detective was amazed at this new information.

Thomas began, "Well, sometimes abusers make their victim go great distances to hospitals out of their area. Then if a search is pulled, nothing is found."

Detective Carter still was not satisfied, "Yes, but don't the hospitals report abuse cases to the statewide database?"

"Well, apparently Margot was very convincing when she told them that she had fallen or tripped. They did not report it." Thomas concluded, "All I know is in a folder I have back at my home. I will be glad to send it to you."

Detective Carter pulled cards from his pocket and handed one to Jadyn and one to Thomas. "My number, fax, and address are on this. If you think of anything else, please let me know. But whatever you do, do not accuse or accost Theo Blodger. If he is innocent, it would be unkind and if he isn't, well, it would put him

200

on his guard. And that is something I want to avoid." The detective held the door for Jadyn and Thomas to exit the building, before continuing. "I want him to settle back into his life and to watch him as if he were in a fishbowl."

He drove them both back to their mother's home. It was not a long drive, but it gave all three of them a chance to talk. Detective Carter was not ready to pass any judgments on the case as of yet— too early to tell. However, it was clear that Jadyn and Thomas did not believe the story that Theo had given. Only time would tell, so they both told the detective that they would keep in touch. When they exited the car, the detective looked long and hard at Jadyn and then finally turned and got back into his police car and drove away.

"What was that about?" Thomas said, looking quizzically at Jadyn.

"No idea. Maybe he finds it disconcerting to look at the face of a dead woman."

"You are not a dead woman! Don't talk like that."

Jadyn smiled slightly, "I meant the twin thing."

"Oh well, maybe. Let's go in and tell Mother what we found out."

They entered the large hallway and headed to the living room. Upon entrance, they found their father and mother together in a rather deep conversation. Both stopped talking when they heard the door open and looked up expectantly. "Hello you two, what did you find out?" Charles spoke directly to the point.

Thomas decided that he would take point on the answer as he felt he might be a little more guarded with his account. "The coroner said that she was probably hit with the boom as Theo said, but she did drown at the end. They still seem to think it was an accident."

"Well, it probably was. Theo seems very upset and had no reason to do anything against Margot. She was very compliant and pleasing." It was obvious that Charles thought Theo innocent. His description of Margot was disconcerting to Jadyn and she turned her head to avoid making it obvious that she did not like her father.

Rachael sat quietly on the sofa watching Jadyn's face while Thomas and Charles were speaking. Her artistic inclinations heightened her observational abilities. She knew something was bugging Jadyn, but did not want to discuss it in front of her husband. Charles stood up and said, "Well, as soon as they are done with their investigation, we will set up the funeral."

"Isn't Theo arranging all that?" Thomas was perplexed. He knew he would want to arrange his wife's funeral if he had a wife.

"No, I told him that we would do that for him. Financially, he does not have the money. Not until he gets the insurance and he can't get that until they make a finalized determination of the cause of death." Charles was the lawyer who had helped Theo setup his estate and insurance policies.

Rachael rose and went into the kitchen to fix supper for her husband and anyone else who might be hungry. Jadyn went into the kitchen and told her mother that she was leaving as she only had wanted to come down to find out what the police knew. She had done that and was now ready to go home. "Father can let me know when the arrangements will be." She kissed her mother on the cheek and then hugged her tightly. Rachael did not seem to want to let go, so Jadyn stood quietly until her mother finally released her. Jadyn could see her mother was crying silently, as Charles had taught her to do.

Jadyn left after saying goodbye to Thomas and her father, both of whom were having a rather terse conversation. After she went outside, Jadyn decided that she would swing by Theo's home, before heading home. She was not going to accuse him of anything—just console him, or so she told herself.

As she drove, she decided to make a list of haunts that Theo might have, based on what little she knew from Margot. As she pulled close to his house, she decided to park near, but not within close observation. She wanted to see who came and went into the house. Yes, a stakeout. That would be one way to see what he was up to if anything.

After about an hour, Jadyn spotted Theo's sports car pulling into the driveway and into the garage. The garage door closed and

202

Jadyn never did really get a look at Theo. She decided to pull up closer and make an attempt at a consoling visit. Knocking on the door, she did not have long to wait. "Jadyn! I did not expect to see you. How nice." Theo was sober but polite. "Come in and I will make some tea."

Jadyn entered through the doorway and into the nicely furnished bungalow. "Theo, I can't stay too long, but I wanted to say how sad and how sorry I am. I lost a sister, but you lost a wife. It must be so hard. Is there anything I can do?" Jadyn looked deeply into Theo's eyes, wondering what was going through his mind.

"Well, thank you Jadyn, but I just want to be left alone for a while. I feel like it didn't happen. Then the next minute, I feel so full of guilt, I don't know if I can bear it." Theo's face looked truly lost. He was definitely hurting, or so it appeared to Jadyn. He walked toward his kitchen and asked if she wanted tea or something stronger, as he definitely did want something strong enough to take off the edge.

"Yes, I could use something too. Maybe a glass of wine?" Jadyn offered hopefully. She did not want any wine but did want a chance to get some questions answered. She sat down on the couch, while Theo disappeared into the kitchen. It did not take more than a minute for him to return with two drinks in his hands.

After handing Jadyn her glass of wine, he took a large gulp from his glass…which looked like straight whiskey. "I can't believe she is gone," he started. "We were having such a good time on the boat. She was thrilled to be sailing and I know she was having a great time." He became silent for a few minutes, which gave Jadyn time to study his face. It seemed to her that he looked like he was thinking of how to phrase what he was going to say as if it was a delicate topic and he did not want to crush the verbal eggs. "When she fell over, I did not even see it. I was not used to the boat and had all I could do to keep it upright in the wind. When I looked at where she was standing, she was gone." Silence again.

"You don't have to talk about it if you don't want to, Theo. I know how hard this must be."

"No, I must tell you. I would never do anything to hurt her. She was my life! She kept me centered and full of encouragement. I don't know what I will do without her!" A tear started down his face as if a final punctuation to his declaration of love.

Jadyn put her hand on his arm to console him. "Don't punish yourself, Theo. I know you would not hurt her. She was too precious to all of us." She let this final thought hang on the air, while she looked around the room. It was a little messy, with his jacket lying on the side of one chair and glasses sitting on a table across the room. He must have been just sitting things down without thought, Jadyn assumed. Maybe he was really in shock. Maybe her gut instincts were wrong.

Standing, she took both of their empty glasses into her hands and went into the kitchen. It was very clean and well cared for, considering he was bachelor-ing it. Odd, it did not match the messed up look of the living room. Maybe he was eating out and not cooking. That would explain the pristine appearance. She went over to the sink and rinsed the glasses and then opened the dishwasher to put them into the top rack.

There was something odd. There were two glasses already in the rack and one had lipstick on it. Very dark lipstick; nothing that Margot would wear. Jadyn closed the dishwasher door and went back into an empty living room. Theo had gone into the hall closet for something, she guessed. She did not see him for a few minutes and when he came back into the room, he seemed recovered from his sorrows.

"I am so sorry, Theo. I did not mean to intrude. I only wanted to see if you were okay or if you needed anything?"

"No, I am fine…considering everything. I will go back to work and try to learn to live with this."

As Jadyn prepared to leave she added a last thought, "Theo, if you need anything, just call. Thomas or I would be happy to help." Then pausing she said, "I understand Father and Mother are making the funeral arrangements. Are you okay with that? Father sometimes can be a little pushy and I don't want you to feel manipulated."

Theo smiled a very odd smile and answered her query, "Don't fret about that. I understand your father very well. He and I are very much alike. I am glad they want to help until all this gets cleared up."

Jadyn gave him a quick peck on the cheek and left wondering if she felt any different about him one way or another. He seemed to be sad one minute and very composed the next. And those glasses…maybe a friend or neighbor? There was no telling at this point. She would just have to wait and do a little sleuthing herself. She knew Thomas would help, too. Yes, Theo would be in a fishbowl, as the detective had offered, observed by extra pairs of eyes.

She drove to the ferry, crossed the Long Island Sound, and headed back to the Boston area. The detective was right—it would be hard to prove anything that a jury could convict on, especially if her father handled the case. And knowing him, he would.

Her thoughts changed over to Detective Carter. The detective seemed nice and genuinely interested in her sister's death. He had a nice face, but it seemed a little tired. Probably too many late night cases. As she drove, she reviewed all she could remember and then decided she would call Thomas when she got home. They would make some plans and test out some theories. Yes, it was going to be a busy time.

Elusive Truths

Search it out, no stone unturned,
Determination of the will.
Seek the truth where ere it lies,
The depths of perdition you must drill.

No matter how much you try,
Or to what lengths you may go.
The truth will constantly elude you,
As down the river it flows.

Chapter XII

James Carter was the youngest member of the detective squad. The other detectives often kidded him about being so enthusiastic in his work, but they had to admit, he was effective. Although he had transferred to Long Island from Boston, he had not acted as if they were small time or less than anyone else he had worked with in the larger city. He was polite, polished and methodical. When he brought someone in on an indictment, they stayed indicted. No loose ends, he always affirmed.

When he had first joined the Police Force, they had teamed him up with an experienced detective, just to make sure he did things correctly—the Long Island way. But that detective found out quickly that James Carter not only was a very good detective but also a pain in the neck. No corner cutting, no guesswork, no jumping to conclusions, no hasty arrests. The experienced detective requested to be relieved of his assignment, stating that James could work very well on his own.

This was against policy, so James was partnered with another young detective, Haley Jackson. After college, Haley had worked her way up the ladder from beat cop to detective in a very short timeframe. She was knowledgeable, stubborn and a bit rash. This amused the other detectives; they assumed that she would drive James as crazy as he would drive her.

However, James did not mind Haley's rash behavior. He enjoyed the constant banter she brought on stakeouts and did not feel intimidated by her insight and education. James was secure in his belief in the system. He believed that Justice would prevail if they did their jobs properly; he was determined that Haley would learn to work the system properly under his tutelage.

After he had left the Martyn house, he headed back to the Police Station. He had not asked Haley to come with him on this long and arduous trip. She had put in long days on several of their cases and needed the day off. He seldom took a day off. If he was not at the station working on a case, he took the case files home, put his feet up and reread the files to make sure he did not miss anything. He may not have the kind of life most young detectives had, but he did not care. His work was as interesting to him as reading a great novel or watching a football game.

There was something about Theo that he wanted to check out and needed the computer at the station to do the research. The victim's brother, Thomas, had stated he had widened his search to find abuse issues in that family. It raised a few questions in James's mind: How many times had he hurt her, what kind of abuse was it, and what was Theo Blodger's background? Where were his parents? What was his father like at home? Did abuse run in the family? Although not directly genetic, it is often a learned behavior and if Theo's father did some of the same things, Theo might have seen it, learned it, and copied it. Or it could be a blind end. You never know about research until you try it.

Once back at the station, James set up several searches for hospitals in the Long Island area, with one hundred mile parameters. It was much more revealing and after he got a list of the hospital names and addresses, he started to look into Theo's background. It was amazing what he found in the computer. Not much is private anymore, he thought. It took him two additional hours of research on abuse victims, Theo's background, and other items before he wrapped up his day. By now it was almost eight-thirty at night and he realized he was very hungry.

He did not live too far from the station and there was a small pub near his apartment, so he decided to stop in for a cheeseburger and beer before going home, as he was not in the mood to cook. As he drove, he wondered why he was so interested in the case. There was a motive if you considered the insurance policy, but it was only two hundred fifty thou, so not a huge amount. Also, if you wanted to kill your spouse, taking them sailing to make it look like an accident was a bit far fetched…although effective.

James drank his beer and waited for his burger in silence. The pub was pleasant enough during the week, but on a Saturday evening, it could get a bit dicey. Tonight was no exception. The boisterous laughter and horsing around made thinking difficult.

208

James decided to take his burger home and told the bartender to wrap it to go. He left with a baggie and headed to his apartment, which was about two blocks south. The neighborhood he lived in was old but safe. Not too much happened around there except for children playing during the day and dogs barking at night.

James lived on the second floor of a courtyard apartment. He had a small balcony, which overlooked an enclosure lined with trees, albeit a bit weedy in the middle. The neighborhood kids played there during the day, while their mothers kept an eye on them from their balconies. It was a nice but somewhat aged setup. As he opened his door, a familiar voice let out a growl. "Hello, Kimble. How was your day?" This was the standard question that James issued upon his return home every night.

Kimble walked up to James and rubbed against his pant legs as if to say good to see you, which Kimble could not do; Kimble was totally blind. James had found him on the street as a kitten, abused and tortured. He took him to a vet, who asked if James wanted him euthanized or fixed up. James took one look at the poor little gray and white kitten and said, "Fix him up, please."

The vet was a good one and in a few short weeks, Kimble as James named him, came home. The vet was able to fix up his wounds, but his eyesight was lost. James did not care. He had a little someone to care for and although he did not realize it, he had needed someone to care for. He was lonely, though unaware of it.

It did not take long before Kimble was walking around the apartment as if he knew where everything was. Although he did most of this by sound and smell, he did it most effectively. He knew where his food was, water, potty box and best of all, how to get up on the bed when it was time for James to go to bed.

James had found Kimble four years previously and Kimble was now his guard cat. If anyone came to the door unannounced, Kimble let out a yell that scared even the most intrepid visitors. Back up and claws out, Kimble approached ready to take on the worst that life could offer unless James told him it was okay. Then and only then would Kimble become a normal looking cat. Well, as normal as a cat can appear without eyes. James had fun with this on occasion. He told his landlady that Kimble was clairvoyant and could think his way around. Although she was skeptical, she did not dare enter the apartment when James was not there, just in case the cat could get into her mind.

James found the cat a perfect house-sitter. He kept the riff-raff away during the day as he had developed a bit of a reputation in the neighborhood. Best of all, he was able to take care of his own needs when James had extra long hours away from the apartment. As per usual, Kimble let James know that he was expecting extra love and petting tonight as James was very late. James opened a small can of tuna and put it on a plate. Kimble literally stood up on his hind legs and faced James. He knew where the smell was coming from and did not want to miss his special treat.

After he fed Kimble, James decided to stick on some shorts before he ate, so he headed into the bedroom, took off his jacket, gun and shoulder holster, pants, shirt, and tie. Shorts on and flip-flops for the feet, he felt comfortable enough to eat and think. He went into the kitchen just as Kimble had finished his tuna and sat purring at James, letting him know that he was a happy cat. James gave him a pat and then sat down to eat. While chewing on his burger, his brain was chewing on the case. Why this case was bugging him he could not tell. And that sister, Jadyn. Wow, what a knockout. If the victim looked like her when she was alive, their father must have been a nervous wreck when they were growing up.

He continued to wonder why the case bothered him. No evidence to prove foul play and no huge motive. But his intuition told him to keep digging, so he decided that on Sunday, he would do a little staking out of Theo. Although it was early in the game, maybe Theo would relax enough to show James something that would point him in the right direction. Or maybe convince him that he was truly a saddened husband mourning his lost love.

The next morning, James rose, showered and ate a quick breakfast. He fed Kimble and explained why he had to leave. He usually discussed his cases with Kimble, who expected full details. Although Kimble seldom said anything while listening, James

210

found his reviewing of a case with the cat often revealed something he had overlooked or missed. So in essence, he credited the cat with clairvoyance… if for no other reason than it attributed to the cat a second sight—since his first sight was lost.

The trip took about half an hour, but James did not mind as it was a beautiful day. Technically, the case was not in his jurisdiction, as the dead woman had lived outside of his precincts, but he still wanted to get to the bottom of what had happened if for no other reason than to give closure to her husband and parents. If he found anything of interest, he would take it to the police in that division of the Suffolk County Police, in hopes that they would act on it. Often, the two police forces worked together on cases, so James knew several of the police on the reciprocating force.

His personal car was a souped-up Camaro with primer black as the paint covering. James was having this worked on over a long period of time as funds would allow, and the final paint job would be completed in a month or two. But the engine was completed and it had a wonderfully throaty roar when he accelerated down the highway. He guessed he was a closet roadster who loved fast cars. One extra advantage, it did not look anything like a police car, so he thought it would be good to use for the stakeout. He parked it half a block away from Theo's home and turning it off, adjusted his mirror so as to see all that was going on in back.

He was sitting there for at least three-quarters of an hour before he saw Theo's sports car back out of the garage and come driving down the road. There were a few cars also coming down the street, so he was able to tail Theo from four cars behind. Theo seemed impervious to anything going on around him. He drove to the local gym and after getting out of his car, gym bag in hand entered the building. James parked down the block and turning off his car, started making some notes as to the name and address of the gym.

An hour later, Theo emerged and headed down the street, passing James as he went by. James followed Theo back to his home, where he pulled into his garage. James did not see him again. He made a mental note to pull Theo's phone records for that day and others. He was curious as to whom he called when all this started.   He then pulled away and headed back to the gym.   He parked near the entrance and went inside.

A young lady was sitting at a counter in an open area just outside of the main workout room.   She looked up, saw the attractive young man and smiled her best smile. "Good afternoon," she offered. "How may I help you?"

"Good afternoon, I am looking into something and was wondering if you might be able to help me."   He took out his badge and said, "I am Detective Carter from the Long Island Police Department, and I was wondering if you know Mr. Theodore Blodger?"

"Well, yes sir, I do. Is anything wrong? Is he okay?"

"Yes, he is fine. We are looking into the death of his wife."

"Wife?" The young lady seemed genuinely confused. "I did not know he was married." She frowned slightly and continued, "I guess she was the lady who came in with him once in a while, but I did not know that they were married. They did not act like it." The young woman realized who she was gossiping with and decided to shut her mouth before she said something that would get her into trouble.

Taking a photo of Margot Blodger out of his jacket, he showed it to the young lady and asked, "Do you recognize her?"

The young lady looked at Margot's picture and said, "No. She is beautiful. I would have remembered her."

"This is not the woman that you saw with Mr. Blodger?" Detective James was now getting somewhere.

"No, I have never seen her before. The woman I saw Mr. Blodger with looked much different."

"Can you describe her?" James was hoping for as much info as possible.

"No, I did not really pay attention to her. I just know that she did not look like that." At this point, the young lady sat down near her computer and said, "Do you need anything else?"

"No, thank you. We are just asking questions of everyone that might help us find answers."

James left the gym and headed back to his car. He realized that if the young woman told Blodger about his questions, it might make him suspicious, but he hoped she would be discreet or just plain scared. He went home and settled in for a nice afternoon nap with Kimble by his side. They could discuss the case later when he was a little more awake.   Sitting around in a car can make one very drowsy.

When he arrived home, Kimble was agitated, which either meant someone had come to the door or the phone had rung. Kimble was not the least bit comfortable with the landline phone that James had in the living room. It made a loud noise that did not sound like anything Kimble could relate to; therefore it was not to be trusted. It might attack when Kimble was not ready. Whenever the phone rang, James tried repeatedly to make Kimble aware of what it was and what it was doing. Kimble did not seem to get it.

James went to his answering machine and listened to his messages. Poor Kimble, there were three messages. No wonder he was spazzed out. The first message was from Haley, wondering if he was working without her over the weekend. The second was from his mother asking him to dinner on the 5th of September. It was his brother's birthday and they were going to throw a party for him. The third call was from Jadyn Martyn. She indicated she wanted to ask him a question, whenever he had time to talk. No hurry.

No hurry? He could not wait to call her back. He entered her number and waited for the machine to connect.   When she answered, he told her that he had just gotten home and wondered how he could help her.

"Well, I was wondering if you would need any other information regarding Theo Blodger's place of birth, parentage, schooling, etc."

Was Jadyn clairvoyant? James was intrigued. "Yes, as a matter of fact, I could use all the information you can give me."

After relating as much of the information as she knew, including wedding dates, birthdates, parent's location, and schooling, Jadyn said, "I hope that helps you."

James felt a little tongue-tied. "Yes, it is perfect. I will keep you posted as to anything that relates."

After they said goodbye, James wondered why he said he would tell her everything. You never give anything away in an ongoing investigation. Looking down at a very disgruntled Kimble, he added, "I must be tired or something." He headed to the bedroom, closely followed by a sleepy, purring cat. Kimble knew James was going to take a nap and that would be followed by takeout Chinese dinner, which the cat loved. Yes, Kimble loved Sundays, even if he did not know what day it was. He loved the routine.

****

Theo stretched out on his sofa, with a large bottle of beer in one hand and a pizza slice in the other. He decided to eat as he had nothing else he could do right at that moment. He knew that his wife's death would either put a cloud over him with some people or would cast a shadow of sadness over him with others. He missed her cooking and cleaning that was true. He missed having someone to talk to also, but once all this was over, he expected Vanessa to join him. After all, they did have so much fun together.

His wife never seemed to get it. He was the boss and she was his wife. Subservient and useful. Her mother knew how to behave with Charles. Theo thought that Margot would have been raised to behave the same. Why did she insist on going back to work? It was her own fault that she was dead. She forced him to do what he had done. She was so disrespectful—always trying to get her own way. She went to lunch with Jadyn the first chance she had gotten —just to gripe about him, no doubt. Jadyn was definitely a bad influence on Margot. Jadyn never followed her mother's behavior. She was way too independent for Theo's taste…but she was gorgeous. He would not mind seeing her once in a while, once the coroner released Margot's body and she was buried. Theo wanted the insurance money. He had plans and he was tired of being bored.

214

When he had returned to work, his colleagues and bosses were very sympathetic, although they said it would be best that he did not take the company boat out anymore. He knew that would happen, liability and all that. As soon as he received the insurance for her death, he would pick up a sailboat of his own. So for today, he resigned himself to working out at the gym and to searching the classifieds for boats for sale. Afterward, he called Vanessa.

"Hey babe, whatcha doing?"

"Well, right this moment I am sitting on the couch doing my nails and waiting for your call."

Theo was pleased to hear she was waiting for him. Maybe she would work out even better than he had hoped. "I really want to see you, but I guess it will be best to wait until this is all over."

"Have you heard anything else from the police? Do you have any kind of a time frame? You know a girl like me needs attention. I don't like being all alone all the time."

"I know, I know. But it can't be helped. I don't think it will take too much longer, now that they have the body and all that. How about we plan to go to dinner tonight? Somewhere far enough from work and our homes to not be seen? We could meet there and that way no one would see me at your home. What do you think?"

Vanessa did not have to think long, "That sounds great. But I want a good dinner, none of that fast foodie."

"No problem. How about Palo's? We have not been there in a long time and it is not too far from your home."

"Works for me, Theo. What time do you want to meet?"

"I will make reservations for seven."

"That is good. It will give me lots of time to fix myself up special for you."

Theo loved the sound of that, so he added, "Not too special or we won't make it home for beddie bye." He hung up and felt much better. Vanessa was great in bed and he knew just the hotel near the restaurant that they could go to. It was neither fancy nor nosy; he and Vanessa had used it once before several months ago. He had told Margot he was going to a short buyer's conference.

Now, he did not have to tell her anything….no more questions. No more lies. He was free! Well, almost.

****

The next day, although Jadyn was back to work and acting normal, her mind was having a very hard time focusing on her little bots. It was time for another set of trials that week and the military would be present for this one. This would have made her nervous as she wanted enough time to finish her trials before putting on any dog and pony shows, but her superiors needed to show progress to the military since they were pouring all the funding into the project. Jadyn had no illusions about how the military wanted to use her little bots, but she was determined to control their use as best she could. At this point and time, the project was still in civilian hands and if she did not antagonize the military staff, perhaps they would leave it that way.

She checked all the tanks that contained her little bots. They had to be programmed, which was to be done using a new Wi-Fi miniature unit that she had developed with the engineering team. This technology alone had so many applications, that the company was patenting it first, before the medical bots. Once the little bots were programmed, they had to be injected into the target ASAP. They did not know that the emulsion in which they were swimming around was a neutral vat of fluid that protected them from disintegration.

Once the bots were injected into the target, they would be compelled to seek out the tumor that they were programmed to find and enter into it. They then would dissolve, which would release the chemical that would attack the tumor. It was a marvelous delivery system taking strong chemo directly to the tumor. Afterward, the little bots, what few of them that was left within the tumor, would act as additional irritants and get flushed out of the system along with the dead tumor cells.

Her first trials were performed on tumor-induced rats. With over eighty percent successfully losing all signs of tumors, the trials looked promising. This week, they wanted to test the bots on the monkeys. If successful, it would take them within six months of human trials on patients that were in stage four cancer.   They already had volunteers who were not able to receive any more chemo in the usual ways, because chemo, when injected into the bloodstream, killed more than its target tumors, leaving the patients in a much-weakened condition, which would cause them to have other issues.

Cancer was the first of the diseases that Jadyn was targeting, but she knew that there were so many more applications that the little bots could be used for, once perfected. Jadyn was determined to succeed. She met with her engineering team for some last minute programming plans and then went back to her office.

She decided to call Thomas and see what his take on everything was up to this point. She wondered if he had uncovered anything new.

"Hello, Jadyn. How is your day progressing?"

"Hi Thomas. Well, I am having a little trouble concentrating. Detective Carter seems to be very capable, but I am not sure how he will handle everything— jurisdictional wise. I spoke to him last night and gave him more background information on Theo. He seemed very glad to receive it, although he did not say much. I wonder if he is shy."

"I think he is when he is around you, my dear." Thomas could not help but tease Jadyn. He knew that her looks caused her more problems than she liked—he could not resist.

"Oh, you think?" Jadyn's sarcastic reply indicated that she knew the detective was uncomfortable around her.

"Well, I would not worry about jurisdiction. I think he is like the proverbial dog with a bone. Once he gets started, he won't quit. He will find a way to get the right things done if Theo actually did anything."

"I guess you are right. But the waiting is killing me. I went to see Theo yesterday before I went home."   Jadyn waited for Thomas to say something.

"Jadyn, was that wise? I mean, as the detective said, he does not want to scare him off. Plus, what if he is a killer? No, when you go over there, you should have me or the detective with you. This is serious business."

"I went alone to give him my condolences. Plus, I wanted to get a read on him, see if he was acting as if he had just lost his wife."

"Well, was he?"

"It was mixed. One minute he was fine and then he went into explanations about it, with tears. The only odd thing that I could not explain was in his dishwasher. Wine glasses, two of them and one had lipstick."

"It is hard to tell at this point. We will have to look into this more. Investigate him."

Jadyn answered slowly, "I am planning to do a stakeout on him. It will be a bit boring, but if he does have someone else, at least it would show probable cause. Like the detective stated, it will be hard to find evidence unless someone saw him."

Thomas loved a challenge. "Why don't we set up a coordinated surveillance schedule? Take turns as it were."

"Great! I will not be able to do too much this week, trials and everything. But I should be able to schedule time next week."

"It might be good to let him breathe for a week and then start. Like the detective said, maybe he will relax and do things that he might not like others knowing." Thomas knew he had vacation time coming, so he decided he would put it to good use. "Meanwhile, I will do some more hospital checking. I want to make sure we have it all."

"Okay, I will call you later this week after my trials and we can plan." Jadyn hung up and felt a bit more relieved. She and Thomas now had an active plan. If they found out anything interesting, she would let Detective Carter know. She left her office and headed down the hall to her lab. She could now concentrate on work and her life—at least for this week.

****

The trials completed, Jadyn would have to wait a week or so to investigate the test results. On Friday, she decided to go to Thomas's place for a quick visit…and a planning session. Thomas was glad for the company and when she arrived, he took her travel bag and set it inside the hallway. "How was your trip? It is quite a long drive to White Plains from Boston."

"It was fine. I left midday, so not quite so much traffic."

"I hope you are hungry. Come on, let's go." Thomas seemed to be in a bit of a hurry as he escorted her to his car.

"Thomas, what is the rush? I just got here."

"We have just enough time to grab a bite to eat and then trail after Theo as he leaves his work. Stakeout time for a Friday night!" He smiled conspiratorially and they jumped into his car happy to have something constructive to do regarding the cause.

After picking up some fast food, they headed out to Theo's place of business. They did not know what to expect, but just like anything else, it was better to be doing something than to be doing nothing. Thomas parked his car down the block from the corporate parking lot. He knew where Theo's special reserved parking space was, so he knew which entrance/exit he would use when he left. They sat and happily ate their takeout while waiting for five o'clock to hit.

It was about five-fifteen when they saw Theo's car turn up the road and head toward his home. He seemed to be in a hurry and it took all that Thomas could do to keep the little sports car in sight. It helped that they knew where he lived as they surmised that he was headed home. They guessed correctly. However, he did not pull into the garage, but parked in the drive and went into the front door.

"He must have plans for tonight, I guess," Thomas offered.

"So it would appear," Jadyn answered.

It was about half an hour later when a fashionably dressed Theo exited his home, jumped into his car and headed down the road, past where they were parked. Both of them scooted down in their seats and hid hoping he did not notice them.

"Whew, he did not lose any time getting down the road," Thomas said as he turned on his car and did a u-turn in the street.

"No, and he is out of sight, so we better get a move on it."

They traveled back into town and came within a block Theo's car, which was sitting at a light. It was just luck that they found him as he turned the corner and went in a different direction out of town. They followed at a very discreet distance and soon saw Theo pull his car over to a curb. There was a young lady standing on the sidewalk with a large shoulder bag and scarf on her head.

"Who do you think that is?" Jadyn wondered out loud.

"No clue and there is no telling from which house she came since there are no houses on this section of the block." Thomas sounded excited and frustrated at the same time.

They continued to follow the car, which headed north toward the Sound. After about half an hour of driving, they pulled into a large boat yard. Thomas was not sure how to follow them without being spotted, so he pulled past the main yard. Parking, he looked out the window in hopes of seeing where they had driven to and parked. No such luck. However, he had a very good view of the main sales office building, which sported the name of the company: the Johnny T's Boat Emporium.

"Well, there is a name we won't have trouble remembering," Jadyn commented.

"There is not much we can do except park and hope we see what they are looking at. Margot did mention Theo loved sailing…. maybe he is looking to buy a boat? Do you think?"

"With what, play money?" Thomas snorted as he remembered Theo did not have enough money to bury his own wife. "He sure is counting his chickens way before they are hatched."

It was a warm night with a gentle breeze. Thomas lowered the windows, lowered the back of his seat for comfort, and pulled a bag of cheese chips from the back seat. "We can nibble while we wait."

"Did you bring something to drink? If not, nibbling will end up torture later."

Thomas reached in back of Jadyn's seat, opened a cooler, and pulled out two bottles of water. Handing one to Jadyn, he smiled and turned back to facing the boatyard. An hour later, they saw Theo and the girl coming out of one of the buildings on the side of the sales office. The girl had her arm in Theo's and seemed very comfortable doing so.

"She sure does seem like she knows Theo well." Jadyn was now very skeptical about Theo's motives.

"A friend?" Thomas said with a twinkle in his eyes.

"Thomas, this is not funny. If he did have a girlfriend while he was married to Margot, it would definitely lead to motive."

"Let us not jump to conclusions." Tomas offered.

"No, lets not!" A voice low and strong said through the open window.

Both Thomas and Jadyn jumped and turned to see the face of Detective Carter. He did not look very happy to see them there as he climbed into the back seat of Thomas's car. "Would you two please explain what you think you are doing?"

"Look, Detective," Jadyn defended. "We are just trying to help. We did not think it fair that you do all the staking out."

"I am sorry Detective, but we are just trying to get an idea of how he is spending his time."

"Come on you two, follow my car. I am ahead of you both on this leg of the trip." Getting out of the car, he walked across the block, got into his Camaro, turned on the throaty engine and pulled away. Thomas followed obediently. He did not want to alienate the young detective, who was obviously going out of his way to help.

"He can't make us stop!" Jadyn was very put out that her first stakeout was brought to such an abrupt conclusion.

They drove two towns over and stopped across from a very nice restaurant. Detective Carter got out of his car, walked over to Thomas's car which had parked two car lengths down the block. Opening the door for Jadyn he said, "Let's go get something to eat." He did not go toward the fancy restaurant across the street but directed them up the street to a small coffee shop. "They serve the best burgers here," was all he offered.

They sat down at the table closest to the window, which had just been vacated. The local customers seemed to enjoy eating at the counter, which worked well for the detective. The young, curvy waitress wiggled her way over and said, "Nice to see you again, detective. What'll you have?"

"Menus for my friends, Beth. I will have my usual."

She handed menus to Thomas and Jadyn and then asked if they wanted anything to drink. Once she had the drink orders, she turned and wiggle-walked her way back to the kitchen.

"A friend of yours?" Jadyn asked as she perused the menu.

"No, but I have been in here a lot lately. You'll see why in a bit."

They placed orders and then the detective decided to catch them up with what he had found thus far. "Look, it is totally wrong for me to share this with you, but if it will keep you two from playing detective—well, it seems the best way to go. I started tailing Blodger a few weeks ago. I did not tell you because I did not want you to act any differently towards him if you saw him." At that point, the waitress returned with their drinks, all smiles for the detective. When she left, he continued, "He stays busy. He started meeting up with this woman about one week ago; although I suspect that he is merely resuming prior behavior."

He took a drink of his coffee and glanced up and down the street. During his pause, Jadyn asked, "Who is she?"

"Her name is Vanessa Gold, although it took me quite a while to figure that out. She always wears a scarf when they meet. I had to get into the restaurant ahead of them one time, behind some plants, to get a picture of her." He smiled at his stealthy behavior, and then continued, "She is his secretary."

"That does make things a little more suspicious, don't you think?" Thomas was getting angry and it showed.

"Yes, and no. He has not broken any laws at this point. Only caused suspicions. I have been taking her picture around to various hotels in the area, but no luck finding out how long they have been an item. All we can prove is that she is recent and they have not been playing house openly. He spends most of his free time at the gym or with her. They have visited that boatyard several times and I think he is planning to buy something there when the insurance is paid. But here again, only suppositions. No proof."

"This is just too frustrating! It is apparent that the most we might ever prove against Theo is infidelity. What good is that?" Jadyn looked as angry as Thomas.

"Well, we must be patient. I will keep an eye on him as well as ask a few more questions. But I want you two to stop investigating on your own. Please…?"

Thomas shook his head in affirmation, slowly. Jadyn merely gazed out the window, as if she did not hear the question. "Look, there they are now!"

Theo's little sports car pulled up to the valet's section in front of the restaurant. After handing the keys over, he helped Vanessa out of the car and they walked into the restaurant together. Jadyn started to stand up, but James put his hand on her shoulder and said, "Not now. That would give it all away. He would know he was being followed and I have more to do in this case."

Jadyn sat back down with a look of fury on her face. It was apparent that she was not about to let this go. Thomas watched her face and then glanced back to the detective. He was watching her face also with a look of consternation on his face. "Jadyn, why don't we go back to my place for tonight? We can wait for more information from Detective Carter and or we could go see Mother."

"No, I don't want Mother to know all this. She is emotionally strained enough as it is." The cloud that was over his sister seemed to dissipate and Jadyn turned to Thomas with a smile, "Let's just go get her and whisk her away. Let's take her to an art gallery near your place and arrange for her to have a showing."

This sudden change in direction completely baffled both James Carter and Thomas. It was like the last hour had never happened. Uh-Oh, what was going on in her mind, was all that James could think. He hoped she did not have a gun. This change was too transparent to him and he knew she was not going to let this go.

All three rose and after paying their checks, went out into the evening air to their separate cars, which were parked around the block. Jadyn said nothing, but Thomas and James continued planning areas that James could look into for hotels and dates. Thomas said, "It might pay for you to go to the boat slip where the company boat is kept. Maybe they could shed some light on how Thomas learned to sail."

"That's a good idea since he did claim that he was new to this. Maybe he did know what he was doing." Both of them looked at Jadyn, to see if she was listening, but she just kept striding alongside Thomas, holding his arm, with a very odd look on her face, which made James very worried. The slight Madonna smile on her face was beautiful and scary at the same time. James knew that no good would come of it.

They parted ways and James headed toward the boat marina that housed the company boat and Thomas and Jadyn headed toward their mother's home. Jadyn hoped that her father was not home, as this was an impromptu visit. If he was—they would just have to come up with a story regarding their visit. If he was not there, then they would pack their mother up for a little trip. Both were plausible goals and Jadyn was content with them.

Yes, Jadyn was content. She had made her mind up regarding the entire situation and she no longer felt angry. She knew where her next trial was going to take place. She just did not know when.

Reflected Choices

The harsh realities of life,
Impact us often like a pinball.
But it is a choice—victim or victor,
How we react will determine it all.

Our daily behavior seems natural,
As we continue steadily on with our lives.
But do not look too closely at our duties,
As a sharpening took place on the glaives.

Chapter XIII

Jadyn worked diligently on her trials analyzing all the data and experimenting on the little bots within the tank. She had successfully completed her initial trial on the monkeys and was awaiting the results; she wanted to see if the tumors that they had were affected. Jadyn had used an intra-venial injection for them. But now she was thinking of something that could be inhaled with a spray, such as a nasal atomizer. She knew that not all medical uses were able to be administered by injection or through ingestion. Some may be needed to go the nasal route, to avoid liver interference.

She found a solution that would prevent the little bots from deteriorating too quickly until they had found their target. Their unique design made them perfect for transporting medications. The oblong bodies and one hundred little legs were made out of a combination of medicine and an iron material that would oxidize once in the bloodstream, adding nutrients to the body. The computer chip that controlled the little legs and the final explosion was made from a calcium and copper base…only a few microns wide. Very tiny indeed, but very effective. The explosion was actually the loosening of the iron bonds that would allow the liquid inside the little bot to enter the target organ.

This guaranteed that all of the chemical would be where it should be, and not leech out into other organs, or in the bloodstream. Ultimately, she wanted her little bots to have arms and to be able to hunt and cut out tumors, but that was years away. The chip that they had developed to perform the machinations for this simple little bot was not capable of that complex of behavior—not yet.

But now, Jadyn was motivated to start anew. She wanted to introduce the little bots through a nasal spray. Theo had a habit of spraying his nasal passage at least three to four times a day, as he had issues with it. Jadyn knew the type of spray he used. She did not even think twice about his motives or hers. She was on a mission. He would not get away with abusing her sister all this time and finally murdering her. Jadyn was calm, cool, and clear of purpose. She had a personal goal, although she did not plan on sharing it with anyone in or outside of the lab. Her superiors would merely think this was an extension to her research. She would only show the mechanisms to them, not the very special chip she would develop for Theo. No, he would have his very own chip.

Jadyn knew this would take many months to develop. It required working on the chip when the lab did not have too many personnel floating about…late nights. Since she and Thomas were not keeping an eye on Theo, she had the time. If Thomas became curious as to why she was not home as much, no problem. She is throwing herself into her work to keep her mind off of Margot's death.

Thomas did ask her about the amount of time she was spending at the lab, but he knew that with time, all things ease. Her pain would subside at some point in time so he would be patient. She still met with him at their mother's home on weekends, which meant time away from the lab, so he was not too worried about her.

Rachael, on the other hand, did not understand Jadyn's behavior at all. She saw things in Jadyn's eyes that reminded her of Charles, but she could not put her finger on what it was, so she kept it to herself. Perhaps it was just Jadyn's way of coping with her twin's death.

James Carter, who had plans to see more of Jadyn on a personal level, found that she was seldom available. The only time he was able to see her was when he had some additional information that he had gathered on Theo and Vanessa, which was not much since they had been very discrete with their affair.

One day in November, Detective Carter called Rachael Martyn and asked if he could meet with the family. All agreed on a time and Jadyn and Thomas drove down to their mother and father's home. When they had all settled into the living room, James Carter dropped the bomb, "The coroner has ruled the death an accident and the case is now officially closed. Although they had released the body, to allow the funeral to take place in September, they still wanted to make sure that all the information had been gathered concerning the August accident.”

“So this means that Theo can date openly, collect the insurance monies, and go on living the life that he deprived Margot of that awful day?” Thomas stated openly what Jadyn and he were thinking. Their mother looked shocked at this statement but said nothing.

“Yes, he can collect the money, and do as he feels.” James Carter knew that this was his last meeting with the family. His chief had closed the case and he was already working on other projects. He was surprised with the varying reactions to his announcement. Charles, who had professed his support of Theo, seemed pleased it was over with and life could resume its normal course. Rachael sat looking very solemn as if life had handed her one too many lemons. Thomas looked outraged and disgusted, but Jadyn revealed no emotion what-so-ever. That one is a cool cucumber, he thought. Why? What is going on in her pretty little mind? No not little, but definitely beautiful.

Yes, it was true; he was totally smitten by the beautiful Jadyn. He wanted to see her again but did not think this was the time to ask her out on a date, so he kept his desires to himself. He only hoped that the closure of the case would help her get past his involvement and let her see him for who he was—an overworked, underpaid detective that lived life as best he could…with his cat. I wonder if she likes cats?

Jadyn was the first to stand to leave, “I must be going. I have a lot of work to do and must start early tomorrow.”

Rachael looked up and said, “We understand, dear. It is such a long trip for you to come all the way down here. You don’t have to come this weekend if you need a break from all the driving.”

“No, that is no problem. It gives me time to think. And I have a lot to think about.”

Thomas rose and stated he would walk her out, but the detective interceded and said, "I must leave also, so I can walk you out if you don't mind Jadyn."

Thomas sat back down, with a slight smile on his face. Jadyn, with no expression on her face, replied, "Of course." She was hoping he had some additional information for her-plus she liked his company. Throughout this entire affair, she had grown fond of the young detective and some of his little quirks. She knew he liked her, but she was used to that and ignored it for the most part.

Charles rose, kissed Jadyn on the cheek, retrieved and handed her the sweater she had put into the hall closet. After they had gone out the door, Charles sat back down and asked Thomas, "Does that young man have a crush on Jadyn?" Thomas smiled and said he thought as much, but did not think anything would come of it. "After all, this is Jadyn—the workaholic. Even if he did want to see her, it would be hard for him to schedule a time that she would be able to see him."

As they walked down the steps toward their autos, James held Jadyn's elbow to ensure she did not slide on the sidewalk. He did not say anything, so Jadyn decided to ask a question to open the door for conversation, "Detective, is there no possible way to prove murder versus an accident?"

James looked down at the sidewalk and shook his head. "Not in this case. If he did kill her, and I did find out he was a much better sailor than he claimed, I still could not prove it—he did it just the right way to not get caught." Jadyn looked at him sternly and he regretted his phraseology. "Not the right way, but a smart way to avoid being caught. There is nothing right about this whole case."

"James, I really appreciate all that you have done, both while you were investigating for the police and while you were on your own time. I know you are as frustrated as we are and maybe you cannot find any peace within as we cannot. But maybe Mother will feel better and I know Father will." She added the Father will with a slightly ironic facial expression.

"Jadyn, I mean Miss Martyn, I was wondering if you would like to go to dinner with me, sometime… not now, but maybe later in the month?" James almost blurted it out before he realized that she had just paid him a compliment.

Jadyn looked at the young detective thoughtfully for a minute, and then offered, "Why not now? I have not eaten much all day and I know a marvelous little place not far from here, which makes great burgers and serves the best ice-cream."

James was so surprised that he forgot to say anything. He just smiled and held her car door open for her. When Jadyn started looking at him oddly, he realized he had not answered. "I would love to. I am hungry. How about I follow you?"

Jadyn smiled, fished out her keys and started her car to let it warm up. James walked rapidly to his car and it was not long before the two of them were headed to the little ice-cream parlor that she and Margot used to frequent as kids. She was not sure why, but she did want to see a little more of this young man. He seemed very nice and not at all like the usual type of man that asked her to go out.

It was an off time in the afternoon, so the little parlor was not crowded. They slid into a booth, and soon the hot burgers, French fries, and pickles replaced their initial awkwardness. Jadyn did not know what to expect, so she kept the conversation centered on the case. "Did you ever find out any more, before your boss shut you down?"

"Not much, other than the fact that Theo had taken sailing lessons for more than a month before he took the company boat out. It looks like he did know what he was doing; however, a rogue wave still can catch the best of sailors off guard. It just can't be proven and the DA said he won't bring it to trial without hard evidence."

"Well, I guess there is not much we can do at this point." Jadyn tried to sound resigned to this news.

"No, not anything we can do. It is one thing to arrest someone on suspicion, but another to get them convicted. Theo will slip up somewhere. They always do. If they kill once, they think they can do it again."

"Well, that doesn't sound good." Jadyn did not find that very comforting, but it did make her feel much more convicted on the course of action that she was planning. She was sure that Theo had caused Margot's death and now Theo was free from suspicion. This was not acceptable to Jadyn, but she did not want anyone else to know of her plans. However, even after she had done the deed, she could not turn the results over to the military. She would have to go through the usual protocols and trials or someone might put two and two together.

"Where did you just go?" James Carter was watching Jadyn's facial expressions.

"Sorry, I was thinking about how much fun we used to have here. After school when it was getting warm, a group of us kids would meet here and have sundaes or fries. We took over the place, more or less. But we were good customers and the owners enjoyed our stories and laughter."

"I imagine those were easier times." James wanted her to relax and try to forget the current situation. He enjoyed watching her eyes as she spoke about her past childhood. She was so marvelous to look at. "Tell me, how did you get into whatever it is that you do?"

"Oh, well I was not sure what I wanted to do when I was in high school. I knew I loved science, but I loved all the sciences. It was hard to pinpoint my favorites. When I went to college, I became a science major and found I really had an interest in human biology. I never wanted to be a doctor, per se but was fascinated by our bodily mechanisms. I wanted to get into research, and it more or less took off from there. My professor/mentor was very much responsible for guiding me in the right direction."

She took a few more bites and then continued, "The Company recruited me after I had gotten my Masters degree. They paid for me to get my doctorate. It was a dream-come-true. I have been with them ever since."

"Yes, but you are so young—how old were you when you got your Masters?"

"Well, I graduated at sixteen from high school, so I was about one and one-half years ahead of my classmates, statistically speaking."

"Did it make it hard for you at work? To be so young I mean. Some places are hard enough for a woman let alone a young one." James seemed well informed on the subject of the glass ceiling for women.

"It did when I was on the West coast. My boss and I had a few problems, but The Company transferred me here and now everything is the way it should be."

James had finished his meal and was happily listening to all that Jadyn had to say. He was hoping this two-way conversation would lead to his ability to see her again. But before he had too much time to think on this, Jadyn asked, "Now tell me about James Carter…what made you go into the police force?"

"Hmm, let me think. Well, when I was a kid, I found I loved old murder mysteries. I read them constantly and soon was able to tell who the guilty ones were before they were unmasked. My parents got a kick out of it when we would watch murder mysteries on television. But I was not allowed to tell who did it because it would spoil their guesses. Instead, we would all write our guess of murderer down and not open them until the mystery was concluded." He smiled as he told the story about his family traditions.

"Anyway, I was like you in that respect, in high school. I knew I wanted to go to college but did not have a clue regarding what I wanted to do. So I joined the navy, thinking that if I saw the world, it might give me a better idea of what I wanted to do when I went to school. I ended up as a Master-of-Arms and found I enjoyed keeping the peace, as it were. When I got out, I got my degree in psychology and my masters in criminology. They more or less go together in a way. If you can figure out the motive, you have a better idea about who the criminal might be."

"Wow, that must have kept you busy. You don't look old enough to have done all that." Jadyn could not get over that he was older than she was and yet looked about the same age.

"My mother tells me I have a baby face. I am not sure what that means, but I guess she means I don't look my age."

Jadyn shifted in her seat to reach for her purse and said casually as she did so, "Well it is a very nice face, even if it does belong to an old fart." She grinned openly for the first time and James beamed. He had made her smile. Jadyn slid out of the booth and stood, "I must go. It is a long drive and I have an early morning tomorrow."

"Oh, that is fine. My apartment guard will be much happier if I show up at a reasonable time."

Jadyn stopped, her brows furrowed in a questioning manner, "Apartment guard?"

"I have a live-in cat, who literally guards the apartment all day when I am not there. I have heard very interesting stories from my landlady and neighbors." He smiled and Jadyn decided right then and there, if he asks me out, I will say yes. It might be a little dangerous, given what she was planning, but Theo was not the only one who could conceive of a perfect murder.

As Jadyn drove home, she started to wonder about herself. What had she turned into, that she could contemplate a cold-blooded murder? What on earth was she turning into? If the murder had to take place right at that moment, Jadyn would not be able to do it. She just could not conceive of such a path in her life, even if Theo did deserve it.

Jadyn pulled into her local grocery store parking lot, just before seven o'clock. She needed a couple of things for the week and thought it would be a good time to pick them up. As she got out of her car, she heard loud voices coming from a few car rows away. A man was shouting at a woman that was standing next to the car. He was using every abusive phrase he could conjure up and people were watching from safe distances. Nowadays, you don't know who has a gun.

Jadyn did not know what he was angry about but could tell it was escalating into something very wrong, so she pulled out her cell phone and dialed 911. Before she could say very much, she looked up and saw the man backhand the woman across the face, so hard that she fell back against the car and then slid down the side to the ground. Jadyn reported the location and some details, then leaving her phone open, she started to run toward the scene. She could not let that man hit that woman anymore. It was like watching her sister or her mother being abused.

As she ran up to the man, she was shouting at the top of her lungs. Her approach surprised the man and he looked up. As Jadyn ran up, another man from a few cars over, also approached and yelled. The abuser stopped, leaned over and pushed the woman away from the car, and then got into it and drove away, leaving the poor woman sitting on the pavement, bleeding profusely from her mouth.

A moment later, Jadyn heard sirens. She handed the woman a clean tissue, which she had in her jacket. The poor thing. Her face was already beginning to swell, and her mouth had a deep gash on the inside where her cheek hit her teeth when his hand made contact. Jadyn was infuriated! How could he? The woman was tiny and very fragile, about five foot three. There was no way she could go up against such an enraged man without training.

After she gave her statement to the police and an ambulance took the injured woman away, Jadyn entered into the store. She could hardly remember what it was that she needed—her mind was on that horrible scene. Then it drifted back to so many scenes that she had witnessed as a child and the scene of her sister's body in the morgue. Jadyn no longer had any compunction about what she was going to do. Her resolve was set stone solid.

****

James drove back to his apartment in a very good mood. He felt relaxed and excited at the same time. He had worried that Jadyn was too intellectual to enjoy time with a dull detective. She might have found his company beneath her. But she not only seemed to enjoy his company, but she had also taken him to a local restaurant where people knew her. She was not embarrassed to be seen with him. That was a big relief.

James was always selling himself short. But others noticed he was handsome of face, well built, and generally well dressed. He knew he did not match the level of Charles Martyn's wardrobe, but his suit was clean, not real expensive, but well fitting. He had many female admirers at the station, but he liked to keep things on a professional level at work. Outside of work, he had little time to socialize or at least that is what he told himself. Actually, he had not really met anyone who interested him as much as Jadyn Martyn.

Funny names… both end in 'yn'. I wonder if that was intentional on the parents' side of it. As he opened his front door, Kimble sat in his usual place directly inside. James had forgotten to announce who it was opening the door, so Kimble was prepared to spring, fur up and claws out. "Whoa boy, it's me!" James hurriedly stated. Kimble's tail flipped back and forth a few times, letting James know that it was James's error not his own for this fierce greeting. He then turned on his heel and headed to the kitchen…he was hungry.

James came into the apartment smiling. He enjoyed this very unusual cat but had no illusions that the cat belonged to him. It was obvious that he belonged to the cat. Kimble had him well trained: time to feed me, time to play with me, time to brush me, and time to give me the back scratch I deserve. And if you are exceptionally good, I will curl up in your lap when you sit down to relax and I will purr in your ear at night to help you go to sleep.

After he changed his clothes and had taken care of Kimble's immediate needs, James sat down on his couch, put his feet on the coffee table and sipped happily from a cold beer. He was content for now, at least for tonight. He was not happy about Theo and the case that was now closed, but Jadyn's opening up to him and their general conversations took over any bad feelings he might have.

James was a determined young man and he now decided that Jadyn was someone of interest to him personally. He had no idea how to make this happen, but he knew she was the most beautiful and fascinating woman he had ever met and if she liked cats—well that would seal the deal. He wondered again… does she like cats? He finished his beer and picked up a folder that was lying on the coffee table.

Although he was off duty so to speak, he always liked to work on a 'who dun it'. He often would grab a cold case file and reexamine everything. On more than one occasion, he was able to get the case reopened and solved. He was occasionally nick-named the Iceman, by his cohorts as he seemed to have a knack for old, cold mysteries. The rest of the evening oscillated between reading the file, scratching Kimble's back, and thinking of Jadyn. James was set for the night.

****

Not far away, Theo was feeling very relaxed. His position with the company seemed solid—at least for now. His relationship with Vanessa was perfect… fun and games with no strings attached. Vanessa was a practical woman. She knew the type of man Theo was and had no illusions what it would be like to be attached to him. She had seen too many domineering men. He was fun to play with, but at the end of the day, she preferred her own company.

Weekends they spent together on the newly acquired sailboat that Theo had been looking at for months. It still had the new boat smell about it on the interior and slept four easily, although Theo only had one other person in mind, at the moment. Financially, he was very solvent thanks to the insurance policy and he started to invest some of the money in various stocks. He felt he had arrived as far as business could offer.

Sunday, February 12, was a cold gray day. Theo did not have any immediate plans for the day other than going to the gym and then taking a ride over to Vanessa's place. They did not have to hide their relationship, so they took turns cooking for one another on the weekend. This was Vanessa's day, so Theo would pick up crusty Italian bread and would select a red wine from his collection to take with him.

He arrived back home from the gym around ten a.m. and took a shower. After dressing, he sat down to pay a few bills before he headed over to Vanessa's when there was a knock on the door. Surprised, he got up and looked out the peephole. Jadyn. Now what does she want? Theo was not too happy to see a reminder of his wife coming to call. He opened the door and put on his best faux smile. "Jadyn, what a nice surprise. I did not know you were in the area. How have you been?"

"Oh, just fine, Theo. I have not heard from you, so I thought I would stop by on my way home from visiting with my mother." Jadyn had no problem lying. She had come directly from her home as she wanted to give as much stability to the little bots as she could. She leaned over and gave Theo a peck on the cheek, then entered into the home of her sister's murderer. Jadyn was not worried about him, as he would have no motive to kill her.

"Theo, we are wondering how you are coping without Margot. Mother and Father want to have you over for supper, but don't want to push you too much. Since it has only been a few months, they more or less wanted to wait to hear from you first."

"Oh, I am coping. I am going through the stages they always tell you about: shock, anger, guilt. I am in the guilt stage, although I think I started with that one too. Odd."

Jadyn did not think it was so odd, as he was the one who killed her; however, she kept her thoughts to herself. Smiling she said, "I can't stay long as I have work to do this evening at the lab, but I just wanted to see you." She noticed he seemed to relax a little bit more when he found she was not staying. She wondered if it was difficult for him to face his wife's twin, so soon. Or was he truly a hard heart.

They talked a little bit more, and then Jadyn asked to use the bathroom before she left. When she came back into the room, Theo was on the phone to someone. He hung up as she entered and said he was meeting a client later that day. "I was making sure the time still worked for them."

Jadyn did not believe that for a moment but did not care. She made her goodbyes and left as abruptly as she had come. Theo was glad to see her leave as she made him very uncomfortable. It was like having his wife around…except this one did not seem enamored with him. It was odd that she had just shown up as she did, but she had left quickly which worked with his plans, so he was not too worried about it.

He told Vanessa about it, but she did not seem to care about it one way or another. Theo and Vanessa had an afternoon and evening of fun and games, and Jadyn went home with a smile on her face. She thought about calling that nice detective to meet for dinner but thought better of it. No need to place herself in the area this weekend. Maybe the next time she visited her Mother with Thomas. Or perhaps for a funeral… she would have to wait and see. Her latest trial had begun.

****

Three days later, as Jadyn was getting ready to drive to work, she received a phone call from Thomas. "Hello Thomas, what's up? Are we to get together this weekend?"

"Well, yes and no, Sis. I have news—Theo's dead."

Silence on Jadyn's end of the phone line. She was going through so many emotions that she did not know how to answer: thrilled the bots did their job, surprised how fast it had happened, curious as to what the coroner would find, sad that she had been made to end a life, but relieved that he would never abuse anyone again. "When Thomas? How?"

"Well, when he did not show up for work, his girlfriend went over to his house. Apparently, she found him sitting in a chair, grasping his chest. The initial thoughts are a heart attack, but the autopsy will reveal more I am sure."

Jadyn said, "It could not have happened to a nicer fellow!"

"Jadyn!" Thomas remonstrated her. "You should not talk like that. Hey, you were not near his place lately were you?" He laughed and added, "Just kidding… sort of."

"Thomas, that is not funny. No, I have been working at the lab most of the last few weeks, so I am innocent." Now she would have to start lying.

"Well, I thought I would let you know. His parents are coming up from Jim Thorpe tomorrow to collect the body. The coroner should be done by then. They will bury him in Pennsylvania. To be truthful, they are the only ones who want him." Thomas had to admit.

"No argument there. Shall we get together this weekend? Do you think this will affect Mother?"

"I don't know, but it would probably be a good idea. I want to work out a time for her to come up and visit me in White Plains. I have two galleries that want to exhibit her work so this will give me a chance to re-promote the idea to her."

"That is wonderful, Thomas. Okay, I will be down sometime Saturday evening. I have a few things I must do first at work. See you soon!" Jadyn hung up and paced around the floor. She had no idea what the little bots had done, but was dying to see the results. The clinical side of her rose up and took control.

This was a remote trial and she had no access to the body…. Unless. She pulled a small card out from her hallway drawer and punched the number into her cell. A few minutes later, she heard a familiar voice. "Jadyn, how nice to hear from you."

"Hello, James. I just received some news. Thomas called me and told me that Theo has died. Have you heard anything about it?"

James, who was thrilled when he had heard her voice, felt somewhat deflated after she asked her question. Nuts, he thought. He had hoped it was to set up a social event. "No, I have not heard. I've been pretty busy and have not read the newspaper. How did he die?"

"I am not sure, Thomas said they initially thought heart attack."

"Well, I am sorry for your loss…but only if you are sorry. I personally did not like him." James was trying to be diplomatic.

"No, I am not sorry at all. You know how I felt about him. However, I am curious about his death. He seemed pretty healthy to me." Jadyn was not sure how to approach the subject without looking too interested.

"Well, I would be happy to look into the death for you."

"That would be wonderful, James. I am coming down to see Mother tomorrow. Maybe we can get together."

"No problem. Give me a call when you get down and we can make arrangements." James hung up and wondered how to approach this. Theo was definitely a bad apple. If the heart attack was natural, okay. But a heart attack could be induced in any number of ways. He would have to do some digging. He hoped it would not cause a problem, but he wanted to see the coroner's report, then when he saw Jadyn, he could answer her questions with as much information as possible. He wanted her to see he had her best interest at heart.

He finished writing the report that he had been working on for the last half hour and then pulled up his contact listings on his cell phone. Finding the County Coroner's phone number, he made the call. Although the body was found outside of Long Island area, it would be the Suffolk County Coroner from his precinct that would be performing the autopsy as the local area was too small to support a large police staff.

Dr. Malory answered after several rings, "Coroner's office."

"Dr. Malory? This is Detective Carter."

"Hello, detective!" Dr. Malory seemed pleased to hear from the young detective.

"Dr. Malory, I was wondering if you were performing an autopsy on a recent death. His name is Theodore Blodger. I understand he died three days ago and was found at his home with an apparent heart attack."

"Funny you should ask about that one. Yes, I did perform an autopsy, but I cannot tell what killed him, other than his heart more or less looks like it is disintegrating." The Coroner seemed puzzled and from his voice, James knew there was a problem.

"Can that happen? I mean, like it did?"

The Coroner hesitated before he answered, "Well if it was an old heart, you might expect the muscles to stiffen or thicken. But I have never seen one like this. It is like the glue that holds the muscle together is letting loose." It was apparent that this intrigued and frightened the doctor.

"Do you think that this was a natural death or will you call it an unnatural death?"

"I am sorry, but I can't say right at this time. I have called in a cardiologist, but he is not available until tomorrow as he has to come down from Boston. I feel bad for the man's parents as they want me to release the body, but I can't until I learn more about this."

The detective was almost as fascinated by this description of death as the Coroner was—it sounded weird. "So the heart did not melt or break or have a blowout?"

Dr. Malory snickered and said, "No, although melting would be interesting too. No, all the matter to the heart is in the pericardial sack…it just is not in the shape of a heart any longer."

"Well, the deceased was a person of interest at one time in a case I was investigating, so would you keep me informed? I am sure that this will roll up into a very interesting ball." James closed his phone and walked back to his desk. He did not realize he had started to pace around the office while he was talking on the phone…a habit he had developed, much to the amusement of his partner and colleagues.

"James, you look like you smell something foul. Is there something going on that I need to know about?" Haley walked around her desk to face her partner.

"We both might have something interesting to look into." James was looking at the floor when he answered her, but then looking up he said, "Let's go get some coffee. I want to tell you some things to see how you react to it."

"Coffee always sounds good to me, especially if a piece of pie goes with it." Haley did not eat meals on a normal schedule, but she never missed an opportunity to eat pie. She claimed it was her secret weight control weapon. It seemed to work for her because she was fit and trim. She never told anyone that she worked out at the gym four times a week and ran five miles every other day. No, she just claimed pie was the answer to all problems.

At this point, James was not going to argue. He had a niggling feeling that something was wrong, but he could not put his finger on it. Maybe pie would kick it out or kick it loose.

They drove to their favorite luncheon diner across town and once they had settled into a booth and ordered, James began his story. He told Haley everything he had done on the Margot Blodger death and his trailing around after Theo and eventually Vanessa, whenever he had free time. "I did not want to involve you, originally, because of all the personal time involved. There was no proof that these two were an item until after the date of his wife's death. No proof and after the coroner declared it an accident, I had no case and finally had to give up."

Haley was slowly chewing her last bite of pie, savoring the fleeting taste. When she had finished she asked, "It does sound like an accident, albeit a convenient one... what makes you think there was something wrong on the husband's part?"

"Hidden abuse. The guy's wife, Margot, had been seen by many doctors in hospitals around the area, but never close to home. It was always reported as an accident, with Margot claiming she fell or ran into something. It was never put into the watch-list database."

Haley's eyes were suddenly very intense, "So he abused his wife over a long period of time and then what—decides he will kill her on a boat? His abuse sounds spontaneous. Anger or control. But the boat part-unless he lost his temper on the boat, it is a rather elaborate way to kill someone."

"Yes, I know." James's brow wrinkled into tight furrows. "I would love to ask a psychiatrist more about abuse."

"That is easily arranged, however, I don't see the connection to the current death you were just on the phone to Dr. Malory about."

"This was the death of the husband, Theodore Blodger. He was young, fit, exercised all the time. And yet he had… well, I don't know what to call it. Heart failure of some kind. It is nothing that Dr. Malory has ever seen. He has called in a cardiologist, who will be in from Boston in a day or so. He does not know what happened to the heart… it kind of melted." James made a face then added, "Well, not melted, but looked like it melted. It was all there in the sack, but not shaped like a heart."

"Geez, I can't un-imagine that!!" She made a disgusted face and continued, "I am glad I finished my pie!"

"He will get the results back to me when it is all finished. For now, I don't know why, but it is bugging me."

"Okay, let's pretend that it is suspicious. Who would you suspect? Who would have the motive? His girlfriend? His wife's parents or siblings? And how on earth do you melt a heart?" At this point, she looked down at her empty plate and then signaled for the waitress. When she came over, Haley ordered a second piece of pie and more coffee. "This is at least a two-piece problem," she explained when she saw James's curious look.

James told the waitress he would have a piece of the pie too and more coffee. When the waitress brought his first piece and Haley's second piece, she smiled at James and said, "I hope you like it. We make all our pies right here in the diner."

"Oh, I am sure I will," he offered. He was used to young women being very polite to him and this one always had something nice to say.

After she left, Haley continued, "So, who do you suspect?"

"I can't suspect anyone until we know how he died. Then we can figure out motive, means, and opportunity. Right now, we don't know anything about the time frame. How it was done, how long it would take, what triggers it."

"I am very glad you finally brought me into the loop. I was feeling estranged." Haley grinned at this point and waited for James to respond. She and James enjoyed their partnership. It was amusing and unencumbered. She knew she had a reputation at the station, but James did not seem to care. The nicest part about it was that her boyfriend had met James and was not jealous. He said that James was too intense to be interested in any kind of relationship.

"Well, it was not intentional. And, until I get the coroner's finding, we are stuck. No case that the chief will approve for us to chase."

"Yeah, but how would you melt just the heart? A new drug or perhaps a ray gun?" Haley was half serious, half joking.

"Beats me, but I want to do some research. Maybe there are new weapons on the market we are not aware of."

"Sounds black opp-ish to me." Haley was done with the pie and ready to go. She rose and grabbed the check. "My turn today."

They went back to the station and resumed their normal duties of police detectives. They would have to wait for more information, which is something detectives have to live with all the time.

****

Jadyn finished up her work fairly early and headed home to pack a carryon bag. She could not wait to hear what her little bots had done and if they left any traces. In a cancerous tumor, it would not matter, but in this incident, it could be dangerous—for her. No one knew what she was working on in the public sector, but the military might frown on her usage of the bots for personal advantage.

When she had finished packing, she called Detective Carter to arrange a time to meet. Out the door and on the road. After she met with him, she would continue down to her mother's home and meet with her and Thomas for a nice weekend. She was curious as to why she did not feel anything about Theo's demise: no guilt, no regret and definitely no sorrow. It almost felt slightly surreal, because there was that three-day delay. Maybe her little bots did not kill him after all. There would be no way to tell until she heard what the detective had to say.

The trip to Long Island took over four hours, so Jadyn decided to fly. Although it was a short flight, it would take a couple of hours by the time she boarded the plane, flew, and then after landing, rented a car. Still, it would give her time to meet with the detective and pick his brain, prior to driving to her mother's.

As she sat back into the plane's narrow seat, she decided to relax. No thinking. That was her mental order to herself. She was to let her brain recharge itself. She would need all her brain functions when she met with the detective. She would have to be careful about how she asked questions. No use making him suspicious. He seemed to be a naturally suspicious type—no use adding fuel to it.

An hour later, she drove into the parking lot of the restaurant that the detective suggested as a meeting place. He said he would treat to a late lunch, and although Jadyn was not starved, she thought it would be a good, relaxed way to ask all her questions. James met her at the door and they went into the quiet dining area. It was early in the day, so the main luncheon crowd had not arrived as of yet.

"It is good to see you, Jadyn. How have you been?"

"I am doing fine, Detective. Busy as usual at work."

"Please, call me James, remember?"

"Oh, yes, I am sorry." Jadyn smiled and looked through the menu hiding her face.

The waitress came over and once they had given their respective orders, Jadyn sat back in her seat and asked, "Did you find anything out from the coroner? Did he have a heart attack?"

"No small-talk huh? Okay, right to the point. Yes, and no. The coroner can't tell what happened to his heart. He is calling in a specialist from Boston, hoping that he might be able to tell him what happened."

Jadyn sat sipping her tea and wondering how to extract more information out of this good looking detective. "Why can't he tell? I thought heart stuff would be fairly standard."

James did not know how much to say at this point. He really liked this young woman. She was smart, beautiful and enjoyable to speak with when he had the nerve. But there was something about her that was intriguing. He decided to answer her without too much detail. "Well, the heart had changed shape and was no longer functional."

"Changed shape?" Jadyn wrinkled her nose when she spoke the words. She was not expecting that as an answer. That is definitely not what she had designed her little bots to do. Now she had to see the pictures of the corpse. The coroner would have taken pictures of the heart, of that she was sure. She had no idea how she was going to find out what went on unless she took possession of the body. She had to do an autopsy on the heart and on other areas, to see if the little bots stayed within the areas that they were programmed to attack.

James pretended to be looking around the room while he had said this, but he really was studying Jadyn's facial expressions of which there were many. She definitely had something going on in that lovely head and he wished he knew what. James said, "I will keep you in the loop during this process—if you would like."

"Oh, yes! I owe it to my parents and brother to find out all I can." She smiled her most charming smile and James decided she was too pretty to interrogate over lunch.

They chatted about James's work, which seemed to interest Jadyn. Toward the end of lunch, James turned the conversation around and asked what Jadyn did for a living. "I know you work in the Boston area for a company and you do research. But that is rather limited. What do you do?"

Jadyn pretended to be chewing while she decided how much to tell the detective about herself. "Well, at the end of the day, I am a nanobiologist."

"A what?" Nano was a term that he had heard before, but not in conjunction with biology.

"I work on biological processes on a very small scale." This seemed as safe an answer as anything else. "I am working on research that will one day help cure cancer. Well, not cure....more like excise." Then after realizing that was too much information, she changed directions. "Our company has already developed new bandages for military use in the field that actually heal the wound. We also have developed new sutures that are like little clamps and can be applied by anyone. Then if there is not a medic around, your military buddy can close your worst wounds until help can come." Jadyn was not giving away any secrets as these were being used currently and had great value, but no security risk.

"Is that the kind of thing you work with? Sutures?" Somehow, James did not think this nanotechnology was needed for this type of thing.

"Well, no. But I can't reveal exactly what I am working on as it is top secret." She smiled and said, "And yes, if I told you…"

"You'd have to kill me, yeah I know." James thought that this was enough prodding for one day. Eventually, he would find out one way or another. He needed more information on the company and the departments contained within it. Haley could help with this part of the project. She was a wiz at research.

They parted ways outside of the restaurant and Jadyn continued on to her mother and father's home and James headed back to his apartment. After all, it was a Saturday and he was off duty until Monday. Besides, he had a lot to think about and the alone time would be useful. Well, not alone. There was always Kimble.

Hidden Truths

You can't undo the past,
Though many have tried.
It is easier to climb a mountain,
Or wade against a flood tide.

So be careful of the path that you choose,
Benign it might seem at first.
But if it hides the truth around a bend,
The direction you chose may be reversed.

Chapter XIV

"I've never seen anything like this before." Dr. White stood over the tray that was holding Theo's heart and continued to shake his head back and forth. "How on earth could a heart do this? It seems to be losing its molecular bonds and the cells are just, well for lack of a better description, the cells are just letting go of one another."

"Now you know why I called you down here," Dr. Malory stated. "The deterioration seems fairly rapid. When he first was opened up, the heart was just sitting there. It looked very oddly shaped, so I called you to confirm a diagnosis of adult congenital heart disease of some sort. But now, it has progressed into something that seems to be the onset of a new type of disease." Dr. Malory cleared his throat and continued, "I cannot tell enough about it as to be sure of anything or to rule out anything."

"Well, don't feel bad, this is new to me, too. I want to film this and photograph it. Don't touch it as of yet. It might be contaminated and I don't want you to be exposed, even though you are wearing gloves and a mask." Dr. White turned from the body and walked across the room. Taking off his gloves, he pulled out his cell phone and punched in a code. It did not take long for someone to answer, and Dr. White spoke only a few words, then gave the address of their location and hung up. "I just called in the CDC" Dr. White offered by way of explanation. "I think that it would be prudent at this point to get many eyes on this before it melts entirely."

"Do you think this is a type of plague? Or large scale epidemic waiting to happen?" Dr. Malory was now looking even more worried than before they had started.

"There is no evidence of that as of yet, but I will be much happier if they take this little puzzle away from here." Dr. White continued to film the heart, which seemed to be slowly dissolving before their eyes. He added, "They have a division for infectious disease and a separate one that works with Homeland Security, in case this was, well, something else."

Two hours later, the initial team of CDC personnel arrived. They came into the room wearing white germ-barrier suits and masks. The first one introduced himself as the team leader, John Jacobs. He addressed Dr. White in a very familiar way, which lead Dr. Malory to feel that they had worked together before.

"Over here, Dr. Jacobs." Dr. White directed their attention to the tray containing Theo's heart.

"What are we looking at, Dr. White? It doesn't look like any organ I have ever seen." Dr. Jacobs stared at the gooey mess lying on the tray.

"Well, not too long ago, it was a heart. But somehow, it is dissolving."

"How long has this taken, to get like this I mean?"

Dr. White looked to Dr. Malory to fill in the missing information. "This man died about fifty-two hours ago. He was found that same day by his girlfriend. We picked up the body and brought it back here. I did not start the autopsy until the next day, on Wednesday. I kept him in the refrigerator until then. When I saw his heart, it was still in the pericardial sack, but it looked misshaped. I had never seen anything like it. That's when I called you to come down to help me with the final diagnosis." He paused, waiting to see if they had any other questions.

"Dr. White, has the degradation been filmed? If so, for how long and how often?" Dr. Jacobs could not take his eyes off the melting mass even while asking questions.

"Oh yes, as soon as I arrived. It has changed a great deal; you should be able to see the transition when you review the file. I've also included all the still shots that Dr. Malory took when he first opened up the victim." Dr. White handed a DVD to Dr. Jacobs.

"All right, let's pack up all this and take it back to the lab." Dr. Jacobs told his two cohorts. It was amazing to Dr. Malory how quickly and efficiently they collected everything that had been exposed to the body, including instrumentation, cell slide samples, and of course the heart.

250

After the CDC left the room, Dr. White looked at Dr. Malory and ordered, "This must be kept quiet for now. Since we don't know what we are dealing with, no one must know anything other than it was his heart that killed him. Leave it at that."

"His parents are looking to take the body back with them to Jim Thorpe in Pennsylvania. What should I tell them?" Dr. Malory was a very open person and was not used to keeping secrets.

"Just tell them you want to have more tests run and you have sent the body to a lab in New York City. Tell them that your medical boss has requested it."

"Who?" Dr. Malory was confused as he did not have a direct superior.

"They won't know you are autonomous in the field here. Just leave it at that." Dr. White looked sympathetically at Dr. Malory's confused look and added, "I am sorry you are in the middle, but this could be a national security issue and we can't be too careful with the information that we do know. We have to look like we think it was an odd heart attack." Dr. White gathered up his briefcase and notes and left before Dr. Malory could protest the nasty position that he was left to defend.

****

Jadyn was as nervous as a cat that was left inside a dog's pen but could not see the dog. She paced back and forth in her office while thinking about her next move. She had to see the body, had to see the heart. The detective said it melted, sort of. That would be amazing. It would mean that the little bots had done exactly what she wanted them to do. They could disassemble cancer cells and destroy tumors. But she would have to study the cells. It was not enough that the tumor was broken up—the cells would have to be dead or they could float to other parts of the body, more or less metastasizing into even more tumors elsewhere.

She had to get samples to study. But how? She needed to get closer to the subject, which fortunately for her, was how she thought of Theo. He was a lab experiment. She seemed able to disassociate her feelings toward Theo from her work; she was now in her clinical mode. Her enemy was dead and she was free to study her work and moderate the mechanical side of her little bots....if she could find out what actually went on in Theo's heart.

The only way she could see to get to the body was through Detective Carter. She smiled when she thought about the young man. He had such a pleasant smile and even though he was a very good looking man, he did not seem conscious of it. He was shy and seemed almost inclined to let a woman make the initial overtures. Well, she had a need to find out more information so she would have to contact him again. Pleasant duty for her.

She pulled her car into the company parking lot and slowly made her way to her assigned parking spot. A note sleeved in a plastic holder was hanging from her nameplate. Uh-oh, she thought. What could that be? Getting out, she went over to the plastic holder and took the note out of the sleeve. It read: Ms. Martyn, please drive over to Section Eight's parking lot. You are to report to Mr. Lambert in the second building.

Putting the note and sleeve in her briefcase, she got back into her car. Pulling out her cell phone, she called her receptionist. "Darla, I am going to be late this morning. I have a meeting in Section Eight."

"I know. They called me a few minutes ago to let me know. I will notify the staff."

"Thank you, Darla. I don't think I will be long." Jadyn stated— more in hopes than with any kind of assurance. She pulled out of her spot and started around the building. It was a huge campus and it took her over five minutes to drive around it and reach the next set of gates. She stopped and the guard asked for her credentials and destination. She showed him the note that was left for her and he pointed and stated, "That low building on the left, Ms. Martyn."

Smiling, she pulled through and headed to the building. By now her heart was pounding so hard she swore it could be heard by anyone near her. Getting out, she took her briefcase and entered the front. Guards stood on the inside and when she showed her badge, they seemed to know where she needed to go. "Private

252

Barnes will escort you to the proper room, Miss." The older guard stated.

The younger guard swept his arm out in an arc, directing her down the hall. She was totally intimidated. She knew that they would not be very pleased if they thought she had stolen some of the bots for her own personal use, but she did not know how they would react. This could not be good. She started down the highly polished green tiled floor, in hopes that the guard could not see that she was about to have a nervous attack.

They went down several hallways. The little building seemed to be set up in a maze pattern; how on earth did the people remember where their offices were? All of the doors were solid with no windows. They finally reached a large brown door with a plaque on it: Mr. Lambert. Jadyn had met Mr. Lambert only once when she had first transferred to her new post. He was introduced as a military advisor, even though he was a civilian.

Jadyn entered through the door and Private Barnes leaned in and told the young man sitting at a desk just inside, "This is Ms. Martyn to see Mr. Lambert." He then ducked back out of the door, closing it behind her. Jadyn hoped he did not go far as she knew she would never find her way back out without a guide.

"Have a seat Ms. Martyn, Mr. Lambert will be with you shortly." The young man, who was in a very strange uniform, smiled and pointed to the small, gray sofa sitting on the side of the office.

Jadyn did as she was told and once seated looked back at the young man and asked, "Your uniform…. I have never seen one like that one before. What branch of the military is it?"

He just smiled and stated, "It will not be long now. Mr. Lambert is very eager to see you." He then looked back at his paperwork and offered no other comment.

Jadyn sat quietly with her hands holding each other in her lap. If she did get arrested, she was willing to go to jail. But she could say nothing about what she had done as it was top secret. However, this did not feel like that. This felt odd. So she sat waiting, speculating wildly in her mind as to all the possibilities.

The inner door opened and a tall, gaunt man in perhaps his early fifties came out. He extended his hand and approached Jadyn with a big smile, "Miss Martyn. It is such a pleasure to see you again. Our last meeting was so very brief."

Jadyn rose and took his outstretched hand, noticing that he gave her a firm shake…not like most men when they shake the hand of a woman. He did not seem afraid to break her. She did not know if that was a good sign or a bad one. The mental speculations continued.

"Please forgive my interruption of your day. I hope it was not too inconvenient?"

Jadyn smiled and answered, "No, I have everything scheduled that needed scheduling. The work is on autopilot, more or less for now." She followed him back into his office, feeling a bit like she was about to be interviewed for something. It did not sit quite right with her, but she had no reason specifically to point to—he was being very courteous.

"Have a seat, please." He indicated the large, overstuffed chair in front of his desk. Jadyn did so, and he continued. "I know this might be a bit over the top as far as a meeting, but I wanted to keep this quiet, more or less."

"I don't understand, sir. You can come to my lab at any time. The military is always welcome."

"Jadyn," he said with a more direct look, "is there something you might want to tell me about your little experiments?"

He looked at her with such piercing, gray eyes that Jadyn thought he knows! But she was not about to assume that openly. "What do you mean, Sir? I submit weekly reports to both the company and to the Pentagon. I am not sure what you are referring to?"

Mr. Lambert smiled and leaned back in his chair, continuing to hold her gaze. He was deciding how he was going to approach this and did not want to hurry the process. This young woman held a very powerful weapon in her hands and he wanted it for the military's use. But he did not want too many people to know anything about it. After a few minutes, he said, "There was a very

254

odd death that the CDC has been looking into up in the Long Island area. You might have heard, as it was your ex-brother-in-law, Theodore Blodger."

He then shut his mouth and waited. From the look on this beautiful young woman's face, she did not know anything about the CDC being involved. "You did not know about that?"

Jadyn looked down at the backside of his desk, staring at nothing. She was not sure why she was there, but this man obviously knew things that she did not. If the CDC was called into the affair, it could get very hairy very quickly. "I did not know about the CDC coming into this," she finally offered.

"Yes, they were amazed at the initial findings, and have not seen anything to explain the happenings. We are fortunate that they do not use electron microscopes, aren't we?" He smiled again, almost conspiratorially.

Jadyn sat back and looked him directly in the eyes and asked, "What can I expect out of this?" She was not going to be intimidated any longer. If he was going to have her arrested, she would not be where she was—in his office, chatting.

"Help, Miss Martyn. You can expect help." He pressed a button on the phone system on the desk and asked, "Burt, can you bring in some coffee? It will help us along." Then turning to Jadyn he said, "You were not able to see the body, were you?"

"No, it was at the morgue and I had decided to go see that young detective that was working on the case. I thought he might be able to get me into the place for a look-see. I did not know the CDC had the body." She looked back down again and said quietly, "Nuts, I won't ever see it."

Mr. Lambert saw her passion and knew he was going to get what he wanted. Just then, Burt, the young man in the strange uniform entered with a pot of coffee, a tray of fixings and cookies. He handed Jadyn a mug of steaming coffee and a spoon, turned and walked out of the room. He also knew that Mr. Lambert would get what he wanted—the coffee was the signal. Now Burt had his orders and started making phone calls as he had been directed to do, previously.

After they had adjusted their coffee, Mr. Lambert said, "Jadyn, you don't mind if I call you Jadyn, do you? Jadyn, I can get you the body, the heart and all the data on it that has been collected thus far." He paused for effect, letting this wonderful news flow over Jadyn like a balm. She obviously was thrilled, and it reflected in her marvelous, blue eyes.

"Sir, I don't know what to say. What I did was reprehensible. I should go to jail, for taking the little bots out of the building and testing them on, well, my sister's husband." She had decided that this man knew enough to incarcerate her if he had wanted to, but he seemed more interested in helping her to obtain the information she was missing.

"Well, yes it was a no-no as far as your protocols are concerned and definitely not good as far as the law would see it. But, it does pose some interesting possibilities for The Company and the military. We certainly would not want you to be jailed for this. We totally understand why you did what you did—we don't condone it, but we do understand."

Jadyn wondered who we were, but decided to keep her mouth shut on the subject, for now. However, it was slowly dawning that she was now in a very precarious position, and then we knew it. "What can I do to see the data? The Body?"

"I know how the timing is essential. From what I understand, the degradation is almost complete. I have arranged for you to use a small lab in this building. I have all the equipment you will need and you have only to ask if you need more." He was enjoying this. She was receptive and he was eager to get this study underway. "By tomorrow, all will be here and ready for your inspection."

Jadyn was speechless. How could this military intermediate get all that done in one day? How did he know what she had done? Who was this guy? As she pondered this quietly, she started in on an oatmeal cookie.   This was a lot to take in and she was not sure how to proceed.

"Mr. Lambert, I find myself at a loss. Who are you, really? And what agency do you represent? I like to know with whom I get in

256

bed, as the expression goes. I don't want to ruin my relationship with The Company if that is possible."

"Don't worry about that. We will keep The Company in the loop, for the most part. But there are certain things they do not need to know, especially concerning your private adventures outside the building with your little bots." He leaned back again and took a very long sip of his coffee. "We will just explain that we feel the next few trials should be under closer guard. They won't mind, as they are used to us doing things like that. And as for who we are, you will be briefed extensively after you have had the opportunity to examine the body and heart."

Jadyn wondered how many times Section Eight had done this type of thing, but decided that she might as well go along with it. "I will need a day to prepare my team in the other building, to keep them moving forward with their work."

"Yes, that is no problem. You will actually be working between both buildings, in a dual role. The cancer research must continue and I am sure you will find a way to do that. But the research you do here will be of a more lethal nature, and the staff and workers, and bosses in the other building are not to know what it is that you are doing here for us."

Jadyn understood that more than he knew. Her entire life had changed and she was now a murderess, even though she did not feel like one. She wondered where this was going to end. She rose and said, "I best be going. I have a lot of work to do before I come over here....oh, yes, I am usually in rather early. What badge will I need to come into the building and all that type of thing? Oh, and where is my lab?"

Mr. Lambert pushed the button on the com again and Burt stuck his head in the door. "Burt, Miss Martyn will need her credentials. She is joining us here tomorrow. Also, you will need to set up her parking space and show her how to enter her lab."

"No problem, Sir." Then looking at Jadyn, who was picking up her briefcase, he said, "If you would follow me."

Jadyn looked at Mr. Lambert and said, "Thank you, sir. It was good to speak with you and I assume I will see you again very soon."

"Oh, don't fear about that. I will pester you enough that you will wish I took vacations." He laughed and Jadyn felt much more relaxed than she had since she read the note pinned to her parking sign. They shook hands and she followed Burt out the door.

Burt, now a different person behavioral wise, smiled and paused by his desk, picking up an envelope. "This contains all of the letters of explanation for your superiors and also a badge. If you let me know what time you think you will be in tomorrow, I will meet you out front and show you how to gain access to the lab and where to park."

"I need a full day at my old lab, so I won't start until the day after tomorrow. I will be here at seven, Burt. I hope that is not too early. I normally start at six, but then I finish up and have all my meetings in the afternoon. There is a great deal of paperwork involved with all the trials, so I finish that up after my meetings and try to leave by six pm."

"That is a long day, miss."

"Yes, but I don't mind. What I do is exciting and I know we are close to a breakthrough."

Burt smiled to himself and walked Jadyn back down all the hallways to the front of the building. After she left, he went back to the office and sat down in his seat. It was not long and his console buzzed. "Yes, Sir?"

"Can you come in, Burt. We have much to do to prep for all that is about to happen." Mr. Lambert was calm, but Burt knew there was an undercurrent that was hidden from view. This would be a wild ride.

****

It was nearly two weeks before Jadyn was able to take a weekend to visit her family. She needed the break, but she had an alternative reason to want to go back to Long Island. She wanted to see Detective Carter. She did not need to use him to see the body or heart. She did not need to have access to the coroner. Although she wanted to see if he would be pursuing Theo's death, she wanted to see him because she liked him. It was a shame that they lived so far apart but probably was safer that way.

Her new exploits with Section Eight were going well and she was busier than ever. Since she was able to autopsy the body of Theo and the heart remains, she was able to determine that the only foreign residual in the goo was iron and a trace of calcium and copper, all of which appeared normal, except the iron level in the heart was higher than the iron level in the bloodstream. But that did not seem to outwardly imply cause. She continued to work long hours investigating the nasal passages, blood-brain barrier, and other areas to see if the little bots became clogged in any of those areas. As far as she could tell, it worked splendidly. If Theo's heart was a cancer tumor, it would have been gone from the body within a few days. Jadyn was very pleased, as was her new overseer, Mr. Lambert.

Mr. Lambert was a true enigma. He seemed like an administrator most of the time, but he had a vast knowledge of anatomy, chemistry, math, and military weaponry. A very odd combination, but then he never told her anything about himself. It more or less just appeared in his questioning sessions.

Although Jadyn was used to working all the time, she knew she had to have some downtime, and a date here and there would help to keep her on a level track. She was not interested in any of the people she had met on the campus, but she knew James and felt comfortable enough with him to relax. Mr. Lambert thought it would be a good idea to survey everyone on the outside involved with the Theo incident (as he liked to refer to it), and decide if there was anything else that needed to be covered… or covered up.

As Jadyn sat in the plane, waiting for it to take off, she started to ponder the events that had taken place over the last month. The one thing that had Jadyn the most curious was her lack of emotional feelings toward the man she had killed. Nothing. No remorse. No guilt. Very little thought. Maybe genetics play a part of that too. She was, after all, her father's daughter and Charles never really regretted anything, that she could tell. Hmm, genetics. Jadyn would have to look into that reasoning. Maybe there was a gene that could be passed on that made people inclined towards being a sociopath. At least to have certain portions of the traits. Not that she was a sociopath. She did not have any intentions of killing anyone else.

Detective Carter was very pleased when he received a call that she was coming. He told her he would pick her up at the airport and take her to a late supper. After he closed off the call, he decided to finish his paperwork early and go home to shower, dress, and prepare for some quality time with this young beauty. "Haley, I am going to pick up Jadyn from the airport at five, so I will be out of the office after three. I want to go home first before I have to meet her."

Haley looked at him with a side glance and then looked back at her piles of paperwork. "You think getting close to her is wise? After all, she did have a motive to kill Mr. Blodger. Even if we could not prove it was a murder."

"Haley, we know her movements during the times in question. She was not anywhere near when he had his heart attack…or whatever it was. She had not been around for days."

"Yes, but I don't like the way the body was removed by the CDC. We had no access to it or their findings. You would think that Dr. Malory would know something or have heard from them by now."

Although James agreed, he did not say anything. Instead of speculating, he picked up the phone and called the coroner. "Dr. Malory, this is Detective Carter. Have you heard anything about Mr. Blodger's odd heart attack?"

There was a long pause as Dr. Malory decided what to offer in answer. "I was getting impatient one day and called the CDC. It was weird. They did not know anything about the location of the body. They had no records on it and did not remember anything. His parents are frantic as they can't have the funeral without a body. So then, I called Dr. White. I asked him if he had heard."

260

At this point, he stopped speaking for almost thirty-seconds before he continued. "He said it was classified and he was not at liberty to discuss it."

"What on earth does that mean?" James was really annoyed that everything always seemed five times more complicated than it needed to be.

"Well, it means a dead end. I don't have any answers for you and unless the information is released, which is doubtful, we will have to close the case unsolved. Death by unknown cause."

James thanked him and then looked at Haley. "This is very suspicious. They are playing it way too close to the vest. They have classified the information and Dr. White won't even talk about it."

"James, I don't like this. And I am not going to make you happy, but my gut tells me that it is too coincidental. Jadyn's work is classified and now this is classified. By whom? Who has this much pull to shut everyone up?"

James smiled. He knew that Haley always rushed to conclusions without proof and although her instincts were good, she would not do herself or him any good dreaming up conspiracies without proof. "Well, for one thing, we don't know if the one classification is related at all with the other. As you pointed out, we don't know who is doing the classifying or why. We will have to establish that first before we take the next step… finding out who it protects."

"I will start seeing if I can determine who is doing some of this classifying. I can't imagine that would be a secret."

"Good. Meanwhile, I will get prepared for my date. I will keep an eye on her and see if I can get any information from her."

"Did it ever occur to you that she might have the same idea?" Haley asked with a chagrinned look on her comely face.

"Absolutely! Won't it be fun to parry with a genius?" James grinned as he stood up from his desk and turned to leave.

Haley was not so sure it would be fun. IF Jadyn was the murderer, she could do the same to her partner, anytime at all. She obviously had found a way to be elsewhere when the victim dies.

Hmm… James is right. I can't condemn her without more proof than the fact that she is working on classified research. Most cancer research was classified or secured until it was patented. Haley decided to delve more into the company she worked for at that moment. Although it had a commercial name, who knew anything about it.

Haley decided she would do more computer work on that first, then see who paid the bills—was it publicly funded or privately. Often, if you chased the money, you found out more than you might if you asked direct questions. Smiling at her plan, Haley started her campaign to find proof of culpability and motive.

James unlocked his front door, speaking out loud to let Kimble know who was invading the premises. Kimble was obviously happy to see James earlier than usual on a work day, and he showed his appreciation by leaping up when James patted his thigh, inviting Kimble to jump. If Kimble was miffed by something, he would turn and walk away. But today, he was very happy to oblige. It amazed James that Kimble could perform such tricks without sight. He figured that Kimble's other senses were taking over where sight left off.

A man, true to his word, James was waiting for Jadyn as she entered the concourse from her arrival gate. Smiling a welcome, James took her carryon bag from her hand and started to guide her toward baggage claim.

"I don't need to pick up anything at baggage claim. I travel very light and I have some clothing I keep at my mother's home."

James noticed that she almost never said her parent's home or her father's home…always her mother's. "Okay, well let's get going. I am hungry and I have the perfect place picked out for dinner."

They soon were driving through the parking lot and out onto the road, the Camaro humming along with its deep throaty buzz. They made small talk as they had walked, but now that they were in the car, they seemed to mutually decide to ask their questions at the same time. They both were eager to find out what the other knew, but James had to consider how he framed his ideas as he might give it away that they thought it was murder.

"James, have they heard anything out about the heart attack?"

"Well, they do not want to give up any information as of yet. Out of curiosity and because I knew you would be coming in to visit, I called the coroner yesterday. It seems that they no longer have the body at the morgue."

Jadyn held her eyes forward but tried to look surprised. "Did Theo's parents take the body?"

"No, and they are up in arms about it. No, Dr. Malory said the CDC came in and claimed the body." James did not offer any additional details. He sort of hoped that Jadyn would add to this.

"That is odd. Maybe they thought that it was contagious or something along those lines." Jadyn was not going to add anything other than typical observations.

James was not sure if he wanted to tell her what Dr. Malory said about his conversation with Dr. White. However, he had to find out what she knew, if anything; he decided to press on with it. "Yes, Dr. Malory was very confused. He called the CDC and they did not seem to know where the body was or have any records of ever receiving it. Dr. Malory thought that was very strange." James decided that was as much as he would offer at the moment. "Mr. Blodger's parents are very, very upset and causing quite a stir locally. They have gone to the papers and complained about every section of our police force and coroner's office. Yay!" He made a face to accent his befuddlement.

Jadyn remained quiet up until this point, but then decided it was a good time to ask, "What do you think happened? Is there anything you can do?"

"Well, we did not really have a reason to keep this as an open case of any kind, since the coroner could not rule it one way or another. My chief wants us to move on, and I am not sure what else we can do without a body or a diagnosis. No teeth to our bite, so to speak."

Jadyn relaxed noticeably and James wondered why. She was so beautiful and he was having a very hard time thinking of her in any other way but as a remarkable date. They continued on in companionable silence for about thirty minutes, until they pulled off the highway into a medium size town. Jadyn did not recognize it, but the detective seemed to know exactly where he was going. Not long afterward, they were sitting comfortably in a very nice restaurant deciding on what to eat.

James decided he would hold off any questions or speculations until after they had had at least one cocktail. Perhaps her guard would come down and he could get information from her about her company. He was as curious about it as he was about her.

When they had finished a few stuffed mushrooms and two very strong daiquiris, James decided he would ask her a few questions. "What is the name of the company you work for? I know you told me before, but I am at a loss to recall it."

"Hmm… I don't remember giving it to you. It is called The Dexler Corporation."

"Oh, well, that sounds fancy. Do you like it?"

"I love my job. It gives me a feeling that I am accomplishing something for humanity. The company itself has a lot of regulations, but that does not bother me, as what I do requires written protocols, which is almost the same thing."

James continued chewing, digesting her words as thoroughly as the hors d'oeuvre he was eating. He loved how her eyes seem to light up when she talked about her work. She truly was an enthusiast. He did not want to interrupt her train of thought, so he continued to chew and smile, nodding in all the appropriate places.

"I was originally in California, but they transferred me. My boss out there was ah… a jack ass. He loved to claim subordinate's work as his own and intimidate those who would not give up their ideas and work to him. It did not work very well with me. The company transferred me to help me avoid his interference."

James was very hopeful at this point. If he got a name, he might be able to get a few more juicy details. "Your boss sounds like someone I knew before, in Boston. Every time I would have a hunch about a case and bring in the perp, he would tell my

264

superiors he thought of it and it was he who solved the case. Very annoying, but when you are a junior detective, you can't really do much about it."

Jadyn smiled. He did understand the awkwardness of an overbearing boss who knew how to take advantage of his workers. "My boss tried to get me fired, in order to keep all my work and take credit for it. But the joke is on him; instead of being fired, I was transferred. He does not even know it as of yet."

Still, no names. Nuts! James would have to take a different approach. "Do you miss the West Coast? It is really nice out there, or so I've heard."

"Well, it was beautiful and for the most part, it was a kind of escape for me. I am not complaining, but my home life left something to be desired. My father made things tense and so, when I got a chance to go to school at Berkley, I jumped at it."

James's mind was running at full speed now. He might be able to find out more about her through her Berkley connections. "Did Berkley steer you into your field? Or did you always want to be a... what are you again?"

"Well, I have had a few titles, but I like to think of myself as a Mechanical Biologist."

"That's not confusing... what might that be?" James knew what that sounded like it meant, but he wanted confirmation.

"Well, I more or less find out how biological cells are put together. The mechanics of a cell. They are very mechanical and if treated like ah, oh, say a car, you can find out a lot about how we work as humans. It will make it easier to get our medications into the cells, break into them as it were. At least that is my hope. Eventually, I hope to break up cancer cells, killing them in the process."

Jadyn started eating her entree quietly. She probably had said way too much, but she really liked James and felt very easy with him. He seemed genuinely interested in her. Most men either tried to compete with her with the one up game or were so intimidated by her that they ran at the very first opportunity. She did not fool herself into thinking that this could lead to anything. After all, she was a murderess, but she intended to enjoy it as long as it lasted.

James was amazed that she opened up as much as she had. He was intrigued by her occupation, but he had come to realize that she had the wherewithal to engineer a delayed death, if she was inclined. He was now as suspicious as Haley and heartbroken about it; he really liked Jadyn.

They both continued the meal with light conversation about the differences between Boston and Long Island, Long Island, and California. Fun topics and very benign. Jadyn did not think these dangerous, but James gathered more about her with every sentence. He was a very good listener; however, he felt like a betrayer as he did so. What he was learning would take him down a path he did not want to travel as he was not sure what he was going to do when he arrived at his destination.

The evening passed quickly and James drove Jadyn to her parent's home by ten. It would be a long drive home for him, but it would give him lots of time to decide on his next steps. His chief would not want him to pursue this line on the police force dime and he knew it would require a lot of effort and research. But even if he got absolute proof that Theo could have been murdered by Jadyn, without a body or a coroner's confirmation of death, it probably would do him no good, unless it happened again.

James drove home, mechanically. His mind was swirling around all the possibilities all the while he continued to hope he could see her again. He really did have it bad and he hated to admit it. Kimble would know. Haley would guess. No secrets with those two.

Jadyn was really pleased with the date but thought the information that she had gleaned from James would be useful to Mr. Lambert, whom she called before she went into the house. It was a nice night outside and there was a hint of spring in the air, which was misleading. She sat down on a chair that was located on the porch and prepared for a conversation. It did not seem to matter what time of the day or night that she called Mr. Lambert— he always was available and interested.

266

"Good evening, Jadyn. How was your date?"

Jadyn thought about her answer. She decided to redact some of the information. "Well, it was fun and relaxing. I did find one thing out you should know. I think we should release the body to the family. They are making a royal stink locally and we don't want the papers to get wind of this."

"I will arrange that tonight… minus the heart. He will be flown out by tomorrow and I will call them and personally give them my condolences. They must feel terrible…I know I would." Mr. Lambert sounded like he had a heart, but Jadyn wondered if it was real.

"Great. That was the main thing I learned. He does not seem like he can do any investigating as there is nothing for him to chase. The coroner's report is inconclusive and he is not allowed to open a case without just cause." Jadyn thought that should end Mr. Lambert's queries on the matter, but it did not.

"Your young detective has a partner does he not?" Mr. Lambert asked off-handedly.

"Yes, her name is Haley Jackson. Why?"

"She does not act like there is no case. She is doing a lot of research on this facility, trying to find out about our funding and other such things. She really does not act like she is interested in this as a hobby."

Jadyn did not know how to react to this new information. Was it possible that James had asked her out just to gather evidence or leads? And now they were going to release the body. "Sir, perhaps you could release a coroner's report from the CDC stating that he died of natural causes?" Jadyn knew that this would make it an obvious illicit ploy if it ever came to light, but she had a feeling that Mr. Lambert had run this race before.

"Good idea. I will have one prepared and sent down to Dr. Malory, the local coroner and to the CDC. They will forward it to Dr. White, the cardiologist. That should shut everyone up. They are very much owned by their necessities and closed reports act as a mental stop sign. Right now, that is what we need. After all, he did die of a heart attack." Mr. Lambert smiled and Jadyn could feel his smile through the receiver.

"Good night, Sir. Thank you for all your help with this." It amazed Jadyn that Mr. Lambert could do the things he could do within other agencies.

"Good night to you, Jadyn. You are worth my efforts!"

Both closed the conversation and Jadyn headed into the house. Thomas was already there and he and Rachael were happily going over plans for her new art exhibit in White Plains this upcoming June. Jadyn joined the conversation and soon all three were engrossed in enjoyable plans. Jadyn would help her mother as best she could with her own time constraints.

Later, they wanted to know how her date had progressed and she expounded on the details, leaving out her duplicitous part with Mr. Lambert. She did not like lying but did get a slight rush when she felt as she was a secret agent. She wondered if all of the personnel in Section Eight had such clandestine positions. She also let it slip that she really did like the young detective and that Theo's parents would get the body back in a day or so. Then they could arrange the funeral and she, Thomas, and parents could fly down to attend.

The weekend passed very quickly and Thomas offered Jadyn a ride back to the airport, as she was eager to work on the project. Although they were months away from human trials, at least the legal ones, she could not wait to make the adjustments in the little bots to avoid the clogging in the blood-brain barrier. The human body has so many protective barriers and the challenge is to find ways around them without teaching viruses to do it. Jadyn knew that this one barrier could block cancer trials on brain tumors. But finding the nose-sinus connection to the brain pushed her experiments forward months in advance, maybe even years.

****

Haley reminded James of a wire-haired terrier that his mother had when he was young. When that dog got something into its mind, it would not let go until it had succeeded in doing whatever it wanted. Resilient, tenacious, and smart… James felt very lucky to have her as his partner. The only problem was that she did not understand his feelings for Jadyn. She could not conceive liking or loving a potential suspect.

As he entered the old station, he realized that he felt very comfortable with the smells and lighting that assailed him. Old time bulbs encased in circular globes hung from the ceiling on long, corroded chains. It reminded him of his junior high, which had a similar entranceway. Perhaps this was once an old school. The township would never consider housing their children in such an old building… but their law enforcement officers, well they did not count as much. James smiled at that thought. He was used to being second fiddle to other people, but it amused him to think kindergarten children were better housed than their police force.

Walking over to his desk, he noticed Haley pounding away on her keyboard. "Hey Haley, whatcha up to? Find anything interesting on our cases?"

Without looking up she said, "Yes and No."

"Well, give me the yes first."

Haley stopped typing and reading long enough to look at James's face. She smiled and said, "I bet I know something you don't know…about your girlfriend."

"That would not surprise me. She keeps most information close."

Haley enjoyed stretching out the moment, which in most cases would not have bothered James, but today it seemed to nettle him. "Please, I am tired from all the driving I did Saturday and I have a lot of research to do."

Haley knew that he was not in the mood, so she shifted gears and began. "I was very curious about where Jadyn works."

"So was I, so I asked her."

"Did she tell you?" Haley said raising her eyebrows in a questioning manner.

"Yes, she did. She works for The Dexler Corporation, up near Boston."

Haley grinned at the news, which made James a bit nervous. "Confirmation is always pleasant to get. I figured that out last night."

"What were you doing here last night?"

"Oh, don't worry about that…. I have a link from home to my computer here. I can log in, whenever I need to. My boyfriend is very good at such things."

"Does the Chief know?"

"No, and I would just assume it stay that way." She grinned conspiratorially and continued, "Do you know what the Dexler Corporation really is? Do you know who funds it?"

James held his breath, knowing instinctively that he was not going to like the answer. Haley was entirely too gleeful in her presentation—she must have found something against Jadyn. James's stomach started to knot up. Geez, why doesn't she just come out with it… why does she always have to play these stupid kid games? "No, I have not had a chance to track that yet."

"Government," was her one-word answer. "It is a governmental research facility."

James was not sure how to receive the information. The government was a bit too general. He would have to find out more than that to feel it a danger to Jadyn. "So what? How does that affect our findings?"

"The deeper I dug, and I might add with a great deal of alacrity, the more I got blocked. It would seem that the military is definitely involved, as well and a few agencies." She leaned back into her chair waiting for this new information to sink into James's brain. She did not have long to wait.

"You mean CIA? Military? Stuff like that?"

"Bingo!" She smiled and then suddenly stopped when she realized that it was causing him stress. "That does not mean that Jadyn is a spy or anything. After all, it is just a research group. Maybe they fund cancer research too…"

"Yes, but it also would explain why she does not tell us anything about her company—funny, she always just calls it The Company, but never names it. Somehow I don't see them doing research for cancer… at least not solely."

Haley wanted to relieve some of the tension that had flown into the conversation. "James, what did you find out on your date? Anything of interest?"

"Well, now that I know what you found out, I can only add to it. She told me what she did, more or less. She is a Mechanical Biologist. She studies cells and how they work, mechanically. She is working on a method for killing cancer cells."

"I don't suppose she elaborated on the subject?" Haley was very intrigued by this idea.

"No. I was surprised she told me what she did for them. She seems to be trusting me a bit more. Oh, yes, she did say something about her old boss in California. He was trying to steal her idea, so the company transferred her to protect her work." He crinkled his face while he thought about what she had said. "Why would they not just kick the guy out? Why was she transferred? And secretly. She said her old boss does not even know they transferred her. He thinks she was fired."

"Secrets within the company?" Haley was ready to investigate full force on this new information. "Where was her old company located?"

"I am not sure. She went to school at Berkley, maybe they know where she went from there. Could be a start. Our only problem is that this is not a viable case. The Chief will have our head if we don't work our other cases on his dime."

Haley went back to work on the keyboard and said, "I tell you what—you work the cases and I will work the noncases." She smiled and winked at him.

"Well, only for the rest of today. I will need you to help me with the other two murders we have to solve. At least they are normal, gunshot murders. The perp did not try to melt them." James sat down at his desk and started reading the statements of the witnesses involved with their immediate cases.

Haley kept digging and digging. She finally accessed some of the Berkley records and started looking into Mechanical Biology, which was not listed. Hmm. Well, biology and engineering were obvious, but combined? "James, have you ever heard of anything dealing with Biomechanics?"

"No, but try nanotechnology. I heard that mentioned somewhere, although I don't remember where. Maybe that is something new. I know I don't know much about it."

Haley continued to look into the Berkley curriculum and when she saw the reference to nanotechnology, she checked out the head of the department—a Professor Bates. She decided to give this man a call. Perhaps he would remember Jadyn from a class. She called the main Berkley number and was eventually given a different number to speak to someone in the science building. As she waited to be connected to the Professor's office, she thought about what she was going to say. She did not want them to think that Jadyn was a fugitive or suspect in anything. She decided that she would say she was investigating a missing person's case and Jadyn was someone that they wanted to speak to.

Although Professor Bates sounded like a very nice gentleman, he did not have any information to give her regarding Jadyn. He did not know where she was working currently. Perhaps if she contacted Jadyn's parents, somewhere on the East Coast, she would have better luck.

Haley knew the run around when she heard it. But since she was playing around in California, she decided to look into the Dexler Corporation to see if it had any California divisions? Again, she was rewarded with some information, but nothing of substance. The company was listed as a technical research group and nothing more. Again with the subterfuge. More digging. More dead ends. Haley finally gave up and decided to give it a rest. She joined James in the other cases, feeling more confident that they would catch those murderers. But she still had a bad feeling about the noncase of Theodore Blodger.

Helping Hand

The hand that guides the path of life,
Grows longer and stronger every day.
It knows the direction of the flow,
And it will guide you on your way.

But just because you find your life,
Headed down a comfortable path.
Remember how you arrived there,
That unseen hand will twist in the last.

Chapter XV

"Mr. Lambert, this is Dr. Jeffries."

"Yes, how are you, Doctor? How is the weather out there?"

"Oh, fine. I will be brief. There has been a development here in the San Rafael Division. I don't know if you know a Dr. Farnot, but he is in charge of our Biology Department."

"I have never met the man, but his reputation I have heard."

"Yes, well, that being said, I thought I would let you know that he has discovered some information about Jadyn Martyn that could lead to an issue for you."

Mr. Lambert never worried about issues if he heard about them in advance. "What kind of information?"

"Dr. Farnot discovered somehow that Jadyn was transferred to your division, secretly. He is on the warpath, and I am not sure why. He always wanted to work at your facility, but this seems more personal. If I did not know better, he is acting like he is on a vendetta."

"Well, I don't see how that can cause us any issues? What is he saying or doing that makes you think it will be a problem?"

"For some reason of which I am not privy, he has been talking with police." Dr. Jeffries did not know why, but he was under no illusions about the nature of the work that was done at the East Coast Plant. If anyone started asking questions, things had to be handled quickly and quietly.

"What Police are you referring to?" Mr. Lambert needed a starting point.

"The Long Island Police. I think it is a division of the Suffolk County Police." Dr. Jeffries declared.

"Did you get a name? Or a department?"

"No, but Dr. Farnot seemed very pleased with himself after he had spoken to them. He informed me that they had contacted him regarding Ms. Martyn and that he knew what she was up to. He looked too smug and I know he is up to something." Dr. Jeffries paused before continuing, "I thought I would give you a heads up.

I will try to find out more, but to be honest, I don't want him to know that I am giving it any attention whatsoever. It would make him too happy."

"Thank you, Dr. Jeffries. I will look into the matter, although I can't imagine why the police would be interested in Ms. Martyn." Mr. Lambert was an expert in deception and could lie with the best of them.

After the phone call with Dr. Jeffries, Mr. Lambert pushed the intercom button and asked Burt to come into his office. Burt came in immediately and Mr. Lambert had him sit down. "Burt, we seem to have an issue coming our way."

"Oh?" Burt said, eyebrows raised in question.

"Yes, it would seem that Ms. Martyn is being investigated by the Long Island Police. I can't imagine why, but I would like to you find out what is going on, if you would… confidentially. I don't want Ms. Martyn bothered at this juncture of her trials. I am sure it is nothing, but I would like to know ahead of time as her previous boss on the West Coast, who would like to cause her trouble, has gotten wind of it. He is very pleased about something and acting like he would be causing her trouble. Jealousy I expect."

"No problem, Sir. I will get right on this. Do you have any names or departments that were involved?"

"No, Burt, I am sorry, but her former boss did not tell anyone at this point. But I would start with Haley Jackson and her partner, James Carter."

Burt rose and headed for the door. "I will get right on this. I should be able to determine more by this afternoon."

****

James went home that evening with a dull headache. Although his current cases were progressing very well, and they already had made an arrest on one of them, he still could not shake the nagging feeling that there was another case he should be investigating. The Blodger killing. It was called a natural death. How on earth could your heart melting or whatever it did, be considered a natural death? Made no sense at all.

Kimble greeted James at the door and then went immediately to his bowl, expecting super. Once he was fed, James changed his suit for a pair of running pants and sneakers. He decided he would go for a run, prior to eating supper. He had to do some thinking. He told Kimble he would return, but Kimble was more interested in his dinner than James's run, so he merely looked in the direction of James's voice and went back to eating.

As James started his run, he decided to mentally look at all the evidence that they had on the Blodger case… noncase:

1.   He died at home alone.
2.   He had no known heart issues.
3.   His only contacts were his girlfriend and coworkers.
4.   He was suspected to have abused his wife.
5.   He lost his wife in a boating accident.
6.   He had taken lessons for sailing for over a month but claimed to   not know much about sailing.
7.   He had bought a sailboat.
8.   Jadyn Martyn was a Mechanical Biologist working for the government.
9.   She studied cell behavior and nanotechnology.
10. They had no proof that Jadyn had seen Blodger just before he died.
11. Blodger's heart melted or something odd. Definitely odd cell behavior.
12. The CDC was pulled in and then the body was not where anyone could find it.
13. Mysteriously, the body was sent home to allow the parents to bury it.

James was not sure what all this added up to, but he knew that all of this led back to Theo Blodger and what he had done before he died.   Haley had found out that Blodger had taken sailing lessons and that he was a very able sailor, considering the length of time he had been at it. And he probably was cheating on his wife prior to her accident, but there was no proof of that either. James

276

did not like conjecture as much as Haley did. He only liked solid evidence. Conjecture could be used to give you new direction only when the facts did not tell you anything.

He finished his run and headed back into his apartment. Kimble was sitting in his usual guard post in front of the door. James wondered if he sat there all day. No way of knowing at this point. He jumped into the shower and after dressing, decided on calling for a Pizza. He wanted to think, not cook. "Kimble, how about a little pizza tonight?"

Kimble licked his jowls as if he understood and James made the call. He grabbed a clipboard and tablet and sat down on the sofa. Kimble joined him and soon they were discussing the evidence in the Blodger Case. Well, James discussed and Kimble listened and made noises at the appropriate times. If James asked him his opinion, Kimble would either shake his head in a no attitude or would look up with his poor blind eyes and make a soft chirping sound. It always amazed James that the cat could actually seem to carry on a conversation when he knew the cat was only responding to his own voice... well maybe.

When the pizza arrived, they both enjoyed the nice hot slices of pepperoni pizza and Kimble seemed to lose interest in James's scribbling on his tablet. Food was always number one in Kimble's heart or so it seemed.

Although there seemed no rational explanation, he would have to give up on the Blodger case. Jadyn was a beautiful woman and he loved being with her, but for now, he would have to let it go. She did not seem like a murderer and the government had her back as far as could be told.

After chasing the pizza down with a beer, James and Kimble retired for the night. He resigned himself to the fact that he would have a cold case, never opened, never solved. It left a bitter taste in his mouth and he fell into a fitful sleep.

****

Burt knocked quietly on Mr. Lambert's door. It was about ten o'clock that night and he had the information that Mr. Lambert had requested regarding the police investigations. "Sir," he began. "Ms. Martyn had a twin sister, Margot Blodger, who died accidentally in a sailing accident last year. She was sailing with her husband and he claimed a rogue wave hit the boat and knocked the boon off to the side, hitting Mrs. Blodger into the water. Her body was not recovered for several days and finally washed up on shore in Norwalk, Connecticut."

"Although it was pronounced an accident, a Detective Carter took it upon himself to do some investigation into her death. Apparently, he was not satisfied it was an accident, but he was never able to prove murder. He and his partner Haley Jackson seemed to give up on that idea until Mr. Blodger died of heart failure of some kind, this past winter."

"This is where it gets a little complicated. Although the local coroner could not say what the actual cause of death was, the CDC got involved and then the body disappeared for a time and then was returned to the family for burial." Burt slowed his dialog at this point to make it a little clearer.

"That detective and his partner seem to be looking into Mr. Blodger's death and researching…the Dexler Corp." He seemed puzzled at this, but not because it was unusual that anyone would look into their company, but that they did it in connection with one of their employees.

"Well, that answers my question." He did not volunteer why he wanted to know and Burt knew not to ask. "I will take care of this. Please call Ms. Martyn in for a conference, with her team. I will let you know when, after I make a few calls."

Burt left the office and Mr. Lambert sat quietly deciding the best way to handle the situation. Then it came to him in a flash! He smiled happily to himself as he decided to make some phone calls in the morning. He had a very wide range of influence and would utilize it at this time.

****

Haley looked at the thick gold-colored envelopes that were on both her desk and James's. She could not imagine what they were about, but she decided she was going to wait for her partner to come into the office before she opened it. No use getting excited over nothing. She did not have to wait long.

"What's this?" James asked as he sat down and picked up the fancy envelope.

"I don't know, but I have one too," she held up her envelope and smiled.

"Well, we may as well open them. It is too fancy to be a pink slip," he said grinning all the while.

They both opened their envelope and read quietly. James was the first to speak, "Well, what do you think of that?"

"I don't know what to think. I am not sure that it is real." Then Haley looked up to see if anyone in the room seemed to be paying any undue attention to them. No one was watching, so she focused back on the large card from inside the envelope. It read: Dear Ms. Jackson. It has come to our attention that your outstanding skills and talents would fit in very well with our team in New Orleans. We would like to extend an invitation for you to join us next week for a get together to discuss the possibilities. It was signed by the Bureau Chief of the New Orleans FBI.

James reiterated "Well, what do you think of that?"

Haley looked up to see his face going through various expressions. He did not know why, but the card inside did not seem to be real: Dear Mr. Carter. After studying your solved-case track record, we are hereby offering you a position with our Washington, DC branch. We would like you to join us as soon as possible to discuss the pertinent details.   Sincerely, Bureau Commander-Washington, DC FBI.

Both were speechless. Haley had applied to the FBI long before but was told she needed more field experience before she could re-apply. However, James had never applied. He did not have the interest needed to become an agent. He liked working in his own back yard, so to speak. He had not been interested in gallivanting all over the country, sleeping out of hotels, and eating takeout more often than was good for you.

Both were shocked at the offers. Haley was the first to ask, "What does yours say?"

"The Washington Bureau of the FBI is looking to recruit me. Interesting."

"New Orleans for me," Haley offered.

"What do you think precipitated all this?" James wondered out loud.

"I don't know and although I love working with you, I will go to hear what they have to say. Just for curiosity's sake." Haley smiled at James when she said this.

"I think it is very obliging of them to send us open-ended plane tickets. Do you suppose they think it is a done deal? That would be a bit presumptive."

Haley looked like she was going to jump out of her chair. Her eyes were wide open with anticipation and she could not wait to set up an appointment. She said, "It is a done deal as far as I am concerned, whatever their reason. I have wanted to work for the bureau for a long time."

James put everything back into his envelope and taking it in his hand, arose and walked toward the Chief's office. Knocking, he entered and asked, "Chief, do you have a minute?"

"Ah, I knew I would see you or Haley sooner or later today. Come in and have a seat."

"Sir, did you know about this invitation from the FBI?"

"Yes and no. I knew they had an opportunity for you, but they did not share what it was about. Are they recruiting?"

"It would appear that way." James seemed amazed that the Chief did not know. He thought it was bad form to recruit from one force to work on another, without notifying the Head of the Department.

"Well, I am not surprised. You two have been very successful these last few years and that type of notoriety travels within agencies." The Chief looked at James kindly and continued, "Of all my men, you deserve it the most. Do you intend to go?"

280

"I intend to go, for a look-see. I can't get it in my head as to why now."

"My advice son: never look a gift horse in the mouth when it is to your advantage."

James smiled and asked, "Would you go, Sir?"

"In a heartbeat!" The Chief did not want the young detective to hesitate out of loyalty or fears.

"Very well, we would like to check it out. We have the one case wrapped up and going to trial. The second murder will…."

"Be given to one of the other detectives." The Chief had anticipated this obstacle and already had it covered. He wanted to have them leave as soon as they could arrange it. No use hemming and hawing around. The Chief was a doer type, not a talker type. Besides, the FBI gentleman, a Mr. Lambert, made it clear that he was to encourage his young detectives to take these opportunities seriously.

James got up and said, "I will let Haley know what you have said. She will let you know when she is ready to go to the meeting with the Bureau." He turned and walked out the door, more interested in the Chief's rousing support of the venture than in the timing of the request. He also wondered what he would tell Kimble. If he did relocate, it would mean Kimble would have an entirely new home to get to know, new people to get to know, new schedule to his life. Scary things for a blind cat, or so James assumed. But that was getting ahead of everything.

He went back out to his desk, sat down and looked at the envelope in his hand.

"So what did the Chief say?" Haley did not want to wait for James to offer.

"He said to go for it, more or less."

"Great!" Then Haley hesitated, "Are you going to go? To see what they want, I mean. Not leave, just check it out."

"Yes, if for no other reason than to find out, if I can, why now?"

Haley sat back in her chair and said, "Yes, it is very interesting, the timing I mean. But what the heck. Who cares?"

"Well, since we have decided to check these offers out, I guess we may as well move forward on them." He picked up his phone and touched in the number that was listed on the card. It did not take long and he had firmed up his appointment. When he hung up, he saw Haley still finalizing her meeting details. He smiled at her enthusiasm for the opportunity. He was glad for her. It would be amazing for her. For him, well, he was not so sure.

Back to work on his last outstanding case. If he was to turn it over to another detective, he may as well try to get all the notes in order and in the computers. He did not know it, but he was about to embark on a new adventure—one of which even Kimble would enjoy.

Turning a Page

Your life is written in a book,
Recorded for all of history to read.
If you waste your time worrying,
Your chapters will be left in need.

So bring joy whenever you can,
Don't cloud the room with smoke.
Life has a way of burning,
And on your choices, you may choke.

Chapter XVI

Christmas had arrived again right at the same time as it did the year before. Jadyn, Thomas, and Rachael were busy prepping the Christmas feast and Charles was sitting on the computer, chasing stock prices all over the boards. It was Christmas Day, but not in Tokyo. Once the meal was prepared, he would enjoy the part he played in eating and critiquing of the food, table appearance, and desserts.

Christmas they spent at the Long Island home and New Years was with Charles's parents in Connecticut. Christmas Eve, Rachael and her grown children would get together and sing carols and drink eggnog. Charles was still in the City and came home late that night, conveniently missing that get together. He was not sentimental at all.

On Christmas Day, while working in the kitchen, Thomas was telling the two ladies about one of his social work cases. He was very disturbed by it and Jadyn was not sure why this one stuck out so very far above the rest.

"I am so frustrated! She does not seem to realize that he will kill her." Thomas spouted his declaration almost to himself.

"Thomas, what makes you think he will kill her?" Jadyn wanted to know.

"He is not afraid to do so. See, sometimes the abusers can be intimidated into behaving somewhat decently, but this guy," Thomas shook his head. "This guy thinks it is funny to threaten the authorities, the hospital staff, and his wife. He seems amused by it all."

"He almost sounds sociopathic, Thomas. No conscience at all and not able to be rationalized with on this subject." Rachael knew something about this subject.

"You are right, Mother." Thomas agreed. "He has no moral compass and does not want one."

Jadyn kept fairly quiet at that moment. It sounded too close to her sister's situation and she did not want to point that out.

Thomas had seen so many abuse cases, but this one had him very concerned.

The Christmas dinner went on as usual and the New Years Affair, as Jadyn always thought of it, was carried off beautifully. The only part of the holidays that Jadyn liked was the togetherness they felt when wrapping presents together or working in the kitchen. She missed seeing Grandpa and Grandma Dickerson on Christmas Eve but reminisced about passed visits with her siblings.

After the holidays were completed, it was time to test her newest little bots. Later on in the week, Thomas called her, upset and sputtering, "He killed her. I know he did, but no one can prove it!"

"Hello, Thomas. What are you talking about?"

"That woman I told you about. The one with two kids and the nutty husband! At Christmas…remember?"

Jadyn did recall the conversation but did not know how to respond. "What happened? How?"

Thomas spoke into the phone so loudly that Jadyn thought he was yelling at her, "They just found her body, along with her two kids up in a quarry. They were cut up in pieces and the coroner guessed that they had been there a while. They cannot pinpoint when they died, because they were submerged in bags in pieces in the cold water." Thomas stopped long enough to catch his breath. "She is dead. Her kids are dead. And that smiling rotter just sits in his house acting as if he really gives a crap!"

Jadyn did not even hesitate, as this was too close to Margot's situation. She could not stand to hear it. "Where did all this take place, Thomas?"

"Near Lake George, in upper New York," Thomas said, a little more quietly. His energy was waning and he sounded like it had exhausted him.

"What is the guy's name? What is the name of the family members?" Jadyn seemed unusually curious.

"His name was Jake Flanners. His wife was Martha. I don't know the kid's names off hand, but is it important?"

"No, just curious. I am sorry Thomas. I really am. I wish you could have done something about it, but you have to work within the parameters of your position. It is not your fault." Jadyn continued to talk Thomas down from his initial fury. She did not want him to get any closer to the situation. Jadyn had a plan. "Thomas, are you going to the funeral?"

"Yes, I feel I should; I feel that I have failed her."

"I will go with you. Just let me know the details and I will make arrangements at work and join you." Yes, Jadyn had a plan.

****

"Detective Carter, please come in," the Bureau Chief invited. "Please, have a seat." The Chief walked around his large cluttered desk and plopped down abruptly in his own seat, not waiting to see if James complied. "How was your flight? How are your accommodations?"

"Everything is fine, Sir. I am curious to ……" James started.

"Yes, I know. You are curious as to why you are here." The Chief anticipated his questioning.

"Well, yes not to put too fine a point on it."

"James, your name was brought to my attention by another member of my team. He seems to feel that you would be a great fit within our organization." He stopped and more or less changed direction, "You know you have quite a reputation for solving the unsolvable."

James turned a shade darker on his face. He was a humble man and did not like to bring up any past exploits. "Well, Sir, I had an excellent partner."

"Yes, but you are the one known as the Iceman, are you not?" The Chief smiled while he was trying to make a point.

"Well, yes. I do enjoy a good mystery… no matter how old it is." James was beginning to get the idea.

"I want you on our team. I have cases that we have been struggling with for months. To be honest, it will save us a tremendous amount of taxpayer dollars if you come into the department and have even half of the success that you have had in the past."

James sat back in his chair to digest what was being told to him. He was intrigued by the request but still wanted to know who had suggested his name. "Sir that does sound inviting; however, I still would like to know who suggested my name." James looked down at his hands and then back to the Chief. "I am really just curious. I don't know anyone down here that I know about…how would they have heard about me?"

"Frankly, I don't remember who it was, but I can try to find out if you like. In the meantime, here is the offer we are making." The Chief slid a large vanilla envelope across the desk to the detective.

James opened it and read carefully. He looked up, rather amazed at the offer. "Sir, you will pay for my relocation, company car, and a bonus for each solved case? Isn't that unusual?"

"Well, I would not say unusual. We have been known to entice new blood this way on occasion, especially when in the long run, we expect you to save us a bundle from our budget. I feel it is an investment well worth making." He seemed pleased with the detective's reaction to the offer and sat back, noticeably relaxing. "Please keep the details of your offer confidential. We obviously did not offer this to everyone."

"When would you like all this to take place?" James was actually starting to warm up to the opportunity. He loved working old cases. He had a unique perspective that seemed to be able to pick out missed facts or overlooked details that were of immense value. And, he did love a good mystery.

"Well, we were hoping within a few weeks. Do you have any open cases that you need to attend to prior to leaving?" The Chief asked this question with what appeared to be mild interest.

"Nothing I can't pass to someone else in the department." James sat on the verge of a dilemma, wanting to take the position and wanting to know why now, why him.

As if he could read James's mind, the Chief said, "Why don't you go back to your hotel and sleep on it. You can give me your answer tomorrow. After all, this is a big change for you. I don't want you to feel pressured."

Pressured? This kind of a decision and in one night... no pressure. James found the whole offer wondrous and tantalizing. But to decide it in one night, well that would require a lot of thought.

The Chief rose from his chair and offered his hand to the detective, "I hope you will come to DC and give us the opportunity to see you in action." He smiled and escorted James to the door. He handed his personal business card to James and said, "Let me know if there is anything else you might need to make your decision."

"Thank you, Sir. I will let you know my decision as soon as I can. It is a wonderful opportunity, but I want to make sure it is the right one for me." What James did not add was and for Kimble.

James headed back to his hotel room to change before he went to dinner. He had more than just a decision to make. He wanted to speak with Haley. She was due to see the New Orleans Bureau Chief soon and James was interested in the offer and information that she would get during her interview. When he got into his room, he decided to call Kimble before he changed.

Although Kimble could not answer the phone, James would often call him and leave a message on the answering machine. Kimble would get freaked out by the phone ringing, but James hoped that once he heard his voice while it was recording on the answering machine, he would relax and know that James was coming home. After he left his message for Kimble, he changed out of his suit and into jeans and a sweatshirt. A run would give him time to think about everything that had transpired over the last few weeks.

The hotel he had been situated in was near the Potomac. A beautiful pathway led quietly along its waterways, allowing passersby to see the activities on the water. Various collegiate teams, rowing in perfect unison practiced for upcoming races. It was gorgeous and very relaxing. James felt not thinking was more relaxing. He knew that if he just relaxed, his decision would come to him, quite naturally. He merely needed to take his mind off of the subject.

Even though he was determined to not think about the DC Bureau offer, his mind wandered back to the timing of the offer and to Jadyn. Could his suspicions and the case/noncase have anything to do with this? That is really reaching, he thought. After all, he had not verbalized any of his thoughts to his Chief or to anyone other than Haley. So how would anyone know?

When he finished his run, he went back to the room to shower and change. He called Haley on the chance that she was still at the office. "Hey, Haley, how is it going?"

"Oh, that is my question, James, how did your meeting go?" Haley was dying to know all about it.

"Well, it certainly was interesting. I am not at liberty to discuss details, but they did make me an offer to come and work at the DC Bureau."

"Wow!" Haley's enthusiasm always superseded her regard for whomever she was speaking to at the time. "Do you plan on taking it?"

"Unknown at this moment. I have to make my mind up and they gave me a whole day to do it."

"One day?" Haley's amazement came through the receiver as clearly as if she were standing next to James.

"Yes. I could not find out how they heard of me, but apparently, they need someone to work on cold cases or any cases that they are stuck on."

"Ah, the Iceman cometh," Haley jokingly quoted a Batman Movie she had seen. "They must have heard your marvelous reputation from somewhere."

"Apparently. When do you leave for your interview?"

"Tonight. I will get in a little late, but I don't meet with the Chief down there until two pm tomorrow. I will be able to relax and eat pie, while I wait." She smiled at her joke, knowing the hotel that they had provided for her contained a swimming pool and a gymnasium. She could work off any pie rampages that she would venture into during this visit.

"Well, I will be back to the office by the time you finish with your meeting. Give me a call, before you leave for home. I will be interested in anything you can glean from their people. You are good at prying information."

"Okay, boss. I will let you know," she answered, and then added, "Say hi to Kimble for me."

James decided to drive into the city to look around for a nice restaurant. He had time on his hands and it would be fun to see the sights at night in the city. He always wanted to photograph the Washington Monument and the White House at night. They would make marvelous screen savers. Maybe he would even visit the Lincoln Memorial. So much to see.

James already knew what he had decided to do, but not for the reasons that the Bureau Chief would suspect. He had the entire night to plan on what he wanted to say, and so it was a very relaxed James that returned to the hotel room that night. He called Kimble once again and offered a lengthy goodnight. It did not take James long to fall asleep. He now had a new direction for his life and new tools that would be at his disposal.

****

"Haley, how did your meeting go?" James was back in the office waiting impatiently for Haley's call.

"Overwhelming. I can't get over how strapped for personnel that division seems to be. They are stretched so thin, that they need to recruit the best that they can get as soon as possible." She waited to organize her thoughts then continued, "I have been offered a nice position, James, and I think I will take it."

"That's great, Haley!" James was genuinely pleased for his young partner but wondered if she truly wanted to leave the area. He knew she was ambitious, but he did not know if she was experienced enough for the big times. He did not want to dampen

290

her enthusiasm, so he asked, "Did you find out how they got your name?'

"Yes.   A detective I used to work with was the one who recommended me.   Apparently, he was recruited a few weeks before I was summoned down to see them.   They must have been looking for other recruits and decided to get recommendations from within."

That sounded very logical to James but a bit convenient; however, he kept his peace. "So, when do they want you?"

Haley gave a little laugh, "Yesterday! They are really desperate. I will be home tonight, late.   I will give the Chief my notice tomorrow and see when he feels he can release me."   Then she stopped talking and realized that she might have offended her partner/boss. "James—I have loved working with you and I have learned so very much about the investigative process. Although I will hate to leave, I can't turn down the offer. It is just too good."

Too good to be true ran through James's mind. Both of these offers were too good to be true, but his Chief's advice ran through his mind, 'Don't look that gift horse in the mouth.' He decided to keep all his suspicions to himself, and merely said, "Great! I am proud of you. I will see you in the office when you get back and we can close off our cases as soon as the Chief allows."

****

It was indeed a rapid change to James's and Kimble's lives. The new apartment that the Bureau had secured for James, as part of his package, was just outside of the City, within easy driving, if you could ever say the Beltway was easy. Kimble was confused by all the noise as they drove to their new apartment, but he was soon prowling around the apartment with all the curiosity of a two-year-old child.

The Bureau seemed to have Kimble in mind when they had picked this apartment. James was not sure if or how they would know about Kimble, but everything was placed in such a way as to invite him to investigate, but not get hurt. No blocked crawling spaces behind things. No long hallways. No noise from the surrounding apartments to frighten Kimble; they did not know that Kimble was fearless when hearing noises that were of human origin. Yes, it was a great choice and James was delighted.

The apartment itself was furnished and it looked as if the plastic coverings had just been removed from the sofa and chairs. If they were not new, they certainly gave the appearance of it. The bedroom sported a king-size bed with two dressers, one tall and one long. The kitchen was a type of galley, with everything placed conveniently for use. The living room and dining room were both furnished in a simple modern taste. James thought that he could not have asked for something more to his liking.

Kimble seemed to like the apartment as much as James did. He did not exhibit any fear as he smelled and felt his way around into all of the different rooms. It was not long and he knew exactly where all of his personal items were housed—especially his food bowl. After two days, he acted as if he had always been in this apartment.

A note was passed under James's door the second day he was there. Animal Services Offered. The number was one located in DC, so James gave it a ring. The woman who answered was pleased to answer all of James's questions and gave him several references, a few of which belonged to people at the Bureau. Unfortunately, travel was a necessity in this new endeavor of his and he had no illusions that he could care for Kimble when he was on a case. The woman arranged to come over and meet with James the next day. He would need someone fairly soon and it would be marvelous if this worked out. But it would be entirely up to Kimble. He would have to approve his newly hired help.

The young woman arrived at exactly the time arranged. James was still unpacking his kitchen and was glad for a break in the action. When he answered the door, Kimble was by his side standing in his usual, menacing stance—back up, fur raised and mouth open in a growl.

The young woman came in and after a quick glance at the puffed up furball, smiled and introduced herself to James, "Hello, I am Jennifer Dancing."

James started this new meeting in his usual tongue-tied way. "Hello, I am James Carter," was all he managed.

The woman was slight in build and seemed to have confidence oozing out of every pore of her being. Jet black hair and a beautiful dark tan, she seemed very much the outdoor type. But her blue eyes caught James's attention. She looked native American, but for her eyes. Well, you could not tell nowadays. "Yes, well, won't you come in?" Then looking down to see how his puffed up friend was doing, he was amazed at the transition that Kimble had made. He no longer looked like the imitation of a puffer fish. Instead, he sat quietly next to James's leg, at attention… as if he was planning to inspect the troops.

"Please don't mind Kimble. He is my guard dog, so-to-speak." James smiled and led her into the living room and offered a chair. As she sat down, putting her purse on the floor, Kimble walked over to her and cautiously started his inspection. "You'll have to forgive Kimble, but he is blind and is a bit wary of all strangers. Once he gets to know you, I am sure that he will be a completely different cat." James stated this more in hopes than in assuredness.

"Your cat is not really blind. He merely does not use his eyes to see." This profound statement caught James off guard.

"Well, I suppose you are right. But however he does it, he does it with alacrity." James was hoping to sound as profound as Jennifer. "So tell me, what kind of services do you offer?" James realized that this was phrased awkwardly so he reiterated, "Ah, I mean pet services."

Jennifer smiled at his stammering and handed him a brochure that she had brought in her handbag. James read the brochure and asked, "How many people do you employ? Are they vetted? What kind of measures do you take to protect your clients?"

"I have three full-time employees that have been with me since I started doing this about five years ago. They are fully vetted as you phrase it, and bonded also."

"Do you assign one person to a pet or do they change around based on need?"

Jennifer knew what he wanted to know…who will be taking care of my pet? "I will be taking care of Kimble. He is a very unusual cat and I think I am the one he will accept the most easily." She looked down at Kimble, but all that was visible was a tail sticking out of her handbag. Kimble had crawled into the bag to investigate it with all the effort that he could muster. When he finished, he jumped out of the bag and sat on the floor, next to Jennifer's legs, leaning up against them while he chewed something.

James said, "Amazing. He never gets friendly with strangers this quickly." Then James realized Kimble was chewing and asked, "What is he eating?"

"Oh, it is a cat treat. Purely organic and wholesome. I put a few in the bottom of my bag before I came into your apartment. I knew you had a cat, and they just love finding ill-begotten gains when they can." She smiled and the confidence radiated off her person and into James. He knew then and there he would hire her. As a matter of fact, he was thinking of adopting her.

"Well, that sounds very good. Your service comes highly recommended and Kimble seems to like you. I will have to show you how to enter the apartment—it has to be done a certain way or his behavior reverts back to prehistoric times." James was obviously pleased with that and he smiled at the cat who seemed to be quietly listening to everything they were saying.

Jennifer spent another hour with Kimble and James. James repeated her name to Kimble many times so he would recognize it. She also repeated, "It's me Kimble, Jennifer, Kimble." To display his trust in Jennifer, he jumped up in her lap curling up in a ball. James was amazed and said so…but secretly, he was a little jealous. He felt like doing the same thing. She was a remarkable young woman and he wanted to get to know her a little more after he got settled.

When she left, he continued with his kitchen arrangements and was ready to order takeout. He was going to try one of the local Chinese restaurants and would pick it up. He preferred to eat at home with Kimble, who loved Chinese. After he left the little restaurant, which was within walking distance of his apartment, he picked up a newspaper from a newspaper box. Slinging it under his arm, he walked contentedly back to his apartment.

"Kimble, it's me," he called out before opening the door. He knew he would have to get Jennifer a key, as he would never know when he would have to take off abruptly. He felt confident that she would know how to handle most of Kimble's little foibles. After setting down the large bag containing the most wonderful smelling food, he went into the kitchen, rummaged around in a box and found two plates (one large, one small), and silverware.

"Our feast is ready," he said to Kimble who was following his every move with his ears. Kimble was not sure where to sit for his treat, so he waited for James to place him. "Okay my friend, up you go." James picked Kimble up and put him on the sofa. They would eat informally tonight. He dished out his own supper and a little bit of each thing for Kimble. Then after they started eating, he sat back against the sofa pillows and opened the newspaper.

The front page contained the usual political propaganda that seemed to be ever so pervasive. It did not interest him, so after glancing through the highlights, he turned the pages to other news sections that carried information from around the states. He was busily eating and reading until a headline stopped him from his contented chewing.

Mystery death kills suspected abuser

From Wire Service News

White Plains, NY - A seemingly healthy man mysteriously dies from a melted heart. Saturday evening, the body of suspected abuser Jake Flanners, was found in his home by his neighbor.

The Coroner stated the death of the man was very unusual as the man's heart seemed to have disintegrated. There is no known medical precedence and he did not know how to rule the death - natural or otherwise.

Flanners was a person of interest in an investigation by the White Plains Homicide Department. The bodies of Flanner's wife and two children were discovered on January 20th, in a quarry near Lake George, NY.

Although Jake Flanners had been questioned, there was not enough evidence to prove his involvement in their murder. It is still under investigation and the police would not comment any further regarding it.

The story hit James almost as hard as if he had been shot. He found breathing difficult and his heart rate climbed with every sentence he read. How could this be? What connection could she possibly have to this guy? James knew then and there that he had to continue the investigation he had started months before. He had to know—her innocence or her guilt. **Jadyn!**

Chills ran up her spine as she nervously moved down the sidewalk, her long, sleek legs pounding to an inaudible beat. She stopped to look in the occasional shop window in hopes of catching sight of him in the reflection. If he was following her, she did not want him to see her get on the train.   He had never gotten this close before. She was not sure if she could avoid him much longer. He was as smart as he was dangerous.

If only she could reach the train before he found her. She hastened down the sidewalk as quickly as she could without attracting too much attention. How had he found her?   Was he close? Was she going to be able to hide once on the train? All these questions buffeted her as she moved in and out of the crowds that were normally found on the public streets of Boston.

She saw a sign that indicated that the train station was very close. She glanced over her shoulder but saw no one looking at her with any undue interest. Good, she thought, maybe I will make it. She rounded the corner and looking up saw the Governor Street entrance looming up in the center of the large courtyard. She trotted up the stairs that lead to the center of the plaza and through the entranceway that lead down to the trains. She knew it would be more difficult to track her once she had headed down below. Too many trains with too many passengers waiting – she could disappear.

Sliding her hand into her pocket, she found the token she needed. It did not matter which train she boarded. The first on the platform would do. He must not catch up to her! Her sense of apprehension was growing as she wavered between the feeling of almost being temporarily free of pursuit and almost being cornered.   She walked swiftly down the first platform and to her relief, saw a train boarding very close to her entry point.   She joined the queue for one of the cars near the back of the train. She did not dare look back for fear of attracting eyes – his eyes. Keeping her head down, she walked onto the train and went quickly to the back of the car. Finding a seat, she looked up and down the platform in search of her pursuer.   No sign.   Not this time. She relaxed slightly into the seat and put her head against the window.

How had he found her? How had he gotten so close? Was it her imagination, this feeling of being watched?   She closed her eyes and let her mind wander.   How had everything become so complicated? How on earth was this all going to end? She relaxed a little more as her thoughts turned to her childhood, where it all began.

9 781732 645028